STORIES
from HISTORY'S
DUST BIN

Also by Wayne Winterton

Whistler's Gold, A Novel of the Southwest
Xlibris, 2005

History's Dust Bin, Volume 2
Xlibris, 2015

History's Dust Bin, Volume 3
Xlibris, 2015

STORIES
from HISTORY'S
DUST BIN

Volume 1

**A book of unusual or forgotten facts, and more,
in the lives of the famous, the infamous, and the obscure.**

to Don & Carol
Partners in raising a couple
of the world's greatest grandkids.
Enjoy the stories

Wayne Winterton
2015 -

Wayne Winterton, Ph.D.

Introduction by Dr. Eduardo Pagán, co-host of the
PBS television series, *History Detectives.*

Rev. date: 11/03/2015

To order additional copies of this book, contact:
Xlibris
1-888-795-4274
www.Xlibris.com
Orders@Xlibris.com
722662

Dedicated to the Memory of
Allen M Winterton
January 31, 1915 – November 29, 2005

Acknowledging those who contributed of their time and expertise in helping to bring the project together.

AZ: Richard H. Atwood, Carolyn Barbier, Sherron Burns, Chip Calamaio, Burrett Clay, June Clay, Glendon E. Collins, Arthur Ferraro, Monica Ferraro, Linda Flake, Matt Flake, Joan Johnson, Stephen G. Johnson, Mary Kelly, Melissa Lehrer, Ellen Martig, Roger M. Martig PhD, Beaumont C. McClure, Dylan Milford, Dennis Oaks, Gary Penney, Prudence Penny, Ken Phillips, Shirl Phillips, Carl W. Reed, Michael G. Simpson DDS MS, Joyce Stewart, Leslie E. Turrin, Roger Van Atta MD, Bryan Watkins, Susan Watkins, Carol Willhoit, Don Willhoit, Darcy Winterton, Jana Winterton, Tami Lyn Winterton, William W. Winterton; **CO:** Terry Baker, Joe Galetovic, Linda Galetovic, Mickey Hammersmith; **MD:** Armand A. Lakner, PhD; **MT:** Ray R. Brubaker; **NC:** Sheri M. Dailey, Beverly B. Mott, Heather N. Shafer; **ND:** Sandra L. Gordon PhD, Sally Friese Hoffman, Esther Rye, Kenneth Rye; **NJ:** John W. Lanza; **NM:** Anthony "Slim" Randles; **NV:** Alene Neilson, Leslie Rash, Shari Shirley; **NY:** Gertrude Gelo, Alfred Zoller; **OK:** Jack Carson, Kenneth Haynes; **OR:** Myrlene Allred; **UT:** Jay L. Atwood, John L. Atwood, Patti A. Atwood, Barbara Benson, Anne Christensen, Roberta "Bobbie" Davis, Jodi T. Kesler, Mary Musselman, Georgie Olson, Merrill H. Olson, Drew Pearce, Janice Pearson, Richard C. Pearson EdD, Lynn O. Poulson JD, Ann Seely, Jennifer Seely, Richard D. Seely, Janice Smouse, Elmo Syme, Janice Thomas, Larry V. Thomas; **VA:** James E. Stone PhD; **WA:** Lydia Chapman, Lynn H. Engdahl, Tanna Engdahl, Weston S. Long, Darlene Simpson, Glenn Waugh, Marci Waugh, Launi Whedon, Shirley Stubben; **WI:** Sunny L. Johnson

Acknowledgement of Cover Artist:

Lydia Chapman is a multitalented artist, ranging from portraits to abstract art. She resides in Bellingham, Washington, with her husband Weston, and a vivid artistic imagination.

INTRODUCTION

I S HISTORY MADE by great individuals or by ordinary women and men? Wayne Winterton's aim is not so grand as to try to settle the debate. Instead, he has assembled a delightful collection of stories that feature those who were great and those who were ordinary, those who were noble and ignoble, and those common and not so common. Each left their mark in their own unique way.

Here in this collection are stories of how people lived their lives, how they struggled with the issues that confronted them and tried to do what they thought was right, or at least necessary, and in some cases, how they wronged society and paid for their misdeeds. These are stories that help explain, in part, why some things in the present are the way they are. Indeed, these are stories that remind us that those who lived before were not all that different from those of us in the present.

In aligning these stories with the calendar year, so you can read what happened on any given day of the year, Winterton reminds us in a subtle way that the past never quite leaves us. In some ways, the past is always present. But consider for a moment, after reading a story for a given day, how many other stories there are to be discovered and told!

Sometimes Winterton's stories remind us that the history commonly remembered is not the history that actually was. Or, at times, we discover that what we thought we understood about the past we did not understand in its entirety.

Something that sets the telling of these stories apart from the presentation you will often find in history textbooks is Winterton's writing style. He occasionally engages the reader with a thoughtful or rhetorical question in mid-story, or inserts a nuanced thought to encourage the reader to imagine beyond the obvious.

One of the things that I most appreciate about this book is that it reminds me of one of the approaches we took on *History Detectives* (PBS), where I worked for four seasons as a cohost. With seemingly ordinary artifacts submitted by our viewers, we began investigations that revealed the larger history behind those items and how ordinary individuals intersected with national events in unexpected ways. What I found so powerful in doing that work were the stories we discovered about the lives of those who lived through the times and events that produced the artifact under investigation. To me, the stories of past lives is what is most motivating in studying history, and that approach to understanding the past is what I strive to bring to the classes that I teach.

History's Dust Bin reminds us that learning about the past is so much more than a dry recitation of names and dates. Here, in this collection, are stories about people from all walks of life and from different backgrounds that reveal the richness of our diversity. Considering such stories in their entirety, *History's Dust Bin* shows how the threads of the past have, from different spools, woven together to create the design of the present.

Walt Whitman once stood back and, looking upon the sweep of the human experience, asked, "The question, O me! so sad, recurring – What good amid these O me, O life? *Answer:* That you are here – that life exists, and identity. That the powerful play goes on, and you will contribute a verse." *History's Dust Bin* illustrates, in its own subtle way, how life exists in the verses each has contributed, and that the powerful play goes on.

Eduardo Obregón Pagán
Associate Dean for Community Engagement
Bob Stump Endowed Professor of History
The New College at Arizona State University

PREFACE

WRITING *HISTORY'S DUST Bin* has been a rewarding adventure, a four-year journey traveling the bone-rattling backroads and bumpy byways of history in search of the unusual and lesser-known features of people's lives and events. Some of what you will find will be uplifting, some humorous, some sad and yet others, thought provoking, but all of it interesting.

The driving force behind the project has been a desire to leave something for the day when I'm no longer around to bounce a grandchild on my knee. My family is now three generations in depth, the oldest great-grandchild, Roni, is already a teenager and in watching her grow up, I'm reminded of Tevya the milkman from *Fiddler on the Roof* who lamented, when he suddenly realized his daughters had blossomed into young women, "I don't remember growing older, when did they?"

If you happen to fall outside the boundaries of my personal family, and you find the musty contents of *History's Dust Bin* as readable and as interesting as I'm hoping you will, know that in spite of what I've told my grandkids, the book was written expressly for people like you.

Each of the stories, except for the Calvin Coolidge offering (July 4), run from 500 to 1,200 words, five to ten minutes reading time each, a perfect alternative to airline on-flight magazines, or for relaxing near the pool, on the sofa, or in bed propped up with cushions against the quiet of the evening. By the way, the Coolidge story, a miserly 443 words is consistent with the man's legacy as *Silent Cal,* America's stingiest president when it came to using words. The lengthiest story is that of William "Billy the Kid" Bonney (November 7), a 1,213 word epic in which your humble author makes an appearance to tell you what he (and others) believe really happened to Billy the Kid, a story guaranteed to surprise you.

Each book in the series is divided into four months of stories, each story tied to a different calendar date. For instance, the first story in the series is about *Betsy Ross* who was born January 1, 1752 and who, contrary to popular belief, didn't sew the first American flag. Do you want to know who the most likely candidate is for having created the *Stars and Stripes*? It's all there in a quick seven-minute, 949-word story, a fun and painless way to expand your knowledge of history. I hope that many of these stories will serve as a springboard to further exploration.

I've tried hard to assure the accuracy of names, dates, events, and other story elements, but since the primary source of information is from the internet, alongside traditionally published works, magazine articles, etc., the possibility of errors does exist for which I apologize.

Early on, I attempted to build a *Reference Section* of internet URLs and citations from print materials. It didn't take long to decide that footnoting, as is done in formal research, wasn't a viable option. Web-based information is often buried behind the homepage and URLs can be as long as a sentence. That, plus the fact that web addresses tend to change over time, made discarding a *research approach* in favor of an *informal, conversational approach*, an easy decision to make, and one that I believe has resulted in more interesting, more readable stories.

It is my hope is that these stories may be read, reread, and enjoyed for years to come by my grandkids, and by all of you who have a fascination with the lesser-known elements of history.

Wayne A. Winterton, Ph.D.
Phoenix, Arizona

CONTENTS OF VOLUME 1

	January	February	March	April
1	Betsy Ross	Frank Buckles	Edwin H. Land	April Fools' Day
2	Dick Powell	Farrah Fawcett	Moe Berg	Buddy Ebsen
3	Dorothy Arzner	Charles Follis	Charles Ponzi	Eddie Robinson
4	Louis Braille	Franz Reichelt	Jack Sheppard	William Henry Harrison
5	King C. Gillette	Daisy & Violet Hilton	Ruth Belville	Howard Hughes
6	Carl Sandburg	Isador & Ida Straus	Pete Gray	Evan O'Neill Kane
7	Sandford Fleming	Thomas Andrews	Joseph N. Niepce	Haym Salomon
8	Joshua A. Norton	Thomas E. Selfridge	Millard Fillmore	Georgia Ann Broadwick
9	Richard Halliburton	Bill Veeck, Jr.	Eddie Foy, Sr.	Carl Perkins
10	Johnnie Ray	St. Scholastica Riot	John Gunby	Joseph Pulitzer
11	Alice Paul	Max Baer	Philo T. Farnsworth	Annie Dodge Wauneka
12	Ira Hayes	Abraham Lincoln	Ion Perdicaris	Henry Darger
13	Ernie Kovacs	Antoine Louis	Susan B. Anthony	Krum the Horrible
14	Mary Ann Butchell	Saint Valentine	J. Fred Muggs	Four Dead in Five Seconds
15	Goodman Ace	Jeremy Bentham	John Snow	Edward Gorey
16	Margaret Corbin & Sarah Wakeman	James Baskett	St. Urho	Isaac Burns Murphy

17	Sir Francis Galton	George E. Dixon	Saint Patrick	Adrian "Cap" Anson
18	Daniel H. Williams	Lavinia Fisher	Rudolf Diesel	Albert Einstein
19	Edgar Allan Poe	Homer Hickam	Richard Francis Burton	Israel Bissell
20	George Burns	Ken Olsen	B. F. Skinner	Henry Nasiff, Jr.
21	Horace Wells	Mary Toft	The Collyer Brothers	Evolution of the Calendar
22	Timothy Dexter	George Washington	David Lunt	Margaret J. Winkler
23	Walter F. Morrison	Paul W. Tibbets, Jr.	Desmond Doss	Herve Villechaize
24	Albert Erskine	The Battle of Los Angeles	The Leatherman	Benjamin Briggs
25	Charles Curtis	Ida Lewis	Robert Cobb Kennedy	Nicolas Jacques Pelletier
26	David R. Atchison	Levi Strauss	Old Abe	Gypsy Rose Lee
27	Last Great Race on Earth	Elizabeth Taylor	Yuri Gagarin	Ulysses S. Grant
28	Collette	Zero Mostel	Marina M. Raskova	Joseph Dunninger
29	Victor Mature	Dinah Shore	Edwin L. Drake	Tad Dorgan
30	John Bigg		Rosa & Josefa Blazek	Eva Braun
31	Andre-Jacques Garnerin		Jack Johnson	

WAYNE WINTERTON, PH.D.

JANUARY 1
She didn't sew that flag, I think

Betsy Ross
(Elizabeth Phoebe Griscom)
Jan 1, 1752 (West Jersey, PA) - Jan 30, 1836 (Philadelphia, PA)

B ETSY, BORN ELIZABETH Phoebe, was the eighth of seventeen children born to Quakers Samuel and Rebecca Griscom.

When Betsy was old enough to learn a trade, upholsterer William Webster took her under his wing as an apprentice. He already had under his tutelage a young man named John Ross, whose father, Aeneas Ross, was an assistant rector at Christ Church (Episcopal), the church where George and Martha Washington worshiped.

It wasn't long before John and Betsy, thrown together as a couple of young upholsterers-in-training, fell in love, and in 1773, they eloped and were married in, of all places, a New Jersey tavern.

It wasn't what Sam and Rebecca had in mind for their little girl, nor did it sit well with the Friends of their Quaker faith, and the Griscom family endured a public shaming that ended with Betsy's name stricken from the church rolls.

The newlyweds opened an upholstery shop and attended Christ Church where they became congregants alongside John's parents and George and Martha Washington.

In 1776, John, a member of the Pennsylvania Provincial Militia died when the munitions he was guarding, exploded, leaving Betsy a youthful widow.

A year later, Betsy married Joseph Ashburn, a man she met at a war rally.

In 1780, while fighting the British, Ashburn and another man, John Claypoole were captured and imprisoned. Ashburn died in prison, but not before asking Claypoole to find Betsy after the war and tell her of his fate. At the end of the war, Claypoole kept his promise, located Betsy, and told her the story of her husband's capture and death.

Claypoole and the twice-widowed Betsy fell in love, and in 1783, they married and raised five children.

So, you ask, when do we get to the part where George Washington asks Betsy to sew the first American flag? The problem with that part of the story is that there's hardly a thimble of credible evidence that Washington, who admittedly knew Betsy from church, ever asked her to sew anything, neither a button on a shirt, nor a hole in his sock, and quite certainly, not a flag.

The story of Betsy Ross, George Washington, and their collaboration in creating the first American flag, was an American textbook staple for more than a hundred years. However, the story was unknown until 1870, ninety-four years after the alleged sewing of the flag in 1776. That's when forty-five year old William J. Canby, Betsy Ross Claypoole's grandson spoke at a meeting of the Pennsylvania Historical Society.

Canby told the group that when he was eleven years old, his Grandmother Betsy (who died in 1836) told him that Washington had visited her in 1776 to discuss making a flag. He said that Betsy and Washington agreed on a flag with seven red and six white stripes and thirteen stars. Canby added that Washington wanted six-point stars, but after his grandmother demonstrated how easily she could make five-point stars, the General agreed and Betsy commenced sewing.

Sometime after Canby told his story to the Historical Society, it found its way into the pages of *Harper's Magazine,* and then into the school books of the next five or six generations of Americans.

One of the difficulties with Canby's story is that although there were plenty of flags flown during the Revolutionary War, sporting everything from pine trees to rattlesnakes, there is no reported instance of a flag that looked anything like the stars and stripes. Neither was there an entry in Washington's 1776 itinerary of places and events that mentioned a meeting with Betsy, or with any seamstress, nor did he make mention of any concern to have a flag designed.

So how did Betsy Ross's flag story become such a celebrated part of American culture? The answer to that rests with America's Centennial in 1876.

As you might imagine, America's first 100 years were a big deal. Every facet of the emergence of the new nation was on display, and there was a need to glorify the men and women who had brought the American dream to life.

As Canby was thrilling the ladies of Pennsylvania with his story, the planners of America's centennial were busy organizing the events to mark the occasion. Loaded with numerous male patriots, such as George Washington, John Hancock, Patrick Henry, and others, the organizers were hard-pressed to come up with a similar list of female patriots.

So think now, whose name was ripe for exploitation? How about a name fresh on the minds of the ladies of the Pennsylvania Historical Society? Right! Canby's story of Betsy and the flag became a favorite during the centennial celebration and overnight Betsy went from an obscure upholsterer of colonial furniture to a starry-eyed flag maker.

Today, most scholars agree that Francis Hopkinson, a signer of the Declaration of Independence is the most likely candidate as the one who designed the first American flag.

Although there are no known Hopkinson flags in existence, his personal notes and a rough sketch of the flag showing the thirteen stripes and thirteen stars, do exist. In addition, the journals of the Continental Congress point to his work in the matter, including his submission of a bill for £2,400 for having designed the American flag, as well as the Great Seal of the United States.

If, on July 4, 1876, Betsy happened to be gazing from the heavens and upon the festivities of the country's first 100 years, she may well have been amazed and delighted, all at the same time.

Then, she just might have gone looking for her grandson, William J. Canby, to see if he had any idea as to how such a story got started.

On **January 1, 1863**, Daniel Freeman of Nebraska was
the first person to submit a claim under the
Homestead Act signed into law by Abraham Lincoln on
May 20, 1862.

JANUARY 2
The Curse of the Conqueror

Dick Powell
(Richard Ewing Powell)
Nov 14, 1904 (Mountain View, AR) – **Jan 2, 1963** (Los Angeles, CA)

D ICK POWELL STARTED his career as a vocalist. He was as popular in the 1920s as a yet to hit the airwaves Frank Sinatra would become in the 1940s. The latter, singing his way to first place on the *Major Bowes Amateur Hour* in 1935 and winning a six-month singing contract from which neither swooning bobbysoxers, nor the world, would ever recover.

Powell would continue to sing, but he didn't intend to leave his mark on the strength of his voice alone. He was anxious to get into the movies, and not only act in them, but to direct them as well. In the 1930s, he appeared in fluffy musicals like *Footlight Parade, Gold Diggers of 1933,* and *Flirtation Walk.*

In the 1940's he received a few meatier roles like that of detective Philip Marlowe in *Murder, My Sweet,* and in tough-guy movies like *Johnny O'Clock,* and although the roles paid the bills, he still wanted to move into the fields of directing and producing.

In the 1950's he co-founded Four Star Television, hosted his own *Dick Powell's Zane Grey Theater* and from 1961 until his unexpected death in 1963, he hosted his own *Dick Powell Show.*

His death in 1963 from stomach cancer at the age of 58 was unexpected. He simply looked too healthy, too active and too vibrant to have died of cancer.

Then, within a decade, an ominous underlying likely cause of the cancer that took his life and possibly many other lives surfaced.

During the 1950s Powell fulfilled one of his dreams, that of becoming a movie director. His credits included *The Enemy Below* with Robert Mitchum and Curt Jurgens, *You Can't Run Away From It* with Jack Lemmon and June Allyson, and *The Conqueror* with John Wayne and Susan Hayward. It was that last film that many people believe may not only have been the cause of his death, but the cause or contributor to the early deaths of as many as 90 of the 220 people who worked on location with that film.

Here is what many suspect may have happened.

The 1956 Howard Hughes financed movie, *The Conqueror,* a flop when measured by box-office receipts, was filmed in the stunningly beautiful Canyonlands of Southern Utah, an expansive area of dazzling red-rock scenery, breathtaking canyons, and blessed with endless days of mild, sun-drenched weather.

The area, for all of its natural beauty, was also downwind from the Yucca Flats (Nevada) nuclear test site.

A mere three years before the filming, the military had tested eleven atomic bombs at Yucca Flats with the heaviest fallout occurring in the Snow Canyon area of Canyonlands National Park where a major portion of *The Conqueror* was shot. During thirteen weeks of dawn to dusk shooting, the actors and crew, all 220 of them, were constantly in the midst of huge quantities of dust kicked up during the film's action scenes, of which there were many, dust that may have been tainted with deadly nuclear residue.

Hughes also had sixty tons of the beautiful, but potentially lethal red dirt hauled to Hollywood for the movie's indoor sets.

In addition to Powell, other notables from the movie who died of cancer include John Wayne, Susan Hayward, John Hoyt, Agnes Moorhead, and Pedro Armendariz, the latter committing suicide after learning he had terminal cancer.

While not all of the 90 early deaths can be assumed to have been caused by the nuclearized Snow Canyon dirt, the deaths represent 40% of the workforce of 220 actors, extras, directors, sound specialists, dialogue coaches, set builders, and others that worked on location, a percentage far too high to be attributed to chance alone.

"If everyone in this town connected with
politics had to leave town
because of chasing women and drinking,
you would have no government."
Barry Goldwater (**Jan 2, 1909** - May 29, 1998) Politician

JANUARY 3
Hollywood's First Lady of Directing

Dorothy Arzner
Jan 3, 1897 (San Francisco, CA) – Oct 1, 1979 (La Quinta, CA)

THE VERY FIRST motion picture produced for a paying audience was filmed in 1910 on the outskirts of the small up-start community of Hollywood, California. It was a seventeen-minute offering titled, *In Old California,* produced by the Biograph Company and directed by D. W. Griffith. Griffith would go on to become a silent film era legend, producing such quiet classics as *The Birth of a Nation* (1915) and *Intolerance* (1916).

The golden era of silent movies that ran from 1914 until the world's first talkie in 1927, *The Jazz Singer* starring Al Jolson, saw a profusion of cinematic offerings that ranged from truly enduring epics to frankly forgettable flops.

Those early days of motion pictures required that the silent on-screen action provide easily interpretable visual clues to keep the story alive in the minds of viewers. When needed, without being too much of a distraction, screen captions superimposed over the action helped to convey dialog or to explain a situation, usually in fifteen words or less. Over all, the success or failure of story continuity rested on the broad shoulders of one person. A man whose job it was to make sure that no theatergoer got lost in the weeds of the story, and that man was the movie's director.

In those early days of cinema, directing a movie was a man's job in much the same way that cooking and caring for the children was women's work.

The message in Hollywood was clear, "Help Wanted. Movie Director. Women need not apply."

It was into this world that a creative, intelligent, and imaginative person with small feminine shoulders entered the scene. She wasn't pushy; she was too smart for that. Instead, she went to Hollywood, found work, listened, studied, and asked questions. With few paying attention to what was happening she worked her way up the cinematic ladder to become one of Hollywood's most respected movie directors. Her name was Dorothy Arzner and if anyone ever suggested to Dorothy that she shouldn't dream about become a movie director because she was a woman, she never listened.

Her first job in the movie industry was as a clerk-typist for William C. deMille, Cecil's older brother, and she was thankful for the job. However, Dorothy didn't take dictation for long.

When given a chance to comment on a script, her spot-on suggestions and later, an ability to improve a script to convey meaning behind an actor's actions, led deMille to assign her to the scriptwriting department. There she learned from the experts, thoughtfully contributing her own ideas to the story's foundation. Her attention to detail made her a natural to move from scriptwriting into the film editor's chair, taking numerous disjointed "takes," and stitching them together in a coherent way to tell the story, and she was outstanding. Nevertheless, there was a problem; she was a woman.

She had done things right. She had won the confidence of her boss, William C. deMille, by being an outstanding clerk-typist. Then, when given the opportunity to take on additional responsibilities, she did so with a personal resolve to learn the process by which movies were made, and then to always go beyond the expected.

Her first solo editing assignment couldn't have come at a better time or with a better movie, and she nailed it! The movie was Rudolph Valentino's *Blood and Sand*, now considered one of the silent era's greatest classics. After editing *Blood and Sand,* and then *Ruggles of Redgap,* and several other films, she asked for a chance to direct a movie.

There was hesitancy on the part of the Hollywood decision makers. No woman had ever directed a movie, and movies represented substantial financial investments from people who are not interested in taking chances. Sure, Arzner was an excellent scriptwriter and she had certainly proven her worth in the cutting (editing) room, but directing! A woman running the show! A woman telling actors, actresses, and extras what to do? Well!

Now, there comes a time in most folk's lives when respect, loyalty and the acknowledged support from others, needs an additional something that can only come from within, and it's called backbone.

That's when Dorothy threatened to quit and go to work for rival studio, Columbia Pictures.

That's when she got her chance.

She was offered the opportunity to direct the movie, *Fashions for Women* (1927), featuring some of the leading fashion models of the day. The movie was successful, proving to the studio that she not only knew how to direct, but that she was good at it.

Next, she made the giant leap from silent movies to movies with sound. The movie would be Clara Bow's first talkie, *The Wild Party,* an edgy offering set in a women's college with distinct lesbian overtones. It surprised everyone, becoming 1929's third top-grossing film.

Dorothy Arzner had broken through the gender barrier of movie direction, and became Hollywood's *First Lady of Directing.*

She was also the first woman accepted into the Directors Guild of America.

Did Dorothy plow new ground in Hollywood? Yes, in part because of her ability to think beyond the boundaries of her peers, and here's one example.

During the filming of *The Wild Party* and dissatisfied with the quality of recorded sound from a single fixed-position microphone, she instructed a technician to go to the prop storage room and find a fishing pole, tape a microphone to the distant end, and hold it over the heads of the actors as they talked and moved around. With that creative act, Dorothy was not only the world's first female movie director, but she invented the boom microphone as well.

"Success seems to be connected with action.
Successful people keep moving.
They make mistakes, but they don't quit."
Conrad Hilton (Dec 25, 1887 - **Jan 3, 1979**)
Hotel developer

JANUARY 4
From tragedy to legacy

Louis Braille
Jan 4, 1809 (Coupvray, France) - Jan 6, 1852 (Paris, France)

WHILE PLAYING IN his father's leather shop, three-year-old Louis suffered a tragic life-altering event. Pushing an awl into a piece of leather as he had seen his father do many times, the unthinkable happened. With his face much too close to the action, the awl slipped, and in a blinding second, the point of the awl penetrated deep into one of his eyes.

His parents, Simon-René and Monique Braille, rushed him to the town doctor, but in 1812, there was little hope, and even less knowledge about antibiotics and eye surgery. The perforated eye was lost and an uncontrollable infection slowly began eating away at the remaining eye.

Louis, intelligent and creative, was fully blind by his fifth birthday. The youngster, however, coped with his blindness remarkably well, and his parents were determined to not let their son's disability interfere with his desire for an education. Unfortunately, in the early 1800s there weren't any educational options for blind children under the age of ten.

When Louis turned ten, he attended the National Institute for Blind Youth in Paris, the first school in the world specifically devoted to teaching the blind.

Linguist Valentin Haüy founded the school after witnessing a group of sightless street musicians taunted by insensitive revelers during a Parisian festival known as St. Ovid's Fair. The musicians, forced to wear dunce caps, donkey ears, and oversized eyeglasses, were at the mercy of the merry-makers. Although many of those who watched the mockery found it funny, Haüy detested the display of poor taste and vowed to do what he could to help the blind.

What he did was to establish a trade school in which blind students learned to weave so they could make their own school uniforms, and to make items for sale to the public, including fishing nets, woven chair cushions, and buggy whips. They also learned to play musical instruments and were in demand to perform outside the school.

For Louis, however, the skill he treasured most was reading.

Reading was taught by a system devised by Haüy in which large books; some so heavy they couldn't be lifted, were read by tracing the shapes of the letters of the alphabet with the fingers. Each letter had to be traced and interpreted, and each letter and word banked in memory until the sentence was clear. Unfortunately, the beginning words of a sentence were often forgotten before the last words of the sentence could be determined.

The system was slow and inefficient.

At the time of Louis's enrollment in 1819, the school's library contained exactly fourteen books. As painfully slow as reading was, Louis quickly read all fourteen and then asked, "Where are the other books that blind persons can read?"

From Louis's point-of-view there was an even greater problem. The complexities of hand-producing Haüy's embossed and confusingly ornate characters meant that the students could only read, not reproduce the writing.

Louis, twelve years old in 1821, wanted to not only read, but to write messages as well, and he knew there had to be a better way.

The beginnings of that better way were under development by a military officer named Charles Barbier at the French Royal Military Academy in Paris. Barbier, a member of Napoleon's Army, had watched (or been told about) the annihilation of an army post when a French soldier had exposed his squad's position by lighting a lamp to read a military dispatch.

Captain Barbier called his experimental writing, *Ecriture Nocturne* (Night Writing). It was a system loosely based on Samuel Morse's *Morse Code* in which two to twelve dots and dashes were used to represent characters of the French alphabet. Barbier's writing also employed the use of an embossing tool to form dots and dashes onto a moistened sheet of thick paper.

In 1823, fourteen-year-old Louis Braille and a few of Haüy's other blind students were guests of the French Museum of Science and Industry to demonstrate Haüy's system of reading.

Also, as a guest, was Captain Charles Barbier who would demonstrate his Night Writing, to the participants.

It was at that gathering that Louis Braille and Charles Barbier's paths crossed. When Barbier presented Braille with a page of his Night Writing, with its raised dots and dashes, Braille knew he had found the basis for a language of his own.

Within a year, Braille had eliminated the dashes and reduced the number of dots from twelve to six. Using the same heavy paper as Barbier had employed, he used a pointed instrument with which he could press upward from beneath the paper to create the dimples (dots) that we're familiar with today.

It would take a hundred years from the time fifteen-year-old Louis Braille established his system of writing, before *braille* would become the universal language of the blind.

Louis Braille never left the National Institute for Blind Youth. Instead, he became one of the school's most dedicated teachers. One week before his death in 1852, he dictated his will. He gave of what wealth he had to his family and his clothing and personal mementos he distributed to his students.

In addition, his will contained a request that struck his family as peculiar. He described a wooden box kept in his room, and without any written explanation, he asked to have the box burned to ashes without opening.

After his death and funeral and when it came time to burn the wooden box, curiosity got the best of his family and an agreement was reached to open the box. Inside were hundreds of IOUs, promissory notes written in Braille from students who had borrowed money over the years from their very generous teacher.

Oh yes, the pointed instrument that Louis Braille used to create those raised dimples? It was a pointed, awl-like stylus. Not unlike the one that had blinded him as a child.

"People, like quilts, are most beautiful
when colors, cultures, and ideas are united
yet remain recognizably unique."
Joyce Stewart (**Jan 4, 1940** -) Quilter, author

JANUARY 5
The man with a disposable idea

King Camp Gillette
Jan 5, 1855 (Fond du Lac, WI) – July 9, 1932 (Los Angeles, CA)

K ING CAMP GILLETTE, born January 5, 1855, was the son of George W. and Fanny Lemira Camp Gillette. His royal-sounding given name, *King*, was the surname of his father's best friend, a man known today only as Judge King. When young Gillette started down the road to a career, shaving was the last thing he had on his mind. Instead, he imagined that one day his name might be associated with something along the lines of social and economic reform.

As a youngster, Gillette and his family lived in Chicago. That was until the Great Chicago Fire of 1871. The family left Chicago with little but the clothes on their backs and relocated in New York, except for sixteen-year-old King who stayed behind to clerk for a Chicago hardware company. Then, in succession, King moved to New York, Kansas City, and eventually to the New England area where he became a traveling salesman for the Baltimore Seal Company.

He was a great salesman. Some people are born with the temperament and personality that make them relatable to others. King Gillette would have been in the top five percent of that group. Author Tim Dowling in his book, *Inventor of the Disposable Culture*, said of Gillette:

> "His biggest asset was his magnetism, an almost hypnotic cloak of easy-going, clubbable charm. Though he spoke softly, it was in a manner that commanded attention. He looked his customers in the eye, used their names, touched their sleeves, and adapted himself to their opinions and prejudices. Above all, he sold himself. The formality of taking an order could wait."

When the head of the Baltimore Seal Company, William Painter, invented the cork-lined crimped bottle cap, he changed more than just the carbonated beverage industry. He gave his best salesman, Gillette, an inspired idea that would make King Gillette a very rich man indeed.

As a salesman for the company's bottle caps, Gillette watched as customer after customer opened a soft drink and tossed the now useless crimped cap in the trash. "That," he realized, "is the secret to success." A two-part product! A reusable component (the soft drink bottle), and a disposable component (the bottle cap).

Because he enjoyed a close personal relationship with company president William Painter, Gillette discussed his theory with him. Painter gave him the encouragement he needed, suggesting he come up with a disposable product that customers would keep coming back for. A product for which there would always be a need.

Excited, he made a list of everything he could think of that could benefit from the two-part product model. Then one morning, while shaving, it came to him. That same day he wrote to his wife who was out of town, telling her, "I've got it! Our fortune is made."

The year was 1895. It would take Gillette six highly focused years to develop the product.

Gillette teamed up with two expert machinists, Steven Porter and William Nickerson. Porter used Gillette's drawings to make the device that would hold the blades (the reusable component), and Nickerson designed the equipment to mass-produce the thin steel blades (the disposable component). The second phase took most of the time because machinery didn't exist in the late 1800s to create the thin steel blades. Nickerson had to first invent the equipment to create the blade, and then create the blade.

Once the elements had all come together, Gillette patented the razor holder and blade. Then, in 1901 with his partners, he founded the American Safety Razor Company and two years later (1903) the company started production. In their first year, they sold 51 razors at five-dollars apiece, and 168 blades. In only its second year of business, sales soared to 90,000 razors and 12,400,000 blades, and it only got better. By 1910, King Gillette had made his first million dollars.

Remember, at the beginning of the story, when it was mentioned that early in his career Gillette would never have imagined his fortune would come from razors and razor blades?

Long before he honed his energies toward giving men that clean-shaven look, Gillette had authored a number of books on his views of Utopian Socialism, to wit, *The Human Drift* (1894); *The Ballot Box* (1897); *World Corporation* (1910); and *The People's Corporation* (1924).

Prior to World War I, Gillette envisioned a socialistic "World Corporation" community in Arizona Territory, even making a pitch for Theodore Roosevelt to consider becoming the community's leader. When Roosevelt failed to show interest, Gillette approached author Sinclair Lewis and later Henry Ford, neither having any more interest in the idea than had Roosevelt, and Gillette abandoned the idea.

Sometime later, Gillette proposed construction of a Utopian city near Niagara Falls. He imagined millions of people living in enormous apartment complexes, deriving their electrical power from Niagara, and everyone living happily under rules of "universal cooperation."

Today, few know about Gillette's hope of changing the economic and social face of America with a communal, communistic model, but everyone knows how he changed the faces of America's men, and America's ladies have to love him for that.

"The art of politics consists in knowing precisely when
to hit an opponent slightly below the belt."
Konrad Adenauer (**Jan 5, 1876** – Apr 19, 1967)
Chancellor, West Germany

Carl August Sandburg
Jan 6, 1878 (Galesburg, IL) - July 22, 1967 (Flat Rock, NC)

CARL SANDBURG ONCE said, "Nearly all the best things that came to me in life have been unexpected, unplanned by me." He was right for himself and probably right for a majority of the rest of us as well.

Nothing in Sandburg's early years, growing up in the drowsy little town of Galesburg, Illinois, would lead anyone to believe he would one day have schools and streets named after him, or that during his lifetime he would receive not one, or two, but three Pulitzer Prizes! Life in those days, in Galesburg, or in most other places in small town America wasn't easy, and that might have been the key to his success. He came to know and understand America. He came to know how to express in words, the way the rest of us felt about the backbone and spirit of our great country.

Carl was born in a three-room cottage not unlike the home of many working class families at the turn of the 20th century. He quit school after the eighth grade, drove a milk wagon, cleaned barbershops, and harvested ice. He laid brick, threshed wheat, mined coal, shined shoes in Galesburg's Union Hotel, and in 1897, he walked out of Galesburg and into the wanderlust life of a hobo. He worked at a Denver hotel, labored in a Nebraska coalmine, and throughout his travels, he memorized the folk songs he would later incorporate into his speaking engagements.

His view of life during those hand-to-mouth early years, and the sharp contrast he saw between the rich and the poor left him questioning the virtues of capitalism.

In 1898, he served in the Spanish-American War and spent most of his time in Puerto Rico battling the heat, the squalor, and worst of all, the mosquitos.

After the war, he enrolled at Lombard College where he became friends with professor Phillip Green Wright, a worthwhile friendship indeed.

After graduation, he sold stereoscope views, worked for the *Chicago Daily News*, and wrote poetry. His friend, Professor Wright, printed Carl's first book of poetry, *In Reckless Ecstasy* in the basement of his home (1904). Sandburg wrote more poetry, *Incidentals* (1907) and *The Plaint of a Rose* (1908). In 1916, he wrote *Chicago Poems*, followed by *Cornhuskers* (1918), and then *Rootabaga Stories* (1922).

At around this time his publisher, Alfred Harcourt, suggested a biography of Lincoln for children, something marketable to America's schools. Sandburg fell in love with the project, meticulously researched his subject, and after three years produced not a children's book, but a two-volume biography for adults and his first true financial success. The work, *Abraham Lincoln: The Prairie Years* (1926) became an instant American classic.

In 1936, he published his best-known book of poetry, *The People, Yes,* and in 1940, he published *Abraham Lincoln: The War Years* and won the first of three Pulitzer Prizes.

In 1954, an Orland Park, Illinois, high school chose to honor his name. Sandburg, thrilled, stretched the one-hour dedication ceremony into several hours of regaling the students and staff with stories from his life. It was a once in a lifetime experience for everyone in attendance.

Years after the school's dedication, Sandburg, driving past *Carl Sandburg High School* made a snap decision to stop and surprise the students and staff with an impromptu visit. Not dressed for the occasion and looking more like an elderly, rumpled citizen than a three-time Pulitzer Prize winner, he was unable to convince the principal of who he was, and he was asked to leave the campus.

He neither fussed nor protested. He just got in his car, drove home, and returned an hour later with proof of his identity. The principal, embarrassed beyond words, instantly cancelled all classes and called an impromptu assembly to honor the school's famous namesake. Once again, and with never a mention of the earlier incident, Sandburg enlightened and enthralled staff and students alike, showing himself to be the class act that he was.

On July 22, 1967, Carl Sandburg, the people's poet, passed away at his home in Flat Rock, North Carolina. As he had directed, his ashes were returned to his birthplace in Galesburg, Illinois, and today rest beneath a large red granite boulder known as "Remembrance Rock."

On **January 6, 2011**, the Romanian
Tax Code was revised
to include the taxable income of witches.

JANUARY 7

It was just a matter of time

Sandford Fleming

Jan 7, 1827 (Kirkcaldy, Scotland) – July 22, 1915 (Halifax, Canada)

IT WAS A matter of *time* that caused engineer, inventor, and railroad man, Sir Sandford Fleming, to shift his energies from surveying, map-making, and bridge design to a project of a cosmic nature. For most of his professional life, he had been an integral part of Canada's railway system, putting into working order the things that needed done to make the system dependable and efficient.

Brilliant at problem solving, Fleming was just as likely to take a crack at finding a solution as most folks are at cussing the problem while watching the clock with their hands in their pockets.

So it was on that day in 1876 when he was in Ireland awaiting the arrival of a train, only to learn that whoever had posted the schedule had forgotten to replace the afternoon designation 'PM' with the morning designation 'AM.'

"Hmmmm," he may have mused, "that wouldn't have happened if railroad schedules were based on a 24-hour clock instead of the family-friendly 12-hour clock." By the time he reached his final destination, his head was full of timely thoughts.

In 1879, three years after his travel schedule had been derailed by a careless railroad employee, Fleming was standing before a meeting of the Royal Canadian Institute sharing his concept of a standardized world-clock he called *Cosmic Time.*

His idea for *Cosmic Time* was to divide the world into 24 time zones to match the 24 hours it takes the earth to circle the sun. He set Zone 1 at the Greenwich (180-degree) meridian, with each successive zone set astronomically one hour apart, taking into account such considerations as geologic land features such as mountains, waterways, and large population centers. For instance, it didn't make sense to run the boundary of two time zones down the middle of Broadway in New York City.

Unfortunately, his concept of a world clock met mostly with ho-hums from folks who thought that he was creating a problem where one didn't exist. After all, why would someone enjoying a mid-morning siesta in Madrid, Spain, care about being on the same time system as someone leaving a New York nightclub near the witching hour of midnight?

Fortunately, his proposal at the Royal Canadian Institute turned out to be a perfect warm-up for a future presentation at the International Meridian Conference in Washington DC, where his well-timed idea found support. As one of the conference planners, he had carefully laid the groundwork for his idea of *Cosmic Time* ahead of his presentation, including courting a few politicians who always have plenty of time to hobnob with voters.

It took six years for the dust of scientific and practical arguments to settle, but on January 1, 1885, Fleming's concept of a 24-hour clock matching 24 around-the-world wedges of time went into effect. His preferred term, *Cosmic Time*, lost out to less imaginative minds who chose the rather mundane term, *Standard Time*, suggesting to Fleming that *Cosmic Time* was just a little too otherworldly for people of the real world to accept.

Now, lest anyone think Sandford Fleming a one-idea man, consider the following. Fleming led the engineering effort of much of the Intercolonial Railway and the Canadian Pacific Railway. He designed Canada's first postage stamp, the reddish three-penny Beaver Stamp. He was a founding member of the Royal Society of Canada. He was Chancellor of Queen's University in Ontario, and in 1897, Queen Victoria decided it was about time to knight her up-to-the-minute man for his timely work in standardizing the world's clocks, and she did.

"Those that don't got it, can't show it.
Those that got it, can't hide it."
Zora Neale Hurston (**Jan 7, 1891** – Jan 28, 1960)
Anthropologist

Joshua Abraham Norton
c. 1818 (London, England) - **Jan 8, 1880** (San Francisco, CA)

S O, HOW DID Joshua Norton become the Emperor of America?

Born in England, Norton spent most of his childhood and early adult life in South Africa.

At the age of thirty, he inherited $40,000 from his father's estate, a sizeable sum of money in 1849. With his inheritance and a sense of adventure, he immigrated to America and settled in San Francisco.

The fortune served him well for a time and he moved about with ease in San Francisco's business community. Then two things happened. First, in an attempt to corner the Peruvian rice market, he lost his fortune. Second, he had already signed a rice-delivery contract, for which he had no rice and no prospect for getting any. He sued to have the contract declared null and void, and when the judge didn't see the matter Norton's way, he disappeared.

A decade later, he reappeared, a changed man, but not as you might think. He was no longer Joshua A. Norton, businessman. He was Norton I, Emperor of the United States, and in a few years, he would add to his responsibilities, "...and Protector of Mexico."

You would think that even folks in San Francisco would concede that Norton I had all the hallmarks of a person delicately teetering on the edge of insanity. However, from the era of Norton I to the present time, San Franciscans have never let a little insanity become an issue when it comes to local governance, thus Norton I had truly found a home.

How did the Emperor rule his empire?

He did it by the issuance of proclamations, edicts, and decrees.

After his ten years of self-imposed exile, he didn't like the way Washington politicians were running the country. Therefore, on September 17, 1859, he issued an edict to let the folks in Washington understand who was in charge. It read (edited):

"At the peremptory request and desire of a large majority of the citizens of these United States, I Joshua A. Norton, formerly of Algoa Bay, Cape of Good Hope and now … of San Francisco, California, declare and proclaim myself Emperor of the United States and in virtue of the authority thereby in me vested, do hereby order and direct the representatives of the different States of the Union to assemble in Musical Hall, of this city, on the 1st day of February next, then and there to make such alterations in the existing laws of the Union as may ameliorate the evils under which the country is laboring…."

Shortly afterward, incensed by the hanging of John Brown in Charles Town, Virginia, he issued an edict in which he fired Governor Henry A. Wise of Virginia, and replaced him with John C. Breckenridge of Kentucky.

On October 1, 1860, he decreed that Congress shall no longer meet in Washington, D.C.

San Francisco was falling in love with their Emperor and on September 17, 1861, the city's newest theater, Tucker Hall, opened with the performance of a comic opera titled, *Norton the First, or An Emperor for a Day.*

Not everyone was pleased with the way *Norton I* was running things and on January 21, 1867, a San Francisco policeman named Armand Barbier arrested the Emperor with the intention of locking him up as a mentally unbalanced public nuisance. The arrest so outraged San Franciscans that something had to be done, and quickly.

Police Chief Patrick Crowley issued an apology to His Majesty for the misunderstanding, noting that the Emperor "had shed no blood; robbed no one; and despoiled no country; which is more than can be said of his fellows in that line." The Emperor, to show he harbored no ill will toward the San Francisco Police Department, granted an Imperial Pardon to Officer Barbier, and from that point forward, without exception, all of San Francisco's police officers would salute His Majesty whenever they passed him on the street.

By the way, during Norton's rule, it was impossible to miss His Majesty's appearances on the street, as his various official uniforms were indeed eye-catchers.

Several photographs of the Emperor are available on the internet and one in particular may have been his favorite. It's one in which he is described as being in full regalia. He is wearing a high-crowned hat adorned with the iridescent tail feathers of a pheasant, and a military-style jacket embellished with two large gold-braid epaulets. His belt, drawn tightly about his waist strains to suppress a middle-aged midsection while supporting a scabbard and sword, the latter of which the Emperor is captured in the feigned act of withdrawing. Overall, the photograph is flattering to the Emperor, even if his thick droopy mustache and untrimmed beard are not.

On August 12, 1869, Norton I ordered the dissolution and abolishment of the Democrat and Republican parties. It was an act that many feel, to this day, should have won him a Nobel Prize. Here is a part of his edict (edited):

> "Norton I, Dei Gratia, Emperor … being desirous of allaying the dissensions of party strife now existing within the realm, do hereby dissolve and abolish the Democrat and Republican parties, and also do hereby decree disfranchisement and imprisonment, for not more than ten nor less than five years, to all persons leading to any violation of this Imperial decree."

Right now, you're probably thinking, where is Norton I when we need him most.

Sadly, on January 8, 1880, the Emperor passed away.

His funeral cortège was two miles long with an estimated 30,000 folks lining the streets to pay homage. Not a bad turnout considering the entire population of San Francisco in 1880 was approximately 190,000 souls.

The Emperor was laid to rest in San Francisco's Masonic Cemetery with all costs paid by the City of San Francisco.

When, in 1934, all of the graves inside San Francisco were transferred to locations outside the city, the Emperor's remains were transferred as well and his Highness now resides at Woodlawn Cemetery in Colma, California, his grave marked by a large headstone inscribed, "Norton I, Emperor of the United States and Protector of Mexico."

On **January 8, 1946**, Gladys Presley gave her son Elvis a $6.95 guitar for his eleventh birthday. Just wait!

JANUARY 9

An adventurer's adventurer

Richard Halliburton

Jan 9, 1900 (Brownsville, TN) – abt Mar 24, 1939 (Pacific Ocean)

RICHARD HALLIBURTON'S LIFE, long on travel and adventure, ended near the Hawaiian Islands in the Pacific Ocean. Years before his death, he had advised his father that,

> ". . . when impulse and spontaneity fail to make my way uneven, then I shall sit up nights inventing the means of making my life as conglomerate and vivid as possible.... And when my time comes to die, I'll be happy, for I will have done and seen and heard and experienced all the joy, pain, and thrills, any emotion that any human ever had, and I'll be especially happy if I am spared a stupid, common death in bed."

Richard was one of two sons born to Wesley and Nellie Halliburton, a family of considerable wealth. At fifteen and the less robust of the two boys, (five foot seven and 140 pounds), Richard developed a heart irregularity and was temporarily confined at John Harvey Kellogg's Battle Creek Sanitarium in Michigan. Not long after Richard's release from the sanitarium, his brother Wesley contracted rheumatic fever and died.

Although Richard had been a good student at a couple of college prep schools and had completed a year or two at Princeton University, he suddenly took time off from his college studies to sign aboard the freighter *Octorara* as a regular seaman and spent a season touring Europe.

When he returned, he completed his Princeton studies (1921) serving also as the editor-in-chief of the *Princetonian Pictorial Magazine*, but the adventure aboard the *Octorara* had ignited a desire in him to do more of the same. He rejected a more sedate lifestyle, finding bachelorhood more to his liking than the prospects of a wife, family and white picket fence. It became his plan to travel extensively and as inexpensively as he could and to earn his living as an author and lecturer about his adventures.

Halliburton took a gentle jab at his more conservative, career and marriage-minded classmates by dedicating his first book, *The Royal Road to Romance,* to those at Princeton, "whose sanity, consistency, and respectability ... drove [him] to [writing] this book."

One of Halliburton's most unusual achievements came in 1928 in Panama when, rather than passing through the canal's locks aboard ship; he registered himself as a ship and over a period of ten days, swam the length of the canal. Doing so, he set the record for paying the lowest passage toll, a miserly 36-cent fee, and a record that stands to this day.

Two years later, Halliburton with aviator Moye Stephens set out to circumnavigate the globe, an eighteen-month odyssey in an open cockpit biplane. The plane, named the *Flying Carpet*, made stops in thirty-four countries and covered 33,660 miles.

Beginning Christmas Day, 1930, they departed Los Angeles and flew to New York, where they crated the aircraft and had it placed aboard the *RMS Majestic* and men and plane sailed to England. From England, they visited France, Spain, Gibraltar, Africa (Morocco), crossed the Atlas Mountains, crossed the Sahara, and then stopped in the West African city of Timbuktu. Continuing, they spent two weeks in Algeria with the French Foreign Legion before flying to Persia (Iran) where they met a German female aviator (Elly Beinhorn) whose plane was grounded with mechanical problems.

They assisted Beinhorn, getting her back in the air, and then it was on to Iraq, followed by India where they buzzed the Taj Mahal, upside down! Next came Nepal where, while flying past Mount Everest, Halliburton stood up in the open cockpit and took the first aerial photograph ever taken of the world's highest mountain. Then, it was on to Borneo and the Rajang River where they took the chief of the Dyak headhunters for a flight, and in return, the chief surprised them with an honored gift of 132-pounds of shrunken heads, which they tossed from the aircraft as soon as they were out of sight.

They were the first Americans to fly to the Philippines, and in Manila, they had the aircraft crated and placed aboard a ship for the final leg of the trip back to America. The flight had cost Halliburton over $50,000 plus the cost of fuel. Halliburton afterward wrote *The*

Flying Carpet: Adventures in a Biplane from Timbuktu to Everest and Beyond, a best-seller that earned him royalties in excess of $100,000.

In 1936, Halliburton completed another of his unusual achievements when he crossed the Swiss Alps on the back of an elephant. On another adventure, he climbed the Matterhorn, and on yet another adventure, he retraced the route followed by Ulysses in Homer's *Odyssey.*

The next plan was to sail a gaudily decorated 75-foot Chinese junk named the *Sea Dragon* from Hong Kong to San Francisco. The junk, manned by a seven-person crew including Halliburton, was a planned publicity stunt to promote the opening of the *Golden Gate International Exposition*, where it would dock and become a part of the exposition.

The preparations involved several delays, including a trial run in Hong Kong harbor that revealed numerous concerns. Haliburton, while waiting for the junk to be repaired, sent the following to the wire services: "If any of my readers wish to be driven rapidly and violently insane, and doesn't know how to go about it, let me make a suggestion: Try building a Chinese junk in a Chinese shipyard during a war with Japan."

On March 3, 1939, the junk, made questionably seaworthy, began its ocean crossing.

The last visual contact made with the *Sea Dragon* was approximately 1,180 miles west of Midway Island by the ocean liner, *SS President Coolidge*, in rough waters. The *Coolidge* also received the following not so cryptic message from Halliburton, "Having a wonderful time. Wish you were here instead of me."

The *Sea Dragon* with Halliburton and his crew were never heard from again, nor were any bodies ever recovered.

As he had once written, he received his wish, "I'll be especially happy if I am spared a stupid, common death in bed."

On **January 9, 1768,** circus performer Philip Astley
discovered that centrifugal force allows performers to ride,
while standing on a horse, when going in a circle.

WAYNE WINTERTON, PH.D.

JANUARY 10
A sobbing success story

Johnnie Ray
(John Alvin Ray)
Jan 10, 1927 (Hopewell, OR) – Feb 24, 1990 (Los Angeles, CA)

F OR THOSE OF you who were around during the Fabulous
'50s when Johnnie Ray came on the scene, you'll remember
him mostly for his unusual voice and his highly charged, emotional
singing style. He often cried, or appeared genuinely upset while
singing the lyrics to his soulful songs, and from a style point-of-view,
he was almost impossible to classify.

He wasn't a pure crooner like Frank Sinatra, Eddie Fisher, or Perry
Como, but in some ways, he fell into the crooning camp. In other ways
his haunting melancholy voice seemed to make him more of a blues
singer, and one website touts Johnnie Ray as "one of the greatest of the
transition singers between the crooners and the rockers." The rockers?

Suffice it to say, Johnnie Ray was a very different kind of vocalist
and as to the origin of his unusual voice, there was an unusual reason,
and one that few who listened to his music knew anything about.

In 1940, Johnnie Ray was a thirteen-year-old Boy Scout attending
a Jamboree for boys from all over the Pacific Northwest. One evening
some of the boys, along with Johnnie, decided it was time for a
blanket toss. Such tosses are generally harmless activities in which
one boy sits on a blanket held taut by the other boys, and then tossed,
trampoline-like, until he yells, "stop," or the boys doing the tossing
become too exhausted to continue.

Nearly every scout during the 1950s took his place on the
blanket at one time or another. However, on this particular occasion,
something went horribly wrong that cost Johnnie the hearing in his
right ear. Yet, what went wrong became the very thing that in a few
short years would make him famous and a household name.

During Johnnie's toss, one or more of the scouts lost their grip on
the blanket and Johnnie hit the floor, hard, and a stiff piece of straw
rammed deep into his right ear. He knew his ear had been hurt, but

being a tough Scout – there isn't a scout on the face of the earth who would admit to not being stronger than a stalk of straw – he didn't say anything to anyone, at least not at first.

He assumed his hearing would return, but it didn't, and it wasn't long before he had to be fitted with an embarrassingly large, cumbersome 1940s-style hearing aid. He solved the problem of having to wear the hearing aid by allowing his hair to grow just long enough to cover the device. It was an unstylish solution for a young man in the Forties and Fifties, when no boy worth his weight in argyle socks would allow his hair to touch his collar.

Johnnie grew up knowing how to belt out a song and as he developed from puberty into manhood, his voice changed. However, it changed not into the typically deeper voice of a young man, but into a voice with a unique sound, the product perhaps of his partial deafness and maturing vocal cords.

In the 1950s, he recorded several hit songs that set him apart from every other singer on the planet. He had this haunting, soulful voice and when he sang *The Little White Cloud that Cried,* or *Cry,* or *Tell the Lady I said Goodbye,* Johnnie would tear up and real tears would flow down his cheeks. Maybe it was an act, and if it was, it was magically effective.

Unlike the other singers of the era who simply stood in front of the microphone and sang, Johnny got emotional. He may have been the first to remove the microphone from the stand and scoot from one side of the stage to the other, sing from his knees while cuddling the microphone, or stroking and weeping into it while playing to the feelings of the audience.

There was no getting around it, Johnnie was mesmerizing and his fans loved him.

Perhaps, if it hadn't been for a couple of butter-fingered Scouts at the blanket toss, we might never have enjoyed the troubled melancholy voice of Johnnie Ray.

On **January 10, 1861**, U. S. Secretary of State
William H. Seward
purchased Alaska from Russia for $0.02 per acre.

WAYNE WINTERTON, PH.D.

Alice Stokes Paul

Jan 11, 1885 (Mt. Laurel NJ) – July 9, 1977 (Moorestown NJ)

A LICE WAS BORN into a prominent Quaker family and raised in a strict religious environment. Among her ancestors were William Penn and the prominent Winthrop family of Massachusetts. She grew up with a keen sense of the Quaker tradition of service, in part because of her mother's involvement as a member of the *National American Woman Suffrage Association.* At times, as a youngster, Alice attended suffrage meetings with her mother.

She graduated at the top of her high school class (Moorestown Friends School), and then attended Swarthmore, a college co-founded in 1864 by her grandfather where she graduated in 1905 with a degree in biology.

After attending a summer session at the New York School of Philanthropy and completing a fellowship program, she realized that her future didn't belong in social work. She stated, "I knew in a very short time I was never going to be a social worker, because I could see that social workers were not doing much good in the world . . . you couldn't change the situation by social work."

For Alice, "changing the situation," meant returning to school and going into a different line of work. She would earn a Master's Degree in sociology from the University of Pennsylvania in 1907, travel to the United Kingdom where she would hold down a job and attend the Woodbrooke Quaker Study Center, and then return to America in 1910 to earn a PhD in economics. Her doctoral dissertation was on *The Legal Position of Women in Pennsylvania.* It was a treatise on women's suffrage and Alice was about to become a national force to be reckoned with.

She became an unforgiving thorn in the side of President Woodrow Wilson for his lack of support for suffrage. On the day before his 1913 inauguration, she stole Wilson's inaugural thunder by leading a massive parade through the streets of Washington. With that singular act, she changed the national conversation from the president's agenda to that of suffrage, the right for women to make their voices heard via the ballot box.

In 1917, she led a group known as the *Silent Sentinels* in picketing the White House. Jailed, she went on a hunger strike, relentlessly attacking the Wilson Administration that already had its hands full with something called World War I. Nevertheless, Alice had her Silent Sentinels well prepared and organized. They began their vigil on January 10, 1917, and they didn't let up until the 19th Amendment, referred to in Congress as the "Susan B. Anthony Amendment," passed in 1919.

By 1918, President Wilson had enough of Alice Paul and the *Silent Sentinels*, whose silence had been deafening, and he agreed to support the 19th Amendment, but not on the merits of the Amendment. No! He supported it by saying the Act was urgently needed as an [undefined] "war measure." However, to Alice Paul, it didn't matter what excuse the president used to sign the measure, just as long as he signed it, and he did.

The 19th Amendment was ratified on August 18, 1920, when Tennessee's Henry Burns, told fellow legislators that he was casting his vote in honor of his mother. He did, and women finally had the right to vote.

Now, with the 19th Amendment the law of the land, Alice Paul formed the *National Women's Party* to support a new initiative, something called the *Equal Rights Amendment*. However, instead of unbridled support from her base, she met fierce opposition from where she least expected. From women!

President Wilson not only opposed her, she had fully expected his lack of support, but what she hadn't expected was opposition from the very women who had stood with her in forcing passage of the 19th Amendment.

The opposition came from every corner of the women's world, including the League of Women Voters, the American Association of University Women, the Parents-Teachers Association, the Women's Christian Temperance Union, the National Council of Jewish Women, and many similar female dominated organizations in what became known in the 1920s as "the Women's War."

So, why did women turn their backs on Alice Paul's cry for an *Equal Rights Amendment*?

In the 1920s, women viewed equal rights as a threat to the "protective labor laws" that limited work hours for females and forbid women from working in male occupations.

"If you want a particular quality, act as if you already have it."
William James (**Jan 11, 1842** – Aug 26, 1910) Philosopher

JANUARY 12

Helped place flag atop Mt. Suribachi on Iwo Jima

Ira Hamilton Hayes
Jan 12, 1923 (Sacaton, AZ) - Jan 24, 1955 (Bapchule, AZ)

I RA WAS A most unlikely war hero.

The oldest of eight children, he was born in the small village of Sacaton on the Gila River Indian Reservation south of Chandler, Arizona. Although described by many as shy and distant, he had mastered the skill of reading and writing in English by the age of four, and by the time he entered school, he was impressively bilingual in English and his native Pima language. Yet, typical of his peers, he was reticent to speak unless spoken to first, a trait often misinterpreted by non-Native Americans as being "slow of thought," instead of being "thoughtful of expression."

He was a good student at the reservation's Sacaton Elementary School and the Phoenix Indian School where he lived on campus. He was athletic in build, but shunned competitive sports and was noticeably one of the shyest students on campus. After completing two years of high school and bothered by the Japanese bombing of Pearl Harbor, he confided to a few of his friends that he intended to join the military.

He dropped out of high school, spent two months in the Civilian Conservation Corps and worked briefly as a carpenter. Then, in an act that many of his friends viewed as out of character for the shy, non-competitive Native American boy, he joined the Marine Corps on August 26, 1942.

Ira thrived on Marine discipline and he liked the camaraderie of his unit. Following a two-month boot camp, he went to Camp Gillespie, near San Diego, to become a paratrooper. After qualifying as a parachutist on November 30, 1942, he was promoted to private first class and assigned to the 3rd Parachute Battalion, 3rd Marine Division.

As a paratrooper, he saw action during the Battle of Vella Lavella (Solomon Islands) and later at Bougainville in the South Pacific.

After eleven months of fighting, his unit was disbanded and he was assigned to the 5th Marine Division and sent to Hawaii for additional training.

On February 19, 1945, he and 70,000 other Marines remained aboard hundreds of ships positioned offshore of the Japanese occupied island of Iwo Jima. There, the Marines waited as the island took a pounding of non-stop bombardment from other offshore ships.

Then it came time to assault the island.

On Day 1, after hours of softening up the island by constant shelling, Ira and the other Marines waded ashore amidst little resistance.

On Days 2 and 3, the Marines secured the southern tip of the island and advanced to Mount Suribachi, an imposing extinct volcano.

On Day 4, forty Marines, including Ira, were given the job of stringing a communications wire up Mt. Suribachi. During the climb, they linked up with Marine private Rene Gagnon, who was carrying a large American flag. When they reached the summit, they hoisted the flag to an avalanche of cheers from the Marines below. Just as one of the soldiers was about to take a picture, a Japanese soldier hurled a grenade at the group, sending the camera careening to the bottom of a seam in the lava flow.

Minutes later, news photographer Joe Rosenthal arrived with his press camera and an even larger flag. Ira and five others hoisted Old Glory for a second time and Rosenthal snapped the now iconic photo of six soldiers (five Marines and a Navy corpsman) raising the American flag on Iwo Jima, the most famous photograph of World War II, and a photo that won a Pulitzer Prize for Rosenthal.

After the war, Ira rarely talked about his wartime experience. He was a national hero, status that he never imagined and was never comfortable in assuming. On the reservation, he had trouble dealing with the demands that came with the national attention he was given. His escape was cheap whiskey, often drinking himself to sleep.

In 1954, following a White House ceremony with others in the photograph who had survived the war, he was his typical quiet self. When asked by a reporter if he liked the "pomp and circumstance" of the ceremony, he responded with a single word, "No."

Less than a year later, he died just outside an abandoned shack not far from where he grew up. The official ruling concluded that Hayes died from exposure and alcohol poisoning.

He was laid to rest at Arlington National Cemetery on February 2, 1955.

"It doesn't matter whether you're rich or poor –
as long as you've got money."
Joe E. Lewis (**Jan 12, 1902** – June 4, 1971) Comedian

JANUARY 13
Ernie's costliest cigar

Ernie Kovacs
(Ernest Edward Kovacs)
Jan 23, 1919 (Trenton, NJ) – **Jan 13, 1962** (Los Angeles, CA)

I F ONLY ERNIE had lit his ever-present cigar before leaving
the party at Milton Berle's home that night. Had he done that
one thing, lit his cigar before leaving, he may well have gone on to
entertain America for another twenty or thirty years or more years.
The epitaph on his tombstone reads, "Nothing in Moderation." That
pretty well summed up Ernie. He worked hard, loved hard, and crashed
hard into an unforgiving power pole. He was forty-two years old.

In his twenties, Ernie worked as a disc jockey, interviewed
personalities on his *Talk of the Town* radio show, wrote a column for
The Trentonian, announced at wrestling matches, and acted in local
theater. Always with his ever-present cigar, his signature prop.

In the 1950s, he took over a cooking show, *Deadline for Dinner*,
renamed it *Dead Lion for Breakfast* and used it to turn honest-to-
goodness chefs into foils for his zany antics. There was something
magical about the cigar-smoking Kovacs, and on the strength of that
wacky cooking show; he launched himself into national fame.

Much of what Kovacs did on national television was impromptu.
He wandered around New York with a cameraman in tow, turning
unsuspecting shoppers and businessmen into stars, if only for a
few minutes. He poked fun at fashion, politics, human foibles, and
whatever else popped into his fertile comic mind, and America loved
his spontaneity.

He got his own show, *The Ernie Kovacs Show* opposite *The
Milton Berle Show*.

He knew that beating out the well-entrenched Berle was a long
shot, something no one else had been able to do, but he gave it his best
shot. The show didn't survive the ratings and became just another
tombstone in Berle's graveyard of busted shows. However, unlike the

hosts of those other failed shows, Berle and Kovacs genuinely liked each other and interacted socially when their schedules permitted.

After the loss of *The Ernie Kovacs Show,* Ernie took no prisoners with *Three to Get Ready,* an early morning wake-up show where viewers never knew what to expect, except the unexpected. They might wake up to someone singing *Mona Lisa,* in Polish, or step from the shower to find someone performing *The Call of the Wild Goose,* in Yiddish.

In the realm of the unexpected, on one occasion when a stage prop failed in the middle of a monologue, Kovacs, without warning, grabbed a cameraman and left the studio in search of something to eat, and you never knew when he might introduce his favorite surprise guest, his wife, popular song stylist Edie Adams.

His spontaneous and sometimes unrestrained monologues and over-the-top stunts plowed virgin soil in the early days of television. Directors and producers yet to direct and produce such imaginative shows as *Laugh-In* and *Saturday Night Live* would later confess they had drawn inspiration from the unbridled and wildly funny mind of Ernie Kovacs.

Then, January 13, 1962, the night of the party at Milton Berle's house.

Everyone had barrels of fun!

There was lots of camaraderie, good friends, good wine, good-natured laughs, and since he and Edie had arrived at the party in separate cars, they left the same way, but only Edie made it home.

A photograph of the accident appeared in the following morning's newspapers. It wasn't pretty. Ernie Kovacs had died instantly of massive chest and head injuries, an unlit cigar mere inches from his outstretched hand.

If only he had lit his cigar before switching on the ignition.

Gambler, buffalo hunter, and the legendary sheriff of
Tombstone, Arizona,
Wyatt Earp died **January 13, 1929**, in Los Angeles
at the age of 80.

WAYNE WINTERTON, PH.D.

JANUARY 14
All because of a clause

Mary van Butchell
(Unknown) – **Jan 14, 1775** (London, England)

MARTIN VAN BUTCHELL, the husband of Mary van Butchell, was an eccentric man. In fact, T. Drew in his (or her) 1852 work, *The Lives and Portraits of Curious and Odd Characters: Compiled from Authentic Sources,* says about Mary's husband, "All the remarkable eccentricities which have yet been the characteristic of any man, however celebrated, may all hide their diminished heads before Martin van Butchell."

After you've read the story of Martin and Mary van Butchell, you'll agree.

We don't know what year Mary was born, but Martin was born in 1735, the son of a tapestry maker in the town of Mayfair, near the city of London.

Martin was a pupil of one of England's most famous surgeons, John Hunter (1728-1793), from whom he learned general medicine and dentistry. When business was slow, he made trusses, custom leather and steel trusses designed to alleviate the intestinal bulging associated with hernias. Thus, Martin could remove an appendix, extract a tooth, truss a man, and afterward conveniently hand the patient a single bill for payment.

By all accounts, Martin was a successful medical practitioner, but his eccentricities would soon overshadow his medical accomplishments; his bedside manner eclipsed by some very odd, socially strange behavior.

Martin loved being the center of attention.

He owned a white pony and on a whim, he might paint the pony purple or pink or some other color, or simply speckle it with varied colored spots. As skillful in play as he was in designing his custom hernia trusses, when his pony showed a tendency to become spooked, he invented a blind, not unlike a window blind, attachable to the pony's bridal. Thus, to prevent the pony from being spooked, he could drop the blind over the horse's eyes by pulling a cord. When the danger had passed, he could pull the cord in the opposite direction to give the pony full vision again.

We don't know when Martin married Mary, but we know she was a woman of means and that she died on January 14, 1775. If you think that painting a pony purple was bizarre, you are going to love what happened next.

Most marriage certificates assure a relationship "until death do you part." Not so Martin van Butchell's marriage certificate. His certificate, a legal document, contained wording to assure him a sustained income (assuredly from Mary's personal source of money), as long as Mary was "above ground." Consequently, Martin fully intended to keep the lovely Mary above ground for the rest of his life, and he did, but as it worked out, she remained above ground not only for the rest of his life, but for a total of 166 years after her demise.

After Mary passed away, Martin contacted his former medical school professor, John Hunter along with famed Scottish anatomist-chemist, William Cruickshank, and asked them to preserve Mary's body. They did so by embalming her with potassium nitrate. They also injected her with preservatives and color additives to give her face, especially her cheeks, a rosy glow. Then they gave her the finest glass eyes available and dressed her in a gown of exquisite lace.

Finally, Mary, on a layer of plaster-of-Paris to simulate fine linen, entered her eternal rest inside a beautiful glass-topped coffin.

Martin put the body on display in the window of his home, which also served as his medical office, and there she stayed for years. Over time, Mary began to look less and less like her old self, but Martin refused to move her until he married a second time to a lady named Elizabeth. Elizabeth, typical of a new bride, refused to have another woman, dead or alive, in the house.

Martin reluctantly gave Mary to William Hunter, the brother of John Hunter, who was also a physician, and who had assisted in the embalming. William kept the body for some time before donating it to the Museum of the Royal College of Surgeons in London, where it remained until May of 1941 when a German bombing raid destroyed the Museum.

"Never in the history of fashion has so little material
been raised so high
to reveal so much that needs to be covered so badly."
Cecil Beaton (**Jan 14, 1904** – Jan 18, 1980)
Fashion photographer

JANUARY 15
Two aces make a pair

Goodman Ace
(Goodman Aiskowitz)
Jan 15, 1899 (Kansas City, MO) - Mar 25, 1982 (New York, NY)

GOODMAN AISKOWITZ, KNOWN in school as "Ace," dreamed of becoming a writer. He enjoyed writing and his classmates liked the way he edited the school newspaper. Among the classmates who admired Ace's writing was Jane Epstein, an attractive blonde, but she had no other interest in her Latvian classmate, well, until . . . but we're getting ahead of the story.

After high school, Ace majored in journalism at Kansas City Polytechnic Institute where he wrote a weekly column with the snappy, but perplexing title, "The Dyspeptic" for the school's newspaper. Following his studies at the Institute, he landed a job with the *Kansas City Journal-Post* as a cub reporter.

One day, his press pass came in handy when that attractive blonde from his high school days, Jane Epstein, wanted to see a sold out Al Jolson concert. Ace had spent hours daydreaming about a date with Jane, but that's all it was ever going to be, a daydream. Jane was pretty and popular and he was, well, bookish, and certainly not the big man on campus. When Ace learned of Jane's plight, he took the initiative and found a way to let her know he could get them into the concert. Surprisingly, she accepted his offer, and six months later, they tied the knot.

Ace's job with the newspaper hardly covered expenses so he took a second job with radio station KMBC. On Sundays, he read the comics over the air, and on Fridays, he hosted a film review called *Ace Goes to the Movies*. The two fifteen minute segments netted the couple an extra $20 and boy, could they use the money.

Then the unexpected happened!

One Friday night, the fifteen-minute radio show that followed Ace's movie review failed to feed from its source. KMBC, with no backup program, was in a desperate bind. That's when Ace, with his wife Jane who was waiting to drive him home, went live on the air. No script, no notes, just dead cold live.

They began the show with a conversation about a game of bridge played earlier in the week. Then they drifted into a discussion about a local murder case in which a wife had shot her husband during an argument over a bridge game. With the clock winding down, the conversation, ad-libbed from the first sentence, ended with Jane asking Ace if "he would care to shoot a game of bridge?" Jane's confusion of words (malapropism), using *shoot* in place of *play* concluded the program. That was it, but . . . .

An enthusiastic response from KMBC's listeners convinced the station to give Ace and Jane a regular fifteen minute slot for a domestic comedy show of their own.

Easy Aces aired in Kansas City for two years. Ace was the straight man to Jane's maloprop-laden offerings, such as "time wounds all heels," and "I look like the wrath of grapes," and "I'm completely uninhabited" and on and on.

The audience loved the show and its success landed Ace and Jane a thirteen-week trial run broadcast from the CBS network out of Chicago. When CBS asked for an audience response, network executives received 100,000 letters of support, and *Easy Aces* and Jane's never-ending string of malapropisms went on to become an American radio fixture for the next fifteen years.

Today is the anniversary of the first appearance
of a donkey to represent
the Democratic Party. The cartoonish image appeared in the
January 15, 1870, issue of *Harper's Weekly* magazine.

JANUARY 16
Heroines who share a date

Margaret Cochran Corbin
and
Sarah Rosetta Wakeman
(Sarah Wakeman also known as Lyons Wakeman)
Margaret: Nov 12, 1751 (Chambersburg, PA) –
Jan 16, 1800 (Highland Falls, NY)
Sarah: **Jan 16, 1843** (Chenango, NY) – June 19, 1864 (New Orleans, LA)

I N THE DAYS of the Revolutionary and Civil Wars, there were no physical examinations to determine whether a person was fit for military duty. A man was fit or he wasn't. Neither was there any need to determine whether a person was a man or a woman. The difference was obvious. Men were men and women were women. Or were they?

To serve their country in war, some women served alongside their husbands, and a few disguised themselves as men. Margaret Corbin was one of those who distinguished herself at the side of her husband during the Revolutionary War. Sarah Wakeman was one of those who disguised herself as a man and fought during the Civil War, never revealing her gender. Coincidently, both women share a common date, as January 16 is the month and day of Margaret's death, and the month and day of Sarah's birth.

First, Margaret Cochran Corbin:

In 1756, Margaret, who went by "Molly," was orphaned when an Indian raiding party killed her father and took her mother captive, leaving Molly to be raised by an uncle. In 1772, she married John Corbin. Corbin enlisted in the Continental Army in 1775 when war with England appeared inevitable.

Like many women during the Revolutionary War, Molly accompanied her husband to war and became a *de facto* member of the military. In fact, she received a soldier's half-ration in return for cooking for the soldiers, washing their clothes and caring for the wounded. Although they were not allowed to participate in military drills, they watched and undoubtedly understood what was necessary to complete many military tasks, including operating a cannon.

On November 16, 1776, British and Hessian soldiers attacked Fort Washington in New York. The Hessians were Germans operating under contract to the British, and during that battle, John Corbin lost his life. Without missing a beat, Molly took over for her fallen husband. She began firing at the encroaching enemy with one of the fort's cannons until a cluster of grapeshot nearly tore her arm off, mangled her chest and lacerating her jaw.

As she was receiving medical attention, the British captured the fort and she became their prisoner. The British afterward released the wounded American soldiers, including Molly, who was ferried across the river to Fort Lee. From Fort Lee, she went by wagon to Philadelphia for additional medical treatment. She never fully recovered from her wounds and was without the use of her left arm for the rest of her life.

For her service, she received a pension of $30 per month for the rest of her life, making her the first woman in the United States to receive a military pension.

In 1926, the Daughters of the American Revolution had her remains moved from an obscure grave to West Point where a monument now stands in her honor behind the Old Cadet Chapel. It states that Margaret Corbin was "the first American woman to take a soldier's part in the War for Liberty."

Now, the story of Sarah Rosetta Wakeman:

Sarah was the eldest of nine children born to Harvey and Emily Wakeman, poor farmers in Bainbridge, New York. At nineteen, she left home to lessen the burden on family finances.

Aware that men earned more than women, she pretended to be a man and worked as a laborer on a coal barge on the Chenango River.

At the outbreak of the Civil War, recruiters from the 153rd New York Infantry Regiment, believing that Sarah was a man, told him he could earn a steady $13 dollars a month as a soldier. It was simply too good an offer to pass up, so on August 30, 1862, describing herself as a five-foot tall, fair-skinned male, she enlisted under the name of Lyons Wakeman.

Wakeman frequently wrote letters home, often asking for the family's forgiveness for leaving and causing them worry, always signing her letters with her birth name.

After serving as a guard in Alexandria, Virginia and Washington, D.C., Wakeman received orders in February of 1864 to join the command of Major General Nathaniel Banks, who was about to leave to fight the Confederates in Louisiana.

Like other soldiers, Wakeman marched hundreds of miles to Louisiana where they fought the mosquitos in harsh swamps and struggled under strength-sapping climatic conditions in the bayous. Through all this, Wakeman fared better than many of the men who died of bad food and water, or from disease brought on by insects.

On April 9, 1864, Wakeman faced the Confederates at Pleasant Hill, firing round after round while standing shoulder-to-shoulder with fellow soldiers. On April 23, at Monett's Bluff, Wakeman engaged the enemy in what would become his (her) final fight on the battlefield.

On May 3, after writing a letter home, vividly describing the horrors of war, Wakeman assured everyone that all was well, and then reported to the regimental hospital with severe diarrhea. From there, weakened and gravely ill, Wakeman was taken to a hospital in New Orleans, where death came on June 19, 1864.

Wakeman's true gender would have been discovered during hospitalization and upon her death. But, in deference to her wishes she died known on the records of the military, only as Private Lyons Wakeman and it is under that name that she is interred at Chalmette National Cemetery near New Orleans.

It was through the letters to her parents and research done years later, that the identities of Sarah Wakeman and Lyons Wakeman became known, positively identifying them as the same person.

"It isn't the mountain that wears you out;
it's the grain of sand in your shoe."
Robert W. Service (**Jan 16, 1874** – Sept 11, 1958) Poet

WAYNE WINTERTON, PH.D.

JANUARY 17
Polymath, inventor, dog lover

Francis Galton
Feb 16, 1822 (England) – **Jan 17, 1911** (Surrey, England)

S IR FRANCIS GALTON was a polymath (a highly intelligent fellow) born into a wealthy family, a good thing when you're very good at almost everything and you enjoy doing many things.

In addition, polymaths are usually interesting people. Not just because of their high intellect, but because there is often a quirky element to their being. Take the case of Sir Francis Galton, who invented something that after two-hundred years is still a doggone good invention. Should you want one, and if you're in the right kind of store, all you need to say is, "Oh, I almost forgot, I need to pick up a new *Galton.*"

Francis Galton was a half-cousin to Charles Darwin. They shared the same grandfather, Erasmus Darwin who, by the way, was no slouch in the intellectual department either. Erasmus was co-founder with Joseph Priestly (the first to recognize oxygen) of *The Lunar Club,* and the two of them were friendly with Josiah Wedgwood, the founder of Wedgwood Pottery and inventor of the pyrometer, a device for measuring extremely high temperatures, such as you'd find in a pottery kiln.

Although Galton and Darwin knew each other as children, it wasn't until they were adults that they grew close. They had their moments however, as they did with Darwin's *Theory of Pangenesis,* an idea that inheritance factors were contained in the blood. Galton disagreed, put Darwin's theory to the test by performing inheritance experiments on rabbits, and then told Darwin, in a cousin-friendly way, that he was nuts.

Following the death of his father, Galton came into a huge fortune that allowed him to live a gentleman's life, meaning lots of friends, lots of travel, and plenty of time to hunt foxes. During the 1840s, as casually as you might plan a family outing, he was touring places like the Middle East, Africa, and Egypt, and once on a whim, he traveled down the Nile.

It was a great life for a guy who didn't have to worry about earning a living.

In the 1850s, perhaps a little bored with just doing things, he made a lifestyle change and decided to apply his ample intellect to a variety of pursuits.

His earlier travels to Africa inspired him to travel there again, but with purpose, and in 1850, he proposed a trip to southern Africa, a trip that met with the approval and sponsorship of the Royal Geographical Society.

During the trip, Galton had maps drawn and he recorded observations of everything from the lives of native peoples to the various flora and fauna. After his return to England, he published *Tropical South Africa* (1853) and two years later followed it with a travel guide, *The Art of Travel: Or, Shifts and Contrivances Available in Wild Countries* (1855). For his work, and it was excellent work, the Royal Geographical Society gave him a gold medal.

Becoming interested in weather prediction, he created the first modern weather mapping system. His system showed changing climatic conditions across broad geographical areas, and in 1863 he published, *Meteorgraphics, or Methods of Mapping the Weather.*

He pioneered the field of *eugenics*, the study of practices aimed at improving the genetic quality of humans, coining the term himself. He proposed improving the human race by promoting reproduction among people with high quality traits while surgically reducing the reproductive potential among people with less desirable traits. He attempted to generate support for his theories, but met with little success.

Galton founded the science of "psychometrics," the measuring of a person's mental capabilities as is done today with IQ (Intelligence Quotient) tests.

In 1869, he published *Hereditary Genius,* the first systematic attempt to study hereditary factors against intellectual abilities, notable for what he called the "Law of Errors," the forerunner of today's bell-shaped Normal Distribution curve.

He studied fingerprints and was the first to classify fingerprints based on the distinctive ridges and valleys of a person's prints.

He conducted studies on the power of prayer, concluding by the way, that prayer has no power. Proof, the devoutly religious would say, that even a polymath has a right to be wrong.

He did research on the human ear and developed a device for determining the hearing range of humans and various animals, including dogs and cats. He was the first to chart those ranges, noting that dogs can hear to an upper level of about 45 kHz (kilohertz), cats to an even higher upper range of about 64 kHz, while a human's upper hearing range taps out at about 20 kHz (kilohertz), much lower than a dog or cat.

We've touched on some of the work done by Sir Francis Galton, but enough to let you see why he was called a polymath, a genius with multiple and varied interests.

In 1909, two years before his death on January 17, 1911, King Edward bestowed knighthood on this remarkable Englishman.

If you're still wondering what it was that Galton invented that is still around today. It's the whistle carried by your local pet store, often identified as a *Galton* or *Galton Whistle,* a whistle that emits sounds too high for humans to hear, but perfectly within the range of canines. It's knowledge like this that can set you apart as a highly intelligent person whenever you take *Barkley* out for his or her daily walk in the park.

"The constitution doesn't guarantee happiness,
only the pursuit of it.
Benjamin Franklin (**Jan 17, 1706** – Apr 17, 1790) Polymath

JANUARY 18
First successful open-heart surgery

Daniel Hale Williams
Jan 18, 1856 (Hollidaysburg, PA) – Aug 4, 1931 (Idlewild, MI)

STEVIE WONDER'S 1976 album, *Songs in the Key of Life*, contains a tribute to the black pioneers of mankind in a song titled simply, *Black Man*. Within the lyrics are the following words, "open heart surgery . . . was first done successfully . . . by a black man."

It's true.

Stevie Wonder's song doesn't name the black man who performed the world's first successful open-heart surgery, but there is no question as to who he was. He was Daniel Hale Williams, and although he wasn't the first to attempt open-heart surgery, he was the first, as Stevie Wonder dutifully notes, to do it successfully.

During a fight, James Cornish took a knife blade through the left fifth costal cartilage, slicing through the pericardium, and into the heart. It was Williams at Chicago's Provident Hospital who opened the heart, and without penicillin or an on-going blood transfusion, successfully performed the operation. The year was 1893, the operation was successful, and Cornish lived for many years afterward, likely much more careful about whom he picked a fight with.

Williams, a graduate of the Chicago Medical College in 1883, was one of only a handful of black surgeons in the nation at that time, but he was certainly one of whom all Americans can be proud.

Williams didn't grow up in an affluent family, nor did he grow up in a medical family unless you count his father, a barber, a skill once considered a part of the medical profession.

When Daniel's father died of tuberculosis, his mother knowing she couldn't care for all seven of her children (Daniel was number five), sent some to live with relatives. Daniel remained at home until his mother apprenticed him to a shoemaker in Baltimore.

It didn't take long before he knew that making and repairing shoes wasn't for him. He ran away from Baltimore and showed up a few days later on the doorstep of his sister's home in Edgerton, Wisconsin. She welcomed him into her home and he supported himself, as his father had done, by cutting hair, setting broken bones, doing a little blood-letting. You know, 1800s medical barbering.

Shortly afterward, he moved again, this time to the nearby town of Janesville. There he met Dr. Henry Palmer, a physician who took him on as an apprentice, and before long, with Dr. Palmer's encouragement, Daniel was considering a career in medicine himself.

In 1880 after a two-year apprenticeship, Williams enrolled at the Chicago Medical College, (today: Northwestern University Medical School). Graduating in 1883, he set up a medical practice in Chicago and the rest is history, but not well-known history.

As a black physician, he couldn't perform surgery in Chicago's hospitals, so he established America's first non-segregated hospital, Provident Hospital in Chicago in 1891, staffing it with a racially integrated medical team.

There's more.

In 1894, Williams moved to Washington, D.C., where he became the chief of surgery at Freedmen's Hospital, a facility established specifically for the care of former slaves. At the time of his appointment, the facility was in disrepair and best known, not for its medical success rate, but for its high mortality rate.

Tirelessly, Williams changed hospital procedures and revitalized its connection to the community. He encouraged the public viewing of surgeries, added ambulance services, and acquired equipment for specialized medical care. Light years ahead of his profession, he served without concern for the racial heritage of his patients.

In 1895, he co-founded the National Medical Association, an alternative to the racially closed American Medical Association that, at that time, refused African-American membership.

In 1912, he received an appointment as "associate attending surgeon" at Chicago's St. Luke's Hospital, the largest, wealthiest, and most influential hospital in the city.

In 1913, he became a charter member and the only African American physician in the American College of Surgeons.

Then, in 1926, he suffered a devastating stroke that left him partially paralyzed and unable to continue his medical career.

Williams died on August 4, 1931, at the age of seventy-one, a true medical pioneer.

"Did you ever stop to think, and forget to start again?"
A. A. Milne (**Jan 18, 1882** – Jan 31, 1956) Author

WAYNE WINTERTON, PH.D.

JANUARY 19
Edgar and the Baltimore Ravens

Edgar Allan Poe
Jan 19, 1809 (Boston, MA) - Oct 7, 1849 (Baltimore, MD)

P OE WAS THE first American author who tried to earn a living by writing alone. It wasn't easy and he wasn't successful, flat broke and dead at forty. Today, over 150 years since his death, few are those who have never heard of him. Most everyone has read at least one of his poems or short stories, or watched at least one football game involving the Baltimore Ravens, a team named in his honor. That's right. The Ravens are Edgar's team.

Poe's was a difficult life. He was orphaned early, depressed often, didn't handle rules well, was kicked out of West Point, was devastated by the loss of his beloved Virginia, wasn't recognized for his genius during his lifetime, and he checked out of this world under mysterious circumstances not knowing who or where he was.

He was born Edgar Poe, the son of actor David Poe and actress Elizabeth Arnold Poe. He was named after the character "Edgar" in Shakespeare's *King Lear,* a stage play in which David and Elizabeth were performers at about the time of Edgar's conception.

David deserted his wife soon after Edgar was born and Elizabeth died a year later of consumption (tuberculosis). That's when John and Frances Allan of Richmond, Virginia, took little Edgar in as a foster child, thus the "Allan" in Edgar *Allan* Poe.

Poe completed part of his early education in Scotland where the family lived briefly, and he later attended the University of Virginia, but quit after one semester following an argument with his foster father over money. He tried gambling to raise enough money to pay his tuition, but it turned out the gambling gods were even less supportive than his foster father.

In 1827, he enlisted in the army drawing a military salary of five dollars a month. When his enlistment was up, the West Point Military Academy accepted his application and he became a cadet. However, once school was underway, he preferred writing poetry to submitting to the school's strict curricular and disciplinary requirements. West Point told him he wasn't military material and they didn't invite him back for a second year.

In 1831, under the penname "A. Bostonian," he published, *Tamerlane and Other Poems*. West Point cadets, 227 of them who enjoyed the writings of their one-time fellow cadet, financed the book by kicking in 75-cents each to raise the necessary $170 for publication.

To give *Tamerlane* the appearance of an already successful offering, Poe added the words, "Second Edition," to the flyleaf, along with the following, "To the United States Corps of Cadets is this volume respectfully dedicated."

That same year, broke, and with no reasonable alternative, he moved to Baltimore to live with an aunt and her family, which included the aunt's eight-year-old daughter, Virginia.

Five years later, Edgar, twenty-seven, married thirteen-year-old Virginia.

To support himself and Virginia, he went to work as a literary critic for the *Southern Literary Messenger*, then for *Burton's Gentleman's Magazine* and the *Broadway Journal*, jobs that allowed him to publish fictional detective stories such as *The Murders in the Rue Morgue* under his own name.

In 1845, he published his poem, *The Raven*, and although he only received nine dollars for its publication, it made him famous, and it is today, considered a masterpiece.

You remember *The Raven*.

Once upon a midnight dreary, while I pondered, weak and weary,
O'er many a quaint and curious volume of forgotten lore,
While I nodded, nearly napping, suddenly there came a tapping,
As of someone gently rapping, rapping at my chamber door.
"'Tis some visitor," I muttered, "tapping at my chamber door –
Only this, and nothing more."

Two years later, his beloved Virginia, died at the age of twenty-seven. Edgar became increasingly despondent and unstable.

Two years after Virginia's death, Poe was wandering Baltimore's streets, delirious, and wearing ill-fitting clothes that were obviously not his. Someone took him to a hospital where he incoherently uttered his final words, "Lord help my soul," and he passed from this life.

The bar where legend claims Poe was last seen alive is still in operation in the part of Baltimore known as Fells Point. The name of the establishment is, "The Horse You Came In On," and locals insist a ghost by the name of "Edgar" still haunts the rooms above the bar.

Remember up front, the comment that the Baltimore Ravens football team was Edgar Allan Poe's team. It's true. It was team owner Art Modell's way of paying respect to the city's most famous citizen. The team name, the *Ravens,* came directly from Poe's famous poem, and the original team mascots were three oversized "birds" named Edgar, Allan, and Poe. Edgar was tall, broad shouldered and represented the Raven's backfield; Allan was thick and quick representing the receivers and backs; and Poe was short and stout representing the linemen.

In 2008, Edgar and Allan retired, leaving Poe to handle the team's mascot duties on his own.

"There is no such thing in anyone's life
as an unimportant day."
Alexander Woollcott (**Jan 19, 1887** – Jan 23, 1943)
Drama critic

JANUARY 20
George finally gave Gracie top billing

George Burns
(Nathan Birnbaum)
Jan 20, 1896 (New York, NY) - Mar 9, 1996 (Beverly Hills, CA)

T O SAY THAT George Burns was a theatrical icon would be an understatement of epic proportions. George died at 100 years of age after spending 93 of those years in show business.

So how did a little Jewish boy named Nathan Birnbaum become George Burns?

George has several stories about how that came to be, each told in typical George Burns' wandering story-telling style. Here is one of them. "My brother Izzy hated his name so he changed it to "George." I liked the name, so I took it from Izzy, leaving him nameless. There was a "Burns Coal Company" delivery truck in our neighborhood. I used to steal coal from that truck to heat our home, but I liked the company name, so I stole it too, and that's how I became George Burns."

At seven, he sang with the *Pee-Wee Quartet*, performing on ferryboats, saloons, street corners, and brothels. Yes, at seven years old, he was singing in brothels! It was a different world in 1903. He says he quit school in the fourth grade because the teachers wouldn't let him smoke cigars, and besides, he would say, he wanted to entertain full-time.

Regarding the *Pee-Wee Quartet*, George, in his distinctive gravelly voice said, "We'd put our hats down for donations. Sometimes the customers tossed something in the hats. Sometimes they took something out of the hats. Sometimes they took the hats."

During the early part of the twentieth century, George tried hard to make it big in Vaudeville. He even tried using different partners in his act, but his success was mediocre at best and he was light years away from being a headliner.

During that same period, Irish Catholic Grace Ethel Allen and her three sisters (Bessie, Hazel, and Pearl) were trying to break into Vaudeville with a song and dance act called *The Four Colleens*.

Grace had already experienced some success and at the age of three had appeared on stage with Eddie Cantor. Now, with her little girl cuteness gone, it was a different world, and although *The Four Colleens* was a decent act, it wasn't doing much better than George Burns' raspy-voiced song and dance and tell a few jokes act.

Then, in the early 1920s in Newark, New Jersey, *George Burns* and *The Four Colleens* appeared on the same billing. George, fresh out of partners, asked Grace to work with him on an act in which she would deliver "straight lines" so he could deliver the punch lines for laughs. However, it didn't work that way. The audience found Grace's ditzy delivery of the straight lines much funnier than George's grinning, cigar ash flicking delivery of the punch lines. Also, at about this time, Grace became the less formal sounding *Gracie.*

George, coming to the realization that he wasn't the key to the act, rewrote the material to capture the essence of Gracie's scatterbrained "illogical logic," writing himself in as the sensible half of the team. Moreover, he did something else; he made himself approachable to the audience, discussing with the audience some of Gracie's foibles while Gracie remained aloof of any knowledge that there was even an audience present.

It was 1922 when they tried the new material out on a fresh audience in Hoboken, New Jersey. Was it an inspired twist to a tried-and-true comedy routine? Some say it was, including that first audience in Hoboken. In fact, audiences everywhere, went nuts over the routine and theatergoers fell in love with Gracie who seemingly lived in a whimsical world of her own. After Gracie passed away, George often explained the secret to their success, "All of a sudden the audience realized I had a talent, and they were right, and I was married to her for 38 years!"

The comedy act of *Burns and Allen* set a new standard and the entertainment world would never the same.

George*: What day is it today?*
Gracie*: I don't know.*
George*: You can find out if you look at the newspaper on the sofa.*
Gracie*: Oh George, it doesn't help. That's yesterday's paper.*

After George and Gracie's turn-around performance in Hoboken and for the next 36 years *Burns and Allen* were headliners in every theatrical venue: vaudeville, stage, film, radio, and television.

In 1958, Gracie, suffering from the heart disease that would take her life six years later, retired. George continued to sing, dance, act, and tell jokes right up to the last year of his life. In his 90s, he told his audiences, "When I was a boy the Dead Sea was only sick."

On his 95th birthday he bragged, "I never felt better, never looked better, never made love better, and never lied better."

Did George love Gracie? Prior to his death, he had the engraving on the family crypt redone to read, *Gracie Allen & George Burns,* explaining he wanted the woman he loved to have the top billing she deserved.

George: *Say goodnight Gracie.*
Gracie: *Goodnight Gracie.*

On **January 20, 1986**, America observed
the first federal holiday
honoring Martin Luther King, Jr.

JANUARY 21

Father of modern anesthesia

Horace Wells

Jan 21, 1815 (Hartford, VT) - Jan 24, 1848 (New York, NY)

IN 1844, "PROFESSOR" Gardner Quincy Colton arrived in Hartford, Connecticut to entertain a theater audience with a demonstration of the effect of nitrous oxide (laughing gas) on human subjects.

Dentist Horace Wells and his wife Elizabeth had tickets, but they almost didn't make the show as Horace had been suffering from a toothache and needed a tooth extraction. Nevertheless, there they were, watching a guy with the dubious title of *professor* entertain them. By show's end, however, Well's mind was racing with an idea that would alter the course of dentistry.

Wells watched as Colton randomly selected a few volunteers from the audience and explained to everyone what to expect, and then the volunteers were instructed to inhale deeply from a container of nitrous oxide gas.

The subjects immediately began speaking in high-pitched voices, doubling with laughter as they bumped into one another drunken-like on the stage. In the midst of hoots from the audience, Wells saw something curious. One of the gas-inhaling volunteers, Sam Cooley, who had been stumbling across the stage, had inadvertently slammed his foot hard into a stage prop with some dangerously protruding nails.

Wells fully expected Cooley to drop to the floor writhing in pain, but instead, he leaped from the stage, frightened a man out of his seat, and chased the man up and down the aisles before sheepishly stopping and plopping in an empty seat right next to Dr. Wells. All of this, of course, to the howling delight of the audience.

As Professor Colton continued to expound on the scientific properties of nitrous oxide, Wells watched Cooley roll up his trouser leg and, in total bewilderment, stare at a deep cut and profuse bleeding coming from his lower leg. He was obviously baffled as to how it happened and why he felt no pain. Wells, however, knew what happened and he thought he knew why Cooley was feeling no pain. He provided first aid to Cooley and then sat quietly enjoying the remainder of the show.

After the show, Wells introduced himself to the professor and asked if he would accompany him to his dental office, and bring with him, one of his containers of nitrous oxide. Colton agreed, and at the office, Wells inhaled deeply from the container and asked his dental partner, Dr. William Morton, to extract his bad tooth, which he did. Sensing a scientific breakthrough in dentistry, Wells reportedly held up the tooth and exclaimed, "Ahhh, a new era of tooth pulling."

Horace Wells had discovered, if not painless dentistry, at least a way to reduce the pain to a tolerable level.

Unfortunately, the story doesn't have a happy conclusion and it's all downhill for Dr. Wells from here.

Wells spent a month experimenting on patients needing extractions and was delighted with the results. Confident in his findings, he and Dr. Morton arranged to demonstrate the painless procedure at Massachusetts General Hospital. The press was invited and the following excerpt is from the December 9, 1849 issue of the *Hartford Courant.*

> "A large number of students with several physicians, met to see the operation performed - one of their own to be the patient. Unfortunately for the experiment, the gas bag was by mistake withdrawn much too soon, and the patient was but partially under its influence when the tooth was extracted."

Use your imagination here, but know the extraction was far from painless, and Dr. Wells left the hospital amongst loud unceremonious jeers.

Wells, in fact, became so distraught over the incident that he sold his share of the dental practice to his partner, Dr. Morton, and became a door-to-door salesman, selling among other things, canaries. Going door to door with some caged birds and introducing himself as Canary Salesman Wells, didn't carry the same professional ring, as being Dr. Horace Wells, Dentist, and it wasn't long before he became despondent.

In 1847, and feeling a change in scenery might do him good, he traveled to Paris where he stayed for some time before returning to America. While in Paris or perhaps right after his return, he became addicted to chloroform, gradually increasing his usage of the substance and becoming more and more irrational.

The final straw to his psyche came when he learned his one-time partner, Dr. William Morton, was claiming credit for having discovered "nitrous oxide anesthesia" for dental patients. It was more than Wells could handle. High on chloroform he filled several empty vials with sulfuric acid, walked outside and threw the acid on two passing women.

Caught and taken to New York's notorious Tombs Prison, he requested that a pair of guards accompany him to his residence so he could pick up a shaving kit and other toiletries.

At his home and with the guards relaxed, he walked out of their view, inhaled deeply from a container of chloroform, allowed time for the anesthetizing process to begin, quickly slit his femoral artery, and departed this world, quite painlessly.

In 1864, the American Dental Association honored Wells posthumously as the discoverer of modern anesthesia. A similar honor took place by the American Medical Association in 1870.

There are today, two statues to honor Dr. Wells. One stands in the *Place des États-Unis* in Paris, France, the other in Bushnell Park in his hometown of Hartford, Connecticut.

"Just because nobody complains doesn't mean all parachutes are perfect."
Benny Hill (**Jan 21, 1924** – Apr 20, 1992) Comedian

JANUARY 22

A most curious man

Timothy Dexter
Jan 22, 1748 (Malden, MA) – Oct 23, 1806 (Newburyport, MA)

AROUND 1770 AN illiterate one-time waif named Timothy Dexter built a mansion in Newburyport, Massachusetts with a commanding view of the Merrimack River and the Atlantic Ocean. The garden of the residence featured a wooden statue of the homeowner, Timothy Dexter, atop a fifteen-foot column with the following inscription on the base:

Lord Timothy Dexter
I am the first in the East, the first in the West,
and the greatest philosopher in the Western World.

Just to show that Dexter was not a total egomaniac, there were thirty-nine other columns in front of the mansion, or within the statuary garden, each supporting a statue. Standing high on one of the columns was General George Washington in full military dress, and on his left, Thomas Jefferson, and on his right, John Adams.

A walk through the statuary took the visitor past the statues of famous generals, philosophers, Indian chiefs, scholars, gods and goddesses.

So, who was this Dexter guy?

He was an eccentric, an oddball for which there isn't space enough to do justice to his life. However, he was also some other things. He was either the luckiest, or the most farsighted, businessman on the planet. He was a man who married far above his station in life, a man who took the time to feign his own death so he could learn how others felt about him, and an author who had no concept of punctuation, but whose books sold anyway.

Timothy Dexter was born in Malden, Massachusetts in 1748 where he received very little, if any formal education. From 1755 to 1761 (ages 8-13) he was sent from the family home to work as a farm hand, and in 1762 he became an apprentice to a leather-dresser, either completing or ending his training after seven months.

In 1769, twenty-one years old, and with no hope of ever being accepted into Boston's affluent society on his own, he headed north to the town of Newburyport, and there met a widow of extreme wealth, Elizabeth Lord Frothingham.

On May 22, 1770, the widow Frothingham became Mrs. Timothy Dexter, and Mr. Timothy Dexter became very, very wealthy.

That same year Timothy and Elizabeth purchased a large parcel of land, built the earlier referenced mansion, and populated it with the 40 columns and statues.

With no formal education, Lord Dexter, like the mythical King Midas, seemed to have the ability to turn everything he touched into wealth.

For instance, just before the Revolutionary War ended, America's money, known at the time as "Continental currency," was so worthless that the words, "not worth a Continental" became an American catch phrase. So what did Lord Dexter do? He bought up every Continental note he could get his hands on at pennies on the dollar. Surprisingly, when the war was over, the federal government honored the notes at face value and Dexter cleaned up.

When trade relations with foreign countries were normalized, he commissioned the building of two ships and started an export business with Europe and the West Indies. On one occasion, he purchased a large supply of warming pans (pans used by New Englanders for heating bed sheets), but instead of shipping them to America as he had planned, he was inspired to ship them to the tropical West Indies, where they were sold as molasses ladles for a healthy profit.

Back in Newburyport, a number of ship's captains, thinking they could pull a joke on their competitor, convinced Dexter to load his ships with coal and sail to Newcastle, England. He did, and had the last laugh when his ships arrived amidst a coalmine strike and his coal, the only coal available, sold for a huge profit.

By mistake, he bought an enormous amount of whalebone. The stiff, but flexible material, used in the making of baskets, was in a depressed market, so he squirreled it away in storage. A few years later, he ended up making an enormous profit when whalebone was suddenly in demand in the manufacture of corsets.

Even with all of his successes in business, life in the Dexter household was not all sugar and spice, and Lord Timothy and Elizabeth split up. It happened right after he faked his own death and funeral without telling his wife about the plan, and she wasn't amused.

Wishing to know what the folks in Newburyport really thought about him, he had his death announced in a newspaper obituary, along with an invitation for everyone within reading distance to drop by the mansion and attend the wake.

An estimated 3,000 mourners, many of whom had never been inside the estate with its many columns and statues, accepted the invitation. Besides learning more than he wanted to know about how others felt about him, most disturbing was his wife's lack of grief over his demise. While the mourners were joyfully partaking of the family's bottomless supply of wine, Dexter found Elizabeth in the kitchen, and for her breach of funerary etiquette, beat her severely with a length of cane.

Now, lest you see Lord Dexter as simply a businessman who married well, but with a propensity for spousal abuse, know also that he was an author who wrote a book about himself that sold well beyond his, or anyone's expectations. Initially, he had no thought that the book would sell at all, giving it away to anyone who wanted a copy.

The book, *A Pickle for the Knowing Ones, or Plain Truth in a Homespun Dress,* addressed his dislike and distrust of politicians, the clergy, and his now former wife. However, the next to most amazing thing about the book was that it consisted of 8,847 words, random capitalization, and not one a punctuation mark. Amazingly, the book went through eight printings, and when a *Second Edition* was printed, it was exactly like the first edition with one exception. Dexter provided one additional page in which he provided thirteen lines of punctuation, no text, just punctuation marks with instructions to the reader to distribute them as they wish.

After his death on October 23, 1806, the Dexter mansion became a hotel and the ravages of time overtook the columns and wooden statues.

Today, Lord Dexter's house, sans statues, is still standing in Newburyport, Massachusetts.

"A bachelor's life is a fine breakfast, a flat lunch, and a miserable dinner."
Francis Bacon (**Jan 22, 1561** – Apr 9, 1626)
Philosopher, statesman

JANUARY 23
Inventor of the Frisbee

Walter Frederick Morrison
Jan 23, 1920 (Richfield, UT) – Feb 9, 2010 (Monroe, UT)

IN 1871, ON Kossuth Street in Bridgeport, Connecticut, pastry-maker William Russell Frisbie opened the Frisbie Baking Company, a business specializing in homemade pies. To remind customers of where to return the used pie tins, he had the words, "Frisbies Pies" embossed on the back of each.

Over sixty years later, 1937, and on the other side of the continent, Fred Morrison was playing catch in the backyard with his fiancée, Lucile (Lu) Nay. They were tossing a popcorn can lid back and forth, in what the mid-1950s would call "frisbee style." In 1937, however, the toss was called "tossing a popcorn lid back and forth" and it was simply something for Fred and Lu to do when they weren't holding hands, stealing kisses, or talking about the future.

When the popcorn can lid became dented beyond straightening, they "borrowed" a few of Mother Nay's cake tins from the kitchen and discovered to their throwing pleasure that they sailed better and further than had the old popcorn can lid.

Fred and Lu took a couple of mom's cake tins to the beach one day and while sailing the tins to each other, a stranger walked up and offered to buy one for a quarter. Well, in 1937, cake tins with a cake sold for a quarter, and anyone could buy the tin at the local five-and-dime for 5¢ each. It didn't take a genius to figure out that buying cake tins for 5¢ each and selling them for 25¢ represented a 400% profit, so Fred and Lu went into business selling "Flyin' Cake Pans" on the beaches near Lu's hometown of Santa Monica.

They did well enough with their beach-based business that it wasn't long before they had enough money to buy a marriage license and a bag of groceries so they got married.

In 1941, the Japanese bombed Pearl Harbor and fun at America's beaches dried up. The Flyin' Cake Pan business folded and to make ends meet, Fred enlisted in the Army Air Corps and became a P-47 Thunderbolt pilot.

Near war's end, he and his plane fell victim to a German anti-aircraft gun and he ended up at the infamous Stalag 13 Prisoner of War (POW) camp. However, his training as a pilot had taught him a few things about aerodynamics and with time on his hands as a POW, he thought about designing cake and pie pans with improved flight characteristics.

In 1945, the war was over and Fred and Lu were back in Santa Monica, where Fred went to work as a Los Angeles building inspector, and in his off hours, he spent time designing a flying disc.

Like Fred, other soldiers were returning home, and many of them were taking advantage of one of the federal government's rare good ideas, something called the *GI Bill*. The GI Bill picked up most, if not all of the costs associated with a college education. Some of those taking advantage of the GI Bill chose Yale University of New Haven, Connecticut, a prestigious institution with something the other universities didn't have. A business next door named the Frisbie Baking Company. That's right, the bakery that William Russell Frisbie founded in 1871 was still in business in 1945 and the pie tins still carried the embossed words, Frisbie's Pies.

That same year, Fred had a design on paper that he labeled the "Whirlo-Way," but it was just that, an unproven idea on paper. Two years later, and right after the reported sighting of a "flying saucer" near Roswell, New Mexico, Morrison met with investor Warren Franscioni. The meeting ended with Franscioni agreeing to pay for the manufacture of an initial batch of Whirlo-Way discs, and to capitalize on the Roswell flying saucer craze, the product received a new name, the *Flyin-Saucer*.

The Flyin-Saucer might have caught on, except for one small detail. It didn't fly as well as those doggone pie tins, and Fred and Warren parted ways.

In 1955, building inspector Fred and the ever-lovely Lu were still at it, designing and testing version after version until they had something that was truly aerodynamic and flew as well as it looked. They named the sleek flyer, the *Pluto Platter*.

A year later, Fred and Lu received U. S. Patent No. 183,626 for the design of the Pluto Platter, which included the outer third of the disc known today as the "Morrison Slope," still a key feature in all aerodynamically sound Frisbees.

Fred and Lu sold the rights for the manufacturing of the Pluto Platter to Richard Knerr and A. K. Melin, the owners of a new toy company named Wham-O. The company kept the name, Pluto Platter, until company president Richard Knerr took a tour of colleges, giving away free Pluto Platters to encourage sales.

During the tour, and to his amazement, Knerr stumbled on a game between some Yale and Harvard students in which metal pie tins that the students called "Frisbie's" were being flip-tossed in a manner that the students called, "Frisbie-ing."

Knerr liked the name better than Pluto Platter and when he returned to his office, the product was renamed the *Frisbee*, a purposeful misspelling of "Frisbie" to avoid any possible name infringement with the New England pie company.

Thus was born the Frisbee, and a new, very long-lasting American craze, and by the way, over the years, Fred and Lu received well in excess of a million dollars in royalties for the invention.

Fred died in 2010 at the age of ninety and is at rest in his hometown of Richfield, Utah.

On **January 23, 1556**, the world's deadliest
recorded earthquake took place.
The epicenter was near Shaanxi, China
killing an estimated 830,000 unsuspecting inhabitants.

WAYNE WINTERTON, PH.D.

JANUARY 24
Hard work, success, downfall, death

Albert Russel Erskine
Jan 24, 1871 (Huntsville, AL) - July 1, 1933 (South Bend, IN)

A LBERT WAS A hard worker.
In 1886 and only fifteen-years-old he worked long hours selling shoes for $1.50 per week.

He quit school to work full time and by the time he was 21, he was earning $7.50 a week keeping books for a business.

In 1898 and twenty-seven, he was the chief clerk for the American Cotton Company and six years after that he was managing three hundred of their cotton gins.

In 1904, he became treasurer of the Yale Lock Company.

In 1910, he was a vice-president of the Underwood Typewriter Company. A year later, he became treasurer and a member of the executive committee of the Studebaker Corporation.

In 1915, he was president of Studebaker, and in 1928, he gained control of the Pierce-Arrow Corporation.

In his spare time, he served on the Board of Trustees at Notre Dame University.

A believer in innovation and quality first, Erskine guided Studebaker, at one time the world's largest manufacturer of horse-drawn wagons, into a position of prominence in the highly competitive world of gasoline-powered automotive manufacturing.

He did extensive research, built numerous experimental models, encouraged the design and production of economically sound automobiles, and conducted exhaustive road tests at Studebaker's million-dollar proving ground and in 1927, the *Erskine,* an independent Studebaker model, was unveiled.

Market timing and the Ford Model 'A' shortened the life of the *Erskine* and only six of the *Erskine Roadster* 50J models with rumble seats exist as of 2015.

In 1932, the company produced the *Rockne,* named for Notre Dame Coach Knute Rockne. It was another short-lived model, in production for only two years except for its engine, the *Rockne 65/10* that became the standard engine for all Studebaker six-cylinder vehicles through 1961.

That Albert Erskine was a respected self-made man with a driven work ethic and persuasive personality is a given. The youngster from Huntsville, Alabama, with almost no formal education had beaten the odds to become a pillar of industry.

Erskine's fall from grace resulted from his failure to recognize the severity of the 1929 stock market crash followed by the Great Depression. In 1930, he paid stockholders a dividend five times the company's net profit, and a year later paid another large dividend that he erroneously thought would be offset with the acquisition of the White Motor Company. He was wrong.

In 1932, Studebaker went into receivership.

He now faced staggering personal debts of $350,000, an overwhelming amount of money in 1932, and he was on his way out as president of Studebaker. In addition, his health was failing with a combined diagnosis of heart disease and diabetes, and for Erskine, even worse, was a heightened sense of personal guilt that he had somehow let his company down and his stockholders holding the bag.

On July 1, 1933, he drove to the company's proving grounds, a testing facility that had become a part of his very soul, and there he sat, contemplating his next move.

To start over, to rise as he had once done, to a position of leadership in the automotive world all seemed so distant now. Faced with a certain loss of control at Studebaker, he reached for the handgun he had brought with him, aimed the barrel squarely at his heart and pulled the trigger.

On **January 24, 1908**, the Boy Scout movement
took a giant leap forward
with Sir Robert Baden-Powell's publication,
Scouting for Boys.

JANUARY 25

America's Native American Vice President

Charles Curtis

Jan 25, 1860 (Topeka, KS) – Feb 8, 1936 (Washington, DC)

CHARLES CURTIS WAS born near Topeka, Kansas Territory, on January 25, 1860, one year before the Territory received statehood (January 29, 1861).

When the presidential ticket of Herbert Hoover and Charles Curtis won the 1928 presidential election, Curtis became the only Executive Branch officer to have been born in a territory rather than a state. In addition, Charles Curtis holds another first, and one that for the past eighty-seven years (1928-2015) has stood unbroken. However, given the right person and the right opportunity, it will be broken and perhaps surpassed as well.

Charles Curtis's rise to success was pure Horatio Alger, a genuine "rags to riches" story.

Curtis grew up on the dusty plains of Kansas. As a young man, he cleaned out livery stables after school for spending money and at one time, was the winningest jockey in Kansas, not the usual benchmarks for climbing bureaucratic ladders and achieving political success.

In 1877, when he outgrew his jockey silks, he went to work as a reporter for the *North Topeka Times* and four years later drove a horse-drawn hack (taxi), a job that allowed him time to hit the books in preparation for passing the Kansas bar exam, which he did in 1881.

At the age of twenty-four (1884), he won his first election becoming the Prosecuting Attorney for Shawnee County, Kansas, and he must have done a few things right because he was returned to office in 1886.

In 1889, he lost a bid to fill a vacant seat in the House of Representatives by a single vote, but the loss only stimulated his appetite for national office.

Three years later and thirty-two years old, he ran and won a seat in the House, afterward winning four more consecutive House terms from 1894 to 1902. In 1903 he made an unsuccessful bid for the U. S.

Senate, lost, and a year later reclaimed his old House seat for a sixth term, 1904-1906.

In 1908, he made another run for the Senate and won, but was defeated when he ran for reelection in 1912, and then reclaimed the seat four years later. Curtis knew how to win elections, and when he lost, he wasted no time feeling sorry for himself. Instead, he examined his losing campaign, refocused, and tried again, usually winning.

In 1924, the talk swirling inside the Senate chambers was that Curtis was presidential timber, smart and electable, but the talk petered out. Then, in 1927, when Herbert Hoover became the Republican nominee, he selected Charles Curtis as his running mate and they won.

However, there's more to the Charles Curtis story and unless you're a history buff or a political junkie, chances are good you might not be aware of an important "first," as mentioned in the opening of the story. It has to do with the election of Charles Curtis as America's 31st vice-president.

Charles' mother, Ellen Pappan Curtis was a woman of blended heritage. She was one-fourth Kaw, one-fourth Osage, one-fourth Potawatomi, and one-fourth French. What all of that means, is that Ellen Pappan Curtis was three-fourths Native American and one-fourth European heritage.

Charles' father, Orren Curtis, was of European heritage only, descended from English, Scots, and Welch ancestors.

With a mother who was three-quarters Native American and a non-Native American father, Charles met the one-quarter blood quantum necessary at the time of his birth to be considered a Native American. He was also an enrolled member of the Kaw Tribe, and thus he was America's first and to the present date (2015) America's only Vice President of Native American heritage.

On **January 25, 1961**, President John F. Kennedy
held America's
first live Presidential news conference,
broadcast simultaneously
by both radio and television.

WAYNE WINTERTON, PH.D.

JANUARY 26
President for one day

David Rice Atchison
Aug 11, 1807 (Lexington, KY) – **Jan 26, 1886** (Gower, MO)

DAVID RICE ATCHISON was President of the United States for exactly one day, March 4, 1849, and he slept through the greater part of his presidency. Some historians have credited Atchison's term in office as the least controversial in history. There are those who say if the politicians running the country today would follow President Atchison's fine example of soporific (sleep inducing) leadership, the country would be better off today.

To put Mr. Atchison's presidency into perspective, his one-day presidency followed the single term of President James K. Polk (1845-1849), and preceded the presidency of Zachary Taylor (1849-1850).

Lest you doubt the veracity of this story, know there are roughly as many historians who accept, as dispute Atchison's fleeting occupancy of the Oval Office. Most of those who refuse to acknowledge Atchison's rightful place as America's 12th president do so on the weak grounds that he was never given the key to the presidential restroom. To quote a former perennial presidential candidate, the late Patrick Layton Paulson, "Picky. Picky. Picky."

Atchison's grave marker in the Greenlawn Cemetery in Plattsburg, Missouri reads, "President of the United States for One Day – Sunday March 4, 1849 – David Rice Atchison," along with the dates of his birth and death. Also in Plattsburg, a statue of President Atchison graces the front of the Clinton County Courthouse. Thus, if the good people of the *Show Me State,* a state full of people who are notorious for not taking anyone's word for anything, can recognize David Rice Atchison as president, then everyone should be able to accept Atchison's presidency.

In 1991, a full 142 years after his single-day service as the leader of the free world, David Rice Atchison was inducted into the *Hall of Famous Missourians* along with a bronze bust that is now on permanent display in the rotunda of the Missouri State Capitol in Jefferson City.

The city of Atchison, Kansas is named for President Atchison, and is home to what has been called the world's smallest presidential library. The *David Rice Atchison Presidential Library* is located inside the historic Santa Fe Depot Museum and is presently (2015) maintained by Chris Taylor, the Executive Director of the Atchison County Historical Society.

Taylor is also the person to see about Library tours, which according to one website, he does with "equal measures of scholarship, conjecture, and good humor." Depending on the number of questions asked, a complete tour of the Presidential Library, including introductions and a restroom break, will take about five minutes. "After all," quips tour guide Taylor, "for a one-day presidency, how much space do you need?"

President Atchison was only forty-one years and six-months old when he had the presidency thrust in his lap, but long enough to make him the country's youngest "appointed" president. John F. Kennedy holds the record as the country's youngest "elected" president at forty-three years and nine-months.

So, how did this quirky bit of Americana come to be?

The Atchison presidency happened when Zachary Taylor refused inauguration on March 4, 1849, because it was a Sunday. The preceding president, James K. Polk, left office right on schedule, but Taylor's demand that his oath of office be delayed until noon on Monday, March 5th, left an unexpected 24-hour vacuum of power.

In 1849, the next in succession to the presidency was the President Pro Tempore of the Senate, who was David Rice Atchison. Atchison never imagined when he went to bed the evening of March 3 that he would awaken the next morning as President of the United States. In fact, he might not have enjoyed his presidency at all if it hadn't been for a certain incident.

According to Achison's personal account printed twenty-three years later in the September 1872 *Plattsburg Lever*, this is how he learned he was in charge of the country.

"... Judge Willie Person Mangum of North Carolina awakened [me] at 3:00 a.m. and said, jocularly, that I was now President of the United States and he wanted me to appoint him as Secretary of State."

In that same article, Atchison said that if he had one boast to make during his presidency, it was "that not a man, woman or a child shed a tear on account of my incumbency."

How many presidents, before or after President Atchison, can make such a claim?

"If you're playing poker and you look around the table and can't tell who the sucker is, it's you."
Paul Newman (**Jan 26, 1925** – Sept 26, 2008) Actor, film director

---

JANUARY 27
... and a husky named Togo

The Last Great Race on Earth
Start: **Jan 27, 1925** (Nenana, AK) – Finish: Feb 2, 1925 (Nome, AK)

T HERE HAVE BEEN a few races over the centuries that have caught the imagination of the public. Some were fictional, such as Phileas Fogg's race in 1872 to circumnavigate the world in eighty days in a hot air balloon. Mr. Fogg was successful because he had the backing of the novel's author, Jules Verne, who wasn't going to let his high-flying protagonist down.

Some were non-fictional, such as Nellie Bly, who had the backing of her boss, newspaper magnate Joseph Pulitzer. In 1889, Nellie traveled around the world covering 24,899 miles in 72 days, thus beating Fogg's famous fictional flight by a full eight days. She even risked a time-consuming side-trip to visit with Jules and Honorine Verne in Amiens, France, where she was entertained and wished God-speed.

There was one race, however, that took place in 1925 for which the sheer boldness of the plan almost overshadowed its purpose. The purpose was to deliver a life-saving vaccine to Nome, Alaska, where an entire community was facing possible death. The boldness being that the only way to deliver the vaccine was to transverse 674 miles of barren waste from Nenana (near Fairbanks) to Nome (100 miles south of the Arctic Circle) by dogsled. Moreover, the serum had to arrive in January when the snow rarely stops falling, the winds never stop howling, and temperatures are typically in the realm of minus-40 to minus-70 degrees.

The race, a relay of twenty teams of sled dogs and mushers, positioned at thirty-five mile intervals across the Alaskan wilderness, were required to pass a twenty-pound canister of serum to the next team, and to do it without going off the trail or losing the canister in the snow. That race, known as the *Great Mercy Race*, ended when Balto, the lead dog of the twentieth team, entered Nome with the serum, on February 2. Total elapsed mushing time: five-and-a-half days.

Although it was Gunnar Kaasen and Balto that entered Nome and thus received national accolades for saving the community, most agree it was Leonhard Seppala and lead dog, Togo, who were the true heroes for having covered the longest and most hazardous portion of the trip.

Imagine if you will, all that had to happen to get the serum across those 674 miles. This wasn't time for a group of planners wearing neckties to hammer out a proposal. It was "decision on the fly" time, with lives at stake, and for Leonhard Seppala, there was extra incentive. There was in Nome, a life more valuable than his own, his only child, eight-year-old Sigrid. Seppala would have attempted the 674 miles on his own, if needed, to prevent her death.

And for Seppala, his portion of that 674 mile race came in the form of being asked to carry the serum over the most daunting portion of the trail, a rarely used shortcut across Norton Sound, which if he were successful would shorten the distance to Nome by a full day.

Seppala wasn't asked because he lived in Nome, and Norton Sound was at his end of the Mercy Run, but because he was recognized as one of Alaska's most experienced and capable mushers. In addition, he had successfully crossed the Sound's ice a few times, something rarely attempted by others.

Unfortunately, there was a mix-up between mushers Myles Gonangnan and Henry Ivanoff, and Ivanoff, who now had the serum, was preparing to follow the trail skirting Norton Sound.

Seppala, who was on his way to receive the serum from Gonangnan before crossing the ice at the Sound, was surprised to hear Ivanoff's voice. "The serum! The serum! I have it here!"

Looking up, Seppala could see Ivanoff anxiously trying to untangle his dogs from a surprise encounter with a reindeer. In retrospect, the problem may have been an act of Providence, as had the reindeer and dogs not become entangled, Seppala, not looking for Ivanoff, may never have received the serum and the *Mercy Run* to Nome may have ended right there, at Norton Sound.

After a few minutes of puzzled discussion and clarification, Ivanoff gave the canister to Seppala, who now faced not only making the dangerous Norton Sound crossing, but also completing both his and Ivanoff's distances before reaching the next musher of the relay team, Charlie Olson.

Seppala began his crossing of the Sound, a particularly difficult task because the ice is constantly in motion from dangerous under-the-ice sea currents. If that wasn't enough, the wind-polished ice made it nearly impossible for man or dog to get a decent foothold, and a flipped sled on undulating ice could have meant a lost serum canister.

It was a matter of only a few hours after Seppala had crossed the Sound, that the ice began breaking up and drifting out to sea. Seppala and his dogs, led by Togo, a dog once thought too small to lead a team, finally arrived at the designated location where musher Charlie Olson waited.

The serum, now in Olson's care, would continue to be handed off like a relay-race baton until it reached Nome and its citizens, including Seppala's daughter Sigrid, all of whom had been praying fervently for the safe passage of the mushers.

Postscript: In commemoration of the Great Mercy Race of 1925, a man named Joe Redington (1917-1999), known today as the *Father of the Iditarod,* along with his wife, Vi, would become the driving force behind the modern Iditarod. The Iditarod, a challenging race of not 674, but 1,100 frozen miles, from Seward to Nome is the "Last Great Race on Earth."

During the first Iditarod in 1973, President Reagan acknowledged the three surviving 1925 heroes: Charlie Evans, Edgar Nollner, and Bill McCarty. The 1973 race also featured the first ever female mushers, Mary Shields and Lolly Medley, who placed next-to-last and last, with signs affixed to the backs of their sleds that read, respectively, "The" and "End."

"When you handle yourself, use your head;
when you handle others, use your heart."
Donna Reed (**Jan 27, 1921** – Jan 14, 1986) Actress

WAYNE WINTERTON, PH.D.

Colette

(Sidonie-Gabrille Colette)

Jan 28, 1873 (Yonne, France) - Aug 3, 1954 (Paris, France)

C OLETTE'S BOOK, *GIGI* (1945) is about a young girl who balks when her grandmother tries to groom her as a courtesan, a prostitute for men of wealth. Gigi, a carefree little girl, isn't much of a student and the purposes of her training in sexuality make little sense to her. Nevertheless, she enjoys the friendship and company of her grandmother's nephew, Gaston, whom she sees as an older brother, and to which he reciprocates by treating her as the little girl she was. That was, until she suddenly blossomed from a little girl into a young woman, and a beautiful one at that.

Lerner and Loewe brought *Gigi* to Broadway. The stage play starred Leslie Caron as the mistress-in-training, Maurice Chevalier as a rakishly charming gentleman who guides the story along, and Louis Jourdan, as the older brother figure whose friendship with Gigi turns into, well, something else. The story takes a few side trips and everyone lives happily ever after, if we might use a fairytale ending, which is exactly what Gigi is, a French fairytale.

As a young girl, Colette (not Gigi) romped and played in the French countryside. Then, into her life came Henri Gauthier-Villars, the French writer and wit known as *Willy*, a bona fide charlatan. In 1893, twenty-year-old Colette and thirty-five year old Henri tie the knot and Colette exchanged a life of pastoral bliss for a whirlwind existence of intoxicating Parisian high-society life.

A gifted writer, Colette quickly learned from Henri what Parisians wanted to read, and she penned a series of racy tales about a girl whose powers to charm were shocking, even to the French, who were not easily shocked by descriptions of sexual indiscretions. Since it was an era when only men wrote books, Colette used Henri's pen name *Willy*, and to Henri's great delight, *Willy,* the assumed author of the country's sauciest stories became the toast of Paris.

By 1910, the wine of marital bliss had turned to vinegar and the couple divorced. To support herself, Colette, under the tutelage of Mathilde de Morny, became a music hall performer and more, inferring a romantic involvement between the two women.

In 1907, a sensuous onstage kiss during a pantomime titled *Revé d'Égypte* (Egyptian Dream) at the Moulin Rouge caused a near riot. The scandalous behavior of the two women exchanging a sensual kiss, led to a ban on all future performances of the production in Paris.

In 1913, she wrote *Music-Hall Sidelights* and later, *Cheri* (1920), *The Last of Cheri* (1926), *Duo* (1934), and of course *Gigi* (1945), which brings our little story of the incomparable Colette full circle.

Well, almost full circle. There is something else about Colette. It's something that might soften your opinion, if it needs softening, of the lady that penned some of France's sauciest novels and performed on stage in unseemly ways.

In 1935, she married Maurice Goudeket, a Jewish man, and during the German occupation of France during World War II (1941-1945), she hid Maurice and many other Jewish people in her attic for the duration of the war.

When Colette died in 1954, she became the first woman given a state funeral in France.

On **January 28, 1986**, the Space Shuttle
Challenger exploded,
killing teacher Christa McAuliffe and six astronauts.

Victor Mature

Jan 29, 1913 (Louisville KY) - Aug 4, 1999 (Rancho Santa Fe CA)

W HEN POPULAR 1950s movie star Victor Mature's application for membership in the swanky Los Angeles Country Club was denied, an accompanying note explained that, "the club did not accept actors into its membership." Mature, respectful and in his usual self-effacing manner, wrote back, "I'm no actor, and I've got sixty-four films to prove it!"

Victor Mature's birth name, as strange as it seems for a Hollywood icon, was "Victor Mature." His father, Marcello Gelindo Maturi, an Italian immigrant and a scissor-grinder by trade, had Americanized his surname to "Mature" before Victor was born. Victor's mother was an American woman of Swiss descent.

Victor grew up independent and undisciplined, and received somewhere between little to no formal education from a variety of schools, and it wasn't because his parents didn't try to get him to study. His lack of interest, stubbornness, and later on, partying, led to expulsions from public and parochial schools alike, including specialized schools like the Spencerian Business School and the Kentucky Military Institute. At the latter, his devil-may-care attitude and a lack of regard for regimentation earned him the disrespectful title, *Cadet Slob.*

By the age of fifteen, Victor had been asked to leave almost every school he attended, so he went to went to work for his father as a refrigeration assistant before moving on to become an elevator operator. When that wore thin, he sold candy for a candy wholesaler, and then something good happened.

Using his good looks, natural charm, a gift for schmooze, and a self-imposed payday savings plan, after four years of saving he had enough money to make a down payment on a restaurant, which he bought and flipped for a small profit. Using the proceeds from the sale, he packed his car with candy for bartering for gas and paying for meals on the road, and he headed for Hollywood. He arrived in tinsel town with a car running on fumes, eleven cents to his name, and few unopened bags of candy.

Showing up at an open audition at the Pasadena Playhouse, he impressed Playhouse founder Gilmore Brown enough to get into a work-study program, doing janitorial work in exchange for acting lessons. Brown also let the homeless candy salesman live in a tent on the property.

In November of 1936, Mature debuted in *Paths of Glory* and received enough critical review that the Playhouse offered him a scholarship, which meant he could put away the toilet bowl brush and devote full time to acting.

In 1939, Frank Ross, a vice-president of Hal Roach Studios liked his performance and especially his impressive physique in *To Quito and Back* and arranged for Mature to make his major film debut as "Lefty" in *The Housekeeper's Daughter.* Lefty was one of five men chasing the housekeeper's daughter who, according to the movie posters, "treated them like she hadn't oughter!"

In the early 1940s, Mature appeared in a variety of films, drama, adventure, and even musicals, and just as it seemed he was on his way to the big time, World War II put his career on ice. He tried to enlist in the Navy where he learned he was color blind, so he walked next door to the Coast Guard recruiting office, took a different eye test, passed, and served his country, including fighting at Normandy and Okinawa.

In 1944, he acted in War Bond films designed to boost military morale, such as the Coast Guard revue, *Tars and Spars* that toured for a year. After the war, he was back in Hollywood, but this time he had an acting résumé.

From 1945 and through the '50s, the ruggedly handsome actor appeared in westerns, including the role of Doc Holiday in *My Darling Clementine.* He appeared in musicals, such as with Esther Williams in *Million Dollar Mermaid.* However, for what he was best known, were his roles in a multitude of Biblical offerings including, *The Robe, Demetrius and the Gladiators, The Egyptian,* and most memorably, that of Samson in Cecil B. DeMille's epic, *Samson and Delilah.*

In the 1960s, with the exception of Neil Simon's *After the Fox*, Mature found golf more to his liking than sound stages and he hung up his shield and mace for good.

Did he need to keep working? Not at all! Perhaps he did learn more from the Spencerian Business School that anyone thought. Mature amassed a fortune in investments and real estate over the years, and the crowning touch, his beloved mansion on a hill above the ninth hole of the Rancho Santa Fe Golf Course.

"When a man's best friend is his dog,
that dog has a problem."
Edward Abbey (**Jan 29, 1927** – Mar 14, 1989)
Author, essayist

JANUARY 30
The Dinton Hermit

John Bigg
Jan 30, 1649 (date of King Charles I execution)

BECAUSE THIS BOOK assumes an associated date for the placement of each story, and because the best that historians can do is to place John Bigg's birth at between 1627-1629, and his death in 1696, it appeared that the story of John Bigg (the Dinton Hermit), might end up in a box overflowing with unused stories.

Then, just as there must be angels watching over odd people like John Bigg, there must be angels watching over equally odd people, like those perpetually hunched over a computer keyboard, because, help arrived in the form of two paragraphs from two different sources.

One was a paragraph about Simon Mayne, a Member of Parliament and one of the judges at the trial of King Charles I of England. The paragraph noted that it was Simon Mayne's law clerk, one John Bigg, who swung the axe in the execution of King Charles I on January 30, 1649.

The other paragraph, from a different source, noted that, "one John Bigg, the 'Dinton Hermit,' who was once the executioner of the King . . . took to living in a cave for his remaining forty years." Thus, there is a place for the story of John Bigg after all, January 30, the date that John Bigg served as the executioner of King Charles I.

As an aside, John Bigg's boss, Simon Mayne, was not only one of the judges at the trial of King Charles I, but he was also one of the signers of the King's death warrant.

On the day of the execution, the weather was cold and King Charles wore two shirts to ward off the chill as he walked from his cell to the executioner's block. It wasn't the biting cold that bothered him as much as a concern that the crowd might interpret his uncontrolled shivering as fear, for he is quoted as saying, "the season is so sharp as probably may make me shake, which some observers may imagine proceeds from fear. I would have no such imputation."

To protect the executioner's identity against those in the crowd sympathetic to the King, the executioner wore a hood through which he could see to do his job, but left him anonymous to others. Some historians say that Richard Brandon, London's most famous hangman, turned down a payment of £200 to perform the beheading. Thus, the executioner could have been just about anyone.

Once on the platform and above the crowd, Charles spoke to the assembly, and then at precisely 2:00 p.m., he laid his head on the block, said a prayer, and signaled his readiness to the executioner by stretching out his arms and hands. A single stroke of the executioner's axe, and the rule of King Charles I belonged to the ages.

With King Charles' death, the British monarchy ended, and in its place, the Commonwealth of England was established. It didn't last long, however, as citizens quickly tired of Oliver Cromwell and his strict Puritan views. Holidays, including Christmas and Easter were suppressed and leisure activities such as theater and gambling were banned. Within ten years the English were ready to return to the good old days and on May 29, 1660, Charles II (the exiled son of Charles I), became King and England entered a period known as the Restoration.

When Charles II assumed the throne, among the first to come under fire were the judges who had convicted and executed his father. Simon Mayne went on trial for his judgment against Charles I, was found guilty of high treason, and was sentenced to death. He died a prisoner in the Tower of London on April 13, 1661 while awaiting his appeal. Mayne's body was then taken to his hometown of Dinton, Buckinghamshire, and was there interred.

Let's return now to the story of John Bigg, the one-time law clerk for Simon Mayne, and the man believed to have been the executioner of Charles I. When Simon Mayne went on trial and was convicted and sentenced to die, Bigg, looking back on his role in the execution, decided it was time to leave town. His clerking days over, Bigg moved into a cave on the side of a mountain near Mayne's hometown of Dinton, and until his death in 1696, that cave was his home.

Some ascribe Bigg's withdrawn behavior to a depression that had come over him at the time of King Charles' beheading; others felt his depression was more recent and due to the conviction of Simon Mayne, his former employer; and still others suggest his change in attitude and lifestyle was simply his way of coping with the need for self-preservation. Whatever it was, Bigg's new lifestyle and eccentricities became the stuff of which legends are made.

He became a tourist attraction in Dinton and as the years wore on; townspeople and visitors alike began to call him the Dinton Hermit. Without a dependable livelihood, the people of Dinton supplied him with food and ale. However, what really set him apart from virtually everyone else on the planet was his homemade clothing and shoes.

His clothing consisted of hundreds of small pieces of leather, one piece attached to another by way of nails bent to hold the pieces together, giving his clothing the odd look of armor. An internet search for the Dinton Hermit should produce an image of Bigg wearing clothing consisting of pieced together leather.

The folks who knew him said he never changed his clothing, but simply replaced decaying scraps of leather with newer scraps

His shoes were handmade of leather as well, held together with bent nails, each shoe containing as many as ten layers of scraps. Both of Bigg's shoes have survived and are on display at the "British Archaeology at the Ashmolean Museum" in Oxford, England.

"I belong to Bridegrooms Anonymous.
Whenever I feel like getting married,
they send over a lady in a housecoat and
curlers to burn my toast for me."
Dick Martin (**Jan 30, 1922** – May 24, 2008) Comedian

WAYNE WINTERTON, PH.D.

JANUARY 31
The man who floated to Earth

André-Jacques Garnerin
Jan 31, 1769 (Paris, France) – Aug 18, 1823 (Paris, France)

ALL OF US have taken part in this same argument. It happens every year on the last day of January. Someone will remember that January 31 is the birthdate of André-Jacques Garnerin. Some say he was the first man to float successfully to earth using a parachute, which he did on October 22, 1797. However, there are those who insist the "floating to earth" honor should go to Louis-Sébastien Lenormand. Thus, whenever Garnerin's name comes up, you can count on someone bringing Lenormand's name into the conversation, and here it comes now.

"Louis-Sébastien Lenormand!" someone yells, and then asks no one in particular. "What about Lenormand? He floated to earth using something like a parachute on December 26, 1783, a full fourteen years before Garnerin."

"Let's not get carried away here," mutters a lady rolling her eyes, remembering last year's fracas.

"Everybody, settle down," comes a voice of reason, adding, "Something *like* a parachute doesn't count. An umbrella isn't a parachute. A parachute is a parachute."

"Not only that," the Lenormand supporter yells, paying no attention to the voice of reason, "Lenormand's the guy what came up with the term *parachute*, shouldn't that count for something?"

"Maybe," says someone looking at their laptop, "It says here that Lenormand was the first to use the word, 'parachute.' Seems he made the word up from the Greek *para*, meaning *against*, and the French *chute*, meaning *fall*. So according to my laptop, the word "parachute" literally means 'against falling.'"

"But," says another, "just because he came up with *parachute*, doesn't mean he should get credit for using one when all he had was a couple of big umbrellas. Besides, he only jumped from the top of the Montpellier Observatory, probably less than a hundred feet above the ground, and that's nowhere near as impressive as Garnerin, who rose 3,000 feet in a balloon before cutting himself loose."

"But if something goes wrong," piped another, "jumping from 100 feet or 3,000 feet, the distance wouldn't matter. I vote for Lenormand."

"This isn't an election," whispers the barely audible lady, still remembering last year's flap.

"I suppose that splattering on the ground from any distance would be a sure ticket to the Pearly Gates," says laptop person, looking at a picture of a man wearing a weird strapped-on contraption. "It was for Franz Reichelt!"

"Who was Franz Reichelt?"

"It says here he was a German tailor who built a "parachute suit" out of a bunch of fabric."

"Three hundred square feet of fabric," says someone just joining the group and the holder of a second laptop.

"Whatever! Anyway, Reichelt stuffed a bunch of fabric inside a metal frame belted to his body and jumped off the Eiffel Tower."

"So, what happened?"

"So, what do you think happened? Ssss-plat."

"Splat? You're putting me on. No German would be crazy enough to jump off the Eiffel Tower."

"He was only half German. His mother was French."

"Okay, that makes sense. A Frenchman would jump off the Eiffel. What then?"

"They say he left a crater under the Eiffel Tower a foot deep."

"A foot deep? Are you sure?"

"I don't know, maybe an inch deep, but anyway, British Pathé Pictures caught the whole thing on film. It's all on the internet. Just punch in Franz Reichelt's name, but don't blink. From jump to ssss-plat takes about three seconds."

"No thanks! Let's get back to Lenormand and our birthday boy, Garnerin."

"So we know that Lenormand invented the word "parachute" and that he jumped from the roof of an 85-foot tall observatory. What else?"

"He jumped using two huge umbrellas tied together, giving him a rigid-frame parachute fourteen feet across, but he wasn't thinking about his invention for balloonists. He was trying to invent a way for people to escape from burning buildings."

"And Garnerin? What about his parachute?"

"Well, Garnerin was an expert balloonist, inventor, and a student of ballooning pioneer Jacques Charles, who made numerous ascents before turning his attention to the development of a parachute. Even his earliest parachutes looked pretty much like those used in World War II, except that instead of being strapped to a man, they were connected to a wicker basket, you know, the kind used by balloonists back in the day."

Here's how it all went down.

On October 22, 1797, Garnerin was ready to demonstrate his parachute.

Visualize, a large hydrogen-filled balloon attached to a wicker basket. Also attached to the wicker basket, is a parachute, limp and dangling half inside and half outside the basket. Next to the limp parachute stands André-Jacques Garnerin flashing a large knife with which, when he reaches 3,000 feet, he will use to sever the rope that connects the basket to the large hydrogen-filled balloon. At that moment, he will be dependent on the parachute, attached to the balloon's wicker basket, to float him to earth.

It's launch time. On signal, the balloon, suspended parachute, and Garnerin ascend skyward. At 3,000 feet, Garnerin severs the rope allowing the balloon to separate from the wicker basket. Now, Garnerin and the wicker basket begin a wild swinging ride earthward, but with each back and forth motion, the parachute canopy takes on more and more air until the swinging lessens to a gentle floating. The descent continues until the parachute, wicker basket and Garnerin all land safely, with Garnerin walking away having achieved what many considered a foolhardy miracle, but a miracle just the same.

From there, Garnerin continued to improve the design of his parachute, and regardless of the varied opinions of your friends, some of whom will always argue on behalf of Lenormand, the majority of historians today agree that André-Jacques Garnerin is in the better position to be the *Father of the Parachute*.

Sadly, as happens so often to people who risk their lives in pursuit of a dream, Garnerin was supervising the construction of another parachute when a wooden beam toppled over. He was simply in the wrong place at the wrong time.

The date was August 18, 1823. He was 54 years old.

"I don't want any 'yes-men' around me.
I want everybody to tell me the truth even
if it costs them their jobs!"
Samuel Goldwyn (Aug 17, 1879 – **Jan 31, 1974**)
Movie producer

WAYNE WINTERTON, PH.D.

FEBRUARY 1
Pershing's last patriot

Frank Buckles
Feb 1, 1901 (Bethany, MO) - Feb 27, 2011 (Charles Town, WV)

F RANK WAS SIXTEEN when he decided to become a "doughboy," the nickname for a World War I soldier, especially one serving in the infantry. All he knew was that bad things were happening "over there," and that "over there" was another name for Europe and that's where his country needed his help. He never thought of himself as a patriot. He might never have used the word himself.

At the Kansas State Fair, he walked into a Marine Corps recruiting office. They asked his age. He lied, telling them he was eighteen, but it wasn't good enough. They were only recruiting twenty-one years and older, they said.

A week later, he returned and waited outside until there was a different sergeant at the front desk, and when that happened, he told the new sergeant he was twenty-one. The sergeant put him on a scale and told him he didn't weigh enough. He walked out of the Marine recruiting office and down the street to its Navy counterpart, passed a written test, but failed the physical examination.

The recruiter said he had flat feet, but Frank wasn't through trying. Not by a long shot.

Two weeks later in Oklahoma City, he walked into and out of the Marine and Navy recruiting offices with no luck. At a nearby Army recruiting office, they said they needed his birth certificate. Buckles had heard about the question and he was ready with his story, "I told them that public records were not made of births in Missouri when I was born and my only record is in the family Bible." They accepted him at his word, which was a mere two years off, and he signed his name. He never forgot the day, "I enlisted in the Army on August 14, 1917," he was fond of telling people, "and my serial number was 15577."

When it came time to choose a military occupation, he asked, "What's the fastest way to get over there?" The sergeant told him the fastest way was by joining the Ambulance Service. Buckles signed another piece of paper and that quick he was on his way to Fort Riley, Kansas, where he received a quick education on *Trench Casualty Retrieval and Ambulance Operations*, and then shipped overseas.

In 1920, three years after his enlistment, he returned home with $143.90 for his military service, which included a $60 bonus, and Frank felt real good inside. Real good! He had served his country.

Twenty years later, he reenlisted to serve in World War II, but ended up a prisoner-of-war in the Philippines where he languished for nearly four years without knowing what might happen to him. Freedom came with the Liberation of Manila on February 23, 1945.

In 1946, he married Audrey Mayo and the couple settled down to farming a piece of land in West Virginia. Audrey passed away in 1999.

In 2004, at the age of 103, Frank was still driving his tractor around his farm.

In a 2007 interview with *The Washington Post,* he said this about serving your country, "If your country needs you, you should be right there, that's the way I felt when I was young and that's the way I feel today."

That same year the Department of Veterans Affairs declared him the last doughboy standing. When visitors stopped at his rural West Virginia home, he'd joke with them, telling them he had "just been declared an endangered species."

When asked the secret to his long life. His response took a mere six words, "When you start to die, don't."

Nevertheless, the day did come when his body wore out for good. It happened right there where he and his bride, Audrey, had started their lives together in West Virginia. He had just recovered from a chest infection and was feeling spry in spite of his 110 years and 26 days. He summoned his live-in nurse and as she walked through the door, she heard his final breath and watched as his eyes closed for the final time.

At the time of his death, a television documentary was in production about America's last doughboy, and Frank would have liked it. His grave at Arlington National Cemetery is within view of the Washington Monument and near the grave of his commander, General John J. Pershing.

Oh yes, the name of the television documentary that Buckles didn't live quite long enough to see, it was a special about him, titled *Pershing's Last Patriot.*

On **February 1, 1887**, a man named Harvey Wilcox began a
project to build a
Christian community on the Pacific coast. His wife Ida,
named it "Hollywood."

FEBRUARY 2
Famous angel

Farrah Fawcett
(Mary Ferrah Leni Fawcett)
Feb 2, 1947 (Corpus Christi, TX) - June 25, 2009 (Santa Monica, CA)

F ARRAH'S METEORIC RISE to success was as close as one can get to having lived a fairytale life. Her passing, unfortunately, came almost as quickly as her ascendancy, and in between the two events, she had become one of the most recognizable women in the world.

Farrah, the daughter of a Texas oil field contractor and a homemaking mother, was the younger of the family's two daughters. Of Irish, French, English, and Choctaw ancestry, she said her mother picked her birth name, "Ferrah," because she liked the way it sounded when spoken with "Fawcett." At some point in her life, the "e" in her given name gave way to an "a" and she became Farrah.

At W. B. Ray High School in Corpus Christi, Texas (1962-65) something that almost never happens in the changeable world of high school attitudes, happened. For four consecutive years, from freshman to senior, she was voted as, "Most Beautiful" by her classmates.

Quick with a quote, Farrah once said, "The reason the all-American boy prefers beauty to brains is because he can see better than he can think."

During her freshman year at the University of Texas, Austin, she was one of the "ten most beautiful coeds" on campus. It was the first time a freshman made the cut for what was typically an exclusive upperclassman honor. After her sophomore year, she passed on college for a crack at making it big in Hollywood, and she probably holds the world's record for the shortest amount of time being in Hollywood before someone noticed.

Within two weeks of her arrival at the Mecca of movies and modeling, she had an agent, a legitimate modeling contract, and was flooded with more offers than she could accept to appear in television commercials.

Farrah, a waterfall of hair cascading to below her shoulders and framing a stunningly wholesome girl-next-door face, was every boy's dream girl in the 1970s and '80s. A person couldn't open a magazine, peer inside a boy's bedroom, or walk into an auto repair shop without finding Farrah smiling back at them.

On television Farrah was Jill Munroe, one of a trio of beautiful take no prisoners crime-fighting females on the hit series, *Charlie's Angels.*

Although an angel for only one season, a fact that most folks don't realize, that television show and a poster of her wearing a red one-piece bathing suit and a million-dollar smile catapulted her into stardom.

Then, a marriage to television's *Six Million Dollar Man* (Lee Majors) that lasted an eternity. Well, a Hollywood eternity, nine years, followed by a romance with actor Ryan O'Neal that produced a son. Then, the devastating news in 2006, that Farrah, the woman who looked like she could never have anything bad, had cancer, and she had it bad, real bad.

A series of treatments by medical doctors and holistic healers bounced her back-and-forth between cancer-free and the discovery of new tumors, one too many times.

On June 25, 2009 with Ryan O'Neal at her side, Farrah quietly slipped out of the room and into a host of real angels, this time far above the streets of Los Angeles where she and a crew of make-believe angels had once fought crime.

"The place where optimism most flourishes
is in the lunatic asylum."
Havelock Ellis (**Feb 2, 1859** – July 8, 1939) Physician

FEBRUARY 3
The Black Cyclone

Charles Follis
Feb 3, 1879 (Cloverdale, VA) – Apr 15, 1910 (Cleveland, OH)

CHARLES FOLLIS. EVER hear the name? No? You're not alone. With the possible exception of a few old-timers who sustain themselves on beer and sports trivia, Charles Follis is a name that just may have slipped past most of the folks who know their sports history.

In 1899 and a junior at Wooster (Ohio) High School, Follis not only helped to organize the school's first varsity football team, but his all-white teammates elected him captain. That inaugural season and with Follis carrying the ball on almost every play, Wooster posted an 8-0 record with a combined score total of 112-0. Wooster High not only won every game, but was never scored on! Not once! The key reason for the latter was that Follis, as did most high school players at that time, played both defense and offense and he was a terror whether coming or going.

In 1901 and out of high school, Follis enrolled at Wooster College, but elected to play for a local amateur ball club, the Wooster Athletic Association. At the end of the season, Wooster AA met the Shelby AA team, the returning amateur champions of Northern Ohio.

Shelby's coach, Frank C. Schiffer, after watching Follis play in those two games, wanted Follis to play for his team, and the September 8, 1902, issue of the *Shelby Daily Globe* carried a story that began, "Manager F. C. Schiffer stated this morning that he had secured Follis, the colored player of Wooster. He knows the game thoroughly [and] will be a valuable addition to the team, and will arrive in Shelby next Sunday."

Follis didn't disappoint!

Shelby's 58-0 rout of rival Fremont, capped by Follis's sixty yard run "with the entire Fremont team as his heels," led one writer to describe Follis as looking like a *Black Cyclone* on the playing field.

The following year, 1903, was a landmark year for the team because a few of Shelby's players received compensation for their play. Follis was not among that group. However, at the beginning of the 1904 season, Follis received a contract, which he signed, and at that moment, the six foot, 200-pound *Black Cyclone* became the first black player in America to sign a professional football contract.

Within two years the Shelby Blues had become, if not the first football team to sport a professional-only roster, at least one of the first. Another of Shelby's outstanding athletes in 1906 was a young man with an odd name, Branch Rickey. Rickey and Follis had once played against each other on opposing college baseball teams, Rickey as the catcher for Ohio Wesleyan, and Follis as the catcher for Wooster College. During 1906, as Shelby Blues teammates, the two men formed a lifetime friendship.

Rickey admired Follis for more than his outstanding athletic ability. He admired him for the unruffled way in which he handled the ugly taunts and verbal abuse that came from opposing players and fans. It wasn't easy being a black athlete, especially an outstanding one, during those turn-of-the-century days.

Rickey would later become famous as the baseball executive who set in motion the breaking of Major League Baseball's color barrier by signing Jackie Robinson as a member of the Brooklyn Dodgers in 1947. Some say it was Rickey's friendship with Follis, and the classy way the latter withstood the taunting public, that helped to pave the way for Robinson.

Although Follis missed most of the first half of the 1906 football season with an injury, he played well during the second half until a serious injury on Thanksgiving Day, 1906, ended his football career for good.

There was no "poor me" in Charles Follis. He turned his attention to professional baseball, and became the holder of another "first." He became the first black baseball catcher to move from college baseball into the Negro Leagues.

Many believe that as talented as Follis was as a football player, his baseball instincts and skills, especially his hitting, made him an even better baseball player. Two of his home runs, described at the time as "moon shots," left the crack of his bat so well hit that those who were there said they went into orbit.

We'll not present Follis's baseball career here, except to mention that he and pitcher Johnny Bright were the ace battery for the Starlight (Cleveland) Champs, and that both men passed away within two years of each other. Twenty-year-old Bright died on June 24, 1908 in a death listed only as "tragic." Follis died on April 5, 1910, of pneumonia, at the age of thirty-one.

While nothing is certain, it's possible that at least one of those two moon shots hit by Follis rolled to a stop somewhere near where St. Peter sits in judgment. If so, when you pass through those Pearlies, look for a large well-built black man playing catch with a younger fellow named Bright.

On **February 3, 1959**, musicians Buddy Holly,
J. P. Richardson (the Big Bopper), and
Richie Valens died in a plane crash
shortly after takeoff from the
Mason City, Iowa airport. The day is known as,
"The Day the Music Died."

WAYNE WINTERTON, PH.D.

FEBRUARY 4
The flying tailor

Franz Reichelt
c. 1879 (Austria) - **Feb 4, 1912** (Paris, France)

O N FEBRUARY 4, 1912, a bitter cold day, Franz Reichelt, a tailor born of a French mother and an Austrian father awaited the clicking of the shutter. The resulting photograph has survived to the present day and is on the internet. It shows Reichelt, standing, wearing a bulky parachute of his own design, his feet apart and his arms outstretched.

Clearly visible is a wood or metal frame attached to his back by means of a broad belt about the waist and perhaps an unseen shoulder harness as well. Reichelt designed the frame to help deploy 320 square feet of fabric, most of which is folded inside an overcoat-type garment he is wearing. The fabric appears strategically tied to his ankles, arms, and wrists.

While working on the development of his newly designed parachute, he likely envisioned a day when it might be standard life-saving equipment for pilots, and toward that end, he had done the needful to clear the way to demonstrate the worthiness of his invention.

In early 1911, he had approached the Parisian Prefecture of Police, asking for authorization to demonstrate the life-saving capabilities of his parachute by allowing him to throw a parachute-wearing mannequin off the Eiffel Tower. It had taken almost a year to work his way through the red tape. Finally, in early 1912, he had approval, and although the mannequin toss would not be from one of the higher platforms as he had requested, he accepted the bureaucracy's decision and took the next step.

He announced his upcoming experimental parachute test to the public, and British Pathé Pictures would be on hand with two cameras to film the event for theater newsreels. One camera would be located on the platform to catch the moment of the mannequin's toss over the tower's protective railing; the other strategically placed on the street to capture the parachuted mannequin's float to earth, and its landing at or near a projected landing spot, depending on the wind.

Reichelt was confident in his parachute and that the 320 feet of fabric would deploy as he had designed. The demonstration would do wonders in attracting an investor, or investors, to help underwrite further development of his invention.

He had conducted multiple experiments by dropping parachute-rigged mannequins from the fifth floor of the apartment building where he lived. With some of the drops, the parachute had deployed as expected, but there had been exceptions, the plaster mannequins literally exploding as they struck the pavement. Those that hadn't deployed, Reichelt concluded, had failed because of a lack of elevation to allow the system to work properly.

February 4, 1912, was just a few days away now, and everything was coming together nicely. Reichelt spent his time talking to people, encouraging their interest and hoping for a sizeable turnout. There's nothing worse than hosting an event, inviting the press, and having no one from the public show up. Reichelt worked hard to assure that wouldn't happen here.

Then, on the day prior to the mannequin toss, Reichelt received a disturbing piece of news.

British Pathé, the same company that would be filming his event, had just filmed a newsreel segment of an American named Frederick Law making a successful parachute jump from the visitor's platform near the top of the Statue of Liberty.

For Reichelt, the news changed everything. It made no sense to have British Pathé film a parachute-wearing mannequin tossed off the Eiffel Tower when only two days earlier, an American had been filmed in a live parachute jump from atop the Statue of Liberty.

On February 4, Reichelt, technicians from British Pathé and a few Parisian dignitaries climbed to the designated platform. Then, to the surprise of everyone, Reichelt set the mannequin off to the side and strapped the parachute to himself, belting it firmly in place. Once satisfied that everything was ready, he climbed onto the railing placed to keep the suicide-prone from doing what he was about to do, jump.

The technicians from Pathé checked and double-checked their equipment, unaware that what they were about to record on film would become historic footage. It would be one of the earliest examples of a true-life tragedy filmed in real time.

Below the Eiffel Tower, milling around and waiting for the demonstration to begin, were a large number of curious Parisians.

Reichelt teetered back and forth on the narrow rail several times. The existing Pathé footage shows someone with their back to the camera talking to Reichelt, a last minute plea perhaps, for him to reconsider what he was about to do. If that were the case, the French tailor wasn't going to let the opportunity go to waste. This was his chance to show off his invention, a chance that had taken a year to get bureaucratic approval.

From the camera on the tower, Reichelt slowly leaned forward and disappeared in a flutter of fabric. The camera on the ground catches two, perhaps three seconds of a man plummeting to his death, striking the frozen February ground with a hard dusty thud, and it's over.

Pathé continued to roll their cameras, as several policemen are seen frantically working in the distance, placing Reichelt's broken body into an ambulance.

The still photographs and the Pathé newsreel showing Reichelt's plunge to his death are reminders of man's desire to rise above the humdrum of everyday life, and thus leave, if not a contribution, at least an impression on the world, and Franz Reichelt certainly did that.

On February 4, 1789, George Washington was elected first
U. S. President with all 69 electoral votes.
The runner up, John Adams, was declared Vice President.

FEBRUARY 5
Lovely ladies joined at the hip, really

Daisy and Violet Hilton
Feb 5, 1908 (Brighton, England) - January 1969 (Charlotte, NC)

U NMARRIED ENGLISH BARMAID Kate Skinner wasn't happy. Not at all!

She wasn't happy because she was pregnant, and she wasn't happy because she suspected her pregnancy was God's punishment for too many indiscretions.

She hadn't meant to get pregnant and barely making ends meet as a barmaid, she couldn't afford to take care of a child. Not now! Nevertheless, Dr. Rooth did what needed done, and although it turned out to be a most unusual delivery, the doctor had done well.

Unbeknownst to Kate, she had been carrying twins, but not an ordinary set of twins.

"Conjoined twins," the doctor said quietly, using the medical term for what most people of the era would refer to as "Siamese twins," and he lifted up the tiny bodies. Two girls oddly attached at the hips and buttocks. When barmaid Kate opened her eyes and looked at her daughters for the first time, she quickly shut her eyes again, tight. She no longer suspected God was punishing her, she knew God was punishing her. How else could such a thing happen?

Kate did everything she could to block out the vision of the tiny connected bodies, but she could still hear their whimpering.

Mary Hilton, the owner of the bar where Kate worked, heard something else.

Ka-ching!

Two weeks later Kate and Mary struck a deal. An unknown amount of cash may, or may not, have exchanged hands, or Kate may have simply handed the babies to Mary, but either way, tavern-owner Mary Hilton viewed the clandestine transaction as her key to easy street.

The twins, Daisy and Violet would grow up calling Mary, "Auntie Lou" and Mary's husband, "Sir," and they would share the surname Hilton, not Skinner.

As soon as they were able, the girls learned to dance and sing, and in spite of their handicap, they were surprisingly well coordinated, had above average voices and each as an individual, was truly attractive! Had it not been for their unusual connection during an era in which sideshows and circus freaks were called just that, they could just as easily been a homecoming queen and first attendant.

By 1911, Mary knew she had cut a good deal with barmaid Skinner, and now it was time to see a return on her investment. She and her daughter Edith prepared to take Daisy and Violet on the road.

Since they were three, the Hilton sisters had been appearing in Mary's pub and by the age of four, they had toured the United Kingdom under the stage name of the *United Twins.*

A year or two later (about 1912-13) and for the next twelve years, the *Brighton United Twins* as they were now calling themselves, added Germany, Australia, and America to the list of countries toured. Successful? They were so well booked in advance, that Mary and Edith hired an agent, Bill Oliver to handle the scheduling of performances.

In 1926, Bob Hope featured them doing a truly amazing four-legged tap dancing routine. At about that time, Mary passed away, but not before signing a will that transferred ownership of the twins to her daughter Edith, who had either just married, or was about to marry, a balloon salesman named Myer Myers.

Myers viewed his role as twofold: (1) that of keeping the twins out of the public eye, reasoning that no one would pay to see them if they could be seen for free on the street, and (2) taking complete control of their earnings.

Business boomed and booking agent Oliver had the girls singing, dancing, and engaged in a busy schedule of extra-curricular activities. When agent Oliver's wife discovered her husband was, literally speaking, two-timing her, she filed for divorce and for good measure, she filed a second lawsuit against those home-wrecking conjoined trollops, Daisy and Violet.

The year was 1931.

With legal problems looming on the horizon, Daisy and Violet contacted Texas lawyer Martin J. Arnold. Arnold was dumbfounded to learn that the girls were included in Mary Hilton's will as if they were an antique desk or a piece of art. He advised the twins to file a counter-suit against their caretakers, Myer and Edith Myers. They did and the court awarded the girls their freedom and $100,000 in damages, a breath-taking amount of money in 1931.

The twins were now in their twenties, on their own, and hopeful of finding the same kind of happiness they saw other young girls enjoying.

In 1936, Violet married Jim Moore in a flashy ceremony on the 50-yard line of the Cotton Bowl at the Texas Centennial Exposition. However, the marriage ended soon afterward.

In 1941, Daisy married Harold Estep in a less public wedding, the marriage lasting less than three weeks.

The twins, no longer the adorable little girls or lively teenagers that they had once been, found little work in Vaudeville or other venues. They had appeared as themselves in the 1932 MGM film, *Freaks,* a movie with a cast made up almost entirely of carnival sideshow performers, and nineteen years later (1951) they appeared in a Classic Pictures release titled *Chained for Life*, an exploitation film based loosely on their lives.

In the 1960s and no longer able to draw an audience, they were down to taking care of the produce section of a North Carolina supermarket. On New Year's Eve, 1968-69, Daisy fell ill with the flu, and when the two ladies failed to report to work on January 4, the store manager alerted police who discovered them inside their small mobile home, deceased. The exact date of their deaths could not be determined.

Born in England, America's Siamese twins were dead, victims of the Hong Kong flu.

"Never rise to speak until you have something to say;
and when you have said it, cease."
John Witherspoon (**Feb 5, 1723** – Nov 15, 1794) Minister

FEBRUARY 6
As we have lived . . . .

Isidor and Ida Straus

Isidor: **Feb 6, 1845** (Otterberg, Germany) – Apr 15, 1912
(Atlantic Ocean)
Ida: **Feb 6, 1849** (Worms, Germany) – Apr 15, 1912, (Atlantic Ocean)

I SIDOR WAS BORN in 1845 to parents Lazarus and Sara Straus, the owners of a successful seed and grain business in Otterberg, Germany. That was, until they supported a failed revolution in Germany in 1848, and with the financial instability that followed, Lazarus immigrated to the United States, relocating in Talbotton, Georgia, southwest of Macon.

In 1854 and finding success in the operation of a small store, Lazarus sent for his wife and four children, which included his oldest son, nine-year-old Isidor.

The store, *L. Straus & Company*, not only grew, but it thrived.

In 1856, Lazarus and Sara enrolled eleven-year-old Isidor at the Collinsworth Institute where he attended classes for five years before the Civil War interrupted everything, including his education.

When Isidor tried to enlist (Confederate), he was turned down because of his age (15 or 16), so he visited the Georgia Military Academy. However, before he could enroll, student pranksters poured a bucket of water on his head and rinsed away his interest in a military future.

In a nearby town, he rented a buggy and purchased on consignment, goods from a mill that he took to Atlanta. After selling the goods to local businesses, he returned to Georgia and paid off the consignment debt and buggy rent, and for his effort, he had turned a nice profit. He was sixteen years old.

In the meantime (1862), Isidor's father, Lazarus opened a second *L. Straus & Company*, this time in the town of Columbus, Georgia.

At eighteen, Isidor went to work selling bonds in England to raise money for the Confederacy, his ship successfully running a Union blockade with him hidden in the ship's hold. Once in England, he proved his money-handling and negotiation skills and sent over $130,000 back to the Confederacy (about $2.5 million in 2015 dollars).

Also in 1863, either on his way to, or when returning from England, Isidor met Ida Blun, the daughter of Nathan and Wilhelmine Blun, residents of New York.

Three years later, the Straus family moved to New York where three important events took place in Isidor's life. First, he became a partner in his father's company, *L. Straus & Company*. Second, in 1871 he married Ida Blun, the young girl he had met on the Atlantic Ocean in 1863. Third, in 1888, along with his younger brother Nathan became partners in the operation of the *R. H. Macy Department Store*, a highly successful business that by 1896 they would own.

The marriage between Isidor and Ida was an uncommonly good one, sharing a lifelong devotion to each other, and although mostly through luck, they shared a few unusual things. For instance, they were both born on the same day, February 6, although he was born in 1845 and she in 1849. Of course, they couldn't know it at the time, but during the year of their 41st wedding anniversary, they would also die on the same day.

During the years 1850 to 1910, Isidor and Nathan had become extremely wealthy and noted for their philanthropy and work in public service. Nathan served in numerous capacities, as New York City Park Commissioner (1889-1893), president of the New York City Board of Health in 1898, and funding the Nathan Straus Pasteurized Milk Laboratory in an effort to combat infant mortality and tuberculosis.

Isidor served as a U.S. Congressman representing New York's 15th Congressional District, served as president of the *Educational Alliance*, supported numerous charitable and educational movements, and President Grover Cleveland once offered him the job of Postmaster General, which he graciously declined.

During the winter of 1911-1912, Isidor, Ida, and their adult daughter Beatrice traveled to Europe for an extended visit. When it came time to return to New York, Beatrice opted to remain in Europe, while Isidor and Ida boarded the *RMS Titanic* and you already how that story ends for 1,517 of the ship's passengers, and unfortunately Isidor and Ida would be among that number.

What you don't know, is how Isidor and Ida died on that fateful night of April 15, 1912.

When it became clear there would be no survivors outside of those aboard the lifeboats, and when asked to board a lifeboat, Ida refused to do so without Isidor. When told he could share a place on a lifeboat with Ida, Isidor declined because there were still women and children waiting to be loaded onto the lifeboats, and it was painfully obvious there were more people than lifeboats. Knowing that neither she nor her husband would be among the survivors, Ida insisted that her personal maid, Ellen Bird, be given her place in a lifeboat, handing Ellen her fur coat saying, "I won't need this." Then Ida turned to family friend and *Titanic* survivor, Colonel Archibald Gracie, and said quite plainly, "I will not be separated from my husband. As we have lived, so will we die, together."

Eyewitness told that the last they saw of Isidor and Ida, was the two of them walking away, arm in arm, describing the act as a "most remarkable exhibition of love and devotion."

Isidor's body was recovered the following day; Ida's body was never recovered.

On the outside of the Straus family mausoleum, with only Isidor within, reads the following inscription from the Song of Solomon, Chapter 8, Verse 7, "Many waters cannot quench love, neither can the floods drown it."

On **February 6, 1971**, Alan Shepard became the first man
to hit a golf ball on the moon.

FEBRUARY 7
Designer of the Titanic

Thomas Andrews, Jr.
Feb 7, 1873 (Comber, Ireland) - Feb 15, 1912 (Atlantic Ocean)

THOMAS ANDREWS, JR., had been attending the Royal Belfast Academical Institution in Belfast, Ireland, but left at the age of sixteen when it became apparent that his uncle, Lord Pirrie, would secure an apprenticeship for him with the Harland and Wolff (H&W) Shipbuilding Company. Arranging for the apprenticeship was easy for Lord Pirrie as he was Chairman of the Board of H&W and his nephew didn't disappoint.

Andrews was a quick study and for the next dozen years, he worked where his uncle felt it would be most beneficial and thus gained valuable experience in a host of various shipbuilding disciplines.

At twenty-eight, he became manager of the company's Construction Works, and at thirty-four, he was in charge of the company's architectural department. He was also granted membership into the prestigious *Institution of Naval Architects,* an honor rarely associated with someone still in his or her early thirties.

Youthful, bright, and energetic, he helped design four of the world's largest ocean liners prior to the announced construction of the Titanic, and when H&W's respected chief designer, Alexander Carlisle left the company, Andrews was asked to take his place.

You might assume that others in the company may have taken umbrage with his quick rise to the position of chief designer, but such was not the case. While there was no question that having Lord Pirrie in his corner was enormously helpful, Andrews had the right personality, the right intellect, and the good sense to not take advantage of his uncle's position. He dirtied his hands and worked long hours as he climbed the ranks, doing everything asked, and always with an eye for perfection. Few who worked for H&W had studied harder or spent more time learning the craft of shipbuilding.

He also kept meticulous notes about the ships he worked on, referring to them often, and he was never without a small notebook that he kept in his shirt pocket for easy reference.

However, building a ship, like building anything of a complicated nature, was a team effort, and although he was the ship's chief designer, engineers and others could still overrule him. Then, there were the construction costs that never went lower than their estimates, and as today, they were always of prime interest to the investors and were tough to factor out of the equation.

Not all of the details regarding his part in designing the Titanic are known, but two things are, and they would become critical as the ship began its maiden voyage. First, Andrews was overruled regarding the number of lifeboats to be placed aboard the Titanic. He wanted forty-six but got twenty, after all, as someone may have reminded him, the ship was unsinkable. In addition, he had argued for the ship's double hull to be built all the way to the "B" deck, but he was again overruled. Too costly he was told.

On April 2, 1912, as was the practice with each H&W ship making its maiden voyage, Andrews and his design team were aboard the Titanic creating a "punch list" of items needing corrective action before the ship made its second and subsequent voyages.

Then, as the world now knows, on the twelfth day at sea, disaster struck, and 1,517 lives were lost.

Andrews knew at once that the "unsinkable" Titanic didn't have a prayer. "Perhaps," he might have mulled, "if only I had argued harder for the more expensive double hull," and he also knew that even if he had been successful in getting the forty-six lifeboats he requested, it would still have been far too few.

A book written by Horace P. Bullock following the disaster, *Thomas Andrews: Shipbuilder* (1912) reported that a ship steward named John Stewart was the last person to see Andrews alive. Stewart had reportedly asked Andrews if he was "going to make a try for a lifeboat," but that the ship's designer never acknowledged his question. The steward noted that Andrews was apparently deep in thought admiring Norman Wilkinson's painting, *The Approach to Plymouth Harbor,* after which he removed a notebook from a shirt pocket, jotted an entry, and put the notebook back into his pocket.

Finally, the steward noted that the lifejacket Andrews should have been wearing was casually tossed onto a nearby table.

Andrews' body was never recovered.

We can only speculate on what his final notebook entry might have said. Perhaps it was something as simple as, "It is over," after which he and the unsinkable Titanic slipped into the sea and into the history books, his empty lifejacket tossed about aimlessly on the undulating waves of the Atlantic.

"When fascism comes to America it will be wrapped in the flag and carrying a cross."
Sinclair Lewis (**Feb 7, 1885** – Jan 10, 1951)
Novelist, playwright

FEBRUARY 8
First powered flight fatality

Thomas E. Selfridge
Feb 8, 1882 (San Francisco, CA) - Sept 17, 1908 (Fort Myer, VA)

ON SEPTEMBER 17, 1908, Thomas E. Selfridge entered the history books as the first person to die in the crash of a heavier-than-air powered aircraft. A dubious honor, especially when you learn the name of the man at the controls of the ill-fated flight.

Raised in a family known at the time for producing men of sound judgment and fine military aptitude, Thomas Etholen Selfridge was a cut above the typical soldier, and he was handsome.

His father was Rear Admiral Thomas Oliver Selfridge, Jr., an 1854 graduate of the U. S. Naval Academy who commanded several Union ships during the Civil War, including the famed Union ironclad *Monitor*. He also commanded the *USS Alligator*, an experimental submarine to help determine its military value.

Thomas's grandfather was Rear Admiral Thomas Oliver Selfridge, Sr., who served admirably in the Mexican-American War and the Civil War. Two U. S. naval ships, both destroyers carry the Selfridge name: the *USS Selfridge* (commissioned in 1921) and another *USS Selfridge* (commissioned in 1936) the latter named jointly for father and son.

Thomas, unlike his father and grandfather who were navy men, chose the army and graduated from West Point in 1903, in the same class as World War II hero, Douglas MacArthur.

Four years after graduation, Lt. Selfridge joined the Aeronautical Division of the U.S. Signal Corps at Fort Myer, Virginia. There he became the pilot of the army's first dirigible, a craft given the extraordinarily sensible, but unimaginably plain name, *Army Dirigible Number One*.

The same year that Selfridge was learning to fly a dirigible, Alexander Graham Bell was organizing an aeronautical research group known as the Aerial Experiment Association (AEA), headquartered at Bell's Nova Scotia residence.

The members of the AEA were a Who's Who of the most notable flight people of the day. They included Frederick Baldwin, the first Canadian to fly an airplane; J. A. D. McCurdy, the first British subject to fly an airplane; and Glenn H. Curtiss, the winner of the world's first international air meet in France. Curtiss also founded America's aircraft industry with the establishment of the Curtiss Aeroplane Company in 1916.

Shortly after the formation of the AEA, Selfridge showed an interest in the organization. Bell, impressed with the young army officer, personally asked President Roosevelt to reassign Selfridge to the AEA as an observer, and that quickly, it was done.

In the spring of 1908, Selfridge received the honor of designing AEA's first powered aircraft, a single-seat biplane named the "Red Wing" because of it red silk wings. On March 12, 1908, piloted by the Canadian AEA member, Frederick Baldwin, the aircraft flew for 319 feet, at a height of twenty feet before crashing. Baldwin survived the crash.

The Red Wing was following by the White Wing, a craft that featured wings equipped with ailerons controlled by a harness worn around the pilot's body. The ailerons worked by following the motion of the pilot's body. Lean to the right, the White Wing banked to the right. On May 18, 1908, Baldwin took the craft on its maiden flight, and the following day, Lt. Selfridge was at the controls, and at that moment, he became the first military officer to fly an airplane.

In September of 1908, at Fort Myer, Virginia, the military was conducting trials of the Wright biplane to determine its feasibility for use as a military aircraft. For two weeks, the aircraft went through its paces, setting record after record to the pleasure of an enthusiastic and ever-growing crowd.

One of the military's tests was to see if the Wright airplane could sustain a speed of forty miles per hour with two persons aboard. The demonstration flight took place on September 17, 1908, and Lt. Thomas Selfridge climbed aboard as the "second person," and in moments, the aircraft was airborne.

Then the unthinkable happened as described in the pilot's report of the accident (edited):

> "On the fourth round, everything seemingly working much better and smoother than any former flight, I started

on a larger circuit with less abrupt turns. It was on the first slow turn that the trouble began.

"… a hurried glance behind revealed nothing wrong, but I decided to shut off the power and descend as soon as the machine could be faced in a direction where a landing could be made. This decision was hardly reached, in fact, I suppose it was not over two or three seconds from the time the first taps were heard, until two big thumps, which gave the machine a terrible shaking, showed that something had broken.

"… the machine suddenly turned to the right and I immediately shut off the power. Quick as a flash, the machine turned down in front and started straight for the ground. Our course for 50 feet was within a very few degrees of the perpendicular. Lt. Selfridge up to this time had not uttered a word, though he took a hasty glance behind me when the propeller broke and turned once or twice to look into my face, evidently to see what I thought of the situation. But when the machine turned head first for the ground, he exclaimed 'Oh! Oh!' in an almost inaudible voice."

With the crash that followed, Lt. Thomas Selfridge suffered a skull fracture and never regained consciousness, thus becoming the first fatality of a heavier-than-air aircraft. The pilot, Orville Wright, yes, Orville Wright, the first man to fly, suffered a broken left thigh, broken ribs, a bruised hip and was hospitalized for seven weeks.

Lt. Selfridge rests at Arlington National Cemetery, not far from the site of the accident.

"If you think its hard meeting new people, try picking up the wrong golf ball."
Jack Lemmon (**Feb 8, 1925** – June 27, 2001) Actor

FEBRUARY 9
Sport Shirt Bill

Bill Veeck, Jr.
Feb 9, 1914 (Chicago IL) – Jan 2, 1986 (Chicago IL)

BILL VEECK (RHYMES with *wreck*) was a promotional genius who, over his lifetime, owned three baseball teams, and if you know anything about baseball, you know he was the game's most incorrigible maverick.

Bill's father, Bill Veeck Sr., was a popular Chicago sportswriter. Once, after writing a series of articles about the Cubs problems and what he would do to fix things, Cubs owner William Wrigley decided to hand him the reins and hired him as the club's vice-president. When the Cubs won the pennant the following year, Wrigley promoted him to president. From birth, Bill Junior grew up on a steady diet of baseball, the official language in the Veeck home, and he would become more famous than his well-known baseball-managing father.

During WWII, Bill Junior served with the Marines in the South Pacific. It was there that a recoiling artillery piece crushed his right foot and leg, requiring immediate amputation of his foot. Sometime later, and after enduring numerous operations in an attempt to save the leg, amputation from above the knee was necessary and he was fitted with a wooden prosthetic leg, the first of many he would use over his lifetime.

He may have gone through life with fewer wooden legs but he was a hard-core chain smoker and he solved the where-is-an-ashtray problem by drilling holes in his wooden leg. That way, by crossing his right leg over his left, he was never without an ashtray.

Following World War II he bought the Cleveland Indians (1946) and signed Larry Doby, the American League's first black player. Manager Lou Boudreau introduced Doby in a baseball ritual where current players, in a one-on-one handshake, welcome new players. All but three of Cleveland's players shook Doby's hand, and they were team history just as soon as Veeck could unload them!

In 1949 Veeck signed 42-year old Negro League pitching sensation Satchel Paige, making Paige the oldest rookie to play in the major leagues.

When a fan named Joe Early complained that Veeck had never honored the "average" Joe at a game, Veeck staged a night in honor of everyone named "Joe" and he packed the stadium.

Once, when ticket sales were sagging, Veeck hired comic Max Patkin, the rubber-faced *Clown Prince of Baseball* and named him as one of his pitching coaches. The comedian delighted the fans with his over-the-top antics in managing the pitchers, but it infuriated the other owners, whom Veeck referred to as "forward-looking fossils that run the game."

Veeck was also the first owner to put players' names on their uniforms.

In an ill-fated 1979 baseball promotion, Veeck, who wasn't a fan of Disco music, sponsored a *Disco Demolition Night* at Chicago's Comiskey Park during a double-header between his Chicago White Sox and the Detroit Tigers. It was a "bring a disco LP for destruction during the lull between the games of the double-header," and get into the ballpark for 98-cents.

White Sox officials expected the promotion to add about 5,000 additional fans to bolster the season's poor gate receipts, but instead of 5,000, an estimated 50,000 showed up. So many, in fact, that the folks at the gates could not collect all of the LPs for "between game" destruction and thousands of 98-cent fans entered the stadium with their LPs in hand.

When the first game of the double-header ended, it was time to destroy the disco LPs that had been collected at the gate. They were destroyed in a controlled, but large and colorful explosion in center field that left smoke and shards of vinyl all over the field. If that wasn't enough of a problem, the thousands of fans that had entered the stadium with their LPs in hand, began throwing them like flying discs from the stands. Then, thousands of fans stormed the playing field, and there was not enough police or security to handle the crowd and pandemonium reigned!

The second game of the double-header never got underway and the following day, American League president Lee MacPhail ordered the game forfeited by the White Sox.

But of all the stunts Veeck pulled, the most memorable was when he sent Eddie Gaedel, a three-foot-seven-inch little person to bat against Detroit's Bob Cain. When Gaedel stepped to the plate wearing number '1/8' on his uniform, umpire Ed Hurley threw up his arms and stopped the game. Veeck ran from the dugout with a copy of Gaedel's legally executed contract and Hurley yelled "Play Ball!" Gaedel, with a strike zone about the size of his uniform number, walked with four straight pitches.

When asked about the audacity of some of his outlandish antics, Veeck would only say, "I try not to break the rules but merely to test their elasticity."

"A man usually falls in love with a woman who asks
the kinds of questions he is able to answer."
Ronald Colman (**Feb 9, 1891** – May 19, 1958) Actor

WAYNE WINTERTON, PH.D.

FEBRUARY 10

... and a grudge that lasted 470 years

The Saint Scholastica Day Riot
Feb 10, 1355 (Oxford, England)

B ASED ON THE assumption that in 1355, only England's wealthiest families could afford to send their sons to Oxford, and that said sons, born into wealth and privilege were likely raised in the rarified air of self-importance, we begin this story.

First, know that Saint Scholastica is the patron saint of nuns and convulsive children and the saint with power over storms and bad weather. Know also, that she has a reflective personality, is typically quiet and not one for raising her voice. Finally and most important, know that she had nothing to do with the bad behavior that has come to be known as the *Saint Scholastica Day Riot*. It's just that the riot took place on her feast day, February 10, 1355.

The origin of the brawl is traceable to a single difference of opinion between John Croidon, the owner of the Swyndlestock Tavern and Oxford University students Walter Spryngeheuse and Roger de Chesterfield, over the quality of ale served to students.

It seems the lads from Oxford, Mr. Spryngeheuse and Mr. de Chesterfield, after noisily making their point regarding the alcoholic content of Croidon's ale, doused the taverner with the contents of their tankards, and afterward assaulted him with a flurry of fisticuffs. To put it plainly, Walt and Rog yelled at Croidon, threw beer in his face, and then beat the crap out of him.

Following the assault on Croidon, Oxford's mayor, John de Bereford demanded that Oxford University Chancellor, Humphrey de Cherlton, bring the two students before the city for arrest.

When the Chancellor refused, Croidon walked to St. Martin's church and began ringing the bell to summon the town's men to arms, and they came, arriving with all manner of weapons. The bell at St. Martin's was still pealing when a number of students began ringing the bell at St. Mary's Church on the Oxford campus, summoning the students to the fight, and they came, about 200 of them, some armed.

It was the mother of all brawls. At first, the students got the better of the fray, forcing the townsmen to retreat. Then things began to spiral out of control.

Taverner Croidon, seeing the townsmen outnumbered by the students, rode into the surrounding towns on a mission of recruitment, and he got what he was looking for. He and 2,000 men, armed and ready for a good fight, rode into town yelling, "Havoc! Havoc! Smyt fast, give gode knocks!"

The donnybrook grew nastier by the minute and when it was over, sixty-three students and thirty townsmen had lost their lives in a full-blown riot, and most of the combatants weren't even sure of why they were fighting.

Because the number of deceased students was greater than the number of deceased townsmen by two to one, the town claimed victory for the battle, but even so, they lost the war.

King Edward III, not pleased with the riot having occurred in England's esteemed town of Oxford, ordered an investigation and the eventual findings favored the University.

Based on those findings, the King had a special edict drawn up, which he signed. The edict set forth that thenceforth, annually, until withdrawn by Royal Order, on each feast day for Saint Scholastica, that the mayor and the councilors of Oxford, march baldheaded (that is, without hats), through the streets to the delight of the citizenry. The King's charter also required that the city of Oxford pay to the University, a fine of one penny for every scholar killed, the penalty amounting to five shillings and three pence.

Incredibly, those annual hatless processions continued for 469 years (1356 to 1825), until the mayor of Oxford, tired of putting up with the absurdity of it all, refused to take part. It took another 130 years, until February 10, 1955, before the British Parliament, in an Act of Conciliation, officially ended King Edward III's edict. To mark the occasion, the Mayor of Oxford received an honorary degree from Oxford University; and the Vice-Chancellor of Oxford was made an "Honorary Freeman" of the city of Oxford.

According to one website, relations between the students of Oxford University and the "townies" of the city of Oxford have never fully mended, and to the present day, there are unofficially, but honored, designated student and town pubs.

"Never invest in anything that eats or needs painting."
Billy Rose (Sept 6, 1899 – **Feb 10, 1966**)
Novelist, playwright

FEBRUARY 11
Boxing's hardest puncher

Max Baer
(Maximilian Adelbert Baer)
Feb 11, 1909 (Omaha, NE) – Nov 21, 1959 (Sacramento, CA)

M AX BAER WAS an American boxer of German descent, best remembered for his fight with another "Max," Max Schmeling. It was a fight that didn't turn out the way that Schmeling's greatest fan, Adolph Hitler, had expected. After all, his Max was of pure Arian stock and America's Max was Jewish.

Ring Magazine ranks heavyweight Max Baer as #22 on its list of boxing's all-time greatest punchers, and some say he had the hardest punch of any boxer in history. His professional record was 68 wins with 13 losses, and of those 68 wins, 52 were by knockouts. That's putting three out of every four opponents on the canvas for the count.

In 1930, Baer fought Frankie Campbell. The fight lasted exactly two punches, both delivered by Baer. Campbell never regained consciousness and died in a local hospital, his brain separated from the connective tissue that anchors it to the cranium.

In 1931, Baer fought Ernie Schaff; nailing Schaff in the temple in what witnesses say was the hardest right hand ever connected in boxing. Afterward, Schaff complained of blinding headaches. Six months later Schaff entered the ring with Primo Carnera. Early in the fight, Schaff collapsed and died after a glancing jab to the head from Carnera. Most agree Schaff's death was the result of Baer's shot to the temple six months earlier.

However, whatever you might think of Baer and boxing, what Baer is best remembered for was his fight with Germany's Max Schmeling. It took place in 1933, hosted at spacious Yankee Stadium to accommodate the turnout, and America's Max won the fight.

Considered a Jew by many because of his father's faith (his mother was Catholic); Baer had a large Star of David embroidered on his trunks. Baer dominated Schmeling, Hitler's most powerful fighter throughout the match. In the 10th round, the referee halted the carnage, rescuing, perhaps, Schmeling from the same fate that had befallen Campbell and Schaff a few years earlier.

Totally forgotten these days, except by boxing aficionados, is that when Baer defeated Hitler's best fighter, der Führer was so outraged and disappointed with his boxer's performance that he never allowed Schmeling in the ring with another Jewish boxer.

That wasn't all.

Baer may have been boxing's most handsome fighter and after hanging up his gloves, he acted in movie and television roles. His movie debut was in, understandably, *The Prizefighter and the Lady* opposite Myrna Loy and Walter Huston, a movie banned in Germany by none other than Joseph Goebbels, the Nazi Minister of Propaganda and Public Entertainment. Goebbels wanted his country to forget the embarrassment felt when an American Jew defeated Nazi Germany's best boxer.

"As a beauty I'm not a great star
There are others more handsome by far
But by face, I don't mind it
Because I'm behind it
'Tis the folks in the front that I jar."
Anthony Euwer (**Feb 11, 1877** – Nov 14, 1955)
Poet, painter, humorist

FEBRUARY 12

He might not have been around to become the nation's 16th president

Abraham Lincoln

Feb 12, 1809 (Hodgenville, KY) – Apr 15, 1865 (Washington, DC)

ABRAHAM LINCOLN CAME within a gnat's eyelash, no, two eyelashes, of not being around to become America's sixteenth president and the savior of the Union.

Gnat's eyelash number one.

Abe's paternal grandfather and namesake, Captain Abraham Lincoln (1744-1786), and his sons, Mordecai, Josiah, and Thomas were planting corn in a field when a group of Indian men attacked them. Abraham, the father, died in the attack. Mordecai, his eldest son ran to the family cabin to grab a loaded rifle, yelling to thirteen-year-old Josiah to run to a place called Hughes Station for help. Thomas, the youngest son and the future father of President Lincoln, ran to his fallen father's side where he stood paralyzed with shock, completely unaware of the danger that he, himself, was in.

Just as Mordecai exited the cabin with the rifle, he saw one of his father's assailants emerge from a wooded area and begin running toward eight-year-old Thomas, most likely to take him captive to his village. Mordecai stopped in his tracks, took aim and pulled the trigger. The Indian, shot in the chest, stumbled and fell before reaching Thomas.

Thus was the life of Thomas Lincoln, the future father of America's sixteenth president, preserved.

Gnat's eyelash number two.

President Lincoln acknowledged that his mother, Nancy Hanks, was born of an illicit relationship, and on one occasion, he described his maternal grandfather as "a well-bred Virginia farmer who had taken advantage of a young woman named Lucy Hanks," and the encounter left Lucy pregnant. On February 5, 1784, Lucy gave birth to a daughter she named Nancy, and being unwed, she gave the newborn her own surname, and thus we are introduced to President Lincoln's future mother, the infant Nancy Hanks.

No one can know, of course, what might have been, had things turned out differently in the life of Lucy Hanks, and there are many "what-if's." What if Lucy and the "well-bred Virginia farmer," had never met, or had married, and what if, following the birth of Nancy Hanks, if Lucy, an unwed girl, had allowed someone else to raise her daughter?

That ends the gnat's eyelashes, but here's what happened next.

Years into the future, Lucy and her daughter Nancy made the long, arduous journey from present-day West Virginia along the Wilderness Road through the Cumberland Gap to Kentucky, and Nancy eventually settled somewhere near where Thomas Lincoln lived.

Thomas Lincoln, described as a "plain, unpretending plodding man," was a carpenter who, among other things, made coffins.

Nancy Hanks was a skilled seamstress and in demand for everything from wedding gowns to funeral clothing. It doesn't require a lot of imagination to suppose that Thomas and Nancy may have become acquainted when a mourning family needed their joint services. However, regardless of how they met, they did, and on June 10, 1806, they became man and wife.

After their marriage, they moved near current-day Hodgenville, Kentucky, and there on Sunday, February 12, 1809, Nancy gave birth to a son. They named him Abraham after the infant's grandfather, the same Captain Abraham Lincoln who died while planting corn in 1786.

Nancy Hanks Lincoln died nine years after Abe's birth. Thomas remarried and Abe and his father grew distant. There is little recorded contact between Abe and his father after the death of Nancy Hanks. When Abe married Mary Todd, he didn't extend an invitation for his father to attend the wedding, nor did Abe attend his father's funeral in 1851.

Of course, what Abraham Lincoln did was nothing short of extraordinary. Poet Rosemary Benet penned the following familiar words about our sixteenth president.

Here's are the opening lines:

If Nancy Hanks came back as a ghost, seeking news of what she loved most,
She'd ask first, "Where's my son? What's happened to Abe? What's he done?"

Equally poignant are a couple of lines of Julius Silberger's, *A Reply to Nancy Hanks:*

Yes, Nancy Hanks, The news we will tell, of your Abe, whom you loved so well. You asked first, "Where's my son?" He lives in the heart of everyone.

On **February 12, 1924**, Calvin Coolidge,
known as "Silent Cal,"
was the first president to speak to the nation via radio.

FEBRUARY 13
So, what exactly is the 'Angle of Louis?'

Antoine Louis
Feb 13, 1723 (Metz, France) – May 20, 1792 (Paris, France)

PHYSICIANS AND MEDICAL students can point out the "sternal angle," also called the "point of junction" between the manubrium (the upper sternum) and the body of the sternum. The medical term for the angle by which the manubrium and the body of the sternum rest against each other is the "angle of Louis," named after French physician Antoine Louis.

Now, if you're neither interested in the medical nor the beheading professions, you might want to skip this story, but if you can handle the unpleasantness associated with losing one's head, and not in a figurative sense, go for it.

Dr. Antoine Louis's "angle of Louis" is medically significant because the "angle" is where the ascending aorta ends, the arch of the aorta starts and stops, and the descending aorta begins, and everyone knows how important an intact aorta is to a properly functioning human body.

During Dr. Louis's lifetime, France used a range of creative ways to punish the guilty, from cutting off the hand of a convicted pickpocket, to the burning of heretics at the stake for serious crimes against the church.

For capital crimes, as dictated by French law, there were two methods employed depending on one's station in life. Commoners guilty of a capital offense could count on a public hanging, a form of execution considered beneath the dignity of those of royal station. Royalty guilty of a capital offense faced decapitation by a hooded axe-wielding executioner, a form of execution for reasons that escape the writer, was somehow considered a "higher-class" way to die, and thus more appropriate for the socially elite.

Although royal executions were well attended, the execution itself was not always a clean-cut affair, if you understand what is meant here. As in any feat of skill in which accuracy is everything, an efficient axe-generated decapitation was largely dependent on the skill of the executioner.

Enter Dr. Antoine Louis who, late in his medical career but knowing precisely where a blade should strike to efficiently sever the manubrium from the body of the sternum, took up the challenge of designing a humane killing machine. To assist him he chose a young colleague, Dr. Joseph Ignace Guillotin who, interestingly, was a vocal opponent of the death penalty.

The two physicians worked together to create a prototype of a killing machine they called the "louisette," after Dr. Antoine Louis's surname. The machine was tested on animals with adjustments made from the shape of the blade (from convex to sloping triangular), to the height of the drop to achieve maximum slicing efficiency. They designed the device so that the precise location and stretch of the neck was determined to assure that the strike of the blade would be at the correct angle for a flawless execution.

In October of 1789, four years before the "louisette" would go into general use and two years prior to the death of Dr. Antoine Louis, its principal designer, Louis's associate Dr. Joseph Guillotin, found himself involved in a debate with the French Parliament regarding capital punishment. Guillotin proposed doing away with beheadings by sword or axe (likely, to the horror of the local Executioner's Union), favoring instead, the use of Dr. Louis's louisette, telling the assembly, "The mechanism falls like lightning; the head flies off; the blood spurts; and the man, beheaded painlessly, no longer exists."

Although Dr. Guillotin, as mentioned, was an outspoken critic of capital punishment, he was hopeful that the use of the more humane and less painful louisette might be a first step toward abolishment of the death penalty altogether.

In December of 1789, Dr. Guillotin made a similar speech to the French Assembly, a speech he would regret, in which he flippantly stated, "Now, with *my machine*, I'll remove your head in a flash, and you won't even feel the slightest pain." It was likely the first time Guillotin had ever referred to the louisette as "his machine." Nevertheless, his "quick as a flash and painless" comment struck a chord with the folks, and someone followed up the comment with a comical song about *Guillotin's Machine* and it was all over. The *louisette* became the *guillotine*, named not after its principal designer, but after the man who deplored the death penalty.

However, Dr. Antoine Louis's name is not forgotten, but immortalized. Because of his work in helping others understand the anatomy of the human being, specifically in understanding the role of the "point of junction" (today: the angle of Louis) in performing a well-executed beheading, executioners knew exactly where to position the subject for the most efficient, most painless execution possible.

"A woman's place is to sit beside her husband, be silent, and be sure her hat is on straight."
Bess Truman (**Feb 13, 1885** – Oct 18, 1982) First Lady

FEBRUARY 14

The man, the saint, the holiday

Saint Valentine

DOB unknown - **Feb 14, c. 270 AD** (The date of his execution)

ALL WE KNOW about the man for whom we celebrate St. Valentine's Day is that he was a Catholic priest named Valentine who defied an order of the Emperor Claudius II, and that his defiance led to his execution. The execution was harsh, consisting of a stoning, followed by a clubbing, and then a beheading, all of which took place on February 14, in either 269, 270, or 273 AD. We also know from tradition that Valentine's final resting place was in a cemetery near the Milvian Bridge on the north side of Rome.

Now that we've established who Valentine was, let's look at why the severity of his execution. Claudius II, it seemed, was having a difficult time getting young Roman men to join the military. To correct the problem, he issued an edict forbidding marriage to which he attached a severe penalty for failure to comply. Claudius, obviously (and erroneously), thought that if a young man couldn't marry the lady of his dreams, he'd forget all about her and sign up for a few years in the military service.

Notwithstanding the serious tone of the edict, Valentine encouraged Rome's young lovers to come to him in the dark of night where he would join them together in the holy sacrament of matrimony. As you might imagine, going from being single one day to married the next was a difficult thing to keep secret, and the Emperor had his spies.

Claudius, knowing that something was amiss regarding the "no marriage" clause in his edict, soon learned that a priest named Valentine was conducting clandestine ceremonies in direct defiance to his order. Claudius was …, well, let's just say he wasn't amused and he had Valentine, arrested and imprisoned.

Legend tells that while incarcerated, Valentine became friends with Asterius, his jailer. Asterius was the father of a blind daughter, and upon learning that his prisoner possessed miraculous healing powers; he brought his daughter to Valentine's jail cell. Valentine, through his strong faith in God, restored the girl's sight. It wasn't long afterward that Valentine and the girl fell in love. When told of his impending execution, Valentine wrote the girl a love letter and signed it, "From Your Valentine."

Because of his willingness to perform marriages for lovers in spite of the Emperor's deadly edict, Valentine has become associated with a tradition of courtship and love. Although never canonized, that is, never made an "official" saint by the Catholic Church, he is a "saint" to many and as such, has his own Feast Day, February 14.

Regardless of religion, one would be hard-pressed to find someone who hasn't been inspired on this day to pen a few lines of poetry, or to leave a message in plain sight to let someone know they are fondly remembered with the kindest of thoughts.

Valentine's Day, as we know it, may have its earliest origins in a poem written by English poet Geoffrey Chaucer. Prior to his poem, *Parliament of Foules,* written about 1375, there was no association of romantic love with St. Valentine's Day. But Chaucer's poem clearly references February 14th, Valentine's Feast Day, as the day in which birds (foules), and perhaps people, come together to find a mate, as he penned, "For this was sent on Seynt Valentyne's day / Whan every foul cometh ther to choose his mate."

In 1415, we have the earliest known sending of a Valentine's Day card. The recipient of the card was sixteen-year-old Bonne d'Armagnac, the wife of twenty-one year old Charles, Duke of Orléans, who at the time was a prisoner in the Tower of London. Today, the card is in the manuscript collection of the British Library.

> Original: *Je suis desja d'amour tanné / Ma tres doulce Valentinée*
> Translated: *I am already sick of love / My very gentle Valentine*

To close, here's a piece of Valentine's Day trivia you may not know. The little cherub named Cupid that often appears on Valentine's Day cards with his bow and arrow. He's a part of the Valentine's Day tradition because in Roman mythology, Cupid, the son of Mars and Venus, was also the god of attraction, affection, and yes, erotic love.

"I may have faults, but being wrong ain't one of them."
Jimmy Hoffa (**Feb 14, 1913** – disappeared July 30, 1975)
Union leader

WAYNE WINTERTON, PH.D.

FEBRUARY 15
Present, but not voting

Jeremy Bentham
Feb 15, 1748 (London, England) – June 6, 1832 (London, England)

AS YOU READ this story, Jeremy Bentham is seated, casually dressed in his stylish 1830s outerwear. On his head is either a leather wide-brim or tightly woven straw hat. He wears a white shirt buttoned at the neck, the ruffled front partially covering a vest over which he wears a black unbuttoned frock coat. His hands, gloved, rest in his lap. His pants, tucked into a pair of white stockings, end high above his ankles and his shoes are low-cut and dark.

He was likely right-handed as the handle of a walking cane rests slightly above his right hand should he decide to exit the wooden cabinet where he has sat in detached quietude for over 180 years.

Alive, Jeremy Bentham was an odd sort of guy. Dead, well, he was still an odd sort of guy. Quite lifelike in appearance, he resides as described above at University College London, an institution he helped to establish in 1826 by donating a sum of money. He and the cabinet wherein he sits, is at the end of the South Cloisters in the main building of the college.

If a trip to London is out of the question, there are numerous websites, all with the same photograph of him sitting attentively inside his cabinet. One website allows a person to rotate Bentham and his chair a full 360-degrees should you be interested in viewing his rather ample backside.

His bony skeleton provides the framework for his likeness; his clothing stuffed with straw to make him appear lifelike. In accordance with his will, written when he was twenty-one, he remains preserved almost as he wished and attired in the clothing he wore when alive.

The phrase, "almost as he wished," is important because one element of his mummification didn't quite turn out as he had envisioned.

Bentham had directed that after his death, his body, including his head remain in a preserved state for use as an *auto-icon,* that is, a lifelike exhibit.

An excerpt from Bentham's will (edited):

> "My body I give to my dear friend Doctor Southwood Smith to be disposed of in a manner hereinafter mentioned . . . . The skeleton he will cause to be put together in such a manner as that the whole figure may be seated in a chair usually occupied by me when living, in the attitude in which I am sitting when engaged in thought in the course of time employed in writing. If it should so happen that my personal friends and other disciples should be disposed to meet together on some day or days of the year . . . my executor will from time to time cause to be conveyed to the room in which they meet, the said box or case with the contents therein to be stationed in such part of the room as to the assembled company shall meet."

However, when the man selected by Bentham to handle the preservation, Thomas Southwood Smith, tried to mummify the head, disaster struck. Although the process produced a well-preserved head, the discoloration and drum-tight skin resulted in a face that looked nothing like Bentham, and today, Bentham's head remains locked away in a cabinet drawer. Instead, a remarkably life-like waxen head, made in the manner of Madame Tussaud's celebrated museum figures, sits atop Bentham's shoulders.

The person who made the Tussaud-type head did use Mr. Bentham's real hair, a decision that might have consoled the subject were he still alive, or perhaps not. Jeremy Bentham was not an easy man to predict.

In life, he was a child prodigy. As a toddler, he enjoyed sitting at his father's desk with a volume of England's history at hand, and at the age of three, tutors assisted him in the study of Latin.

His elementary education was at the Westminster School where he learned Greek and Latin and reportedly wrote poetry in both languages. At twelve (1760), he was admitted to Queen's College (later Oxford University) where he graduated at the age of fifteen with a Bachelor's degree. A Master's degree was awarded three years later. In 1766, he studied law and in 1769, he passed the British bar.

Regarding his position on social standards, he was ahead of his time. He was an outspoken proponent of equal rights for women. He believed that couples in untenable marriages should separate or divorce, and he was firmly against the criminalization of homosexuals. He supported the abolishment of slavery, was against the death penalty, against corporal punishment of children, and a strong advocate of animal rights.

At the age of 28, he wrote his first book, *A Fragment on Government: Being an Examination of What is Delivered, on the Subject of Government in General, in the Introduction to Sir William Blackstone's Commentaries.*

In the book, the upstart Bentham took on the noted British jurist, judge, and politician, Sir William Blackstone. While the treatise did little to win friends and influence those who supported the British status-quo, it firmly established Bentham as an intellectual free thinker and gained him a sizeable following.

The list of Bentham's accomplishments and foibles is lengthy, but know that he is still involved in the decision-making process at University College London.

On the 100th and 150th anniversaries of the college, and again in 2013, he was taken from his cabinet and seated at a meeting of the College Council where it was recorded he was "present, but not voting."

"If a dog jumps into your lap,
it's because he's fond of you;
but if a cat does the same thing,
it's because your lap is warmer."
Alfred North Whitehead (**Feb 15, 1861** – Dec 30, 1947)
Mathematician

James Baskett
Feb 16, 1904 (Indianapolis, IN) – July 9, 1948 (Los Angeles, CA)

W HO WAS THE first male performer of African heritage to win an Academy Award?

Clue: He won the award for his 1946 portrayal of Uncle Remus in Walt Disney's *Song of the South,* where he portrayed a warm, story-telling, song-singing black man.

So, who was he?

He was James Baskett. If you knew his name, you would be somewhere in the top 5% of movie trivia buffs, an expert in the knowledge of silver screen personalities.

Don't feel bad if you didn't know the answer. Nearly everyone who went to the movie had never heard of James Baskett either. That's because before *Song of the South* became a movie, Baskett had been studying to become a pharmacist, but had dropped out of school for lack of funds.

To help make ends meet, he joined up with a fellow named Bill Robinson, an entertainer better known as Mr. Bojangles. Blessed with a one of a kind mellow voice, Baskett appeared on Broadway with Louis Armstrong in an all-black revue named *Hot Chocolates.* He also acted in a few all-black productions in New York, moved to Los Angeles and got a bit part in *Revenge of the Zombies* (1943), the latter telling you that life for the man with the platinum pipes wasn't easy.

Life got a little better in 1944 when Freeman Gosden gave him a chance to play lawyer Gabby Gibson on the hit radio show, *Amos 'n' Andy*. Gosden, a white man, was one of the show's writers and the voice actor who played Amos on the show.

Maybe it was his voice characterization of Gabby Gibson that caught the attention of the folks at Disney? Whatever it was, someone heard Baskett's voice and invited the one time aspiring pharmacist to try out for the voice of Brer Fox, one of the animated characters that brought the *Song of the South* to life. Baskett won the role. Granted, it wasn't much of a role, but then he won another voice role as well, that of Brer Rabbit, one of the story's main characters.

Then, something special happened.

Walt Disney himself, walked into the recording studio and was so impressed with Baskett's voice and especially his stage presence that he hired him to not only do the voices for Brer Rabbit and his antagonist, Brer Fox, but he hired him on the spot to play the film's leading role, that of the movie's storyteller, Uncle Remus.

The rest, as the old saying goes, is history.

Only Baskett's future didn't last all that long. To begin with, he wasn't allowed to attend the movie's premier, more about that later; and second, he had been in poor health throughout much of the filming and suffered a heart attack either just before the filming was completed or immediately afterwards. His health, further complicated by diabetes, continued to deteriorate and two years later, July 9, 1948, James Baskett passed away.

Let's talk about the movie for a minute.

The movie was Disney's first feature-length film that used live actors. Live actors, that is, who shared the screen with dozens of Disney's wonderfully animated cartoon characters. Not only Brer Rabbit and Brer Fox, but also hundreds of butterflies, and an assortment of woodland creatures, all of whom were blessed with the ability to carry a tune.

The movie is about Uncle Remus, a former slave who shares with a number of children, the adventures and misadventures of an anthropomorphic rabbit and his friends. The movie's very upbeat song, *Zip-a-Dee-Doo-Dah,* sung to perfection by Baskett, won the Academy Award for Best Song. Perhaps you've heard it:

> *Zip-a-dee-doo-dah, zip-a-dee-ay; My, oh my what a wonderful day!*
> *Plenty of sunshine heading my way; Zip-a-dee-doo-dah, zip-a-dee-ay.*
> *Mister Bluebird on my shoulder;*
> *It's the truth, it's actch'll,*
> *Everything is satisfactch'll*
> *Zip-a-dee-doo-dah, zip-a-dee-ay; Won-der-ful feeling, wonderful day!*

The film was a box-office smash and few were the number of moviegoers that didn't leave the theater humming or singing the cheery and optimistic song on their way home.

Now to the question we left hanging earlier, why it was that James Baskett, the star of the movie and the winner of an Academy Award for his portrayal of Uncle Remus, couldn't attend the movie's premier.

The premier of *Song of the South* took place in Atlanta, Georgia, a city racially segregated by law. In 1946, the thought that a black man, even one personally acquainted with a thousand animated woodland creatures could sit in the same theater as white folk, was unimaginable. We've come a very long way as a nation since 1946.

On **February 16, 1925**, archaeologist
Howard Carter entered the
sealed burial chamber of Egyptian King Tutankhamen.

George E. Dixon

c. 1838 (KY or SC) – **Feb 17, 1864** (near Sullivan's Island, SC)

G EORGE DIXON WAS a first lieutenant in the Confederate Army, best remembered as the commander of the *H. L. Hunley*, the submarine that successfully sunk the *USS Housatonic* off the coast of Charleston, South Carolina on February 17, 1864. Dixon and his men never returned from that mission. One hundred thirty-six years later (2000), the Smithsonian would raise the Hunley from its watery grave and discover a most interesting artifact, George Dixon's personal life preserver.

In addition to the aforementioned artifact, Doug Owsley of the Smithsonian would also conclude that Dixon was evidently a man of means, recovering some gold fillings from his teeth, some diamond-studded jewelry on his person and a handful of Civil War artifacts from his pockets.

With the completion of the salvage work in 2004, Dixon's remains, along with the other crewmembers of the Hunley received full military honors before their interment in the Magnolia Cemetery in Charleston, South Carolina.

This would be the end of our story about Lt. George Dixon if it were not that he and the youthful Queen (Queenie) Bennett of Mobile, Alabama had become romantically involved. Dixon likely met Queenie, whose father was a steamboat pilot prior to the war, while he was moonlighting as a security guard to earn extra money. Regardless, George and Queenie became an item and once the war was in full swing, he proposed to his southern belle and she agreed to become his wife, but only after the war.

As a gift to seal her part of the engagement she gave George a $20-dollar gold piece, making him promise to carry it always for good luck.

As it turned out, the $20 gold piece was a very lucky coin indeed.

On April 6, 1862, at the Battle of Shiloh, Dixon, shot at point blank range in the upper thigh, would almost certainly have required amputation of his leg, except that Queenie's engagement gift had absorbed enough of the ball's impact to negate the need for surgery. As a result, Dixon limped away from the medical tent with a badly dented gold coin, and with his leg still attached to his body.

In celebration of the luck of Queenie's gift, George had the gold coin straightened, as best possible and inscribed with a personal message, one that he knew would bring a smile to her face when the day came that he would be able to show it to her. Right now, there was a war needing fought.

While recuperating from his injury, Dixon served garrison duty at Mobile, Alabama, and it was there where he learned of the submarine that Horace L. Hunley was building, a craft he would soon command, the *H. L. Hunley*.

By February of 1864, Hunley had made the final changes to the converted boiler tank he had turned into a submarine. It was an odd-looking seafaring craft, twenty-five feet long, and barely big enough to carry a crew of eight volunteers. Of the eight volunteers, six were responsible for hand cranking a primitive propeller, a seventh steered the craft by alternately looking through a tiny glass window while holding a small compass, and the eighth, George E. Dixon, to command the craft and to monitor a crude depth gauge.

On February 17, the moon rose over Charleston harbor as the men took their places in the craft, fitted now with a live torpedo attached to her bow. On signal, six men began cranking the propeller and the mission was underway.

Dixon directed the craft away from the ironclads in the harbor and headed for the nearest of the wooden ships. He feared the moonlight, and the ghostly underwater shadow that his submarine might make to anyone looking, but there was no turning back. After striking their target, the Hunley would turn and crank for shore, but the men would probably have to await the incoming tide before completing the mission.

At 8:45 p.m., the Hunley was approaching the 1,240 ton, thirteen-gun wooden steam sloop *Housatonic*, and unaware the moon had already betrayed their presence, Dixon had the navigator steer straight toward the enemy ship. Suddenly, the *Housatonic* turned in the direction of the tiny submarine, the captain increasing the ship's power and Dixon's men pouring every ounce of energy from their exhausted bodies into cranking the propeller of their small craft.

The instant the explosive touched the bow of the *Housatonic* there was a tremendous explosion. The air filled with pieces of timber and there was a great rushing of water into the ship and heavy black smoke roiled from the stack. The ship began to sink in twenty-eight feet of water and the disabled *Hunley* would sink as well.

Until the advent of World War II, the *H. L. Hunley* would remain the only American submarine to sink an enemy vessel.

It wouldn't be until the Smithsonian Institution's raising of the *Hunley* in August of 2000 that the inside the small submarine would reveal its secrets. Do you remember the $20 gold piece that Queenie had given Dixon, the one that saved his leg?

Among the handful of artifacts found near George Dixon's remains, was a slightly bent $20 dollar gold piece, inscribed: "Shiloh – April 6, 1862 – My life preserver – G.E.D." Queenie would have loved knowing that her lover considered her gift as his personal life preserver.

Maria Jacobsen, Senior Archaeologist for the Smithsonian was the person who recovered the coin. On the day after the discovery, she suggested, "Some people may think this is a stroke of luck, but perhaps it's something else. They tell me that Lieutenant Dixon was a lady's man, perhaps he winked at us yesterday to remind us that he still is."

"Money is just a way of keeping score."
H. L. Hunt (**Feb 17, 1889** – Nov 29, 1974) Oil tycoon

Lavinia Fisher
1793 (Charleston, SC) – **Feb 18, 1820** (Charleston, SC)

T HE WHOLE TRUTH about Lavinia Fisher may never be known.

After all, it's been almost 200 years since her hanging, and there are varied tales about how she went from being the respected hostess of Charleston, South Carolina's "Six Mile Wayfarer House," to recognition as America's first female mass murderer.

Know also, that whatever Lavinia did, she didn't do it alone. She had help from her husband John, who, depending on which version of the story you read, either (1) died on the gallows one day before Lavinia; or (2) died immediately before Lavinia's execution, but on the same day. The reason for John's execution needing to take place prior to Lavinia's was that 1820s South Carolina law didn't permit the hanging of a married woman. Lavinia needed to become a widow first, and the state's judicial system was more than willing to take care of that detail.

Lavinia, however, didn't make it easy!

Her execution wasn't exactly the outing that the estimated crowd of 2,000 expected. Some claim Lavinia arrived at the gallows wearing a white wedding gown. Others say she wore a loose-fitting white robe. Regardless, she arrived on schedule, and she was not pleased with the crowd, especially with some of the faces she recognized.

She preferred to be somewhere else, anywhere, but her presence was central to the occasion and when the carriage pulled up next to the gallows, all hell was about to break loose. When she refused to exit the carriage, she was physically extracted, an ugly ten to fifteen minutes at best. Then, when she refused to walk from the carriage to the gallows she had to be carried, literally kicking and screaming to the foot of the gallows stairway.

Use your imagination here, but wearing either a wedding gown or a loose-fitting white robe, and not inclined to be the least bit helpful,

Lavinia made sure the authorities had all they could handle getting her up the narrow stairway to the gallows platform. All of this in front of families, some with children, who had come to witness the hanging while relaxing with a picnic lunch.

On the platform when given an opportunity to say a few final words, she did, verbally ripping the crowd, pointing and screaming at Charleston's most socially prominent ladies. Many of those who were the object of her scorn, had been her friends, and all of them were there to see her off, so to speak. Lavinia blamed everyone and everything from society to the governor for her conviction. Here's how one observer put it:

> "She stomped in rage and swore with all the vehemence of her amazing vocabulary, calling down damnation on a governor who would let a woman swing. The crowd stood shocked into silence, while she cut short one curse with another and ended with a volley of shrieks."

As the noose was placed around her neck, she screamed to the crowd, "If you have a message you want sent to Hell, give it to me – I'll carry it," and she jumped from the scaffold.

Fortunately, or unfortunately, depending on your point of view, she barely cleared the platform and was suspended, dangling in midair, her legs kicking frantically until she could be rescued and once again pushed, shoved, and carried up those narrow stairs.

This time there was no speaking to the crowd and twenty-seven year old Lavinia Fisher exited this life.

So what did she and John do to warrant such a disgraceful final chapter? As mentioned, they owned an inn, the Six Mile Wayfarer House, just six miles north of Charleston.

Reports over the years talked about guests who had stayed at the Wayfarer, yet never showed up at their final destinations the following morning. However, because of John and Lavinia's social prominence and apparent law-abiding nature, nothing ever came of the stories.

Lavinia, an attractive woman, often invited men who checked into the inn to share dinner and tea with her. At dinner, she would inquire about their occupations and interests, and ask questions that might give an indication of their wealth, or of how much money they might be carrying.

As the evening would end, she would send the guest to his room with a freshly brewed cup of tea laced with a powerful sedative. John would later enter the room, stab the sleeping guest to death, remove his valuables, and then dispose of the body.

One story recalls a man named John Peeples, and it was his story that brought about the end for the Fishers.

Peeples had stopped at the Wayfarer House for the night and was told by the Fishers that there were no available rooms. The Fishers, however, did invite him to join them for a cup of tea and some dessert. John disliked tea, but took a cup to look sociable and poured its contents down the kitchen drain when Lavinia stepped out of the room for a moment. Her numerous questions made Peeples nervous, but when she announced that a guest had departed making a room available, the weary Peeples decided to stay and he was shown to his room.

Exhausted, he fell asleep in a chair, and was awakened to a swishing sound and the bed swinging back-and-forth on hinges. Beneath the bed, he could see a gaping hole in the floor. Peeples climbed out a window and rode to Charleston where he told authorities of what he had just experienced.

A search of the Wayfarer House turned up hidden passages and approximately a hundred sets of human remains, many in a pit filled with quicklime to speed decomposition and reduce odor. In the room once occupied by John Peeples, a mechanism, when activated, opened the floorboards beneath a hinged bed, thus dumping the guest into the pit.

The Fishers were arrested and jailed.

In May of 1819, both were found guilty of multiple robberies and murders and sentenced to death. In September, they tried to break out of jail using tied-together bed linens. John went out first and was able to get part way down before the linens gave way. Being the gentleman that he was, he refused to escape without the lovely Lavinia and he returned to his cell to await the outcome of an appeal.

In February of 1820, their appeals were denied and their executions scheduled and carried out, John solemnly accepting his fate first, Lavinia vehemently rejecting hers afterward.

If ever in Charleston, South Carolina, it's claimed that Lavinia's ghost is still angry about the hanging and occasionally haunts the old jail on Charleston's Magazine Street and when not there, her ghost wanders the tombstones at the Unitarian Cemetery.

On **February 18, 1881**, Jefferson Davis
is inaugurated as the
provisional President of the Confederate
States of America.

FEBRUARY 19
The 'October Sky' guy

Homer Hickam
(Homer Hadley Hickam, Jr.)
Feb 19, 1943 (Coalwood WV) Engineer, author

N OW, THIS IS interesting!
Just came across it the other day.

So, what are the chances that something like this could happen? A million to one? Certainly someone didn't just walk into a committee meeting one day and say, "Hey guys, let's see what happens if we turn the computer loose to create an alternative title for Homer's book, *Rocket Boys*."

Homer Hickam is a bona fide rocket scientist. That's right. After checking out everything available by science-fiction writers Jules Verne, Isaac Asimov, and Robert Heinlein in the Coalwood (West Virginia) Public Library, he and his high school friends established the Big Creek Missile Agency (BCMA). Then, under the youthful "authority" of the BCMA, they built and fired off rockets in a vacant field.

But being a teenage rocket scientist can also have a downside, especially when a few of the homemade rockets had minds of their own, upsetting Hickam's mine superintendent father and some of the local residents when they fell from the sky and landed in places they shouldn't.

However, the budding scientists had an all-important friend in high school teacher Miss Frieda Riley who not only supported them, but also gave them a book on *Guided Missile Design* and then helped them create projects for consideration at the National Science Awards competition.

Just how good were Hickam and his fellow rocket scientists? During Hickam's senior year at Big Creek High School, he and his fellow scientists won gold and silver medals for propulsion with their, *A Study of Amateur Rocketry Techniques,* at the 1960 National Science Fair.

After high school, Hickam graduated from Virginia Polytechnic Institute earning a degree in Industrial Engineering (1964) and then he enlisted in the military, serving six years in Vietnam as an infantry officer.

Following his military tour, he went to work for the Army Aviation and Missile Command at Redstone Arsenal (Huntsville, Alabama), followed by a tour of duty with the 7th Army Training Command in West Germany, and then on to the National Aeronautics and Space Administration (NASA) at the Marshall Space Flight Center back in Huntsville where he trained astronauts.

In 1998, as mentioned up front, NASA engineer Homer Hickam wrote a book titled *Rocket Boys.* It was his second non-fiction book. His first, *Torpedo Junction,* was published by the Naval Institute Press in 1989, the story of U-boat activity on America's east coast during World War II. It sold well enough to be considered a best seller and further encouraged the now grown up, and very real, rocket scientist to continue writing.

His second book, *Rocket Boys,* is a biography. It's the story of what it was like to grow up in a small West Virginia coal-mining town under the watchful eye of a domineering coal-mining superintendent father.

Rocket Boys lifted off as a selection by the *New York Times* as one of its Great Books of 1998. It was also an alternative Book-of-the-Month selection for both the Literary Guild and the Book of the Month Club. Next, came a nomination by the National Book Critics Circle as the Best Biography of 1998, and then came talk about turning it into a movie.

Someone in Hollywood decided the book's title, *Rocket Boys,* wasn't quite right for a movie title and so a committee discussed the matter and some alternatives were bandied about, the group settling on the rather odd title, *October Sky,* understandable, maybe, but only after you've seen the movie.

Now, here's the interesting thing about the two titles. *Rocket Boys* and *October Sky* are anagrams of each other. That is, the same ten characters [b,c,e,k,o,o,r,s,t,y] are used in writing both titles. What a covertly intriguing thing to do, establish an unmistakable, but veiled, relationship between the two titles of a singular story, which of course, required a healthy dose of imagination, some creativity, and a lot of smiles.

"To know that we know what we know,
and to know that we do not know what we do not know,
that is true knowledge."
Nicolaus Copernicus (**Feb 19, 1473** – May 24, 1543)
Mathematician, astronomer

FEBRUARY 20
The evolution of a quote

Ken Olsen
(Kenneth Harry Olsen)
Feb 20, 1926 (Bridgeport, CT) – Feb 6, 2011 (Indianapolis, IN)

K EN OLSEN, THE founder of Digital Equipment Corporation, made a statement in 1977 before the *World Future Society* that is often quoted today for its "shock value" at conferences and other venues. But don't be deceived into thinking that Olsen didn't know what he was talking about. Ken Olsen was one of the brightest minds of his generation and he knew exactly what he was talking about, and so did everyone at the conference who was listening to him and nodding in agreement. It's just that the quote is a perfect illustration of a changing concept.

For example, during the Civil War, the term *torpedo* referred to a floating explosive device, and the sentence, "Be careful, the boys have seen some torpedos floating in the harbor," would have made perfect sense to the boys in blue or gray. However, that same sentence, if spoken today doesn't make sense because our concept of a torpedo brings to mind a self-propelled underwater explosive device, not a static, floating device.

Here is Ken Olsen's oft-quoted quote:

> "There is no reason for any individual to have a computer in his home."

Olsen was one of the 20th century's finest minds in computer science. He was educated at the Massachusetts Institute of Technology (MIT) and as a graduate student was part of the team that furthered the concept of core memory, what we call RAM (Random Access Memory) today.

While at MIT, the Office of Naval Research recruited him to help build a computerized flight simulator, which he did. He also directed the building of the first transistorized research computer, and while all of that was going on, he was working toward an advanced degree in electrical engineering, graduating in 1952.

So let's return to that strange quote of Olsen's uttered in 1977.

"There is no reason for any individual to have a computer in his home."

In 1977, at the time the statement was made, a computer was a large, complex piece of technology, a "mainframe," that most housewives wouldn't have allowed inside the home anyway. Besides, it would have taken up a whole bedroom and would have needed a temperature-controlled environment.

Olsen wasn't opposed to doing a little "computing at home," as he once explained when defending his famous quote. He explained that he, in fact, had installed a "computer terminal" at home so his wife could play Scrabble with one of MIT's time-share machines. And, in the same breath, mentioned that his sixth grade son was "networking with the MIT and the DEC mainframe computers, hopefully, without doing mischief," while at home.

The problem with the quote wasn't with Olsen's words, but with what "a computer was" in 1977; as compared with what "a computer is" today.

Olsen was right, but in trying to put computing into a sensible context and one that was clear in his visionary mind, he gave the world a very funny quote that far outlived his 1977 speech.

In 2011, in honor of the 150th anniversary of the Massachusetts Institute of Technology, MIT published a listing of 150 of the most significant innovators, inventions, or ideas to have come from alumni, faculty, and students of MIT. Ken Olsen is #6 on that list.

"It is easier to build strong children than
to repair broken men."
Frederick Douglass (c. Feb 1818 – **Feb 20, 1895**) Abolitionist

---

WAYNE WINTERTON, PH.D.

FEBRUARY 21
One harebrained scheme

Mary Toft
Baptized: **Feb 21, 1703** (Unknown) – 1763 (Unknown)

RABBITS? YES, THAT'S rabbits, plural, as in "Mary gave birth to more than one rabbit." Believable? Not in the 21st century. However, in 1726, it was believable, and Mary Toft of the village of Godalming, England, was quite convincing in her claim that she had given birth to rabbits. And just as amazing, those births took place after she had already given birth to three normal children, Mary, Anne, and James, all fathered by Joshua Toft, a clothier by trade and a non-rabbit by birth.

On September 27, 1726, pregnant and with her mother-in-law Ann Toft, and a neighbor, Mary Gill, both present, Mary felt the unmistakable urges of delivery. When it was over, she had given birth to what the other women described as a "half-cat." As you might imagine, disturbed by the strange delivery, they asked a respected male-midwife, John Howard, to render an opinion. He examined Mary and the stillborn creature, and that's not all, over the next thirty days, Howard delivered a rabbit's head, a set of cat legs, and nine dead baby rabbits.

Bizarre births always rate high on the scale of tabloid newsworthiness, regardless of century, and any time a woman gives birth to a warren of rabbits, you can rest assured the tabloids will pick up the story. Thus, it was no surprise when the November 19, 1726, issue of *Mist's Weekly Journal* reported the delivery of nine stillborn rabbits by a pregnant lady from Godalming. Just as surprising to the readers, was the fact that the delivery had occurred in the presence of a well-known and esteemed male-midwife. Here's a portion of the text from the above article.

> "From Guildford comes a strange but well-attested piece of News. That a poor woman who lives at Godalmin [sic] … about a Month past delivered by Mr. John Howard,

an Eminent Surgeon and Man-Midwife, of a creature resembling a Rabbit ... [and] about fourteen days since was delivered by the same Person, of a perfect Rabbit: and in a few Days after of 4 more ... [until] in all nine. They died all in bringing into the world.

"The woman hath made Oath, that two Months ago, being working in a Field with other Women, they put up a Rabbit, who running from them, they pursued it, but to no purpose. This created ... such a Longing to it, that she (being with Child) was taken ill and miscarried, and from that Time she hath not been able to avoid thinking of Rabbits."

Easily one of the more unusual pieces of news to reach the court of King George I, the hare-raising births generated enough discussion that the esteemed Henry Davenant of the King's inner circle traveled to Guildford to check out the story. After visiting with John Howard, the male-midwife, Davenant returned to London a believer in the unusual, but miraculous births.

Reluctant to believe Davenant's assessment, but not wanting to embarrass him, King George asked one of his personal physicians, Dr. Nathaniel St. André and an astronomer, Samuel Molyneux to go to Godalming to see what they could learn about the story.

The two men were eager to resolve the question as to whether a woman, who had already given birth to normal children, could also give birth to rabbits. After exchanging greetings with Mary, the two men got right to the point. Mary responded by telling them, quite convincingly, that prior to the birth of the rabbits, she had experienced a strong craving for rabbit meat and had spent much time trying to catch one of the long-eared rascals in her garden.

After listening, Dr. St. André decided that nothing short of a full scientific and medical evaluation could determine the veracity of Mary's story. After placing one of the dead rabbit's lungs in a bowl of water and seeing it float, he was almost convinced. To verify his findings, he examined Mary and concluded that indeed, the rabbits had formed within her Fallopian tubes. The doctor was convinced!

WAYNE WINTERTON, PH.D.

Dr. St. André reported his findings to King George, and the King, to his royal credit decided to get a second opinion (a third, if you count Henry Davenant's opinion), so he sent another of his surgeons, Cyriacus Ahlers, to look further into the matter. Ahlers gave Toft a thorough examination and found no evidence of a pregnancy that would have produced any kind of offspring, hare, hamster, or human.

Certain that Toft was perpetrating a hoax, Dr. Ahlers feigned agreement with Mary and asked if he could take a couple of the dead rabbits back to London with him. Mary willingly gave Ahlers two of the rabbits.

In London, Ahlers opened the stomachs of the rabbits and found grain and other evidence of outside the womb activity, and on December 4, 1726, he had Mary brought to London.

Mary, sure she had Ahlers' support, stuck to her story. That was, until she learned that yet another doctor, Sir Richard Manningham had been brought in to perform a particularly painful exploratory surgery on her reproductive organs. The purpose, as explained to Mary, was to determine how her reproductive organs were different from the reproductive organs of other women.

It was a ruse of course, but after a few minutes of thoughtful consideration, Mary opted to forego the painful surgery in favor of confessing to the hoax.

On December 9, 1726, Mary Toft was convicted in court of being, "a notorious and vile cheat," and was incarcerated at Bridewell Prison where she was exhibited before numerous onlookers who wanted to see the woman who once claimed to have given birth to rabbits.

Mary Toft's hoax became the subject of cartoons, writings, and even a ribald ballad composed by famed poet Alexander Pope titled, *The Discovery; or, The Squire Turn'd Ferret.* Most of the ballad's stanzas are unpublishable here, but the opening is G-Rated and acceptable to all. In fact, you might have heard it before, but just didn't know of its origin.

> "Most true it is, I dare to say / E'er since the Days of Eve, The weakest Woman sometimes may / The wisest Man deceive."

The hoax proved to be damaging, not only to Mary Toft who served jail time, but also to the respected Dr. Nathaniel St. André who, only four days before Mary's confession, published a forty page scientific booklet titled, "A Short Narrative of an Extraordinary Delivery of Rabbits."

"We are all here on earth to help others;
what on earth the 'others' are here for, I don't know."
W. H. Auden (**Feb 21, 1907** – Sept 29, 1973) Poet

WAYNE WINTERTON, PH.D.

FEBRUARY 22
By George, I didn't know that

George Washington
Feb 22, 1732 (Westmoreland, VA) – Dec 14, 1799 (Mt. Vernon, VA)

MOST EVERYONE IS familiar with George Washington's life from the time of the Revolutionary War (1775-1783) forward, but few know much about him prior to that time.

George was the oldest of Augustine and Mary Ball Washington's children. He had two older half-brothers, Lawrence and Augustine, as his mother had been married prior to her marriage to George's father. Considered an "old" family, George's great-grandfather had immigrated to America in 1657 and settled in what is now Virginia.

In 1735, the family moved to a place called *Little Hunting Creek Plantation*, and later to another family property, *Ferry Farm* near Fredericksburg, both in today's Virginia. The latter is where George was home-schooled and tutored by a schoolmaster in math, geography, and Latin and English classics, receiving a "basic education."

In 1743, when George was eleven his father died. George's half-brother Lawrence, being the eldest male in the family, assumed the role of surrogate father to George and his siblings. In addition, by virtue of his senior position in the family, Lawrence inherited the family's oldest and largest property, the approximate 5,000-acre Little Hunting Creek Plantation. George, as the eldest of his father's and Mary Ball's children, inherited the Fredericksburg property, the approximate 3,000 acre Ferry Farm, a sizeable parcel of property for an eleven year old to own.

Both of George's older half-brothers received their advanced education at the Appleby School in England, a school that George would have attended as well, had his father lived. Unfortunately, from an educational standpoint, the death of his father dictated that George not travel to England, but remain at home, helping with family matters.

At sixteen, George joined a survey crew that mapped Virginia's western territory, and a year later, he became the official surveyor of Culpepper County.

At nineteen, when Lawrence became seriously ill with tuberculosis, George accompanied him to Barbados where the family hoped a change in climate would cure Lawrence of the disease. It didn't and Lawrence's problems only worsened so the two returned to the Little Hunting Creek Plantation (1751).

After his return from Barbados, and shortly before his death less than a year later, Lawrence put his affairs in order. That included renaming the 5,000-acre Little Hunting Creek Plantation in honor of the British naval commander he had served under during the *War of Jenkins Ear* (1739-1748), an admiral fondly known as *Old Grog* by his men because of his preference for long coats made of "grogram" fabric.

When Lawrence died, George acquired his property, which together with Ferry Farm, brought his total land holdings to 8,000 acres.

Now, keep in mind that in the 1750s, what would become the United States in 1776, was still a British colony. Thus, in 1752 when Virginia's Lieutenant Governor made twenty-year-old George Washington a major in the Virginia militia, it meant that Major George Washington was an officer in the British Army.

A year later, Major Washington and his men fought in the French and Indian War, and on one occasion, Washington surrendered to the French. The French, however, were willing to turn him loose, but only after they secured a solemn promise that the colonies would construct no more forts along the Ohio River.

In 1755, Washington, still fighting the French, became Colonel Washington. During one particularly nasty skirmish, Washington almost didn't survive to become the leader of the Revolutionary War, as he was the target of a volley of French bullets. When he was safely away from the skirmish, he found four bullet holes in his long cloak, but not a scratch on his body. That same year, Washington, now a very experienced twenty-three year old military officer, became commander of the Virginia militia.

In 1758, with the French and Indian War over, George, twenty-six, resigned his military commission. A year later, he married Martha

Custis, a wealthy widow with 2 children and the owner of an 18,000-acre estate. Martha's land holdings, when combined with the 8,000 acres that George owned, plus land he received as payment for his military service, made the future *Father of his Country* and first lady one of the wealthiest families in Virginia.

Skipping ahead now, beyond the Revolutionary War (1775-1783) we arrive at Washington's final days.

On December 12, 1799, and in a freezing rain, sixty-seven year old George Washington rode his plantation marking the trees he wished to have removed. The following morning he arose with a terrible sore throat. Washington called three physicians and ordered them to perform bloodletting, a standard medical procedure of the era intended to "remove bad blood."

On December 14, and with nearly half the blood in his body gone, and with no improvement in his condition, he summoned his personal secretary, Tobias Lear. "I am just going," he said, "have me decently buried, and do not let my body be put into the vault in less than three days after I'm dead." Lear nodded in agreement. "Do you understand?" asked Washington. "Yes, sir," replied Lear. "'Tis well," breathed Washington with a long sigh, and he was gone.

Remember the land that George inherited on the death of his brother Lawrence, the 5,000-acre parcel that Lawrence renamed in honor of his naval commander, a man known affectionately by his men as *Old Grog.* Well, *Old Grog* was Admiral Edward "Old Grog" Vernon, and thus the Little Hunting Creek Plantation when renamed, became the Mount Vernon Estate, and the home of the first president of the United States.

"Age doesn't matter unless you're a cheese."
Luis Buñuel (**Feb 22, 1900** – July 29, 1983)
Spanish filmmaker

FEBRUARY 23

He delivered a 'Little Boy' to the Emperor

Paul Tibbets

(Paul Warfield Tibbets, Jr.)

Feb 23, 1915 (Quincy, IL) – Nov 1, 2007 (Columbus, OH)

COLONEL PAUL W. Tibbets was the son of Paul and Enola Gay Tibbets. The name, "Enola Gay," would become familiar to the world as the name of Colonel Tibbets B-29 Superfortress bomber, the airplane that carried the world's first atomic bomb, codenamed *Little Boy*, to the doomed city of Hiroshima.

Overwhelming in its destructive power, *Little Boy* was a one-way passenger on April 6, 1945, when Colonel Tippets and his crew of eleven flew straight into the history books as the first to release the awesome power of an atomic weapon on the earth. The devastation was harsh and immediate. The population of the city of Hiroshima dropped from 340,000 to an estimated 166,000 by year's end, a combination of immediate deaths and the slow deaths of thousands of others from radiation. The bomb also leveled an estimated 75% of the city's structures.

Now, it was up to the Emperor of Japan to make a decision. Given three days to consider what had just happened to Hiroshima, and informed that a second bomb, one with even greater destructive power than the first was awaiting his decision, the world held its breath.

So, as promised, a second and more destructive atomic bomb was prepared. With the code name *Fat Man*, it would detonate a plutonium core, instead of a uranium core as was used in *Little Boy*. America and the Allies waited the promised three days, hopeful the Emperor would surrender to prevent the destruction of another Japanese city and the unnecessary deaths of another hundred thousand or more people. However, nothing was forthcoming.

Thus, in the early morning hours of August 9, *Fat Man* was loaded into a B-29 Superfortress and armed. At precisely 3:47 in the morning, with Major Charles W. Sweeney at the controls, the plane lifted off and set a course for its principal target, the city of Kokura, Japan. When the B-29 reached its target, the city was "socked-in" and after several passes in an effort to find a hole in the clouds, Major Sweeney turned the B-29 toward its secondary target, Nagasaki.

As the plane reached its new target, bombardier Kermit Beahan spotted a hole in the clouds, directed the plane to that location, and *Fat Man* was on its way. It took the bomb exactly forty-three seconds to fall to the proper elevation above the city and detonate. Although the bomb did not hit the preferred target directly, it got the Emperor's attention and the world was shocked back to its collective sensibilities.

Now was a time of thanks for America and its allies, but it was also a sobering time for the world. Far too many lives on both sides of the conflict had been lost during too many years of fighting. While there are some who questioned then, and question today, it is impossible to know how many lives were spared by the use of the world's most powerful weapon at that point in time.

Colonel Tibbets put it this way, "I knew when I got the assignment it was going to be an emotional thing. We had feelings, but we had to put them in the background. We knew it was going to kill people. But my one driving interest was to do the best job I could so we could end the killing as quickly as possible."

Emperor Hirohito had finally made a right choice. The alternative to bombing Hiroshima and Nagasaki would have been an all-out assault on the Japanese mainland. It would have cost the lives of an unknown number of American and Allied soldiers, as well as Japanese soldiers and civilians, far more than had been lost to the power of *Little Boy* and *Fat Man.*

General Paul Tibbets (he was promoted to "General" prior to his retirement in 1966), on the 50th anniversary of the bombing of Hiroshima, told an interviewer for the documentary, *The Men Who Brought the Dawn,* "It would have been morally wrong if we would have had that weapon and not used it and allowed a million more people to die."

On **February 23, 1954**, the children of Arsenal School in Pennsylvania
became the first to receive Dr. Jonas Salk's
new polio vaccine.

The Battle of Los Angeles
Feb 24, 1942 (Los Angeles CA)

TO UNDERSTAND WHAT the Battle of Los Angeles was, and how it happened, it's important to understand the context of the times.

One day after the Japanese bombed Pearl Harbor, President Franklin D. Roosevelt gave his famous speech that began, "Yesterday, December 7th, 1941, a date which will live in infamy, the United States of America was suddenly and deliberately attacked by naval and air forces of the Empire of Japan," and America geared up for war with Japan.

Seventy-eight days later (February 23, 1942), a Japanese submarine commanded by Kozo Nishino surfaced approximately twelve miles off the coast of California, west of Santa Barbara, and within sight of the Ellwood oil fields. The submarine crew, after surfacing, using 5.5-inch deck guns fired 20 to 25 shells at two oil storage tanks on the mainland, hitting neither, but damaging one well, Luton-Bell #17, an adjacent catwalk and a pumping station.

Nishino, after sending a message to Tokyo that he had "left Santa Barbara in flames," submerged and was gone.

Kozo Nashino's raid on Ellwood was the first attack on American soil by an enemy force since the War of 1812.

Although the cost in dollars to repair the damages was negligible, the damage to the psyche of the American public was high. Those living along the California coast suddenly realized that "the war over there," just might be "coming over here." It was an anxious time.

As the sun was setting on February 24, one day after the shelling of the Ellwood oil fields, people in the Los Angeles area began seeing things in the sky, and most prominent among the reports, were the sightings of a giant craft hovering in the night sky. The first thought in the minds of most Californians was, "What are the Japanese up to now, and what will happen next?"

Was the giant craft an illusion? Was it simply mass hysteria coming on the heels of the Ellwood attack?

No, it was not, because whatever the civilians were watching from their backyards was also under surveillance by military radar.

At 2:25 in the morning, air raid sirens started to wail and a full blackout went into effect for Los Angeles County. Powerful spotlights lit up the night sky, and thousands of newly trained air raid wardens took up their positions at pre-determined lookout locations.

People watching from their homes or front yards saw a sky full of searchlights, most converging on a single giant craft that whenever illuminated would begin taking on a barrage of anti-aircraft fire. Civilians watched as tracer bullets preceding live rounds seemed to disappear inside the huge craft.

[Note: A news photo taken of searchlights converging on the unidentified craft is available on the internet.]

Fighter pilots of the 4th Interceptor Command went on alert; aircraft were readied, positioned for takeoff, but never used.

At 3:16 am, the 37th Coast Artillery Brigade began firing each time the craft was illuminated. Using .50-caliber machine guns and eight-pound anti-aircraft shells, the 37th was relentless in its attempt to bring the craft down and by morning had fired over 1,400 shells and nothing fell from the sky.

At 4:14 am, the "all clear" sounded.

Eyewitnesses to the nightlong fight, as one-sided as any fight in history, were certain they had seen something. Whatever it was, it had been impervious to the barrage of shelling, and at 4:30, just before dawn, the craft moved from the Santa Monica area toward Long Beach before it disappeared from view.

In the aftermath, five civilians were dead of indirect causes, three were involved in deadly automobile accidents during the chaos, and two of heart attacks believed caused by stress.

Shortly after the all clear had sounded, Secretary of the Navy Frank Knox held a press conference, claiming the entire incident was the result of war nerves.

This brought about instant shouts of government cover-up. Sound familiar?

Other notables weighed in, including General George C. Marshall who suggested the incident might have been part of a psychological warfare campaign to generate panic.

Representative Leland Merritt Ford of Santa Monica called for a full Congressional investigation, believing that what had happened, might have been part of a plan to get California citizens to reject the location of war industries in their state.

Whatever scared the dickens out of the citizenry of Los Angeles on the night of February 24, 1942, remains as one of the nation's most interesting Unidentified Flying Object mysteries.

Something hovered in the California sky for hours that night. Whatever it was, it was photographed by a news reporter, fired on repeatedly by military guns, seen by thousands of civilians, and then went on its merry way.

"The depressing thing about tennis is that
no matter how good I get,
I'll never be as good as the wall."
Mitch Hedberg (**Feb 24, 1968** – March 30, 2005) Comedian

FEBRUARY 25
The "Minder of the Light"

Ida Lewis
(Idawalley Zorada Lewis)
Feb 25, 1842 (Newport, RI) – Oct 25, 1911 (Lime Rock, RI)

MINDING THE LIGHT on Lime Rock Island, Rhode Island, was the only life Ida Lewis knew.

If a young lady needs a role model for what it means to be the big sister, or to pull one's weight in a struggling family, or to take responsibility when a challenge needs met, you couldn't find a better role model than Ida.

The lighthouse known as the "Lime Rock Light" is two hundred yards of churning water from the mainland at Newport Harbor.

Erected in 1854, the first *keeper-of-the-light* was James Stockbridge Lewis, Ida's father. The original lighthouse was a short stone tower equipped with a standard Fresnel (pronounced fruh-nel) lens in front of an oil-burning lantern.

Every day, seven days a week, James Lewis rowed the 200 yards from Newport Harbor to Lime Rock Island to make certain the lantern had sufficient oil, and he cleaned the lens if necessary to assure a good beacon for passing ships.

Six months into the job, James suffered a stroke and could no longer work, so his elderly father, Hosea Lewis took over *keeper-of-the-light* responsibilities. The only help that James could offer was his daily reminder to, "mind the light." To accommodate the Lewis family, a two-story house was erected on the island, and in 1857 grandfather Hosea, James and his wife Ida and their four children, including fifteen-year-old Ida, a daughter named for her mother, moved into the house.

If you've ever rowed a small boat in choppy water, you'll appreciate the physical effort it took for teenager Ida to row her three younger siblings to shore each morning for school, and to make another round-trip after school to row them home safely for dinner. Think about it, Ida, fifteen, rowed the equivalent of two football fields twice each day, in dangerous waters, to take her three younger siblings to and from school.

In 1858, one year after they moved onto the island, Ida saw four young men recklessly sailing in the area of the lighthouse. She watched as one of the boys climbed the mast and began rocking the boat to the dismay of his friends, and then it happened. The sailboat capsized and the four boys were splashing, shouting, and struggling to hold onto the disabled boat. Ida made a run for her boat and rowed to where the exhausted boys were about to give up. She pulled all four of them into her boat, not an easy task, and rowed them back to the lighthouse.

Within a few years, the appointment for the *keeper-of-the-light* went from grandfather Hosea to James' wife, Ida, who was in poor health herself. Thus, it fell on daughter Ida to not only care for her three siblings, including the two daily round trips to the mainland, but to care for her aging grandfather, her partially paralyzed father, and to share with her ailing mother, the critical light-keeping duties. Until his death, Ida's father James faithfully reminded the two Ida's in his life "to always mind the light."

Over time, Ida's prowess in rescuing individuals in the waters around the lighthouse became legendary. Her most famous rescue took place on March 29, 1869, when a boat carrying two soldiers and a fourteen-year-old boy capsized in a snowstorm. In spite of the snow and the extreme temperature, and suffering from a cold herself, Ida went into action calling for a younger brother to assist her.

Without considering the danger involved, she and her brother rowed to the capsized boat. Although it was too late to save the life of the fourteen-year-old boy, they were able to get the soldiers into the boat and back to the safety of the lighthouse.

The story about the rescue of the soldiers made national headlines. Ida received a medal from Congress for the rescue and the story made the *New York Tribune*. A month later, the Lewis family received President Ulysses S. Grant and Vice-president Schuyler Colfax as guests on the island. Shortly afterward, the *Life Saving Benevolent Association of New York* presented Ida with a silver medal and a check for $100, the most money she'd seen in one place, at one time, ever. A few months later, on the Fourth of July, the city of Newport held a parade in her honor and presented her with a new mahogany rowboat with gold-plated oarlocks.

Ten years later, in 1879, Ida, now thirty-seven years old, became the *keeper-of-the-light*, faithfully following her deceased father's admonition to "mind the light," which she did for another thirty-two years before suffering a stroke and passing away on October 25, 1911, at the age of sixty-nine.

At the time of her death, she was the highest paid lighthouse keeper in the United States, earning $750 per year.

On her death, artillery practice stopped at nearby Fort Adams and all of the ships in Newport Harbor tolled their bells in respect for Ida Lewis. The city's flags flew at half-staff. An estimated 1,500 people viewed her body as she lay in repose before interment at a prominent location in Newport's *Common Burying Ground*. During her lifetime at Lime Rock, Ida rescued thirty-six people. After her death, stories of her heroism were widely published in national magazines such as *Harper's Weekly*.

In 1924, the Rhode Island state legislature officially changed the name of the Lime Rock Lighthouse to the Ida Lewis Rock Lighthouse, the only time that such an honor has been bestowed on a *keeper-of-the-light*.

On **February 25, 1913**, the 16th Amendment to the
Constitution was ratified,
paving the way for something new in America,
the income tax.

FEBRUARY 26

It pays to listen, and pays well

Levi Strauss

Feb 26, 1829 (Buttenheim, Bavaria) – Sept 26, 1902 (San Francisco, CA)

T HE STORY OF Levi Strauss is a true American success story. When laid to rest in Colma, California in 1902, Levi Strauss's six million dollars, if converted to 2015 dollars, would amount to roughly $160 million.

Levi, his mother and his sisters left Bavaria in 1847 because of the severe discrimination of people of the Jewish faith. America, they knew, was a different kind of place. It was where anyone willing to work hard, regardless of ethnic background or religious belief, could succeed.

At eighteen, Levi went to work in the family dry goods business, J. Strauss Brother & Company, with his brothers, Jonas and Louis who had emigrated earlier.

In 1853, two months after receiving citizenship, Levi sailed for San Francisco taking with him a supply of dry goods, some fashionable clothing, and a variety of fabrics on bolts, canvas for tents and wagon covers, important items needed to open a branch of the family business in California.

When Levi arrived, the gold rush was in full swing and with more men arriving daily, everything was in short supply. It was the perfect environment for a merchant who knew that the secret to selling was in offering what customers needed.

That's when a prospector struck up a conversation with the twenty-five year old dry goods proprietor and asked what he had brought from the east that might be useful in the gold fields. Levi showed the prospector his goods, and the prospector looked at him and said, "You should have brought pants with you," adding, "nowhere can a guy find a pair of pants strong enough to withstand the rigors of panning."

Levi was a good listener and he took the message to heart. He looked through the bolts of fabric he had with him, but found nothing that would withstand the hard work of prospecting. That's when he put the bolts of fabric away and turned his attention to the heavy, highly durable canvas he had brought to sell for making tents and wagon covers.

Levi took some of the canvas and made it into waist overalls, a work pant without an attached bib. The miners liked the durability but they didn't care for the stiffness of the canvas that chafed their legs. Levi began a search for a substitute fabric and found it in France. It was almost as strong as canvas, twilled, but considerably more supple, and it was called (in French) "serge de Nimes." The miners loved the fabric, which they mispronounced as "serbe de-nim." It wasn't long before the "serbe" was lost altogether, and when the miners wanted a pair of pants made from the fabric, "de-nim" soon became "denim."

By 1873, the company had become Levi Strauss & Company, and among its many employees was Jacob Davis, a Latvian tailor. Davis came up with the idea of riveting, rather than double stitching the stress areas of the pants for greater strength. The U. S. Patent Office awarded Patent No. 139,121 to the company on May 20, 1873, a date now considered by the Levi Company as the official birthday of America's original blue jeans, Levis.

As mentioned up front, at the time of Levi's death in 1902 he was worth about $6 million dollars. Although much of his wealth remained with his family, he never forgot that his piece of the American dream came from the dedicated support of his customers of many faiths.

Levi had a soft spot in his heart for the most vulnerable; children and the elderly, and he directed sizeable gifts to the Pacific Hebrew Orphan's Asylum and the Home for Aged Israelites. Neither did he slight those of other faiths, leaving gifts to Catholic and Protestant Orphan Asylums – a testimony of his love for his fellow man.

Today, prospectors for gold, people with golden parachutes, Las Vegas gold-diggers, owners of golden retrievers, retirees with gold watches, kids who collect fool's gold, old-timers with gold fillings, people who eat at the Golden Arches, and Goldie Hawn, all love their denims.

It was all because of a comment made by a crusty old prospector who wanted nothing more than a pair of pants that wouldn't wear out before he did, and a businessman named Levi, who was dedicated to providing what it was his customers wanted and needed.

"Money can't buy love, but it improves
your bargaining position."
Christopher Marlowe (**Feb 26, 1564** – May 30, 1593)
Playwright

Elizabeth Taylor

Feb 27, 1932 (London, England) – Mar 23, 2011 (Los Angeles, CA)

K NOWN TO THE medical world is an unusual genetic mutation called "distichiasis," a hereditary condition that affects about ten breeds of dogs.

The condition, technically a genetic frameshift mutation near the tip of chromosome sixteen, can also affect humans, although it does so with much less frequency than with canines. The condition is correctable by surgery or localized cryotherapy, the latter a medical term for the treatment of problems such as warts, moles, skin tags, solar keratosis, etc.

Now, if you're trying to get ahead of the story, let's take care of that right now. Yes, Elizabeth Taylor was born with distichiasis, and she preferred to live with the mutation rather than to have it medically treated, and for a very good reason.

Were you a friend of Miss Taylor's and aware of the condition, you would recognize its presence at will. However, to everyone else whose contact with the movie star was through photographs in glamour magazines, or watching her on the silver screen, the mutation, although noticeable, wouldn't so much as raise an eyebrow. All you'd see would be Miss Taylor's undeniable beauty.

Elizabeth Rosemond Taylor, named for her paternal grandmother, was born in London, England, the daughter of Francis and Sara Taylor, an American couple from Arkansas City, Kansas. Elizabeth's father, Francis Taylor, was a well-respected art dealer who had decided to open a gallery in London. Her mother was a former Broadway actress, Sara Sothern, who gave up acting after the birth of her first child, Howard Taylor. Elizabeth was the couple's second child.

The Taylor's enjoyed England, in part because the art gallery had attracted an outstanding clientele of notables, including Victor Cazalet, a wealthy and well-connected Member of Parliament. It was Cazalet who introduced the Taylor's to Winston Churchill and to the British Royal family, good names to have associated with any British business. The associations weren't casual either, and on one occasion, three-year-old Elizabeth Taylor performed a dance recital for Britain's two princesses, Elizabeth and Margaret.

Cazalet, who was also Elizabeth Taylor's godfather, had spent more than one evening in the Taylor home trying to convince Francis and Sara to move permanently to England.

Little Elizabeth and the Taylor family might have stayed in England except for one thing, World War II. When things began heating up in Europe, the Taylor's began thinking about returning to the United States. In 1939, just two years before the Japanese bombed Pearl Harbor, they established another art gallery, this time in Los Angeles.

The gallery, ideally located to attract the Los Angeles and Hollywood affluent, was a success. It opened doors and led to introductions that would turn Elizabeth into a future movie star. One of the Taylors' new friends was Hollywood gossip columnist Hedda Hopper who loved the little girl with the biggest blue eyes she had ever seen. Hopper also introduced the family to Andrea Berens whose fiancée was John Cheever Cowdin, a major stockholder of Universal Pictures.

Metro-Goldwin-Mayer was also interested in Elizabeth and when John Cowdin learned of MGM's interest, he had Universal sign her sight unseen, an action that irritated the studio's casting director. Thus, at the age of ten (1942) without so much as an audition, Elizabeth Taylor appeared in her first movie, Universal's *There's One Born Every Minute*, and she wasn't cast as an extra. She had a credited role, playing the part of Gloria Twine, the on-screen daughter of the movie's two stars, Hugh Herbert and Peggy Moran.

Perhaps Elizabeth was too mature for what Universal's casting director had in mind for the part of Gloria Twine. Perhaps he was still miffed that stockholder Cowdin had gone over his head to have the unknown girl hired without reading a single line. Whatever it was, Universal's casting director told the front office: "The kid has nothing! Her eyes are too old and she doesn't have the face of a child," and ten-year-old Elizabeth Taylor was asked to remove the coloring books and paper dolls from her locker. She had been fired!

The following day MGM signed her to a contract and the rest is history.

In 1943, MGM cast eleven-year-old Elizabeth in *Lassie Come Home* with another child star, Roddy McDowell. Many years later, McDowell would write about Taylor, recalling her beauty with a question.

Now, you're about to learn what *distichiasis* is, the genetic mutation that Elizabeth Taylor was born with, because here is the question that Roddy McDowell asked, "Who has double eyelashes except a girl who was absolutely born to be on the big screen?"

That's right, Elizabeth Taylor was born with a mutant second row of eyelashes right above the first row, giving her the fullest eyelashes in Hollywood.

It's no wonder that those meeting Miss Taylor for the first time often came away with, "Ohhhh, my gosh! Can you believe those eyes? And those 'lashes! How does she do that?"

On **February 27, 1922**, the Supreme Court upheld
the 19th Amendment
to the Constitution. Women could finally vote!

FEBRUARY 28
The Zero who finally amounted to something

Zero Mostel
(Samuel Joel Mostel)
Feb 28, 1915 (Brooklyn, NY) – Sept 8, 1977 (Philadelphia, PA)

ZERO MOSTEL WAS the son of Israel Mostel, who immigrated to the United States in 1898, and Cina "Celia" Druchs, a Polish Jew raised in Vienna, Austria, who came to America in 1908. Israel and Celia met sometime after 1908, were married, with Celia assuming the motherly duties for Israel's four children from a previous marriage. The couple would go on to have four children of their own, with Samuel Joel (Zero) being Israel's seventh child.

If ever there was a performer with stage presence, one would be hard pressed to find anyone better than Zero Mostel in his finest role, that of "Tevya," the opinionated and pious Jewish milkman in the Broadway production of *Fiddler on the Roof.*

The play, adapted from Sholem Aleichem's fictional memoir, *Tevya and his Daughters,* is the story of a loving but culturally demanding father and his strong-willed daughters, especially the eldest, "Tzeitel." No amount of explanation here can do justice to the story and the interwoven conflict as non-Jewish influences encroach into Jewish family life, including Tzeitel's love for a Russian soldier whose responsibility it is to enforce the Tsar's edict to evict all Jews from Tevya's village.

Samuel (Zero) was born in the Brownsville section of Brooklyn, a neighborhood populated by families as poor as his. He grew up multilingual, as English, Italian, German, and Yiddish were all spoken in the home, an asset that would do wonders in helping him connect with New York's varied ethnic population.

Before he was of school age, Samuel's father bought a small farm in Connecticut, and when his dream of farming turned into a financial nightmare, the family returned to New York, but this time on the Lower East Side of Manhattan, and that's where young Samuel first attended school, or more accurately, began his education.

An average student at best, his mother was constantly after him to do his studies, warning that without a good education, he'd never amount to anything, but her encouragement did little to spur the youngster to academic greatness at New York's Public School #188.

However, Samuel was good at one thing, art, so his mother arranged for professional art lessons from the "Educational Alliance," to be included with his public school studies, and it proved to be a winning combination. Samuel learned geography, history, and other standard public school fare, and became a competent artist, all at the same time.

There is a story told by New York journalist Roger Butterfield that Samuel's mother would dress her son up in a velvet suit, not unlike Gainsborough's *The Blue Boy,* and take him to the Metropolitan Museum of Art and have him practice painting copies of the masterpieces.

What better way for a child to study artistic technique at virtually no cost?

At any rate, Samuel's favorite was John White Alexander's *Study in Black and Green,* a painting he reproduced almost brush-stroke perfect at least once daily to the applause of curious onlookers. The velvet-clad youngster became so good at matching the elements of Alexander's painting, paint dab by paint dab that on one occasion, as a sizeable crowd gathered, he tried something different, he painted the entire *Study in Black and Green,* upside-down, to the amazement of his audience.

He attended the City College of New York and taught art on the side for New York's "Public Works of Art Project" to help finance his studies.

Before long, Samuel Mostel was giving lectures at New York's art museums, and having discovered an ability to combine a knowledge of art with his natural comedic personality, his lectures became noted, as much for the artistic commentary as for the entertainment value of his presentations.

Samuel began to receive more invitations to entertain as a stand-up comedian than he did for his museum lectures, and in 1941, a Manhattan nightclub, the *Café Society,* offered him a regular job as a comedian and he took it. He quickly became the club's main attraction, and since being a comedian was a much less formal occupation than lecturing at museums, he dropped *Samuel* in favor of the informal *Sam*.

Nevertheless, the proprietor of *Café Society*, Barney Josephson, felt that the name "Sam" lacked marquee presence, or something, and that may have been when Sam himself suggested "Zero" and the name stuck.

Why "Zero?" Remember the difficult time that Celia Mostel, Sam's mother had in trying to get her son to do his homework, suggesting that if he didn't do his studies he would never amount to anything?

According to Sam's brother, Bill Mostel, a more exact phrasing of what Mrs. Mostel said countless times to her son Samuel, was that if he didn't do his studies he would amount to Zero (with an exclamation mark)! And that, according to Sam's brother who should know, is how the world ended up with a very gifted actor named Zero Mostel.

"A good marriage would be between a blind wife
and a deaf husband."
Michel de Montaigne (**Feb 28, 1553** – Sept 13, 1592)
Philosopher

FEBRUARY 29
America's Sweetheart

Dinah Shore
(Frances Rose Shore)
Feb 29, 1916 (Winchester, TN) – Feb 24, 1994 (Beverly Hills, CA)

F RANCES ROSE SHORE grew up with a nickname that no one would suppose for the classy lady who invited folks in the 1950s to "See the USA in your Chevrolet." Frances Rose grew up as "Fanny" Shore.

Fanny was also a victim of polio (infantile paralysis), stricken by the debilitating disease when she was eighteen months old. Instead of following the conventional wisdom of the day and confining Fanny to bed rest, Solomon and Anna Shore chose to have their daughter undergo a new and controversial treatment promoted by Elizabeth Kenny. Kenny, a self-taught Australian nurse, believed the affected muscles needed hot packs and exercise, lots of it, not bed-ridden immobilization.

The decision turned out to be a good one, and although Fanny went through life with a deformed foot and slight limp, the disease never affected her voice.

When Fanny was eight the family moved to Nashville, where she completed her elementary education and attended Hume Fogg High School. In high school, she won a spot on the cheerleading team, took private voice lessons, and in the community, she was always available to belt out a song, whenever a song needed belted.

Her talent for singing and her love for performing once landed her in trouble with her parents, enough trouble that both she and her voice were "grounded" for a while.

On the sly and only fourteen years old, Fanny showed up at a Nashville nightclub to audition as a torch singer. After stepping on stage and allowing her eyes to adjust to the darkened room, there, in the front row amidst the cabaret patrons, were her parents.

Tipped off to their daughter's late night escapade, they were not pleased. However, to their credit, they chose not to embarrass Fanny, but to let her sing and collect the ten dollars for showing up for the audition, and then they took her straight home without stopping for a treat. There, they had a heart-to-heart talk about what had just taken place and their barely teenaged daughter's singing career was put on ice until she was older.

When her mother died unexpectedly of a heart attack in 1932, Fanny enrolled at Vanderbilt University in Nashville. Her education at Vanderbilt included a few study breaks at the nearby Grand Ole Opry, where the show's stars came to know her, and when invited, she gladly hopped onto the stage and sang a song or two. After graduating in 1938, she went to work for WSM, the radio home of the Grand Ole Opry where her new job included a few opportunities to sing on the air.

In 1940, after getting a taste of success in Nashville, Fanny went to New York where she auditioned, along with a skinny young vocalist named Frank Sinatra, for a job with radio station WNEW. During the course of her audition, she sang the song, *Dinah*. When Martin Block, the radio station's disk jockey in charge of the auditions couldn't remember her name, he simply announced her as "the Dinah girl." The name stuck and Fanny Shore became "Dinah Shore." The newly minted Dinah Shore beat out the competition, won the audition, and signed a contract to sing with Xavier Cugat's orchestra. She was grateful for both the new name and her first contract.

Whether the skinny kid who appeared malnourished and shared the audition stage with Dinah that day, ever amounted to anything, it's hard to tell. But Dinah's start into the big time as Xavier Cugat's female vocalist, got her career off to a great start.

By the way, if you were around in 1991 and happened to watch Dinah's final television special, and wondered why it originated from the stage of the Grand Ole Opry in Nashville, and was named *Dinah Comes Home*, well, now you know.

Dinah had truly come home.

"The secrets of success are a good wife and a steady job.
My wife told me that."
Howard Nemerov (**Feb 29, 1920** – July 5, 1991)
Novelist, playwright

MARCH 1

A 20th Century minute man

Edwin H. Land

May 7, 1909 (Bridgeport, CT) – **Mar 1, 1991** (Cambridge, MA)

E DWIN WAS THE son of Harry and Matha Land, owners of a scrap metal yard, a slightly upscale term for junkyard. Nevertheless, Harry was a good businessman and he knew how to turn scrap metal into money, enough that he was able to send Edwin to a semi-private high school, Norwich (Connecticut) Free Academy, from which he graduated in 1927.

After high school Edwin enrolled at Harvard to study chemistry, became interested in polarized light (technically: light transmitted through a media so that all vibrations are restricted to a single plane), and then at the end of his freshman year, he dropped out of college.

After several years of using the New York Public Library as his personal base of operations, and clandestinely entering a Columbia University laboratory at night to use equipment he had no other way of accessing, he discovered a process by which he could align millions of polarizing crystals onto the surface of film.

However, he needed help, so what did he do? He re-enrolled at Harvard.

There, and interacting with some of the world's finest minds, he was able to focus on exactly what it was he needed to do. He was never very good about writing things down, but it was soon apparent to his professors that he had an abundance of intellect.

Some professors (reportedly) even worked with Land's wife to get her to extract what she could from her husband as it pertained to his study assignments. She'd write it down as best she could remember and give it to the professors to prevent her husband from failing. Land didn't care whether he failed a course or not, as long as he came away with the knowledge he was interesting in learning. He was a strange student indeed, but carried the mark of pure genius.

Then, as soon as he had the answers to his questions, what did he do next?

He dropped out of Harvard for a second time.

Edwin Land would never receive a degree from any college, but he would eventually garner enough honorary degrees to wallpaper a room, or perhaps his entire house, had he cared to do so.

At about the time he dropped out of college the second time, he and one of Harvard's professors, a physicist named George Wheelwright, founded Land-Wheelwright Laboratories.

Using Land's newly discovered technology and Wheelwright's ability to secure funding, the company began to produce a wide range of Polaroid products, such as sunglasses, photographic filters, night-vision goggles, and a viewing system known as Vectography that was capable of revealing enemy camouflage during aerial photography.

In 1937, Land-Wheelwright Labs became the "Polaroid Corporation," and the number of products for which the technology was key, grew exponentially.

The story goes that in 1943, during a trip to Santa Fe, Land's three-year-old daughter asked why she had to wait to see the pictures they were taking. Land considered the question and in his mind began formulating a process that would take care of his daughter's concern. In four years (1947), he had created an instant camera that he named the "Land Camera," later changing the name to the "Polaroid Land Camera."

The initial production run for the camera was 60 units, of which 57 went to the Jordan Marsh Department Store in Boston in time for the 1948 Christmas holidays.

Land underestimated the public's interest and every camera and every box of film sold the first day, and although the cost of the camera and its special film kept it out of the hands of the average consumer, the idea of instant photography took the country by storm.

So, what was it like to be around one of those first *Polaroid Land Cameras* in the 1950s?

Imagine yourself a Connecticut Yankee (as Edwin Land was) and waking up to find yourself in King Arthur's court around 500 AD. Imagine the look on King Arthur's face, or better yet, on Merlin's face as you hold up a small stick, scratch it across a rock and have it magically burst into flame! To Merlin, scratching a stick across a rock and producing fire shouldn't be possible, but it was, and it was pure magic. For those of you who were fortunate enough to be somewhere near a 1950s demonstration of Edwin Land's camera, the click of the shutter and the withdrawal of a blank piece of paper that turned into a picture, in daylight, shouldn't have been possible either, but it was. Pure magic!

You had to see it to believe it.

Of course, the finished picture took sixty-seconds to "develop," before the "developing paper" was pulled away to reveal a black and white photograph. The sixty-second wait only heightened your anticipation for seeing the finished product. The downside to being the first among your friends to own a "Land" camera was not only the cost of film, but also the fact that everyone expected you to take an instant photo of them, so they could show it to others.

And, oh yes, there was the final step, and that was for the photographer to coat the picture with a smelly chemical-laden sponge to stabilize the image.

If you come away with the idea that Edwin Land was a one-idea guy, forget it. He is best known for the Polaroid Instant Camera, that's true, but at the time of his death, he held an astonishing 535 patents!

When Edwin Land died on March 1, 1991, in accordance with his personal wishes, all of his personal papers and notes were shredded.

"I wonder why it is, that young men are always cautioned
against bad girls.
Anyone can handle a bad girl. It's the good girls men should
be warned against."
David Niven (**Mar 1, 1910** – July 29, 1983) Actor

MARCH 2
Linguist, ballplayer, secret agent

Moe Berg
Mar 2, 1902 (New York, NY) – May 29, 1972 (Belleville, NJ)

ACCORDING TO MANAGER Casey Stengel, Morris "Moe" Berg was the strangest man ever to play baseball, and Casey was around baseball long enough to know strange when he saw it.

Berg graduated magna cum laude from Princeton University in 1923 with a major in modern languages. He was fluent in Greek, French, Spanish, Italian, German, Latin, Japanese, and he could read Sanskrit. During his collegiate years, he played shortstop for Princeton and was the team captain during his senior year. Baseball wise, he had an accurate throwing arm, good baseball instincts, and average hitting, the weakest part of his game.

At Princeton, he and another linguist communicated on the playing field in Latin. A teammate once said of Berg, "He can speak seven languages, but he can't hit in any of them." Yet, his skill as a catcher and his baseball instincts were good enough to satisfy the scouts, and after graduation in 1923, he signed with the pre-Dodger era Brooklyn Robins.

During his first season in the majors, he batted a puny .186. So what did he do in the off-season to improve his batting average? Spend hours in a batting cage? No, he went to Europe, enrolled at the Sorbonne in Paris, took a few philosophy classes and toured Switzerland and Italy before sailing back to Brooklyn.

In 1926, the White Sox bought Moe's contract but he failed to show at spring training.

Why?

He had enrolled in Columbia University's law program and insisted on finishing the semester. White Sox management grudgingly agreed and when he finally showed up, they indignantly parked his butt on the bench. When all three White Sox catchers fell to injuries, the manager, with zero options, called on Berg to catch for the final

41 games of the season. Berg was happy, the infield liked his cannon arm, and management put up with his miserly .221 batting average.

In 1928, Berg spent the summer at a lumber camp in the Adirondack Mountains and the clear air and hard work did wonders for him. He reported to spring training on time and in the best physical shape of his life. By season's end, he had won the starting catcher's position and the following year he batted a very respectable .287 in 107 games, and received two votes as the American League's Most Valuable Player.

In 1929, a year before finishing his law studies, Berg took the New York bar exam and passed. However, back at school he flunked a course on handling evidence and failed to graduate. Although licensed to practice law, he returned to Columbia, retook the course, and graduated. Berg, having satisfied all of the requirements to become a lawyer never opened a law office. It was as if he became a lawyer just to prove he could do it.

In 1931, the White Sox placed him on waivers and the Cleveland Indians picked him up.

In 1932, Moe with two other big leaguers, Lefty O'Doul (Dodgers) and Ted Lyons (White Sox) spent the off-season in Japan giving baseball seminars. When done, O'Doul and Lyons returned home, but Moe, true-to-form, stayed behind and toured Japan, Manchuria, Shanghai, Peking, Indochina, Siam, India, Egypt, and visited Berlin.

In 1933, Cleveland traded him to the Senators who released him in 1934, and he once again became the property of Cleveland who refused to renew his contract at season's end.

By 1934, things were beginning to sour in Europe, but America was still above the fray so Major League Baseball organized a good-will baseball tour to Tokyo. Moe, playing for Cleveland and nearing the end of a ho-hum career was, for some strange reason, added to an All-Star roster that featured the likes of Babe Ruth, Lou Gehrig, Jimmie Foxx, Lefty Gomez, and others.

Now, and the reason you've read this far, the stuff of legends.

When the team arrived in Tokyo, a welcoming committee of Japanese dignitaries welcomed the ball players, to which Berg responded on behalf of the team in flawless Japanese. Berg also gave a goodwill speech before the Japanese legislature.

A week later, on November 29, 1934, after the team without Berg, was on its way to play an exhibition game, Berg, dressed in a long black kimono, traveled to Tsukiji, a Tokyo suburb. There, he walked into Tokyo's tallest building, St. Luke's Hospital, and in perfect Japanese asked for the room of U. S. Ambassador Joseph Grew's daughter, who had just given birth.

After bowing deeply and thanking the Japanese clerk, he took the elevator, bypassed the floor where Ambassador Grew's daughter and baby were resting, and went straight to the hospital's roof. There, using a 16mm Bell & Howell movie camera he had hidden under his kimono, he photographed the entire Tokyo skyline, with particular interest in the industrial areas where munition factories might be located.

Upon his return to the United States, the White Sox released him and thus ended his baseball career.

When World War II came to America, Berg's film of the Tokyo skyline was among the footage used by Jimmy Doolittle and his pilots in preparation for their famous Tokyo raid in April 1942.

On January 5, 1942, Nelson Rockefeller, then head of the Office of Inter-American Affairs, hired Moe in some capacity. About six months later (August 2, 1943), Moe went to work for the Office of Strategic Services, the predecessor of the Central Intelligence Agency, his extensive linguistic skills making him a valued operative in numerous countries.

On October 10, 1945, six months after he tendered his resignation to the Office of Strategic Services, he received the Medal of Freedom, which he rejected. His sister, on his behalf, accepted the award after his death on May 29, 1972.

Moe Berg was either a baseball player who was a spy, or a spy who could play baseball, but either way he was as manager Casey Stengel once noted, "The strangest man ever to play baseball."

"If you could choose one characteristic that would get you through life, choose a sense of humor."
Jennifer Jones (**Mar 2, 1919** – Dec 17, 2009) Actress

Charles Ponzi

Mar 3, 1882 (Lugo, Italy) – Jan 18, 1949 (Rio de Janeiro, Brazil)

CHARLES PONZI, BORN March 3, 1882, was a con artist as slimy and free of conscience as they come. Today, his surname is synonymous with crimes in which honest investors are fleeced of their life savings, inheritances, and homes by financial sleight-of-hand. That's what a "Ponzi scheme" is, financial sleight-of-hand.

Ponzi arrived in America as an Italian immigrant in 1903 with exactly $2.51 in his pocket. Hungry, he needed to find work in a hurry, and he did, washing dishes in a restaurant. He worked his way up to waiter and did well until he was caught short-changing customers and lifting patron's wallets from jackets placed on the backs of chairs.

In 1907, he went to Canada and worked for a bank that catered to Italian clientele, his native language serving him well. When the bank failed, he stopped to see one of his former customers, the director of a company named, Canadian Warehousing. Finding the director's office empty but a checkbook in view, he wrote a $400 check to himself forging the director's name and walked out.

When he tried to cash the check, the police, tipped off about the theft of the check, confronted him. He calmly stuck out his hands for cuffing, and said, "I'm guilty." He spent three years in a Canadian prison. He wrote to his mother, assuring her he was doing just fine, saying he had found employment as an assistant to a prison warden.

After release from prison, he was caught smuggling Italian immigrants into the United States and spent two years in federal prison in Atlanta.

After Atlanta (1917), he returned to Boston, married and tried to go straight by working for his father-in-law. He later went to work as a clerk for a company that needed someone who could respond to foreign mail. Here he discovered a new way to make money, a lot of money, by gaming the international postal system.

Shortly after starting his new job, he opened a letter that contained an "International Reply Coupon" (IRC) inside. It was a coupon purchased in the sender's country for use by the respondent to purchase U. S. postage, useful for sending a reply back to the original sender. The cost of an IRC depended on the cost of postage in the country of purchase, but redeemable at the rate of postage in whatever country it was received.

To test a theory that there was money to be made by buying IRCs in Europe and cashing them in America, he sent money to his relatives in Italy, told them to purchase IRCs and send them back to him. They did, and although he didn't redeem all of them for cash, he realized a substantial profit and a new idea.

With his new idea, Ponzi was on his way to fortune, fame, failure, and infamy, and in that order, but not with IRCs, with stocks.

On December 26, 1919, he hired a staff and established the Security Exchange Company, claiming a return on investment of 50% interest in 90 days. After an initial success of paying 50% interest on 90-day investments, he had more customers than he could handle, with investments ranging from $10 to $50,000, the average being $325 per transaction.

In less than a year, Ponzi and his staff were bringing in a million dollars a week. There was no investment of course, only what buyers thought was an "investment." Checks were cashed and the cash stashed everywhere, in filing cabinets, closets, and with so much money and so little space, they even began depositing it in banks.

In 1920, Ponzi paid $3 million for a controlling interest in the Hanover Trust Bank of Boston, and because most of his investors preferred to "reinvest" rather than withdraw, hoping for an even greater return, his cash reserves continued to pile up. He hired more and more agents to work for him, his scope of business now covered most of New England and New Jersey.

People were mortgaging their homes and investing their entire retirement savings with Ponzi's company, but underneath all of the excitement, there were signs of crumbling within his organization and rumblings within Boston's financial community.

A financial writer for the *Boston Post* said it was impossible for anyone, including Ponzi, to deliver such high returns in so short a time, and some investors cashed out, Ponzi paid off, and the sailing was smooth again. Then, a lowly furniture dealer filed a lawsuit when Ponzi kept delaying payment of his bill. Ponzi paid the bill, but finally, something didn't smell right.

The *Post* stayed the course, hiring Clarence Barron, of *Barron's Financial*, to look into Ponzi's operation and on August 11, 1920, it all came crashing down. Ponzi who had claimed liquidity of $7 million was actually $7 million in debt. Then came the stories about Ponzi's years spent in Canadian and American prisons and there was a run on the Security Exchange Company that nearly brought the building down, literally.

Ponzi's fall from grace was lightning quick and with it, the failure of five other banks in addition to Hanover Trust. His investors, many of whom had invested everything they had, received on average of 25-cents on the dollar.

After doing some prison time, Ponzi spent his final years in poverty, dying in a Rio de Janeiro hospital charity ward on January 18, 1949.

About the heartbreak and poor financial condition of those who had trusted and invested their life savings and homes with him, he showed no remorse during his final interview, saying, "I had given them the best show that was ever staged in their territory since the landing of the Pilgrims! It was easily worth fifteen million bucks to watch me put the thing over."

This story could end with information about Ponzi's death and where he was laid to rest, but few care and it's not worth the ink.

Now you know the origin of the term, *Ponzi Scheme.*

"It does not require many words to speak the truth."
Chief Joseph (**Mar 3, 1840** – Sept 21, 1904)
Leader of Nez Perce

Jack Sheppard

Mar 4, 1702 (Spitalfields, England) – Nov 16, 1724 (Tyburn, England)

D ASTARDLY JACK SHEPPARD was born March 4, 1702. His father died shortly after his birth, leaving his mother to care for him and his siblings. When he turned six, the workhouse for orphans was for him. There, he worked wickedly long hours for a child, stripping cane for making furniture. At ten, he was a helper to a fabric-maker, and later did the same for a carpenter, where he remained for ten years until he started looking for an easier way to turn a schilling.

And he found it, in a yearlong crime spree, and he had help.

Elizabeth Lyon, London's most notorious 1700s prostitute, saw to it that Jack discovered the good life in the seedy taverns along Drury Lane. One in particular, the *Black Lion,* was also a favorite haunt of Jonathan Wild, London's "Thief Taker General," a man who secretly ruled a criminal empire while posing as a public-spirited crime fighter.

That Jack was boyishly handsome is undeniable, confirmable by checking out his likeness on the internet. Deceptively strong and slightly built at only five foot four, Jack was even more adept at escaping from jails than he was at committing crimes. In fact, his ability to escape from "escape proof" cells would eventually elevate him from common thief status into a popular counter-culture icon. Well into the twentieth century, writers continued to spin tales of his escapades, most with little concern for accuracy.

Officially, Jack's first crime occurred in the spring of 1723 while working as a carpenter's apprentice. That's when he stole two silver spoons from Rummer's Tavern near Trafalgar Square. They would show up again during his final day in court.

Needing cover to support their way of life, Jack and Elizabeth lived together as a married couple. Jack's earnings came from shoplifting and picking pockets; and Elizabeth's from doing what she did best, afterward picking the pockets of her clients as they slept. All went well with their career choices until Elizabeth picked the wrong pocket and found herself looking out through the bars at St. Giles Roundhouse.

Jack, refused visitation by the St. Giles guard, tipped his cap in respect and walked away whistling. Then, in the dead of night, he returned, broke into St. Giles' (that's right, Jack broke into the prison), found a way to free Elizabeth, and the two escaped.

Remember Jonathan Wild, the so-called Thief Taker General and master criminal that Jack befriended at the Black Lyon? About midway into his one-year crime spree, Jack began breaking into homes and picking pockets in the part of London that "crime fighter" Jonathan Wild had reserved for himself, an act that would be Jack's downfall.

Jack was a busy little thief, taking nothing too big, committing no major crimes, but keeping his equally industrious sweetheart well-kept and fashionably clothed. The sheer number of Jack's petty crimes infuriated the Bobbies. Eventually caught, searched, and bound in chains, Jack's cell was special; twenty-five feet above the ground at the escape proof New Bridewell Prison.

During a routine inspection the day after his incarceration, all that remained in Jack's cell were his irons. By some means, he had cut his way through the bars of his cell and then climbed onto the prison roof. From there, he descended or scaled walls, one after the other as needed, until he could finally drop to the ground and freedom.

London police, embarrassed and determined, made Jack the prime suspect for every highway robbery, every picked pocket, every theft, and every burglary, but he remained elusive. That was until his old friend Jonathan Wild decided that Jack's lack of respect for the "criminal way" was out of hand.

The short of the story is that Wild betrayed Jack on July 23, 1724, and this time in addition to making sure he had nothing on his person that could aid an escape, Jack was securely locked in his cell with around the clock guards.

On August 12, Jack went on trial, was found guilty and sentenced to die on September 1. His new residence was the famed Old Bailey courthouse, an 18th century version of death row.

On the day before his scheduled execution, Elizabeth and another trollop, Polly Maggott, arrived to say their goodbyes to Jack. After Elizabeth entered Jack's cell, Polly (use your imagination here) distracted the guard. Inside, Elizabeth and Jack created a large opening in the cell's ventilation grille and Jack was gone.

Elizabeth exited the cell weeping uncontrollably; slamming the cell door behind her to prevent the guard from discovering too quickly, Jack disappearance. Polly, with a sudden loss of interest in the love-struck guard, shifted her attention to consoling an inconsolable Elizabeth as they bawled, sniffed, and walked out of Old Bailey together.

The authorities were furious when Jack wasn't available for his date with the executioner. Stories circulated about his ability to escape London's prisons, and tavern minstrels took to singing the praises of Jack Sheppard, London's criminal escape artist.

Freedom was fleeting and in nine days, the long arm of the law reeled him in again. He was placed in solitary confinement in the break-out proof "Stone Castle" at Newgate Prison, where he was chained and padlocked, inside a chained and padlocked cell, and although nothing is mentioned, it's unlikely he was allowed visitors either.

No one was sure when he escaped, but it soon became obvious how he escaped. After shedding his chains, he exited through the cell roof, scaled a chimney, and worked his way onto the roof. Too high up to escape, he returned to his cell, wove a rope from his bedsheets, returned to the roof and lowered himself to where he could safely descend a prison wall.

Two or three days later, badly hung over, he awakened inside another prison cell.

There would be no more escapes.

The Reverend Wagstaffe asked Jack if he would like a Bible. Jack reportedly told the Reverend, "One file is worth all the Bibles in the World."

Jack died at Tyburn gallows on November 16, 1724, before an estimated crowd of 200,000 onlookers, approximately one-third of London's population. When he reached the end of his rope (now you know the origin of that phrase), the weight of the slightly built thief was insufficient to break his neck, resulting in a long and painfully slow strangulation.

Many of those attending the hanging reportedly bought a copy of his autobiography, ghostwritten, it's believed, by Daniel Defoe, the author of *Robinson Crusoe*.

It wasn't Jack's crimes, but his escapes and the embarrassment he caused the Queen's judicial system that was his downfall. His crimes of record for which he received the death penalty, were the theft of a silk handkerchief, some fabric, and the two silver spoons he had stolen from Rummer's Tavern.

"We learn more from our epic failures than we do from our blazing triumphs."
Chip Calamaio (**Mar 4, 1951** -) Videographer, educator

MARCH 5
It's about time

Ruth Belville
Mar 5, 1854 (Unknown) – Dec 7, 1943 (London, England)

DURING THE MIDDLE Ages (500-1500), someone had to specialize in body armor alterations to accommodate the knight whose appetite for ale and lard-laden pastries required the services of a metalworking tailor.

During the Victorian era (1837-1901), someone had to know how to repair high-button shoes. Another had to know how to block stovepipe hats, and someone had to know how to work with the multiple weaving shuttles that warped and woofed their way through giant industrial looms to create tapestries and sewing fabric.

During the 1850s through the early 1900s, traveling salesmen sold everything from anvils to zippers, from straw hats for dandies to chin-to-shin swimming attire for ladies. In the midst of it all, one lady sold something that no one else sold, time.

Ruth Naomi Belville was a lady from London who not only sold the time of day to those who paid for her services; but also later in life, she could have passed for a feminine version of Father Time.

Ruth's father John Henry Belville established the family's timely business in the early 1800s as a way to supplement the income from his job at the Greenwich Observatory in London.

After work each day, John Belville would match his timepiece to the Greenwich clock and travel by buggy to each of his clients' shops, homes, and offices, setting their clocks to the precise time. Upon his death in 1856 and without missing a tick or a tock, John's wife, Maria Elizabeth continued the routine, showing up at the Observatory each day at precisely 9:00 am, matching the family timepiece to the Greenwich clock, and making the rounds to the subscribers of the service.

In 1892, daughter Ruth took over the job from her mother who was now well into her eighties, and she continued in her mother and father's footsteps with no change in the procedure.

Known locally as the *Greenwich Time Lady*, she went each day to the Observatory, set the family timepiece and traveled to each of her clients, adjusting each clock to Greenwich perfection, and she did that faithfully for forty-two years.

During her years as the Greenwich Time Lady, all went well except for one time when the Standard Time Company, a firm that provided a similar, but electronically run service, entered the picture. John Wynne, one of Standard Time Company's directors, gave a speech in London in which he poked fun at Ruth's manual approach to maintaining the accuracy of her customer's clocks. He belittled her as "amusingly out of date," and even implied she might be using her "femininity to gain business."

The London newspapers wrote about the speech and Ruth was suddenly the center of interest with reporters asking about her business and inquiring about an alleged scandal, to which the Mother Time look-alike smiled all the way to the bank, with a fistful of new customers.

In 1940, the Greenwich Time Lady was running out of time herself, and on December 7, 1943, her mainspring finally ran down for good. She was 89 years old.

"I'm at the age where I've got to prove that
I'm just as good as I never was."
Rex Harrison (**Mar 5, 1908** – June 2, 1990) Actor

MARCH 6
A one-armed success story

Pete Gray
(Peter James Wyshner)
Mar 6, 1915 (Nanticoke, PA) – June 30, 2002 (Nanticoke, PA)

A RE YOU READY for a tale of pluck and perseverance involving a six-year-old who lost his arm in a childhood accident but went on to fulfill a dream of playing in the big leagues?

This is such a story.

In 1921, six-year-old Pete was doing what all energetic little boys do best, run, play, and jump. Unfortunately, one of those jumps was from the bed (or hood) of a pre-1920s truck, one with large, old-fashioned spoked wheels. Either Pete slipped or simply failed to put enough distance between himself and the truck's wheels, but before he hit the ground, his right arm had wedged tightly between the spokes of a wheel bringing his body to a painful midair stop. The accident had jerked, twisted and mangled his arm so badly that the town's doctors had no option but to amputate, which they did, taking Pete's right arm off just above the elbow.

That left a right handed six-year-old boy, who dreamed of playing big league baseball, with a sudden need to become left-handed, just to handle the day-to-day needs of living.

Think of the hopeless feeling of being six and not having an arm and hand where both had existed a few days before, and now needing to do everything from tying shoes to buttoning a shirt with one poorly coordinated hand that seemed oddly detached from his brain.

Pete mastered those tasks and a whole lot more.

It was never easy!

Growing up in a hardscrabble Pennsylvania coal-mining town didn't help and during those early years, "one-armed Pete," had to overcome the cruel and relentless teasing of the other children.

Pete never ceased to think about playing baseball and he never ceased to work on the skills he needed to play the game.

He mastered the ability to catch a fly ball in a thin, lightly padded glove. Then, in a single fluid motion that must be seen to be believed, allow the ball to drop onto his chest for an instant as he whisked his glove under the stump of his right arm, scoop the ball from his chest, and throw in a single motion, fast and accurately, in the blink of an eye.

He fielded grounders with a similar motion, catching and then flipping the ball in the air as he threw off his loosely fitting glove, catching the ball in his freshly un-gloved hand and throwing to the infield. Woe to the base runner who assumed he could beat one-armed Pete's unorthodox throw. Pete only needed to embarrass a couple of base runners before gaining the respect of the entire opposing team.

His ability with a bat was equally amazing with the lone exception of curve balls. With one arm, he sprayed line drives all over the field. To bunt, he planted the knob of the bat against his side, sliding his hand about a third the way up the shaft to control the swing. However, those darn curve balls! With only one arm, he had no way to adequately adjust or check his swing during mid-pitch, a skill needed to compensate for the movement of the pitch.

In 1938, the *Three Rivers* (a Pittsburgh minor league team) signed Pete sight unseen and they couldn't believe their eyes when he showed up at spring training with only one arm. He surprised everyone, however, batting .381 in his first season in 42 games.

In 1943, playing for the *Memphis Chicks,* he hit .289.

In 1944 he was named Most Valuable Player of the Southern Association, hitting .333, scoring 119 runs in 129 games (almost a run per game), and leading the league with 68 steals.

Yes! He was that fast!

The next season he signed with the American League Champion *St. Louis Browns.* He had realized his dream. The one armed kid from a tough coal-mining town in Pennsylvania had become a major leaguer. Unfortunately, once opposing big league pitchers learned about his single batting weakness, his inability to react to the ever-changing nuances of curve balls, he got a steady diet of wickedly thrown curves and his baseball playing days were numbered.

It was now 1945.

World War II was over, as was Pete's baseball career.

The war might be over, but one-armed Pete knew there was still work to do before America's soldiers, the wounded ones, could go back to a normal life.

To the troops returning from the battlefields, many with amputated limbs and dashed dreams, Pete Gray was a living inspiration. Movie theater newsreels featured his comeback from the childhood loss of his arm to go on and play in the big leagues. He spent hours visiting the wounded in veteran's hospitals and rehabilitation centers, a living example of what man can do in spite of the worst of odds.

In 1986, Hollywood produced a made-for-Television movie of his life, titled, *A Winner Never Quits,* starring Keith Carradine and Mare Winningham. That same year, author William C. Kashatus published a biography of Gray, titled, *One-Armed Wonder: Pete Gray, Wartime Baseball and the American Dream.*

Pete Gray died June 30, 2002 in his hometown of Nanticoke, Pennsylvania.

His glove is enshrined in the National Baseball Hall of Fame and Museum in Cooperstown, New York.

On **March 6, 1857**, the Supreme Court ruled against former
slave Dred Scott,
saying he did not have standing to request
his own freedom.

WAYNE WINTERTON, PH.D.

Nicéphore Niépce
(Joseph Niépce)
Mar 7, 1765 (France) – July 5, 1833 (France)

JOSEPH NIÉPCE WAS the second of four children born into a wealthy French family. Named Joseph at birth, he took the unusual step of renaming himself, and thus sometime in his teens or early twenties, he became Nicéphore Niépce in honor of Saint Nicéphorus, the Patriarch Saint of Constantinople.

Unless you really know your inventors, Nicéphore Niépce just might be the best inventor that you've never heard about.

In 1807, with assistance from his brother Claude, Niépce invented the world's first internal combustion engine, the "Pyréolophore," the Greek word for "wind bearer." After the Pyréolophore successfully powered a six-foot boat up the River Saône to the astonishment of onlookers, including Napoleon Bonaparte, the emperor granted Niépce a ten year patent dated July 20, 1807, for the ground-breaking engine.

Niépce's French patent came fifty-three years before Belgian engineer Jean Joseph Étienne Lenoir patented a single-cylinder, 2-stroke engine in 1860 that ran on coal gas ignited by a spark; and fifty-five years before Nikolaus Otto, considered by most as the *Father of the Internal Combustion Engine*, received a German patent for his spark-ignited engine.

So why doesn't Niépce get the respect given to Jean Joseph Lenoir and Nikolaus Otto? Perhaps it's because of what he used as fuel. Whereas Lenoir and Otto's engines burned variants of coal gas, principally methane, Niépce's internal combustion engine burned a dry mixture of Lycopodium (the dusty yellowish powder of moss and fern spores), a few cups of finely crushed coal dust, and a pinch of resin.

To power his boat upstream and to earn Napoleon's praise, the Pyréolophore delivered its dry powdery fuel every six seconds into two connected ignition/combustion chambers where an ignition device (think ultra-primitive sparkplug here) would create a mini-explosion timed to match the six-second fuel delivery. The gaseous exhaust from the burn was expelled from the engine into an under the boat tailpipe positioned to push the boat continuously forward.

To Niépce's supporters, the creativity and intelligence required to design the Pyréolophore, at a minimum, matches or exceeds the creativity and intelligence of design of petroleum-powered engines.

To show that Niépce was not a one-dimensional guy, in addition to being the first to invent the internal combustion engine, he was also the first to capture a photographic image, doing so with what he called the "camera obscura," Latin for "dark chamber."

Sometime around 1816, Niépce began to look at ways to capture the images he was able to project onto the back of his camera obscura. As you might expect, he met with failure after failure, until in 1818 he got his first taste of success by capturing an image that remained stable for three months.

Later, in 1822, by coating a glass plate with Bitumen of Judah, an asphalt-like substance with light-sensitive properties, he captured a picture of a drawing of Pope Pius VII, the image remaining on the glass for a full year.

From 1822 until about 1827, the determined Niépce continued to experiment with a variety of materials, making mechanical adjustments to his camera obscura along the way.

Whether he achieved a permanent image prior to 1827, we can't be sure, although correspondence with his brother Claude seems to say that he successfully created a permanent photograph in 1824.

What we do know is that Niépce captured, onto a tin plate in 1827, an image that is still viewable today. That image, titled *Du vue de la Fenetre* (View from the Window), is currently at the Harry Ransom Humanities Research Center at the University of Texas. You can view the image on the internet by searching for Niepce or by using the image name.

Nicéphore Niépce, the best inventor you have never heard of, died July 5, 1833, at the age of sixty-eight.

"A divorcée is a woman, who got married so
she didn't have to work,
but now works so she doesn't have to get married."
Anna Magnani (**Mar 7, 1908** – Sept 26, 1973) Actress

MARCH 8
The accidental president

Millard Fillmore
Jan 7, 1800 (Moravia, NY) - **Mar 8, 1874** (Buffalo, NY)

MILLARD FILLMORE BECAME the "accidental president," when Zachary Taylor died unexpectedly in 1850, setting in motion the most abrupt political shift in American history. Without exception, every member of Taylor's cabinet tendered their resignation and Fillmore quickly accepted each. Every member of his new cabinet (except Treasury Secretary Thomas Corwin) favored the "Compromise of 1850," a bill famous for kicking the Civil War can four years down the road.

Fillmore attempted to appease the South by supporting the "Fugitive Slave Act" that required all runaway slaves, upon capture, be returned to their masters. As might be expected, his attempt to appease the South met with fierce opposition from Northerners when he tried to enforce the Act in their states.

Then he angered the South when he refused to back an invasion of Cuba to expand the South by acquiring the slave-based Caribbean island as a new U. S. territory. The anti-slavery North wouldn't hear of it and brought the idea to an immediate halt. The result was that both North and South were unhappy with Fillmore, and the stress began to pull his own party, the Whigs, apart at the seams.

Fillmore may have believed he was safeguarding the Union, but in reality, he had given everyone in the Union something to dislike about his presidency.

At some point in his presidency, he said, "It is not strange . . . to mistake change for progress," perhaps the only profound statement he made during his term in office.

Fillmore served only the balance of Taylor's term, failed to gain the Whig nomination in 1852, and became the last member of the Whig Party to be president.

As if his time in office hadn't been curious enough, following his stint in the White House, he became a member of the "American Party," better known as the "Know-Nothings." The Know-Nothings were a regressive political party, its nickname coming from the party's preferred answer to political questions with a simple, "I know nothing."

The Know Nothings favored temperance, were anti-immigration and recommended a twenty-one year residency requirement prior to citizenship. They also wanted to "purify" American politics by limiting or ending the influence of Catholics, especially Irish Catholics from holding public office. Fillmore served as the party's presidential nominee in 1856. He carried one state, Maryland, and won 22% of the vote, losing to Democrat James Buchanan (45%) and Republican, John C. Fremont (33%).

Although his childhood and education was similar to that of Lincoln, both were born in log cabins and both were self-taught lawyers, the two men had starkly different views of the presidency. When Lincoln became president in 1861, Fillmore, a strident opponent of the Civil War, was a constant thorn in Lincoln's side.

Today, although Fillmore consistently ranks at or near the bottom of the presidential ladder, he did have a few moments in the sun, one of them coming in the Utah Territory.

In 1851, after President Fillmore signed legislation to create the Utah Territory, Territorial Governor Brigham Young honored the president by laying out a spanking new town and naming it, what else, but Fillmore, and the town would be the county seat for a brand new Utah county, Millard County.

Then to cap off the festivities, Young had yet another surprise. He announced to President Fillmore that the town of Fillmore, since it was near the geographical center of the Territory, would become the Territorial capital. A state house was built and for four years the affairs of government were managed from the tiny farming community of Fillmore, a settlement about 150 miles due South of Salt Lake. Keep in mind that in the 1850s, a hundred and fifty miles meant a very long, dusty day's travel over rutted and bumpy dirt roads by horse and buggy.

After four years of putting up with the inconvenient commute, Utah's legislators decided it was time to revisit Young's decision. In 1855, a legislative Act established Salt Lake City as the Territorial capital, and forty-one years later, January 4, 1896, Utah received statehood, keeping Salt Lake City as the capital of the new state.

By the way, the original Utah statehouse in Fillmore is still standing, and is a museum these days worthy of a visit.

On **March 8, 1910**, French aviatrix Raymonde de Laroche became the first woman in the world issued a pilot's license.

MARCH 9
Legendary Vaudevillian

Eddie Foy, Sr.
(Edwin Fitzgerald)
Mar 9, 1856 (Manhattan, NY) – Feb 16, 1928 (Kansas City, MO)

EDWIN (EDDIE) FITZGERALD, the second of four children, was born to Irish immigrants Richard and Mary Fitzgerald in 1856. Six years later, Eddie's father died in a New York insane asylum after losing his mind to syphilis-induced dementia.

The family moved from New York to Illinois where Mary Fitzgerald found work at the Bellevue insane asylum in Batavia. There, in 1875, she, with others, took care for the facility's most famous patient, President Lincoln's widow, Mary Todd Lincoln. The experience was short-lived however, as Mrs. Lincoln made good her escape three months after being committed, and spent the remainder of her life with her sister, Elizabeth, in Springfield.

Supporting a family of five proved a difficult task for the widowed Fitzgerald and by the age of eight Eddie was helping to support the family by dancing for tips on Chicago's streets.

In 1871, and fifteen-years-old, Eddie changed his surname from Fitzgerald to Foy and, with a partner, picked up a few bucks by singing and dancing in bars and when the opportunity arose, as an extra in stage productions. Working on the stage also gave him a chance to watch and borrow techniques from such notable performers as comedian Joe Jefferson and Shakespearean actor Edwin Booth, whose brother, John Wilkes Booth, had assassinated President Lincoln a few years earlier.

In the 1870s Eddie headed west with partner Jim Thompson where they put on shows at mining camps and frontier towns, including Dodge City, Kansas. In Dodge City, Foy and Thompson had enough success to allow them to hang around for a while. There, Eddie became friends with the likes of Wyatt Earp, Bat Masterson, and a gun-fighter dentist named John Holliday, known around town as "Doc."

Once, in Dodge City, Foy and another entertainer got into a fight over a girl. When the altercation escalated and a few rounds fired in Foy's direction, Sheriff Earp disarmed the situation by taking the six-shooter away from the irate actor and locking it up. Then telling Foy and his antagonist to go to their rooms and sleep it off, which they did.

A decade later, on October 26, 1881, Foy and another of his partners, songwriter Arthur J. Lamb, just happened to be in Tombstone, Arizona when an altercation called the Gunfight at the O.K. Corral took place.

The place in Tombstone where Foy and Lamb were entertaining was the *Elite Theater Opera House*. Inside, there were a dozen draped box seats extending outward from the balcony, giving them the appearance of "cages." The cages were popular as places where customers and their *dames du jour* could relax, watch the entertainment on the stage, or close the drapes and create their own entertainment.

One day, as songwriters sometimes do whenever a piano is handy, Lamb was tapping the ivories as he, Foy, and a few patrons were discussing the virtues of the ladies of Tombstone. During the discussion, Lamb looked up from the keyboard and made the comment that the girls of Tombstone were like "birds in gilded cages."

As the others continued their conversation, Lamb's creative juices ran free and he wrote the words and music to one of America's best-known sad songs, *A Bird in a Gilded Cage*.

She's only a bird in a gilded cage, a beautiful sight to see,
You may think she's happy and free from
care – She's not, tho' she seems to be,
'Tis sad when you think of her wasted life,
for youth cannot mate with age,
And her beauty was sold, for an old man's
gold – She's a bird in a gilded cage.

Although it's only speculation, Foy and Lamb may have performed the song during their engagement at the *Elite*. A year later (1882), owners Billy and Lottie Hutchinson sold the *Elite* to Joe and Minnie

WAYNE WINTERTON, PH.D.

Bignon, who kept the name for a few years before renaming it "The Bird Cage Theater."

The theater became one of the wildest venues of the old west, its walls containing no less than 120 bullet holes at one count. Today the Bird Cage is a Tombstone, Arizona tourist attraction and worth the visit. If you're there, and listen closely, you just might hear Arthur Lamb at the piano, the soft-stepping Eddie Foy on stage, and the eerie lyrics of *A Bird in a Gilded Cage* wafting from within the walls.

After successfully touring the west, Foy returned to the Chicago area in 1888 as the star comedian of a number of variety shows.

In 1896, he married Madeline Morando, a dancer in his production company. They became the parents of eleven children, of whom seven survived, and those seven became a part of his most famous act, *Eddie Foy and the Seven Little Foys,* a national sensation.

Eddie performed right up to his death, suffering a heart attack in 1928 while performing in Kansas City, Missouri.

"The first page sells this book.
The last page sells your next book.
Nobody reads a book to get to the middle."
Mickey Spillane (**Mar 9, 1918** – July 17, 2006) Author

John Gunby
Mar 10, 1745 (Somerset, MD) – May 17, 1807 (Snow Hill, MD)

IN 458 BC, the Roman army found itself trapped in a narrow valley by a very hostile Aequian army. Members of the Senate rode to the home of one of their own, Cincinnatus, a retired senator and former military general who was busy plowing his land. The senators told Cincinnatus of the army's plight, asked for his help, and told him if he could rescue the Roman army, the senate would make him king. He agreed, left his plow in the middle of the field, raised an army of volunteers, rescued the Roman soldiers, turned down the kingship, and went right back to being a gentleman farmer, plowing his field.

On May 13, 1783, a group of patriots founded an organization they named the *Society of the Cincinnati*. It was an organization dedicated to the preservation of the ideals as exemplified by Cincinnatus and it is still open for membership, but only to descendants of Revolutionary War officers, making it the oldest "hereditary" society in North America.

The Gunby family from Yorkshire, England, set foot on American soil around 1660 and settled near present-day Crisfield on the southern tip of the Maryland peninsula. During the eighty-five years the family was in America prior to the birth of John Gunby (1745), it had acquired considerable property and was running a fleet of merchant ships along the eastern seaboard.

In 1775, John was thirty, wealthy, influential, and by all measures could have remained aloof of the fight that was brewing between Great Britain and the American colonies. However, John didn't see it that way and volunteered as a civilian willing to take time from his daily routine to receive military training in his hometown. The underlying idea of the group he trained with was an ability to be ready in a minute should the need arise, hence the famous nickname, "Minutemen."

John's father, a British loyalist tried to talk his son out of his involvement, warning if caught by the British he faced almost certain death by hanging. John reportedly told his father, "I am determined to join [the] American forces, come what will. We have little fear, for justice will dominate …. For me, I would rather sink into a patriot's grave than wear the crown of England."

When it was evident, there would be no middle ground between England's desire to rule America as a colony and America's desire to rule itself, the inevitable happened.

War!

Overnight John Gunby went from plowing his fields to plowing much of his personal wealth into the creation of an independent military company. This included personally paying to equip and maintain a fighting force of 103 men, and then serving as the group's leader as Captain of the 2nd Independent Maryland Company.

Initially, Gunby's group raised havoc with British encampments on Maryland's Lower Peninsula, and then on August 16, 1776, General Washington absorbed the group into the Continental Army where they saw numerous battles up front and personal. This included the Battle of Long Island where the Maryland Line, as the 2nd Independent Maryland Company became known, achieved fame. However, the fame didn't come from a major victory; it came from the successful rescue of Washington's army in retreat.

The Battle of Long Island was lost because of tactical errors made by General Horatio Gates, and the loss left much of Washington's Army in an indefensible position. The bravery of Gunby and the Maryland Line made possible Washington's retreat, but it was costly as about a third of Gunby's troops died in the process.

About the battle, one man wrote: "Wherever the Maryland Line met the enemy they made their mark and wrote their names high in the annals of fame," and General Johann de Kalb, who was mortally wounded gave high praise to the Maryland Line before he passed away.

In 1783 after serving seven years in the cause of freedom, Gunby resigned and returned to his Maryland farm, becoming once again a gentleman farmer, plowing his land and helping poor families build homes, giving generously to places of worship, and not surprisingly, becoming one of the Charter Members of the Maryland Chapter of the *Society of the Cincinnati*.

Alexander Graham Bell made the world's
first telephone call,
calling his assistant, Thomas A. Watson
on **March 10, 1848,**
and saying, "Mr. Watson, come here, I want to see you."

MARCH 11
An American genius

Philo T. Farnsworth
Aug 19, 1906 (Beaver, UT) – **Mar 11, 1971** (Salt Lake City, UT)

ALTHOUGH IT DOESN'T seem possible in the twentieth century, it's true. The man who invented television, Philo T. Farnsworth, was born in a log cabin in an isolated place called Indian Creek, the nearest town being Beaver, Utah. At the age of ten, Philo and his family moved to Rigby, Idaho, where they sharecropped on his Uncle Albert's 240-acre farm, and when the opportunity presented itself, Philo's father bolstered the family's income by hauling freight.

With ingenuity beyond his years, after watching his mother struggle with a hand-cranked washing machine, twelve-year-old Philo rigged a discarded electric motor and a few spare parts he found to power-agitate the tub of the family's washing machine.

This was only the first of many mechanical improvements he would make around the farm. While his pre-teen friends were busy seeing how far they could throw a cow pie, Philo rigged power to his mother's treadle sewing machine and installed electric lighting in his uncle's barn.

At thirteen, he entered a contest and won $25 for his invention of a theft-proof ignition switch for automobiles. That same year, while rummaging the contents of a stack of magazines in his uncle's attic, he found an issue of *Popular Science* in which inventor and science fiction writer Hugo Gernsback described an interesting concept. Gernsback suggested a future in which, just as the sounds of radio can now travel through the air, "pictures" could travel through the air, and he even had a name for his futuristic concept, "television."

Philo read the article a dozen times.

At fifteen, while working a potato field with a horse-drawn harrow, he imagined an image "sliced" into a series of rows the same way a harrow slices a potato field into rows, back-and-forth, back-and-forth.

That night his mind was full of "what-ifs."

What if a light and a lens could direct the image of an object into a vacuum tube, and then slice the image, and transmit the slices as a stream of electrons to be reassembled, back-and-forth, line-by-line, later? He got out of bed and drew a diagram of his idea so as not to forget his thoughts, and then he went to sleep.

The next day he showed the diagram to Rigby High School science teacher Justin Tolman, who marveled as he always did, at the newest idea to come from Philo's mind, a mind as fertile as the farmland he plowed. Tolman sensed from the first time he met Philo, that the kid was not your average science student. Consequently, he and Philo spent many hours together, each sharing their thoughts about various scientific concepts. Philo had become such an advanced, out of the box thinker, that Tolman allowed him to sit in on his senior-level science classes.

Moving ahead to 1927, Philo now twenty-one had patented what he called an "image dissector tube" that, using sixty constantly refreshing lines, could electronically transmit an image. The first image he successfully transmitted, perhaps prophetically, was a hand-drawn dollar sign. The second image was that of his wife Pem, making her in a manner of speaking, televisions first star.

However, not everything was rosy!

In 1935, seven years after Philo patented his image dissector tube, David Sarnoff and the Radio Corporation of America (RCA), unhappy with the idea of having to pay royalties to some hick named Farnsworth, challenged the patent. The case was hard-fought in court and RCA had deep financial pockets. However, when Rigby High School science teacher Justin Tolman took the stand and produced Philo's original fifteen-year-old diagram, something happened. The diagram clearly described the concept under debate, and the mood in the courtroom shifted. Those present could sense the argument moving in favor of the man who, as a boy, had seen the future in the furrows of an Idaho potato field.

RCA, in a last ditch attempt to prove their case, argued that a fifteen-year-old diagram, drawn by a fifteen-year-old farm boy didn't constitute "legal proof," but the U. S. Patent Office had seen and heard enough and the case was decided in Farnsworth's favor, recognizing him as the rightful inventor of television.

WAYNE WINTERTON, PH.D.

It was proof that anyone, regardless of whether born in a stately mansion or a log cabin, can still achieve greatness in America.

Thirty-four years later (July 20, 1969) while watching Neil Armstrong's live televised first step on the moon, Farnsworth reportedly leaned back in his recliner and told his family, "This has made it all worthwhile."

Farnsworth is a member of the Television Academy Hall of Fame and a statue of him graces the Letterman Digital Arts Center in San Francisco.

Farnsworth's statue is one of two allowed each state inside the National Statuary Hall Collection inside the Capitol Building in Washington, D. C. Utah's other statue is that of colonizer and religious leader, Brigham Young.

Farnsworth died on March 11, 1971 in Salt Lake City at the age of sixty-four.

On **March 11, 1918**, the first case of the Great Influenza Epidemic of 1918 was reported at Fort Riley, Kansas. The disease would kill 20 million worldwide.

MARCH 12
Perdicaris Alive or Raisuli Dead

Ion Perdicaris
1840 (Unknown) - **Mar 12, 1925** (Kent, England)

SOMETIMES HISTORY IS altered by the most unrelated of events. Such was the so-called "Perdicaris Incident" that may have been the feather that tipped the balance of American politics in favor of Theodore Roosevelt during the election of 1904.

Ion Perdicaris was born to privilege. His father, a former Greek Consul to the U. S. remained in America after marrying into a wealthy South Carolina family. Set for life, Ion was living as only a well-heeled playboy can, spending freely, eating well, and enjoying the ladies. That was, until a blip on his social calendar threatened his world.

Ion's blip, known to the rest of us as the Civil War, meant Ion needed a way of staying clear of the brawl and equally important, of protecting his inheritance. So he traveled to his father's homeland, gave up his American citizenship for Greek citizenship to protect his fortune, secure in his belief that the South wouldn't seize the estate of a foreign national.

Years passed and Ion moved to Tangier, Morocco, and began a two-year affair with Ellen Varley, the wife of transatlantic cable engineer C. F. Varley. In 1873, Ellen divorced her husband, married Ion, and the two of them built a palatial residence in Tangier known locally as the *Palace of Nightingales*.

Life was good.

All went well for the couple until 1903 when Barbary pirate Sharif Mulai Ahmed er-Raisuli took Ion and Ellen hostage and demanded that the Sultan of Morocco pay a ransom of $70,000 for their release. The Sultan of Morocco couldn't have cared less, but . . . .

Back in the United States, a heated presidential campaign was underway between the incumbent Theodore Roosevelt and the challenger Alton B. Parker, and the stakes were high.

When Roosevelt learned that a Moroccan pirate had abducted a prominent American, he was outraged. After all, it was an election year and he needed some outrage to divert America's attention away from election facts. To show his anger and to bolster his no-nonsense presidential image, he ordered seven warships and a contingent of Marines to Morocco.

By the time the warships docked in Morocco, the State Department had become aware that Perdicaris had previously dumped his American citizenship and was now a Greek citizen. Roosevelt, when advised of the fact, reasoned that as long as the pirate and the world cared little about whether the hostages were Americans or otherwise, there was no reason to make an issue of the matter, especially during an election year, and the facts surrounding Perdicaris's national allegiance remained under wraps.

The pirate Raisuli continued to make his demands and the Sultan of Morocco continued to ignore the pirate. That was, until England and France covertly agreed to help the United States twist the Sultan's arm.

Back at the Republican National Convention, Vice-president John Hay, in describing Roosevelt's tireless efforts to free "Americans" Ion and Ellen Perdicaris from the bloody hands of the pirate, brought the delegates to their feet when he ended his speech with, "This government wants Perdicaris alive or Raisuli dead." The catchphrase, "Perdicaris Alive or Raisuli Dead" caught the imagination of the delegates and helped to secure Roosevelt's reelection.

The fact that Ion Perdicaris was not an American citizen remained a secret until historian Tyler Dennett mentioned the incident in his 1933 biography of John Hay, titled, *John Hay: From Poetry to Politics.*

On **March 12, 2009**, financier Bernard Madoff pled guilty in New York to taking $18 billion from clients in the largest swindle in Wall Street history.

MARCH 13

A lady with a strong inner light

Susan B. Anthony
Feb 15, 1820 (Adams, MA) – **Mar 13, 1906** (Rochester, NY)

S USAN B. ANTHONY was the second child born to Daniel Anthony, a Quaker, and Lucy Reed Anthony, a non-Quaker. Daniel Anthony's marriage to Lucy was obviously not one approvable by the Quakers, a group not known for showing tolerance toward those who marry "out of unity," their term for a marriage outside the faith. Therefore, it might have been Daniel's strong personality, after a formal rebuke by church leaders that allowed him to retain his Quaker membership.

A few years later Daniel was once again on the Discipline Committee's hot seat, this time for allowing a dance school to operate within his residence. With their patience toward Daniel growing thin, church leaders held the requisite rebuke and then "disowned" him, meaning he could not be reinstated until he admitted his errant behavior, and even then only if church leaders were willing to take him back. None of this bothered Anthony who continued to attend Quaker meetings, although gradually moving further and further away from traditional Quaker values.

Lucy and Daniel raised the family's seven children in Daniel's rather relaxed version of the Quaker religion. They saw to it that their children had family chores and were taught to be self-reliant and as they matured, to be self-supporting. They were also taught, in accordance with tenets of the Quaker faith, that an individual's inner light (conscience) should govern their individual actions, and that God didn't recognize a hierarchy that placed one person, male or female, above any other person.

Equality was a particular tenant of the faith that ran true in the mind of young Susan.

In 1837, seventeen-year-old Susan went to a Quaker boarding school in Philadelphia, an ultra-strict school that she tolerated for a single term before the financial *Panic of 1837* forced the Anthony family into bankruptcy and she returned home. Now, instead of furthering her education, she became a teacher at a Quaker boarding school.

In 1845, with help from a windfall inheritance, the family moved to New York where they joined with a group of like-minded former Quakers that had formed their own church. The church, the "Congregational Friends," included among its members, Frederick Douglass, the former slave and prominent abolitionist who became a friend of the Anthony family, especially Susan.

In 1848, the Congregational Friends hosted a women's rights convention, patterned after the country's first such convention held earlier at Seneca Falls, New York. Susan, finding herself surprisingly liberated and well-accepted, replaced her Quaker-plain wardrobe with the stylish outerwear of the era and soon discovered she could support herself on the fees she received for speaking in favor of those things she believed in.

That inner light she had trusted as a young girl was now directing her toward anti-slavery activism and temperance, and she became fully engaged in both arenas.

Then, in the early 1850s, her inner light didn't just come on – it began flashing. It all happened when she was denied an opportunity to speak at a temperance convention because she was a woman.

Anthony, taught from birth that God didn't impose a hierarchy on the power of the human mind, wondered why the organizers of a temperance convention thought they could. After mulling those thoughts over for a few minutes, she added a third purpose to her life, equal rights for women, and the fight was on!

In 1868, Anthony began publishing *The Revolution,* a weekly women's rights journal, its motto, "The true republic – men, their rights and nothing more; women their rights and nothing less."

"Women, we may as well be dogs baying at the moon
as petitioners without the right to vote."
Susan B. Anthony (Feb 15, 1820 – **Mar 13, 1906**)
Social reformer

J. Fred Muggs
Mar 14, 1952 (French Cameroon) –

IN 1953, A chimpanzee saved NBC's *The Today Show*, a show, by the way that is still on the air (2015).

It seemed that *The Today Show,* which had debuted on January 14, 1952, was in deep trouble from consistently poor ratings. In fact, it was about to be sacked. The show, the brainchild of NBC president Pat Weaver, was the early-morning companion to the network's successful *The Tonight Show,* with its captive audience and hosted by the versatile Steve Allen.

However, life wasn't as easy for *The Today Show.* There wasn't a captive audience. Oh, perhaps a small number of childless housewives with nothing to do but eat bon-bons and watch the tube, but that was it. Then as now, daytime television was subject to a completely different set of variables as nighttime television, and in early 1953, *The Today Show* was having difficulty sustaining a dependable audience.

The Tonight Show had a ready-made audience of folks propped up in their beds with pillows, relaxed and ready for a monologue covering the day's foibles, whereas *The Today Show* was searching for a way to capture an audience when half of America's adults were out of the house earning a paycheck. These were also the hours filled with running errands, taking kids to school, showing up for medical appointments, and for refereeing the antics of pre-school age children.

Nevertheless, advertisers weren't interested in excuses for the poor showing of a television program. They were only interested in the bottom line, and the bottom line in television, then as now, was ratings.

Enter the savior of NBC's *The Today Show.* A year-old chimpanzee ingloriously adorned in a baby diaper, with the highly improbable chimpanzee name, J. Fred Muggs. Muggs' handler, Carmine 'Bud' Mennella, had just introduced his trained chimp to the delight of the audience of the *Perry Como Show,* and that's where NBC President

Pat Weaver first saw him. Weaver, thinking the chimp might just have what his failing show needed, went to work.

At a press conference where it was announced that J. Fred Muggs would be joining Dave Garroway as co-host of the show, J. Fred unceremoniously grabbed Garroway's signature glasses from his face and refused to give them back. The public loved the antics, both from Muggs and Garroway, and from across picket fences America's housewives began to talk about the show. "Did you see what Muggs' did to Garroway this morning? I love it!" Moreover, the ratings not only improved, but J. Fred with his sidekick Garroway, carried the show to new heights.

In time, the diaper gave way to trousers, suspenders, shoes, and pullover sweaters.

About two years into the show, America was introduced to J. Fred's live-in girlfriend, Phoebe B. Beebe, and the lady chimp became a frequent guest on the show, and she was every bit as endearing as J. Fred.

Today, on the internet, you can find numerous stills and videos of the simian couple indulging in everything from friendly play to a tender kiss.

As of 2015, J. Fred and his lady friend, Phoebe, were both still alive and doing well in Citrus Park, Florida, in the care of Gerald Preis, the son of their original trainer and handler, Carmine 'Bud' Menella who passed away in 2002.

Muggs, according to reports, is beginning to show some signs of aging, specifically a little gray in his beard. So, welcome, J. Fred Muggs and the lovely Phoebe to the world of senior citizenry.

"The difference between genius and stupidity is that
genius has its limits."
Albert Einstein (**Mar 14, 1879** – Apr 18, 1955)
Theoretical physicist

John Snow

Mar 15, 1813 (York, England) – June 16, 1858 (London, England)

THE AVAILABILITY OF public water pumps was just one of a growing number of modern conveniences that made life easier for England's city folks in the 1800s.

Today, walking down Broad Street (1800s: Broadwick Street) in London's Soho District, one will notice what seems to be an out of place old-fashioned public water pump. In fact, it appears that someone might have vandalized the pump because the pump's handle is missing.

A closer examination reveals that the pump is a replica, erected in 1992 in commemoration of the work done by Dr. John Snow, the physician who discovered the cause of London's deadly cholera outbreaks of the 1800s. Why a water pump and one built without a handle?

John Snow was the first of nine children born to William and Frances Snow in what was the poorest community in the town of York, England, a community on the River Ouse that was in constant threat of flooding.

Initially educated at a "common" school for the children of poor families, John's intellect must have caught someone's attention because in 1827 at the age of fourteen, he was taken to Newcastle-on-Tyne, eighty miles away – a far distance in the 1820s, and there began a six year apprenticeship in medicine under the supervision of Dr. William Hardcastle.

In 1831, and well into his apprenticeship, Snow experienced a horrific cholera outbreak in the nearby town of Newcastle. The town, savagely attacked by the disease, had a mortality rate of 50% among those contracting the disease. Not a good outlook for members of the community.

He shared the feelings of hopelessness felt by the town's physicians who, for two long years, had done their professional best to battle the unseen odoriferous "miasma" in the air, the smelly cause of the deadly cholera. At least that's what the doctors of the 1820s believed caused the disease.

After his apprenticeship (1833), and only twenty years old, Snow practiced medicine in several small towns around North Yorkshire before returning to his hometown of York and joining the practice of physician, Dr. Joseph Warburton.

In 1836 and feeling the need for additional training, Snow closed his practice and walked 200 miles from York to London where he enrolled at the Hunterian School of Medicine, and began a study of the toxicity of arsenic.

In 1837, he began working at the Westminster Hospital, and in 1838, became a member of the Royal College of Surgeons of England, and then, instead of returning to his hometown of York, he established a practice in the Soho District of London, and that's where he was when the Broad Street Cholera Outbreak occurred in 1854.

During the years from 1837 to 1854, Snow never forgot the devastation wrought by the two-year cholera epidemic that had struck Newcastle while he was in his apprenticeship, and he began keeping meticulous records on each occurrence of the disease throughout England.

In 1849, he published a pamphlet that ran counter to the prevalent thinking of his profession. The pamphlet, *On the Mode of Communication of Cholera*, based on his carefully kept notes, showed that the disease occurred more in the late summer and most often in the poorest parts of England. He concluded by saying that he believed cholera was caused by a poison that reproduced in the human body, that it was carried through the vomit and stools of cholera patients, and that it ultimately found its way into the water source.

He received equal portions of criticism and acclaim for his conclusions and all the while, he continued to research his hypothesis.

Then the Broad Street Cholera Outbreak, right in his own backyard, the Soho District of London. With the help of a friend, a church pastor, the two began pinpointing on a map, the residences of the deceased. As rapidly as the deaths were piling up, 500 in the first ten days alone, it didn't take long to determine the area around the Broad Street pump as the area of greatest concern.

Although his testing of water samples taken from the pump were not conclusive, he had enough circumstantial evidence to convince the town council to disable the pump and force the local citizens to go elsewhere for their water.

With the removal of the pump handle, the rate of deaths began to decline, producing only 161 more deaths after the initial ten-day count of 500.

An examination of the well that supplied water to the Broad Street community revealed the culprit. The well was very shallow and dug adjacent to an old cesspit that was leaking fecal matter into the water supply.

Dr. Snow's findings and the sudden ceasing of the Broad Street Outbreak, less than a month after it had started, as opposed to the Newcastle outbreak that lasted two years, got the attention of London's sanitation officials. A complete renovation of the city's water and sewage systems resulted in a virtual stoppage of the dreaded cholera that had plagued the city for generations.

Dr. John Snow died on June 16, 1858, of kidney disease. He was 45 years old.

"The true purpose of education is to teach a man
to carry himself triumphant to the sunset."
Liberty Hyde Bailey (**Mar 15, 1858** – Dec 25, 1954)
Horticulturist

WAYNE WINTERTON, PH.D.

MARCH 16
For the fun-loving Finn in everyone

Saint Urho
1956 (MN or MI) – **Mar 16** (St. Urho's Feast Day)

S T. URHO'S DAY is the brainchild of either Richard Mattson or Kenneth Brist, depending on whose brain you believe conceived the child that became St. Urho in 1956. Either Mattson, then a Minnesota department store employee, or Brist, a teacher on Michigan's Upper Peninsula, decided that Finland's lack of a patron saint required corrective action. So, since you already know about Ireland's St. Patrick, meet Finland's St. Urho. Whereas St. Patrick was supposedly responsible for banishing snakes from the Emerald Isle, St. Urho was responsible for saving Finland's grape crop by ridding that country of grasshoppers.

Here is some background information for your edification.

First, historically, post-glacial Ireland has never had a snake population, and although Finland may sport a grasshopper here and there, the Finn's are neither major grape growers, nor wine producers.

St. Patrick supposedly drove all of Ireland's snakes and toads to a single location where he commanded them to slither off a cliff or hop into the sea, as told in a popular Irish ballad, "Success to bold St. Patty's fist / he was a Saint so clever / He gave the snakes and toads a twist / and banished them forever."

St. Urho supposedly put the kibosh on a plague of giant grape-eating grasshoppers by attacking them with a pitchfork while chanting in Finnish, "Heinäsirkka, heinäsirkka, mene täältä hiiteen!" (Grasshopper, grasshopper, go from hence to Hell!)

Also, unlike St. Patrick's Ireland, which is 90% Catholic, a religion that believes in the power of Saints, St. Urho's Finland is 80% Lutheran, a religion that does not believe in saints in the upper-case sense, although it does acknowledge individuals who have lived saintly lives, which may or may not include Finland's only upper-case pseudo-saint, St. Urho.

It should be no surprise that most of the Finns in Finland are unaware of the existence of St. Urho. However, to an increasing number of Finnish-Americans, and Americans who claim Finnish heritage for a day, St. Urho is real, and to prove it they honor him with revelry each March 16. Afterwards, they spend the bulk of the following day, March 17, St. Patrick's Day, with icepacks on their heads all in the name of frisky festive Finnish fun.

And, in the category of *just so you know*, the word "urho" in Finnish means "hero."

Now, in the event you've concluded that St. Urho is hardly worth writing about and has no place in an authoritative, highly respected tome such as the one you're holding, be assured there are people and places for which St. Urho is honored.

For instance, there's a statue on Highway 71 just outside of Menahga, Minnesota erected to the memory of St. Urho. The statue is a twelve-foot man in traditional Finnish dress, standing tall and holding a pitchfork upon which is speared one enormous grasshopper. The original statue, fashioned by chainsaw sculptor Jerry Ward, now resides in a protected mausoleum in the Menahga cemetery. The current roadside statue is a weather-resistant fiberglass replica of the original.

There is another statue to St. Urho, this one at the intersection of Minnesota Highway 1 and Lake County Road 7, just outside of Finland, Minnesota. Like the original Menahga sculpture, it is a chainsaw product, but this one carved by Don Osborn in 1982. It is eighteen feet tall, but thirty years of standing in the harsh Minnesota climate has taken its toll. If you look carefully, however, you'll see a tall St. Urho shouting at the top of his lungs in an effort to rid the countryside of hordes of ravaging grasshoppers, while a large grasshopper with a broad smile is happily relaxing atop his hat.

From poet Linda Johnson comes the following, *The Legend of St. Urho*, to tell the Saint's story, in which the final three couplets read:

> As Finland was freed from the insects so vile,
> They pronounced Urho a saint and not just a child.
> The legend has grown and spread through the years,
> Of a brave Finnish boy without any fears.
> Now each March 16 we celebrate this way,
> Wearing purple and green for St. Urho's Day.

Regardless of how St. Urho came to be, March 16 is a good reason for America's Finns to do a little celebrating and for the rest of us to be a Finn for a day.

U. S. Scientist Robert Goddard successfully launched the world's first liquid-fueled rocket on **March 16, 1926**, at Auburn, Massachusetts.

MARCH 17

Everyone's Irish on St. Patrick's Day

Saint Patrick

c. 385 (Banwen, Wales) – **Mar 17, 461** (Saul, Ireland)

P ATRICK'S PARENTS, CALPURNIUS and Conchessa, were Roman citizens living in Britain during the period of Roman occupation. Those were difficult times for British families as war with someone (Rome, Ireland, etc), was a way of life. Around 400 AD, fifteen-year-old Patrick, kidnapped by an Irish raiding party, ended up in Ireland to perform slave labor as a shepherd. There he became fluent in the Gaelic (Irish) language and knowledgeable regarding the religious practices of the Druids (a pagan, pre-Christian religion).

Around his fifth year in Ireland, he heard a voice promising to help him escape. The voice told him to flee toward the Irish coast where a ship would be available to return him to England. He followed the instructions and when he reached the coast, he met some sailors who were preparing to sail to France. They took him as far as they were going, after which he wandered lost for twenty-eight days before making it to England and a cheerful reunion with his family.

Thankful to be back on British soil and no longer a slave, he professed his faith in God and became a Catholic priest. Shortly after taking his vows, he experienced a second dream. This time, instead of hearing a single voice, there were multitudinous voices, all calling him by name and pleading with him in the Gaelic language to return to Ireland. "We beg you, holy youth, to come and walk among us once more."

Remaining in England until he was ordained a bishop, he departed for Ireland. Once there, in part because of his fluency in Gaelic, he experienced remarkable success in converting the pagan Irish to Christianity. There were also times he felt miraculously delivered from death.

In one such instance, legend tells of his near demise at the hand of a local chieftain. When the chieftain raised his arm to slay Patrick with his knife, his arm locked in the upward position and he was unable to plunge the knife into Patrick's body, or to lower his arm to his side. It was only after he professed a change in heart that he regained the normal use of his arm.

Conversions continued throughout Patrick's forty years of service and he credited much of his success to a prop that was available everywhere on the Emerald Isle, the lowly shamrock. The shamrock, with its three leaves, served as the perfect visual aide for helping him explain the doctrine of the Holy Trinity.

In 461 AD, after performing numerous miracles among the Irish and personally enduring much suffering, he passed away. The day of his death was March 17, the day we now celebrate as St. Patrick's Day.

And now, for a small bit of truth that probably isn't worth the time it will take to divulge, and it surely won't change anyone's feelings about St. Patrick, who is right up there in popularity with other saintly notables such as St. Valentine and St. Nicholas.

You see, Patrick isn't one of the Catholic Church's full-fledged Saints. Instead, he's a saint spelled with a lower-case "s," as in, "Considering all that Patrick accomplished among the handsome lads and lovely Irish cuties on the Emerald Isle, he was truly a saint among men."

The problem is that although the folks who knew him best, the early Christians, called him Saint Patrick, he has never been canonized, the process by which the Catholic Church exalts someone to sainthood.

Thankfully, few are the number of folks who care about such details. In the hearts and minds of most of us, Catholic, Mormon, Methodist, or Moonie, Patrick will always be one of our favorite Saints (with a capital "S"), a good man who helped others, who walked among the poor and performed miracles, and who found a special reason to wear the shamrock.

"Careers, like rockets, don't always take off on time.
The trick is to always keep the engine running."
Gary Sinese (**Mar 17, 1955** –) Actor

Rudolf Diesel

(Rudolf Christian Karl Diesel)

Mar 18, 1858 (Paris, France) – Sept 29, 1913 (English Channel)

IF SOMEONE WERE to ask you to name the inventor of the diesel engine, you might not know, but if someone were to ask you what Rudolf Diesel was famous for inventing, those same chances would be greatly improved, at least you could suggest it might be the diesel engine, and you would be right.

In 1848 Theodor Diesel, a Bavarian bookbinder immigrated to France and there met Elise Strobel, the daughter of a Nuremberg merchant. The two fell in love, married, and in 1858, Elise gave birth to Rudolf.

When the Franco-Prussian War broke out in 1870, Germans living in France had no choice but to leave the country and the Diesel family moved to London. That same year Rudolf, now twelve, went to Bavaria to live with his uncle in hopes he would learn two things: the German language, and a trade at the Royal County Trade School where his uncle taught mathematics.

Rudolf proved to be a quick learner, mastering German and graduating at the top of his class in 1873. He immediately enrolled at the Industrial School of Augsburg and two years later received a scholarship from the Royal Bavarian Polytechnic of Munich. Although his parents tried to talk him out of the scholarship, feeling it was time for him to begin earning some money, he accepted and in 1880 again graduated at the top of his class.

After graduation, he went to Paris where he worked as a refrigerant engineer for one of his former professors, Carl von Linde. It was here with Professor von Linde where, if there were any gaps in the thermodynamics portion of his education, they quickly filled.

In 1893, well before the era of the gasoline-powered internal-combustion engine, he published a paper in which he described such an engine, suggesting that an electrical spark could ignite the engine's fuel. Well ahead of his time, he also wrote about a solar-powered air engine. However, the engine for which he became famous, and to which he would lend his name, was an engine powered, not by a spark, but by the compression of gaseous vapors.

His *compression engine*, scoffed at by many, almost remained theoretical when a prototype of the engine he was working on, exploded! Diesel didn't view the explosion as a bad thing, instead, he viewed it as proof he had been right. He now knew without a doubt, that compression alone could ignite fuel and he resumed his work with even more passion and energy.

By 1897, Diesel had his engine perfected and ready to turn the heads of those interested in watching it run, and he displayed it at the Munich Exhibition of 1898. The engine he developed used a fuel less refined than the more-volatile and more expensive gasoline. Its fuel economy was remarkable and the engine ran quietly. The engine went from "Diesel's Folly" to the engine that has powered the trucking industry and many of the world's electric generating plants.

By the early 1900s, Diesel's health had taken a beating from the exhausting work schedule he had forced upon himself during the development and refinement of the engine. Later, demands on his time as a lecturer were cutting into what was most important to him, his engineering time.

In 1913, he participated in a meeting of the Consolidated Diesel Manufacturing Company (London) and afterward boarded the steamer *Dresden* in Antwerp to make a crossing of the English Channel. He ate dinner aboard ship, visited, and excused himself to go to bed around 10 p.m., asking for a 6:45 wake-up call.

He was never seen again, alive.

Diesel had not slept in his bed, although his watch was on a nightstand positioned so it was visible from where he would have slept. His hat and coat were outside his room, and tucked underneath the afterdeck railing.

Two weeks later a Dutch ship discovered a body floating in the North Sea near Norway. Inside the pockets of the deceased was Diesel's wallet and identification card. The body was so badly decomposed that after removing all of the personal effects from the clothing, it was returned to the sea.

Foul play? Suicide? The mystery as to his death, how and why, has never been solved.

"We are most alive when we're in love."
John Updike (**Mar 18, 1932** – Jan 27, 2009) Novelist

WAYNE WINTERTON, PH.D.

MARCH 19
The infidel who visited Mecca

Richard Francis Burton
Mar 19, 1821 (Devon, England) – Oct 20, 1890 (Trieste, Austria)

S IR RICHARD FRANCIS Burton was an early 19th century international man-of-mystery with a dash of daring for whom even the literary James Bond would have approved.

Wikipedia lists Burton's occupations as spy, explorer, writer, geographer, translator, soldier, orientalist, cartographer, ethnologist, linguist, poet, fencer, and diplomat. Then, add to that his knowledge of numerous cultures and languages, and you have a one-of-a-kind guy.

Richard's father was a Lieutenant Colonel in the British army, a job that saw the Burton family bouncing from England to France and to Italy, where young Richard showed an early propensity for acquiring languages. By his teens, he had mastered French, Italian, Neapolitan, and Latin.

In 1840, he enrolled at Trinity College (Oxford) and was nearly expelled after challenging another student to a duel for making fun of his mustache. He did, however, get the boot in 1842 for attending a steeplechase in direct violation of college rules. That left him with a disheartened father and few options, so he enlisted in the East Indian army.

While in India, he added Hindustani, Guajarati, Punjabi, Sindhi, Saraiki, Marathi, Persian, and Arabic to his list of mastered languages. He also kept a menagerie of tame monkeys in his residence, hopeful of mastering their language as well.

Toward the end of his military service, he went to Sindh, one of Pakistan's four provinces where he learned surveying, a skill that would serve him well during his career as an explorer. In Sindh, he adopted the identity of Mirza Abdullah, and his dark complexion and flawless command of the language was such that he easily fooled the locals, and his co-workers, into thinking he was of Pakistani heritage.

In March of 1849, he became ill, received extended leave from the military and began to plan the mother of all dangerous missions.

He wanted to be the first non-Muslim to enter the sacred city of Mecca and he would do it by making the *hajj*, the sacred pilgrimage to Mecca expected of every adult. If caught, he knew an immediate execution would end his life. He wrote in his journal, "A blunder, a hasty action, a misjudged word, a prayer or bow not strictly the right shibboleth, and my bones would have whitened the desert sand."

In addition to a need for flawless speech, he would need to be authentically Muslim in other ways as well. This included the proper wearing of the pilgrim's traditional two white seamless sheets, and at the age of thirty-two, he carried method acting to new heights by having a circumcision performed in the event the wind should blow his cover, so to speak.

In 1852, Burton approached England's Royal Geographical Society about funding the adventure. They were skeptical at first, given the odds that he could actually pull off an incursion into the holiest of Muslim cities. However, the allure of being the first to publish a true glimpse into the Forbidden City was too tempting, and Burton had his funding.

In 1853 and calling himself Abdullah, he joined a caravan and began his pilgrimage. He disguised himself as a Pashtun, having mastered the Pashto language by spending a great deal of time among ethnic Afghans, and constantly perfecting the subtle nuances of the language.

Inside Mecca, he pushed and shoved his way, as did everyone, through the swarm of pilgrims to the Black Stone, and once there he kissed it. He made his way to Mount Arafat, and then he was on to the holiest of Muslim holies, the *Kaaba*, a square structure inside the Great Mosque. In keeping with sacred tradition, he walked around the structure exactly seven times, and just as he was about to enter, he was accosted by two guards.

Without blinking, Burton flawlessly answered the guards' questions and continued into the Kaaba, where he prayed while keeping one eye open to memorize the floor plan that he would later sketch.

Back in England, he met with the Royal Geographical Society and collected the money owed him for his successful venture, after which he published his meticulously detailed papers in a book titled, *Personal Narrative of a Pilgrimage to Al-Madinah and Meccah.*

The book made Burton famous and led to funding other adventures.

He died of a heart attack on October 20, 1890 in Trieste, Italy, and is at rest alongside his wife, Isabel in St. Mary Magdalen's cemetery in southwest London, in a tomb shaped as a Bedouin tent, their coffins visible through a window at the rear of the tent.

"Fast is fine, but accuracy is everything."
Wyatt Earp (**Mar 19, 1848** – Jan 13, 1929) Lawman, gambler

B. F. Skinner

(Burrhus Frederic Skinner)
Mar 20, 1904 (Sesquehanna, PA) – Aug 18, 1990 (Cambridge, MA)

T HROUGHOUT THE AGES, mankind (heavy on *man*; light
on *kind*) has come up with some ingenious ways to use
animals in an attempt to gain the upper hand on the battlefield.
As you know, war is nasty business and even worse than man's
inhumanity to man, has been man's callous attitude toward animals.

For instance, it's reported that during Hannibal's march across the
Alps in 218 BC that 50,000 infantry, 9,000 cavalry, and 37 elephants
accompanied him. "Why the elephants?" They were the military
tanks of the time, their skin impervious to hand-thrown spears and
the willingness for elephants to use their heads to gain entrance to
enemy fortifications was legendary.

When Hannibal was about to storm the gates of Rome, the
Romans knowing of an elephant's fear of squealing pigs, slathered
dozens of little porkers with tar and set them ablaze amidst the
elephants. According to Pliny the Elder, the pigs, the world's first
anti-tank missiles, caused unprecedented pachyderm panic within
Hannibal's army to say nothing of the number of disabled elephants
and pigs that had to be put to sleep afterward.

Hannibal also used snakes as weapons of war. He filled earthen
pots with venomous snakes and had his men lob them onto the decks
of enemy ships as his ships pulled aside. The demoralizing effect of
being at sea with a shipload of poisonous vipers in 200 BC wouldn't
be very different than, say, being aboard a Boeing 747 in 2006 with
a similar problem. Both situations would make for great movie plots.
Remember, you read it here first!

During World War II, dogs became anti-tank weapons. Dogs,
trained by the Soviets to expect food underneath German tanks,
were denied food for days. When the dogs were turned loose, high-
powered explosives strapped to their backs would detonate on contact.

An estimated 300 German tanks were disabled by the Soviets in this manner.

During the 1960s, both the United States and the Soviet Union used dolphins as military tools. Both countries trained them to detect underwater mines and to attack enemy divers. The Soviets, being the more creative of the antagonists, attached hook-like devices to the backs of dolphins for snaring dead, and on occasion, living soldiers. The catch then searched or interrogated for intelligence.

There were also some plans to use animals in warfare that were never used. One of those was America's idea during World War II to drop "bat bombs," containers carrying 1,000 bats each, to which were attached small timed incendiary devices. After deployment, the bats would roost in the eaves and attics of buildings, setting fires in inaccessible places as their timers went off. The idea, however, never took off.

There was also "Project Pigeon," the World War II brainchild of noted psychologist-behaviorist B. F. Skinner of Harvard University.

The Navy was in search of a weapon for use against Germany's behemoth battleships, such as the Bismarck and the Tirpitz. Those ships, the terrors of the seas, seemed impenetrable, and threatened the Allies path to victory. The generals needed help and that's when they decided to listen to Dr. Skinner's idea of how to neutralize German battleships.

Skinner, based on his work in the field of operant conditioning, (a learning model based on reward or punishment), suggested that pigeons could be conditioned (trained) to guide warhead-loaded missiles to a target.

The generals, desperate for a solution, provided Skinner with $25,000 to develop a prototype of his idea. He began by taking a mock-up of the nose cone of a missile and dividing it into three chambers, one chamber for each of three pigeons, and a window from which each pigeon could view forward.

Then he trained each pigeon to peck at a picture of a battleship. Whenever the battleship strayed out of view of the nose cone, the pigeons learned that by "pecking" the battleship back into the center of the screen, they would receive a reward, perhaps a kernel of corn.

By using three pigeons in the nose cone at the same time, Skinner believed that the redundancy of multiple pigeons working together to keep the battleship in the center of the screen would eliminate any possibility of error. Of course, what looked like a battleship moving out of position to the pigeons was in reality, their missile straying from a direct hit.

Correcting their position meant steadying the flight of the missile. The pigeons, of course, had no idea they were on a one-way mission, so they would continuously peek out of their little windows and peck, peck, peck as necessary until BAM! Pigeon Pearly Gates.

However, Skinner's pigeons never made it into battle.

Why?

Few, if not all of the generals, were unwilling to put their faith and confidence in a lowly pigeon, no matter how well the pigeon performed in the laboratory.

The real winners in all of this, of course, were the pigeons who lived to peek and peck another day.

Harriet Beecher Stowe's anti-slavery novel,
Uncle Tom's Cabin, was published
on **March 20, 1852**, becoming the best-selling novel
of the 19th century.

MARCH 21
Don't bother us

Homer Lusk Collyer
and
Langley Wakeman Collyer
Homer: Nov 6, 1881 (Manhattan, NY) – **Mar 21, 1947** (Manhattan, NY)
Langley: Oct 3, 1885 (Manhattan, NY) – c. February 1947 (Manhattan, NY)

COMMON BROTHERS WITH uncommon brotherly love. That was the Collyer brothers, Homer Lusk and Langley Wakeman. They were also two men with a complete distrust of everything beyond the boundaries of their massive New York brownstone home. Until their deaths in 1947, they were the unknown hoarders of over 280,000 pounds, that's over 140 ton of everything from tin cans to pianos, fourteen of the latter, grand and upright, and that's just for openers.

As odd as the brothers became late in life, their youth was typical of most who grew up in New York under relatively affluent conditions. Their father, Dr. Herman Livingston Collyer was a successful, if not slightly eccentric, gynecologist who worked at the famed Bellevue Hospital. Their mother, Susie Gage Frost was a former opera singer.

Respected and wealthy, Herman and Susie saw to it that their two boys would become successful. Homer, bright and articulate, was fourteen when he enrolled as a "sub-freshman" at the College of the City of New York where he earned a bachelor's degree. He went on to receive a law degree from Columbia University. Langley also attended Columbia, earning degrees in chemistry and engineering. He was also a talented concert pianist and played professionally, including one performance at Carnegie Hall.

Once the boys were well on their way toward their careers, and still living at home, the family moved into a spacious brownstone on Fifth Avenue in Harlem, an elite upper-class neighborhood in the early 1900s.

Life was good, that was, until marital problems beset Herman and Susie. By 1920, the marriage was over and the once happy couple separated. Herman moved out, leaving Susie in the family home with Homer and Langley, now 39 and 35 years old, respectively.

In 1923, three years after his separation from Susie, Herman died, leaving the items of his medical practice to his sons, which they dutifully stored in the brownstone. Six years later Susie died, and the brothers, now 48 and 44, had the enormous home to themselves.

Now, just the two of them and lacking badly in domestic skills, they became socially distant. Homer continued to practice law until 1933 when he lost his eyesight to disease. Langley, a partner in a piano dealership, sold his interest in the company so he could take care of his blind brother full time.

Elusive when asked about his brother's health, Langley once told a reporter, "You must remember we are the sons of a doctor. We have a medical library of 15,000 books in the house," assuring the reporter that Homer was well cared for, his blindness improving, he said, "from a diet of oranges, black bread, and peanut butter."

With the 1930s, came the effects of the stock market crash of October 29, 1929, and the beginning of the Great Depression. It was during this time that the brothers, who could have weathered the depression better than most, went from being socially distant to fully withdrawing from society.

Once when asked why they had shut themselves off from the world, Langley coolly replied, "We don't want to be bothered."

Yet, they had the money to buy and to have delivered to the brownstone, those things they deemed necessary. If Langley wanted a new piano, he had one delivered to the house.

The community surrounding the brownstone grew suspicious about the occupants, and they wondered what was going on inside.

There were a few attempted burglaries, sparked by rumors of valuable jewelry and buckets of cash, but none were successful. Nevertheless, the attempts were indications to the brothers that something needed to done. Langley, with his engineering skills, began to build a system of tunnels and mazes throughout the mansion, complete with trip-wire activated booby traps designed to drop something heavy and lethal on the head of anyone trying to break in.

Failure to pay their bills brought more isolation, with telephone, gas, electricity, and water all eventually disconnected. To compensate,

Langley adapted a Model T Ford engine to generate electricity for the house.

In 1942, when the bank holding the mortgage began proceedings to evict the brothers for non-payment, Langley simply wrote a check for $6,700 (equivalent to $97,000 in 2015 dollars) and paid off the mortgage in full.

Then, on March 21, 1947, an anonymous person called the police to complain about a ghastly stench emanating from the residence. After breaking into the home, it took Officer William Barker two hours of crawling through the tunnels, careful of the booby traps, to locate Homer, who had apparently starved to death. The medical examiner placed his death at less than ten hours.

It took another eighteen days and the removal of 84 ton of rubbish before they could find Langley, who had been dead for a month, pinned beneath one of his own booby-traps, and a mere ten feet from his disabled and starving brother.

In the 1960s, the site of the Collyer home (2078 Fifth Avenue, New York) became *Collyer Park,* a permanent neighborhood park, a quiet place for folks to sit, relax, and contemplate the vagaries of humanity and the universe.

On **March 21, 1871**, journalist Henry Morton Stanley
began his odyssey
to locate missionary and explorer David Livingstone.

David Lunt

(Unknown) – **Mar 22, 1877** (Deadwood, SD)

NO ONE KNEW where David Lunt called home, but in the mid-1800s, no one much cared where anyone came from, as long as the "someone" wasn't a problem, and that was David Lunt. He wasn't a problem. He was a congenial man, agreeable and well liked around Deadwood, and what happened to him shouldn't have happened to a dog.

Irish immigrant Con Stapleton was Deadwood's first marshal. Well, actually Deadwood's second marshal if you count Isaac Brown. Two weeks and a day after Deadwood pinned a star on Isaac Brown, he with Reverend Brown, Charles Mason, and Charles Holland arrived at the Pearly Gates, instead of at Crook City as they had intended when they left Deadwood that morning, all victims of lead poisoning, shot to death.

Just three days before Brown's appointment as sheriff there had been the famous incident in which Jack McCall, in a Deadwood saloon, shot Wild Bill Hickok in the back.

To give you a flavor of 1870s justice, a jury found McCall "not guilty" when he claimed all he was trying to do was even the score after Hickok killed his brother.

McCall was in Wyoming Territory when he was arrested a second time for Hickok's murder. Wyoming, not certain if the Deadwood ruling was legal, held McCall while it awaited a South Dakota ruling regarding double jeopardy. When South Dakota ruled that double jeopardy didn't apply in McCall's case since Deadwood didn't have an approved judicial system, McCall was sent to Yankton, South Dakota to be tried a second time. This time, McCall was found guilty, sentenced, and hanged. When McCall was exhumed in 1881 for reburial in a new cemetery, he still had the noose around his neck.

Let's return to the story about David Lunt, a guy liked by everyone, who was central to one of the strangest incidents that ever took place when the west was wild.

Right after the last shovel of dirt graced the top of Isaac Brown's grave, a town meeting to appoint a new sheriff ended with Brown's barely used star pinned on Con Stapleton, a good choice.

During the evening of January 14, 1877, Sheriff Stapleton and a group of locals, including David Lunt, were inside Al Chapman's Saloon swapping stories and sipping suds when suddenly, the saloon doors burst open. Standing in the doorway was Tom Smith aiming his revolver first at one patron, and then another and another, screaming, "Anyone who moves gets shot!"

When he approached the table where Sheriff Stapleton was sitting, the sheriff moved quickly to disarm the wild man and in the fracas, Smith's revolver discharged. The bullet narrowly missed Stapleton's head but struck Lunt squarely in the forehead. Smith, overpowered and pinned to the floor was quickly disarmed and handcuffed.

Certain that Lunt was dead from a head wound that was oozing blood, the crowd, who was now standing around his body, were shocked when he sat up, and then stood up and brushed the floor's sawdust from his clothing as if nothing had happened.

Tom Smith, charged with discharging a weapon at a law officer went free because no one was hurt in the incident. Never mind that David Lunt had a hole in his forehead and another in the back of his head. He was still alive and in the old west, just being alive counted for a lot.

Then, on March 22, 1877, sixty-seven days after the bullet had passed through his head; David Lunt complaining of a severe headache, laid down to rest and died. An autopsy revealed that the bullet that passed through Lunt's head, had also forced a piece of bone deep into the brain. That piece of bone had caused an abscess, filling his brain with water, and was ruled the cause of death.

The most amazing thing, of course, was that David Lunt had lived at all after having a bullet pass completely through his head.

"   ,   ,   ."

Marcel Marceau (**Mar 22, 1923** – Sept 22, 2007) Mime

MARCH 23

Conscientious objector, Medal of Honor winner

Desmond Thomas Doss
Feb 7, 1919 (Lynchburg, VA) - **Mar 23, 2006** (Piedmont, AL)

D ESMOND DOSS WAS born into a family and into a religion, Seventh-day Adventist, whose tenets of faith does not prohibit military service, leaving that decision to the conscience of the individual, but it does prohibit the taking of a human life and the carrying of a weapon, and it does require strict adherence to honoring the Sabbath.

Doss, well grounded in his faith, was equally firm in his belief that living in America came with responsibilities, one of which was the requirement to register for the draft on his eighteenth birthday (February 7, 1937), which he did.

It was at a time when battles were raging in Europe, and America was somehow hoping to escape being drawn into war. That hope ended on December 7, 1941, when the Japanese air force bombed the naval base at Pearl Harbor, Hawaii. The following day President Roosevelt asked Congress to declare war against Japan, and it did. Doss, like other American men, wondered when the Selective Service System, a lottery used to activate men into the service, would call his "draft" number.

In the meantime, he continued to work at the Newport News (Virginia) docks and to take advantage of the advanced first aid medical training offered.

Doss's number came up in 1942. He reported to the Army Recruiting Office, filled out the paperwork to request "non-combatant status," and when the sergeant-in-charge looked at the skinny kid, he said nothing and stamped "Conscientious Objector" on the paperwork.

Doss shipped out for basic training but it wasn't a pleasant experience. Some of the men in his unit ridiculed him for his non-combatant status and for his refusal to "qualify" on the shooting range. From their point of view, every active weapon moved the odds of survival one notch in their favor; but from Doss's point of view, it made no sense to learn to fire a rifle when he wasn't going to carry one. His fellow soldiers also poked fun at him in the chow hall because of his religion's dietary restrictions, and kneeling in prayer at night occasionally brought a friendly boot tossed in his direction.

The unit's commanding officer, in a move he thought would alleviate the problem, prepared the paperwork to give Doss a "Section 8 discharge." A Section 8 referred to a person's unsuitability for military service and he scheduled a hearing with Doss.

At the hearing, Doss explained his beliefs and assured the officer that it was never a question of "suitability," or of his willingness to pull his own weight. However, pulling his weight would have to be in a capacity where he wouldn't have to take a human life. Doss also explained that he had joined the military to serve his country and he didn't want a discharge that might reflect poorly on his Seventh-day Adventist religion.

The commanding office never submitted the paperwork, and instead sent Doss for training as an infantry medic. Upon completion of his training, Doss became a corpsman in the Army's 77th Division and shipped overseas.

About being a medic, Doss wrote:

> "The Japanese were out to get the medics. To them, the most hated men in our army were the medics and the BAR [Browning Automatic Rifle] men . . . they would let anybody get by just to pick us off. They were taught to kill the medics for the reason it broke down the morale of the men, because if the medic was gone they had no one to take care of them. All the medics were armed, except me."

Then, at Leyte on the Island of Guam, Doss proved himself the equal of any man on the battlefield. Think about it! It's one thing to be shooting at an enemy from the safety of a camouflaged bunker; it's another to be running into the open to pull a wounded soldier to safety carrying only a syrette of morphine, a roll of gauze, and some adhesive tape.

Repeatedly he rescued the wounded, each time becoming the target of sniper fire that kicked sand up all around him.

On one occasion, his fellow soldiers watched in horror as a Japanese sniper popped up at relatively close range, aimed his weapon directly at their medic . . . but never fired. Doss pulled the wounded soldier to safety and returned to rescue another.

One of the sergeants told Doss what he had seen, about the sniper that aimed but never fired. "Didn't you see him?" the sergeant asked, "He had his weapon aimed directly at you, point blank!" Doss said he had seen nothing, his attention solely on the wounded soldier.

Years later, a missionary in Japan told the above story during a church service. Afterward, a Japanese man in the congregation stood and told the parishioners that the sniper may have been him. He said he was at Leyte at the time of the incident and that he had observed an American medic rescuing wounded soldiers. He remembered leveling his sights on the medic, but then the strangest thing happened. No matter how hard he squeezed the trigger, the weapon wouldn't fire and he could only watch as the medic dragged the injured man to safety.

On October 12, 1945, President Harry Truman presented Doss with the Congressional Medal of Honor, making him the first conscientious objector to receive the award.

With typical Doss humility, the one-time medic grinned, and said, "Oh shucks," proving that serving in the military as a conscientious objector has nothing to do with one's courage, valor, or patriotism.

If you have occasion to visit the Walter Reed Army Medical Center in Washington D.C., you'll now know a little about the man for whom *Doss Memorial Hall* is named.

"Immature love says: 'I love you because I need you.'
Mature love says: 'I need you because I love you.'"
Erich Fromm (**Mar 23, 1900** – Mar 18, 1980) Psychologist

WAYNE WINTERTON, PH.D.

MARCH 24
Wandering vagrant

The Leatherman
c. 1839 (Unknown) – **Mar 24, 1889** (Ossining, NY)

ON MARCH 24, 1889, they found the Leatherman's lifeless body inside a cave he frequented in the "Saw Mill Woods" area near Ossining, New York, thus the origin of the date we use to present his story, as best we know it.

The identity of the Leatherman is unknown; although he may have been Jules Bourglay, an identity based on an 1884 *Waterbury (Connecticut) Daily American* account of his life.

One version of the *Jules Bourglay* story tells that young Jules had fallen in love with Margaret Laron, the daughter of a wealthy leather merchant. The merchant, however, refused to allow Jules to wed his daughter until he could prove a worthy son-in-law. The merchant, likely at the insistence of the daughter, hired Jules to give him a chance at proving himself. Jules did fine until he tipped over a lantern and burned the leather factory to the ground. Jules' eligibility for Margaret's hand in marriage went up in smoke as fast as had the leather factory, and without the lovely Margaret at his side, he chose a life of self-imposed isolation as the Leatherman.

At least one researcher (and possibly others) has discounted the above story, as well as other stories, as to the origin of the Leatherman. If interested, you might consider Dan W. DeLuca's book, *The Old Leather Man: Historical Accounts of a Connecticut and New York Legend.*

However, the fact that there once lived an itinerant man known only as the Leatherman is not in dispute.

No one knows from whence he came, although his speech when he spoke, which wasn't often, was guttural English punctuated with appreciative gestures and grunts. Found with his body was a French-language prayer book, so perhaps he was from a French-speaking province in Canada. It was also known that while alive, he refused meat on Fridays, an indication he may have been Catholic.

So, you may ask, what sets the Leatherman apart from thousands of others who have traipsed through the American landscape for centuries? Well, let's start with his clothing. His shoes were clogs, wooden soles with leather uppers; his hat was crudely stitched leather; his pants, which extended to his armpits, were made of stitched together pieces of raw leather and held in place by broad leather suspenders; and his long coat was of similar handiwork.

He wore the above clothing regardless of season, with the occasional addition of a neck scarf in the wintertime. Collectively his clothing weighed over sixty pounds.

He also carried a walking stick and a leather bag that upon his death contained leather-working tools, a small axe for cutting firewood, and the aforementioned prayer book.

However, as unique as his clothing was, the Leatherman's most unique characteristic was not his odd fashion statement, but his unwavering attention to schedule and his incredible punctuality.

For thirty-one years, from 1858 until 1889, regardless of the time of year, he walked the same circuitous 365-mile route, bounded on the East by the Connecticut River and on the West by the Hudson River, crossing the Housatonic River twice each trip. He never failed to make the 365 miles in exactly 34 days, each day's travel averaging 10.73 miles.

He was so punctual that if you were from Stamford, Connecticut, one of his many stops, and gave him a loaf of bread on June 24 and wished to do the same on his next visit, you could count 34 days and mark July 28 as bread-baking day, because without fail, he would return to Stamford on that day. The folks along his never-altered route claimed they could set, not only their calendars, but also their clocks, by his visits.

Where did the Leatherman stay in each of the towns and villages that were regular stops on his route? He lived mostly in abandoned animal dens, caves and other natural shelters known locally then, and to this day, as "Leatherman caves."

The Leatherman was laid to rest in the Sparta Cemetery in Scarborough, New York, his tombstone identifying him as the aforementioned Jules Bourglay.

In 2011, the body at rest underneath the Jules Bourglay headstone was exhumed and assigned a new plot, reburied, and a new headstone prepared; one that refers to the occupant of the grave simply as *The Leatherman.*

"One of the most attractive things about writing your autobiography is that you're not dead."
Joseph Barbera (**Mar 24, 1911** – Dec 18, 2006)
Cartoon artist

Robert Cobb Kennedy
About 1835 (Unknown) – **Mar 25, 1865** (Fort Lafayette, NY)

R OBERT COBB KENNEDY finally made the front page of the *New York Times*, but the headline wasn't what he had looked forward to reading. He would have preferred a description of the destruction of New York City. How the city had been burned to the ground with fires started at the same time in the city's great hotels, of the screams of the city's citizenry as chaos erupted everywhere, and all of it the work of a half dozen patriots, himself the leader, because that's how he viewed his role in the plot – as a patriot.

But given all that had transpired, and that he in death would no longer be troubled by the events that had destroyed his beloved South, he would let history sort things out, and only then would his actions be understood and appreciated.

> **KENNEDY'S EXECUTION** (The New York Times, March 27, 1865); Singular Conduct of the Prisoner – Confession of His Guilt – A Full and Voluntary Statement of the Great Incendiary Plot – He Dies a Death of Bravado – Scenes at the Scaffold. Confession.

Kennedy wasn't the only conspirator in the plot, but he was the only one caught in what was the most daring covert operation of the Civil War, the intended destruction of the entire city of New York by fire.

Confederate President Jefferson Davis blessed the operation when he assigned Jacob Thompson the task of leading an 1800s Delta Force type operation known as the Confederate Army of Manhattan into Canada, for the purpose of staging raids against the Union from Canadian soil.

Jacob Thompson was a no small potatoes guy. Prior to the Civil War, he served as President James Buchanan's Secretary of the Interior. At the outbreak of the war, he resigned his post with the Union to become Jefferson Davis's Inspector General of the Confederate Army, a post in which he primarily served as the head of what might have been called, during a different time, the Confederate's States Secret Service.

It was the first of November 1864, election month, and the war that had started three-and-a-half years previous was showing serious signs of stress and an ultimate victory for the Union. However, as far as Thompson and his raiders were concerned, it was payback time for what they considered as the Union's scorched-earth policy, in particular, the burning of Atlanta.

The pay-back? It would be a literal scorched-earth policy of their own.

A decision was made. If Lincoln wins the November 8, 1864 election, they'll burn New York to the ground using "Greek Fire," a flammable substance consisting primarily of phosphorus. The group would target hotels and other large structures to strain the city's capacity to fight fires. When the chemicals needed to make Greek Fire didn't arrive on schedule, the group merely changed the date. New York would burn on November 25.

At this time, two of the eight raiders quit the project and fled further into Canada, leaving an army of six, including the aforementioned Robert Cobb Kennedy, the group's de-facto leader, to carry out the mission.

When the 402 bottles of Greek Fire finally arrived, the six raiders traveled to New York, with Kennedy pretending to be a French-Canadian businessman. In the city, they checked into their assigned hotels. When the time came to carry out the deed, Kennedy set fire to the Lovejoy Hotel, the Everett House, the Tammany Hotel, the New-England House, and Barnum's Museum. Altogether, the six raiders set fire to nineteen structures and then disappeared into the night, all fleeing back to Canada.

However, unknown to them, the flames didn't spread as they had anticipated and at some locations, hotel employees using brooms and water extinguished the fires before any damage of consequence was done.

The New York police identified a few of the raiders, but they were unable to locate any of them.

In January of 1865, Kennedy, a native of Louisiana, decided to return home for a visit. He boarded a train for Detroit, but as soon as the train pulled into the station, he found himself surrounded and arrested. After his conviction, confinement followed at Fort Lafayette, a prison facility surrounded by water in New York harbor.

The judgment on Kennedy from General John A. Dix, commander of the Department of the East, read, "The attempt to set fire to the city of New York is one of the greatest atrocities of the age. There is nothing in the annals of barbarism that evinces greater vindictiveness. It was not a mere attempt to destroy the city, but to set fire to crowded hotels and places of public resort, in order to secure the greatest possible destruction of human life."

After the hood was pulled over his face, and just before he was executed, Kennedy sang the words to a few lines of verse: "Trust to luck, trust to luck, stare fate in the face, for your heart will be easy, if it's in the right place."

Immediately following the word, "place," the gallows counterweight was released and Kennedy's body was yanked hard and upward of the floorboards, the severe movement breaking his neck instantly.

Robert Cobb Kennedy, America's first "home-grown" terrorist, became the last Confederate soldier executed by the Union during the Civil War.

On **March 25, 1965**, civil rights activists led
by Martin Luther King, Jr.
successfully completed their 4-day, 50-mile march from
Selma to Montgomery, Alabama.

WAYNE WINTERTON, PH.D.

MARCH 26
Mascot extraordinaire

Old Abe
May 1861 (Flambeau River, WI) – **Mar 26, 1881** (Washington, DC)

A ROADSIDE MARKER about Old Abe stands at a wayside pull-off on Highway 178, just south of its intersection with 150th Avenue (Barn Road), Jim Falls, Wisconsin.

OLD ABE, THE WAR EAGLE

"This wayside is part of the old McCann farm, childhood home of Old Abe, the War Eagle. In the spring of 1861 a band of hungry Chippewa came to the McCann farm and traded a young eagle for corn. The eagle became a family pet. When Company C, Eighth Wisconsin was organized at Eau Claire for Civil War duty, the crippled Dan McCann offered his eagle's services as mascot, feeling that 'someone from the family ought to go.' On October 12, 1861, the Eagle Regiment started for the front. In action, Old Abe spread his wings and screamed encouragement to his men. The louder the noise of battle, the louder and fiercer were his screams. The eagle served with the regiment in 42 skirmishes and battles and lost only a few feathers. After three years' service, Old Abe was formally presented to the State of Wisconsin on September 26, 1864. A room was equipped for him in the Capitol and a man employed to care for him. His last public appearance occurred at the National Encampment of the G.A.R. (Grand Army of the Republic) in Milwaukee in 1880, where he and General U.S. Grant were honored guests. After a brief illness, Old Abe died March 26, 1881."

In the spring of 1861, Old Abe, who was just an eaglet at the time, was inside an aerie at the very top of a pine tree near the north fork of the Flambeau River near the town of Eau Claire, Wisconsin. Two young Chippewa boys spotted the aerie and chopped the tree down to capture the eaglets. Unfortunately, one of the eaglets died when the tree fell, but the other survived and the boys took it to their village where it became a pet.

Toward the end of the summer, one of the boys who had captured the eaglet, Chief Sky, and his father, Bee Thunder, made a trip down the Chippewa River to do some trading and they had the young eagle with them. At Jim Falls, Wisconsin they met Daniel McCann who traded a bushel of corn for the bird.

At the same time that McCann took possession of the two-month old eagle, a company of Civil War volunteers were being recruited into the 8th Wisconsin Infantry.

McCann approached some of the newly trained soldiers and asked if they were interested in purchasing the eagle for a mascot. A civilian spoke up and purchased the eagle for five dollars. He then turned around and gave the bird to the military unit for their mascot. The unit named the eagle, "Old Abe" in honor of the President, and the newly formed company became the Eau Claire Eagles.

Old Abe was fitted with a red, white, and blue ribbon around its neck, to which was attached a rose-shaped medal. Rigged atop a pole was a perch so Old Abe could stand next to the flag for parades. It wasn't long before the mascot was full-grown, sporting a six-and-a-half-foot wingspan, and large round, clear, intelligent eyes.

Once, during a march through a now-forgotten town, an irreverent spectator called Old Abe a buzzard. Several men of the 8th Wisconsin stepped out of rank and convinced the spectator that disrespect toward their mascot would not be tolerated. The irreverent spectator remained crumpled on the ground rubbing multiple knots about his head and wiping the blood from his face until all of the men of the 8th Wisconsin had passed by.

On another occasion, when he shared the Guest of Honor position at the head table alongside Generals Ulysses S. Grant and William Tecumseh Sherman, Old Abe attempted to bite both men. The host of the occasion explained, to the delight of the gathering, that Old Abe never did cotton much to generals. Even the generals took Old Abe's conduct in stride, saying there was nothing they could do about it, as he outranked both of them.

In 1881, sixteen years after the end of the Civil War, Old Abe was still going strong when a fire broke out in the basement of the Wisconsin Capitol Building where he resided. He sounded the alarm and the fire was extinguished, but not before the country's most famous eagle had inhaled large quantities of thick black smoke.

On March 26, 1881, despite the best efforts of veterinarians and physicians alike, and while being held by George Gilles, his caretaker, Old Abe's spirit soared toward the great aerie in the sky.

Six months later, a local taxidermist restored his feathered remains to his once handsome self and he looked superb in his glass case inside the rotunda of the Wisconsin State Capitol Building. Unfortunately, on February 26, 1904, a fire burned the Capitol Building to the ground, destroying the once glorious eagle with it.

There is one thing not generally known about Old Abe and it is this. Old Abe wasn't guy at all, but a lady eagle, which makes one wonder what it was she had against the two generals, Grant and Sherman, since like herself, they had both fought on the side of the Union, once again proving it's never easy to understand the mind of a lady.

"The house of delusions is cheap to build
but drafty to live in."
A. E. Housman (**Mar 26, 1859** – Apr 30, 1936) Poet

MARCH 27

First man in space

Yuri Gagarin

Mar 9, 1934 (Klushino, USSR) – **Mar 27, 1968** (Novosyolovo, USSR)

YURI GAGARIN WAS a small child who grew up to be a less-than-average height man at five-foot-two inches tall. His was a difficult start in life and no one could have predicted that one day he would have a profound effect on the American space program, and even more than that, on the world.

Yuri was born in 1934 to parents Alexey Ivanovich and Anna Timofeyevna Gagarin, workers at a Russian communal farm in the village of Klushino, where Alexey was a construction worker and Anna a milkmaid. Yuri was the third of the Gagarin's four children.

In 1941, at the beginning of World War II, the residents of Klushino felt the nasty brunt of the Nazi war machine when the German army commandeered many of their homes for offices and sleeping quarters.

Overnight, the Gagarin's went from a comfortable home to a small, ten-by-ten foot mud hut on their property. The hut barely slept the family's two adults and four children, and inside space for food and clothing was minimal or nonexistent.

The Gagarin's lived in that hut for twenty-one months, at which time the Nazi occupation of their village ended. But, just as the Nazi's were ready to leave Klushino, they lined up the Gagarin's four children, in order of age: Valentin, Zoya (female), Yuri, and Boris, and against the desperate pleadings of the Gagarin family, Valentin and Zoya were forced into a truck and shipped to a slave labor camp in Poland. Yuri remained with his parents, likely because of his deceivingly small stature, and Boris, because he was too young.

Moving ahead, at the age of sixteen Yuri apprenticed as a metalworker and went for training at the Saratov Industrial Technical School where he became a tractor mechanic. At Saratov, he volunteered for weekend training as a Soviet air cadet where he learned to fly a biplane and later a Russian Yak-18 trainer.

After Saratov, he went into the Soviet military and ended up at the First Chkalov Air Force Pilot's School, soloing in a MiG-15 fighter in 1957.

In 1960, the Russians were searching for men for the Soviet Space Program, and Gagarin became one of the program's first six cadets. They were known as the *Sochi Six*.

As potential cosmonauts (the equivalent of America's astronauts), Gagarin passed all of the physical endurance and psychological tests well enough to become one of two finalists for making the world's first space flight. Gagarin's size was a key selection factor due to the limited size of the cockpit of Russia's *Vostok,* the spacecraft that would propel the first man into space.

Gagarin received the nod, and it was he inside Vostok 1 when it launched from Russia's *Baikonur Cosmodrome* and entered space and the history books on April 12, 1961.

After exiting Earth's atmosphere, Gagarin made a single orbit around the earth, reaching a speed of 17,560 miles per hour. At the conclusion of the orbit, the Vostok 1 reentered the atmosphere and began its tumble to earth.

At about four miles above the earth, Gagarin ejected and parachuted to safety, landing near a Russian farmhouse where, clad in an orange spacesuit and wearing what was unmistakably a space helmet, he terrified two women until he could convince them that he too, was Russian.

The next day, the headline of the communist newspaper, *The Daily Worker,* proclaimed:

A Communist in Space
Soviet Union Wild with Joy at First Trip Outside this World

Below the headline appeared an article titled, *Now for a Man on the Moon.* The article opened with the following statement by a Professor Lovell, "There might be a man on the moon in four or five years, and American chances of getting there first are negligible."

It didn't matter in which language the newspaper was printed, the message was the same, "Russia Puts a Man in Space," adorned with a photograph of the handsome young Russian Cosmonaut, Yuri Gagarin.

The *Huntsville (Alabama) Times* headline of April 12, 1961 was only three words long, "Man Enters Space," followed by an article clearly expressing the disappointment of America's citizens: "So Close, Yet So Far, Sighs Cape," the "Cape" of course, meaning Cape Canaveral, the nerve center of America's space program in 1961.

Then, the *coup de grâce*, as far as America's space community was concerned, was another article in America's newspapers, this one carrying the reaction of the country's foremost name in space science, Wernher Von Braun. "Von Braun's Reaction: To Keep Up, U.S.A. Must Run Like Hell," and it might have been that headline and article that caught the attention of America's newest president, John F. Kennedy, who had been sworn in as the nation's 35th president only four months earlier.

In a Joint Session of Congress on May 25, 1961, President Kennedy stated:

> "First, I believe that this nation should commit itself to achieving the goal, before this decade is out, of landing a man on the Moon and returning him safely to the Earth. No single space project in this period will be more impressive to mankind, or more important for the long-range exploration of space; and none will be so difficult or expensive to accomplish."

It was clear to the new president that America's prestige was at stake, and he wasn't about to see it diminished on his watch.

Americans and American expertise came together in an effort to assure that President Kennedy's vision did not fall short. At least some of the credit should go to the small Russian cosmonaut who had once lived in a mud hut, and who showed the world what is possible when a nation and its people get behind a project with a common goal.

America's space program did come to life and in keeping with President Kennedy's dream, America landed Neil Armstrong on the moon, on July 20, 1969, and the country had done it before the end of the decade just as the President had predicted.

Yuri Gagarin died in 1968 at the age of thirty-four, during a routine training flight in a MiG-15UTI fighter plane. In recognition

WAYNE WINTERTON, PH.D.

for his achievements as a Russian Cosmonaut, America's National Aeronautics and Space Administration erected at its original spaceflight headquarters in Houston, a statue of Gagarin, which was dedicated on October 15, 2012.

"A committee is a group of men who keep minutes
and waste hours."
Milton Berle (July 12, 1908 – **Mar 27, 2002**) Comedian

MARCH 28
Hero of the Soviet Union

Marina Raskova
Mar 28, 1912 (Moscow, Russia) – Jan 4, 1943 (Saratov, Russia)

MARINA, THE DAUGHTER of Mikhail Mikhailovna, a Russian opera singer, and his wife Anna, a schoolteacher, was one of Russia's most decorated female aviators during World War II, and among her honors, in 1939 she received the Soviet Union's highest military honor, "Hero of the Soviet Union." Such an honor does not come lightly in the Soviet Union, and that award presented to Marina and two other women on the same day, made the trio the first women so honored.

Marina has appeared on Soviet postage stamps, twice, once in 1939, and a second time in 2012, the latter in observance of the 100th anniversary of her birth. There's also a square in Moscow named after her; and until it closed its doors in 1997, there was the M. M. Raskova Higher Air Force School in Tambov, Russia.

Marina was seven when her father died after struck by a motorcyclist. In school, she studied drama and voice, but finding vocal studies stressful, she switched to chemistry and graduated from high school in 1929. Because her mother needed help to meet family expenses, Marina went to work as a chemist in a dye factory.

At the dye factory, she met Sergey Raskov, married, and in 1930 gave birth to a daughter.

In 1931, and for the next ten years, her life was a whirlwind. She quit the dye factory and went to work as a draftsman in the Aero Navigation Lab of Russia's Air Force Academy. She learned navigation and piloting skills and in 1933, became the first woman navigator in the Soviet Air Force and the first female instructor at Russia's Zhukovski Air Academy.

In 1935, she and Sergey divorced, and she added an "a" to Raskov, thus becoming Marina Raskova.

She taught at the Air Academy (1937-1938) and while there, she set a host of long-distance flight records.

In 1938, with Marina as navigator, she and two other female aviators set an international women's record for distance. However, experiencing poor visibility on the return flight, and the crew's inability to locate the airport, Marina decided to parachute to safety. Only moments after Marina exited the plane, the pilot saw through the soup and landed the plane safely. Marina, however, spent ten days without food or water before finding her way to the airport. It was because of this flight, the new women's record and the stressful low visibility return, that the Russian government presented the women with the "Hero of the Soviet Union" award.

On December 18, 1940, Adolph Hitler authorized Operation Barbarossa against the Soviet Union. It would be the largest invasion in the history of warfare. Imagine four million German troops lined along a 1,864-mile border, supported by 600,000 motor vehicles and 750,000 horses. Although the invasion ultimately failed, its initial victories were devastating with three million Russian prisoners taken and the Soviet military in disarray. It was under those circumstances that Marina Raskova began her greatest hour.

She met with Joseph Stalin and proposed establishing three combat-ready regiments of top flight Russian women aviators, including a total of 1,200 female officers, pilots, navigators, ground crews, and mechanics, and to complement the above womanpower, she wanted ninety aircraft and the authority to slice through Russian red tape like a knife through over-cooked borscht.

Stalin decided, wisely, that he had little choice. Much of his military had been decimated during Operation Barbarossa, and what little was left was in shambles with marginal leadership.

He gave Raskova the green light.

In a matter of months, she had put into place what would have taken government bureaucrats at least four years to do, and even more time would have been lost if she'd had to deal with self-serving labor unions and corrupt political hacks.

Raskova's three combat-equipped regiments consisted of the 586th Fighter Aviation Regiment; the 46th Taman Guards Night Bomber Aviation Regiment; and the 125th Guards Bomber Aviation Regiment, the latter being the Regiment that Marina would command until her death in January of 1943.

Although Marina's 125th Guards were responsible for 1,134 missions and the dropping of 980 ton of bombs, it was another of her regiments that truly caught the imagination and respect of the enemy, the 46th Taman Guards Night Bombers.

The 46th flew biplanes, slow, aging aircraft with dual wings, one above the other, that were like giant gnats and mosquitos that buzzed and bombed the hell out of specific German targets. Capable of carrying only six bombs at a time, they typically flew 15 to 18 missions a night, and therein rested the magic of what the Germans came to call the "Nachthexen" (the night witches), and from the 46th Taman Guards Night Bombers alone, came 24 new Heroes of the Soviet Union.

Following Martina Raskova's death on January 4, 1943, when her aircraft crashed near the Volga River, her ashes received a special place of repose, entombed inside the Kremlin Wall on Red Square.

Following her death the United States honored her life by naming one of its World War II Liberty Ships in her honor, the *SS Marina Raskova*. Thus, Marina Raskova continued to serve the cause of freedom, ferrying American warriors to Europe to fight, returning from each trip with the remains of American heroes for return to their families.

"Love people, not things; use things, not people."
Spencer W. Kimball (**Mar 28, 1895** – Nov 5, 1985)
12th President, LDS Church

MARCH 29

Drilled America's first successful oil well

Edwin L. Drake

Mar 29, 1819 (Greenville, NY) – Nov 9, 1880 (Bethlehem, PA)

EDWIN LAURENTINE DRAKE grew up in New York and Vermont, but restless at nineteen, he left home to seek his fortune. When the fortune wasn't forthcoming, he had the good sense to find a job, which he did, going to work in New Haven, Connecticut as a railway clerk, conductor, and express agent.

Around 1854 he experienced an unspecified medical problem for which the railroad company let him go, but allowed him to keep the free travel privileges he had as an employee. Those who knew Edwin Drake, described him as friendly, a convincing conversationalist, and when focused on a project, any project, a doggedly stubborn guy.

The freshly unemployed Drake, now spending much of his time leaning against the wall inside New Haven's Tontine Hotel, met James M. Townsend, a wealthy financier-speculator and long-time hotel resident. The two exchanged pleasantries, visited, and the talkative Drake and the well-heeled banker hit it off. By the end of the evening, Townsend had hired Drake as an agent of his newly formed Pennsylvania Oil Company of Connecticut.

Earlier in the day, Townsend had read a report from a professor who claimed that rock oil, as he called it, had value, and that it could be refined and used for lighting and lubrication. Drake's job was to learn what he could about the nasty oil seepages that dotted the landscape around Titusville, Pennsylvania.

In December 1857 and using his railroad privileges, Drake traveled to Titusville and to insure immediate credibility, he had the forethought to send a few letters to himself before he left. The letters, addressed to "Colonel E. L. Drake" and carrying a New Haven postmark, arrived at the Titusville Post Office ahead of Drake. As soon as he stepped off the train and picked up his mail, everyone in town knew the "Colonel" had arrived.

The first thing Drake did was to have some locals show him the seepages that Townsend mentioned. They were nasty, smelly, bubbling pits of oily sludge that ran alongside Oil Creek, an appropriately named slow flowing body of water nearby. It was a scene unchanged from what it may have looked like ten thousand years earlier.

When the locals learned the Colonel was interested in extracting and collecting the nasty stuff, they hooted, poked fun at him, and when he was beyond earshot, they called him "Crazy Drake."

Drake leased a parcel of land along Oil Creek and hired some workers to dig a few trenches that he hoped would drain the oil into collection pits. While his men were digging, he returned to New Haven, reported to Townsend that he had secured a lease for a promising extraction operation, and from that conversation was born the Seneca Oil Company.

Drake returned to Titusville, this time taking his wife and kids with him, and the little town became their home.

When the trench-digging operation didn't pan out, Drake changed the operation from trenching to drilling, paying his workers $1.25 each for the first 100 feet they drilled, and $1.00 per foot afterward. The only thing the operation produced was blisters, and the so-called hometown experts grinned and told the Colonel, "We told you so!"

Undaunted, Drake bought a steam engine to power the drill, but by fall, the unstable sides of the well hole were caving in. Drake halted drilling and waited for spring.

The next year (1859), the stubborn Colonel, still funded by Townsend, had a new plan. He had a derrick built that the locals derisively called "Drake's Folly." He also constructed a well house and an out-building to house the steam boiler and engine, and he resumed drilling.

The effort produced only water.

Then he had ten-foot, cast-iron pipes, one on top of the other, driven into the ground.

One day, as he started to drive the next in his series of pipes, the pipe at the greatest depth struck bedrock.

Looking the situation over, Drake had his men pump the water out of the pipe and the hole. Then, for whatever reason, he decided to insert the drill inside the pipe, lower the drill to the bedrock, and while continuing to pump water out of the hole, he began drilling into the bedrock.

Ol' Crazy Drake, it seemed to the folks of Titusville, just didn't know when to quit, and as long as Townsend and the investors kept sending money, Drake kept up his efforts.

And guess what!

More nothing!

Not so much as a teaspoon of oil, not that the townsfolk of Titusville thought it would be worth anything even if ol' Crazy Drake found oil. The stuff was just black waste from God's good earth. That's all.

By the middle of the summer, all of Townsend's investors had bailed, leaving only himself and Drake in the effort.

By the middle of August, even Townsend called it quits. Disheartened, he sent Drake a letter telling him to pay the bills, shut down the operation, and return to New Haven.

Drake read Townsend's letter and did what all good self-proclaimed Colonels do.

He pretended he hadn't seen it.

He continued to work the operation and a couple of weeks later, August 27, 1859, and seventy feet beneath the Earth's surface, the drill slipped crazily into an unseen underground crevice, bringing the day's work to an abrupt halt. The following day, August 28, as the men arrived to resume work, it was evident that something had happened while they were sleeping; the pipe was full of black liquid.

Colonel Drake and his men had done it. They had struck oil and the Pennsylvania Oil Rush was about to begin.

John D. Rockefeller would make millions, but that's another story.

Time would pass and Edwin L. Drake, the man whose dogged determination led to the discovery of Pennsylvania oil, lost all of his money on bad investments. Had he protected his oil-drilling methods, it might have been different, but as too many others have learned, there is no future in "what if's."

The man, who had drilled America's first oil well, was broke.

In 1873, fifty-four years old and destitute, the Pennsylvania legislature voted an annuity of $1,500 yearly to Colonel Drake, whose one-time dogged determination had founded an industry.

On **March 29, 1806**, Congress authorized surveying to start on the 620-mile 'Cumberland Road' connecting the Potomac and Ohio Rivers, which in essence became America's first federal highway.

WAYNE WINTERTON, PH.D.

MARCH 30
Joined together for life

Rosa and Josefa Blažek
Jan 20, 1878 (Skrejšov, Bohemia) – **Mar 30, 1922** (Chicago, IL)

R OSA AND JOSEFA Blažek were twins, conjoined at their backsides. Although a cartilaginous ligament at the base of the spine connects most conjoined twins, as with the famous Siamese twins, Eng and Chang Bunker, Rosa and Josefa were fused together at the 9th thoracic vertebra, making separation impossible.

Mother Blažek, a superstitious woman, consulted a local medical woman regarding what to do. You can draw your own conclusion here, but the medicine woman advised the parents to withhold nourishment for eight days, which they did. Somehow, the girls survived and the parents considered it a sign from God that the girls were on earth for a purpose, but what purpose?

Before they could walk, they had become popular exhibits at small town fairs. Whether the parents profited from the display of their unusual daughters is unknown.

By the time they were two, they had learned to walk, positioning themselves against each other, stepping first with their front legs, then their back legs. Josefa's left leg was considerably shorter than her right, a problem corrected with an orthopedic shoe.

Of the two girls, Rosa was the stronger, both from a personality standpoint and physically, and less deformed than Josefa. As they grew into their teen years, Rosa was witty and would banter freely with those who came to visit, while Josefa remained quiet and introspective. They also learned to play the xylophone and violin and were proficient enough to play duets, amazing their audiences.

In their late teens, they developed different tastes in food and personal habits. One would often sleep while the other was awake and they were hungry and thirsty at different times. Rosa, the dominant personality, could think about something and Josefa would do it. If Rosa wanted to go somewhere, all she had to do was think about it and Josefa would step forward, and from that first step, they would walk accordant with each other.

In promoting the appearances of the sisters, theater posters, particularly those from places like the *Gaiety Theater* in France emphasized their sexuality, portraying them with skimpy tops and bare midriffs, shocking at the time, or wearing ultra-tight corsets and little else.

In 1893, the Blažek sisters traveled to the United States and were successful headliners at the 1893 *World Columbian Exposition* in Chicago. Afterward, they returned to Europe always looking for ways to increase interest in their act, but as they approached their thirties, public interest dwindled and they faded from the limelight.

That was until 1909 when Rosa, now thirty-one, announced she was pregnant. Suddenly the Blažek's were headline news. Speculation was rampant as to who had fathered the child. There were rumors circulated that a soldier named Franz Dvorak was the responsible party, or perhaps, their theatrical agent was the father.

Because of Rosa's delicate condition the twins made no public appearances and on April 16, 1910, it was announced that little Franz had entered the world. Almost as fast as he had arrived, the little guy became the star of a new traveling show called the *Son of Two Mothers.*

After a successful tour in Europe, the sisters decided it was time to make a permanent move to the United States, and they did, settling in a Czech community in Chicago. Although many believed they had already amassed a fortune, the sisters set their sights on making it big in Vaudeville.

The dream, however, was cut short when Rosa fell ill to influenza, and just as she was on the mend, Josefa fell victim to the same illness. On March 22, 1922, with both ladies weakened from the illness and doctors at Chicago's West End Hospital uncertain as to what to do next, Rosa fell into a coma.

That's when Frank, who introduced himself as Rosa and Josefa's hitherto unknown brother, showed up. At the hospital, he took immediate charge of the sisters. When the doctors suggested that Josefa's only chance would be a separation, Frank took issue, claiming that Rosa would insist on dying with her sister.

On March 30, 1922, Josefa Blažek died first, followed twelve minutes later by Rosa.

Their deaths opened a Pandora's Box of medical and legal questions. There was no will so who would inherit the Blažek fortune? Brother Frank? Twelve-year-old Franz, Rosa's son?

The issues sparked numerous debates.

Was Franz, who had been billed as the "son of two mothers," truly the biological son of both women? If so, he would be heir to both fortunes.

Was Frank, who showed up just in time to be there when Rosa and Josefa approached the Pearly Gates, truly their biological brother? If so, he would be heir to both fortunes.

To clear up the question, Frank ordered an autopsy to settle the question as to which of his sisters had conceived and given birth to Franz.

Three well-respected physicians performed an autopsy on April 2, 1922. They determined that Rosa and Josefa's uteri were independent of each other, proof that Rosa alone could have given birth to Franz. But then the bad news, if you're Franz; or the good news, if you're Frank. During the autopsy, the doctors found that neither Rosa nor Josefa had ever been pregnant. Frank was thrilled beyond words.

Rosa and Josefa were cremated and their ashes placed at the Bohemian National Cemetery.

Attention now focused on the sisters' fortune, estimated by some as upward of $200,000 or more. Imagine now, the disappointment on Frank's face when he learned the actual amount of his inheritance was $400 and change.

An investigation found that little Franz was from a Chicago orphanage. His supposed birth had been a planned publicity stunt to launch a second career for the Blažek sisters.

Interestingly, according to a contributor to the *Find-A-Grave* website, the Krasca Funeral Home that handled the cremation, retrieved the ashes from the Bohemian National Cemetery on April 22, 1922, and gave them to Frank, the man who claimed to have been the sisters' brother.

So, who was Frank? Could he have actually been Rosa and Josefa's brother?

Why else would he want their ashes?

"No man is so old as to believe he cannot
live one more year."
Seán O'Casey (**Mar 30, 1880** – Sept 18, 1964) Dramatist

WAYNE WINTERTON, PH.D.

MARCH 31
The Galveston Giant

Jack Johnson
Mar 31, 1878 (Galveston, TX) – June 10, 1946 (Raleigh, NC)

JOHN "JACK" JOHNSON was born in 1878, the third of nine children to former slaves, Henry and Tina Johnson. Thirty years into the future (1908), he would become the first African-American to win the world heavyweight boxing title. He would do it by defeating the reigning champion, Tommy Burns, the first fighter to agree to a championship bout with a Negro boxer.

Johnson's win against Burns, however, wasn't a satisfying one to the white public who defiantly held it impossible that a black man could defeat a boxer of Burns' stature. Burns, some were contending, was still suffering from the effects of the flu, weighing in at 168 pounds, well below his usual 190 pounds. Moreover, there was the way the fight ended. The fight, cut short when the police, not the referee, stopped the fight in the 14th round, the referee afterward awarding the fight to Johnson as a knockout.

Johnson needed a decisive win to gain the respect of the public, and the chance would come.

Johnson, like many youngsters of his era, got off to a tough start. He dropped out of school early. At twelve, he hopped a freight train to get out of Galveston. When discovered hiding in a boxcar, railway security guards beat him severely before advising him against hopping a freight in the future.

Then came a job in a carriage-shop where the owner, an ex-boxer, gave Johnson a few pointers. Later, on the Galveston docks, he honed his skills by fighting other dockworkers for money tossed in a jar by coworkers.

In 1898, he entered the ring for the first time as a professional boxer and made short work of a fighter named Charley Brooks, defeating him in Round 2 of a fifteen rounder. For the next several years, he fought numerous fights, winning most.

In 1901, he knocked out Joe Choynski, an experienced heavyweight, but both he and Choynski were thrown in jail because prizefighting was illegal in Texas at the time. With bail set at $5,000, well beyond the means of either, they agreed to spar in the jail cell to the appreciation of large crowds who came to watch. After twenty-three days, a grand jury refused to indict either and they were set free.

In 1903, Johnson defeated Denver Ed Martin in a 20-rounder for the "World Colored Heavyweight Championship," a title he held for 5 years 3 months, vacating the title in 1908 when, as described up front, he defeated Tommy Burns for the World Heavyweight Title.

Also, as mentioned earlier, the white public didn't take kindly to Johnson's win over Tommy Burns and racial animosity ran deep, with whites calling for a *Great White Hope* to wrest the title from the black man.

During the year that followed, Johnson received more press than all other notable black men in the country combined, much of it peppered with racist comments. Take this sentence for instance, from a newspaper editorial, "If the black man wins, thousands and thousands of his ignorant brothers will misinterpret his victory as justifying claims to much more than mere physical equality with their white neighbors."

In 1909, Johnson fought mostly exhibition matches, each opponent touted as a *Great White Hope*, but each losing to the champion. Then, in 1910, the former undefeated heavyweight champion James J. Jeffries, who planned to stay out of the discussion, was enticed to come out of retirement when offered an incredible $120,000 to fight Johnson.

Jeffries, who hadn't fought in six years, began a rigorous regimen to work himself back into shape. Johnson, on the other hand, was in excellent shape, having fought continuously since his first professional bout. The fight took place in Reno, Nevada on July 4, 1910 with an audience of 20,000. Outside the ring, tensions were running high. Inside, guns were prohibited and alcohol was banned. Nevada gamblers had placed the odds at 10-7 in favor of Jeffries.

However, the aging Jeffries, knocked down twice for the first time in his career, was unable to take control of the fight and just before the bell sounded for the 15th round, Jeffries manager tossed in the towel. After the match, the classy Jeffries told the press, "I could never have whipped Johnson at my best – not in a thousand years." The fight was over and there would be no *Great White Hope* to defeat the powerful Jack Johnson. Another classy boxer, the great John L. Sullivan, told the world that the match had been "played fairly at all times and fought fairly."

Jack Johnson's personal life was more difficult for him to master than the pugilists he fought in the ring. He was married three times, each time to a white woman, a highly unacceptable act to the people of the era in which he lived.

In 1913, an all-white jury convicted Johnson of violating the Mann Act, a law prohibiting the transporting of women across state lines for immoral (prostitution) purposes. In Johnson's case, the white woman he was with when arrested for crossing a state line, was a woman he was dating and would later marry.

Johnson died in 1946 in a car crash on U.S. Highway 1 after angrily speeding away from a Franklinton, North Carolina restaurant that refused to serve him.

Since 2004, Senator John McCain (R-AZ) and Representative Peter King (R-NY) have introduced legislation asking for a presidential pardon for Jack Johnson. President George W. Bush failed to act on the legislation during his term in office, and thus far (2015) President Barack Obama has failed to act as well.

On **March 31, 1951**, the UNIVAC was America's
first commercially built computer.
The size of a two-car garage, it was purchased
by the U.S. Census Bureau for $159,000.

APRIL 1
Fool me once, and . . . .

April Fools' Day
April 1st occurs during odd years only. April Fools!

O N APRIL 1, 1950, the sleepy town of Hot Springs, New Mexico officially changed its name to Truth or Consequences, New Mexico. Here's how it happened.

In March of 1950, to promote the tenth anniversary of the popular radio game show, *Truth or Consequences,* host Ralph Edwards promised to broadcast an episode of the program from the first town in America that would rename itself after the show. The citizens of Hot Springs, 150 miles south of Albuquerque, put the question on a ballot and voted 1,294 to 295 in favor of renaming the town, it did, and Edwards kept his promise.

The broadcast took place on April 1, 1950, leading some radio listeners to think the whole thing was an April Fools' stunt. But here we are, over sixty years later, and the central New Mexico resort town is still "Truth or Consequences," although most everyone in New Mexico, including postal employees, simply refer to it as "T or C" to save time and ink.

Ever since that broadcast in 1950, the town has celebrated a Fiesta, a wonderful throwback to small town America, held in Ralph Edward's Park the first weekend in May. The Fiesta is complete with a parade and a beauty pageant. Although there was nothing in the original deal that said he would do as much, Ralph Edwards showed up in Truth or Consequences for every Fiesta from 1951 until 1999 when illness overcame his ability to travel.

Edwards died in 2005 of heart failure at the age of ninety-two.

Although April 1, 1950, was no joke for Ralph Edwards or the citizenry of Hot Springs, it is a day of pranks, hopefully sane and harmless pranks, and hopefully always in good taste.

The origin of the day is cloudy, but here is one theory as to how April 1 became April Fool's Day.

It all has to do with the changeover from the use of the Julian calendar to the current Gregorian calendar in 1582.

When the Julian calendar was in use, each year began on March 25.

When Pope Gregory issued the edict that replaced the Julian calendar with the Gregorian calendar, the new calendar called for the year to begin on January 1. As you might expect, switching from one calendar system to another in the 1500s was no easy task. Many people refused to make the change. Or, just as likely, they never got the word and continued to celebrate March 25 as the beginning of the "new year" with its traditional "new year" celebration that lasted for eight days, ending on April 1.

According to tradition, those slow to adopt the new calendar were made to feel the sting of embarrassment by being sent on "Fool's Errands," making them "April's Fool," or if more than one fool was fooled, as "April's Fools." Over time, the day became "April Fools' Day," and it has become a day of fun for those who delight in catering to the gullibility in all of us.

To wit:

On April 1, 1957, British television played a hoax on its viewers by showing a video of Swiss peasant women harvesting spaghetti from trees. The images provided the backdrop for a story on the eradication of the dreaded "spaghetti weevil" by Swiss scientists. Following the airing of the report, viewers called the station wanting to know where they might buy their own spaghetti trees and asking for suggestions on cultivation.

On April 1, 1996, the Taco Bell Corporation took out a full-page ad that appeared in six major newspapers to announce the company's purchase of the Liberty Bell. Not only had the Bell been purchased, according to the announcement, it was soon to be renamed the Taco Liberty Bell. Outraged citizens called the National Historic Park in Philadelphia to express their anger. Taco Bell followed their original announcement by assuring the public that the historic Bell would remain accessible to the public, and that, "While some may find this controversial, we hope our move will prompt other corporations to take similar action to do their part to reduce the country's debt."

When asked about the sale of the Liberty Bell, White House press secretary Mike McCurry couldn't resist, replying that in addition to the sale of the Liberty Bell, the Lincoln Memorial had just been sold to the Ford Motor Company and was in the process of being renamed the "Lincoln Mercury Memorial."

And what about the full-page ad that appeared in the April 1, 1998, edition of *USA Today* that announced the introduction of a "Left-Handed Whopper," a hamburger specifically designed for the thirty-two million American lefties who have had to "struggle in the past with right-handed hamburgers."

The ad went on to say that, "all condiments were being rotated 180 degrees, thereby redistributing the weight of the sandwich so the bulk of the condiments will skew to the left, thereby reducing the amount of lettuce and other toppings from spilling out the right side of the burger."

And the list goes on.

"Beware of the first one through the door with
his or her view of events."
Lynn Engdahl (**Apr 1, 1938** -) Rancher, educator

APRIL 2

'That damned movie!'

Buddy Ebsen

(Christian Ludolf Ebsen, Jr.)

Apr 2, 1908 (Belleville, IL) – July 6, 2003 (Torrance, CA)

BUDDY EBSEN WAS one of those incredibly talented performers that never seemed to wear thin. He could dance and sing and he was a capable performer in virtually every role he was offered, that was, except one! That role literally made him so sick that he almost lost his life and afterwards rarely referred to the movie by name, calling it just "that damned movie!" Any idea which movie?

Born Christian Ludolf Ebsen, Jr., Buddy Ebsen was cut from the same cloth as George Burns, Mickey Rooney, and Abe Vigoda (okay, so Vigoda only looks old), but like Burns and Rooney, Ebsen's remarkable talent sustained a career that spanned over seventy years.

Buddy, and his sister Vilma, were natural-born performers who learned to dance at a very early age from their father, a professional dancer who operated the *Ebsen School of Dance* in Orlando, Florida.

By 1928, Buddy and Vilma were performing in Vaudeville and supper clubs as *The Baby Astaires,* a crowd-pleasing seemingly lighter than air dancing couple. That same year, they auditioned and won a dancing spot in the chorus of Broadway's 1928 hit, *Whoopee!*

In 1930, they performed their own choreographed version of *Ain't Misbehavin'* and according to newspaper columnist and radio commentator Walter Winchell, he couldn't believe what he was seeing. The sparkling, high-energy dance absolutely mesmerized Winchell and the audience. The following day, Winchell literally put the Ebsen's on the show-business map with a rave review of their performance in the *New York Daily Mirror.*

The review led to parts in Broadway's *Flying Colors* (1932), where they introduced the song, *A Shine on Your Shoes,* and two years later in *The Ziegfeld Follies of 1934,* where they helped to popularize the song: *I Like the Likes of You.*

In 1936, MGM approached the brother and sister act, gave them a screen test and awarded them a two-year contract at $1,500 a week, big money at the time. That same year they played Ted and Sally in the movie *Broadway Melody of 1936,* and helped to popularize, *On a Sunday Afternoon,* with a stunning dance routine. It was one of Vilma's last performances as she left the stage to settle down, marry, have children, and to take over operation of the family run Ebsen School of Dance, now located in Pacific Palisades, California.

Buddy however, was never able to get the entertainment bug out of his blood and he went on to become a major Hollywood star. Still with MGM, he appeared with Frances Langford in *Born to Dance* (1936), that same year he was one of Shirley Temple's dancing partners in *Captain January,* and in 1938, he played an ex-vaudevillian in *Broadway Melody of 1938,* starring Judy Garland.

In 1938, the head of MGM, Louis B. Mayer offered Buddy a lucrative "exclusive contract," but Buddy turned him down. From Ebsen's point-of-view, he didn't want to be limited to an exclusive contract, although most actors at the time would have given their left arm to sign such a document. The powerful Louis B. Mayer, on the other hand, felt snubbed by Ebsen and he was furious. He told Ebsen that he would never work in Hollywood again!

Mayer was wrong, and within a year (1939), Warner Brothers offered Ebsen the role of the Scarecrow in *The Wizard of Oz*, playing opposite his former co-star, Judy Garland. Another co-star was Ray Bolger, just offered the part of the Tin Woodman. Bolger, however, had grown up watching, and emulating, his childhood idol, Fred Stone, who had been the Scarecrow during a long run of the *Wizard of Oz* on Broadway back in 1902.

Bolger convinced the movie's producer, Mervyn LeRoy, to allow him to change parts with Ebsen so he could do on the silver screen what he had seen Fred Stone do on Broadway. When asked, Ebsen said he didn't care, even thinking the Tin Woodman was a better role.

Ten days into the filming, however, Ebsen began to suffer a severe reaction to the aluminum powder applied to his body to give him the metallic look of the Tinman. Without realizing it, Ebsen had been inhaling the powder. So much that it was coating his lungs. Hospitalized in critical condition, Ebsen required placement in an "iron lung," a mechanical ventilator that enabled a person to breathe in the absence of normal muscle control.

The part of the Tinman went to actor Jack Haley, who assumed Ebsen had been fired since the studio never bothered to inform him of the latter's hospitalization. The studio, somewhat to their credit, replaced the inhalable aluminum powder with an aluminum paste and Haley never experienced the ill effects that nearly took Ebsen's life.

Until Ebsen's dying day, although he outlived every major cast member of *The Wizard of Oz* by at least 16 years, he complained of experiencing lung problems from his involvement in "that damned movie!"

"If you shut up the truth and bury it underground,
it will but grow."
Émile Zola (**Apr 2, 1840** – Sept 29, 1902) Author

APRIL 3
You can't coach people unless you love them.

Eddie Robinson
Feb 13, 1919 (Jackson, LA) – **Apr 3, 2007** (Ruston, LA)

R OBINSON WAS THE head football coach at Grambling State University for fifty-six years. When he retired in 1997, his teams had won 408 games, more than any other football coach in the history of the game.

Robinson's record of 408 wins was eclipsed in 2011 when Joe Paterno's Penn State Nittany Lions defeated Illinois, giving Paterno 409 wins. However, a scandal at Penn State a year later, in which Paterno looked the other way while his friend Jerry Sandusky was sexually abusing young boys, caused the NCAA to vacate 111 of Paterno's victories, reestablishing Robinson as America's winningest coach.

In 1940, after earning a bachelor's degree from tiny Leland College in Baker, Louisiana, Robinson began coaching at Louisiana's *Negro Normal and Industrial Institute* in Grambling, Louisiana. The school today is *Grambling State University*, a place according to the school's motto: "Where everybody is somebody." Robinson, who would become vice-president of athletics, quite literally built the school's athletic program from scratch, and in doing so, became a nationally known somebody, and was inducted into the College Football Hall of Fame in 1997.

During that first year at Louisiana Negro Normal, he coached football, basketball and baseball for a monthly salary of $63.75. That wasn't all. He also put the chalk lines on the field before the game, led the drill team at halftime, and after each game was over, he wrote up the game stories that appeared in the local newspaper.

In his second season, his football team went undefeated, holding opponents scoreless in every game. Every game! Eventually Robinson's duties were limited to football but it was never easy. On one occasion his two star players, brothers, were unable to practice because they had to help harvest the family's cotton crop. When

Robinson learned about it, he bussed the entire team to where the brothers lived and everyone, including Coach Robinson, picked cotton until the crop was in.

Above all, Robinson stressed a well-rounded education. He instituted an "Everyday Living" course for his players, many of whom were unsophisticated in the social graces. He abhorred profanity and if he caught a player using words he felt inappropriate, they ran wind sprints until he told them to quit. Some of the players that Robinson coached claimed he literally ran the profanity out of their character.

Robinson coached over 200 players drafted into the NFL, including four Hall of Famers, Buck Buchanan, Charlie Joiner, Willie Brown, and Willie Davis.

Robinson's last game was a loss to Southern University. His amassed record was 408 wins, 165 losses and 15 ties. It was his last season, a season for which he had been under fire for two losing seasons in a row.

Asked if he was bitter about losing his job, he replied, "I've been here all my life. I've had one job and one wife. I've coached some of the finest players who have ever played the game. I've been at Grambling for 56 years and my paycheck has never been late. Do I need to say anything else?"

Coach Eddie Robinson was pure class.

On **April 3, 1981**, the Osborne 1, the world's
first successful portable
computer was unveiled at the West Coast Computer Faire
in San Francisco. Weight: 23.5 lbs.

APRIL 4
One tough ol' bird

William Henry Harrison
Feb 9, 1773 (Charles City, VA) – **Apr 4, 1841** (Washington, DC)

WILLIAM HENRY HARRISON was a tough ol' bird, and that was the image he wanted presented to the American people during his run for the presidency. He was going to become the ninth president of the United States if it killed him.

Prior to the Revolutionary War, some of the colonists agreed that a portion of the Northwest Territory should remain Indian land. But after the war, citing a provision in the "Treaty of Paris of 1783" in which the defeated British gave lands once inhabited by the Indians to the colonists, the colonists began to look at things differently.

This turn of events had to have the Native Americans shaking their heads. From where they stood, they had be asking, "What is this nonsense? A treaty between the British and the colonists regarding land that doesn't belong to either? A treaty? Signed where? In France! What is this France? What kind of agreement is it that says the British, who never owned the land in the first place, can sit down in this France, and give our land to the colonists?" However, in 1783 it mattered little what Native Americans thought.

In 1794, Harrison had served under "Mad" Anthony Wayne at the Battle of Fallen Timbers, a campaign that had taken the fight out of the Indians in the Northwest Territory.

In 1801, Harrison became governor of the Northwest Territory where he built the territory's first brick home at Grouseland (today: Vincennes, Indiana), a home with enormously thick walls to protect against Indian raids.

The situation remained calm until 1810 when a Shawnee leader by the name of Tecumseh surfaced, established an American Indian Confederacy, and on November 7, 1811, attacked an encampment on the Tippecanoe River. The battle was fierce with 190 dead and wounded, leaving Tecumseh and his warriors defeated. It was here that Harrison earned the nickname *Old Tippecanoe* and the name would provide the basis for a future presidential slogan.

In October 1813, with the War of 1812 a year old, the British with the assistance of a still determined and charismatic Tecumseh engaged the colonists at the Battle of the Thames. It was here that (1) Tecumseh would die in battle, an unrecoverable blow to the Indians of the Northwest Territory, and (2) Harrison would defeat the British, firmly establishing himself as a military hero.

As Harrison's military career wound down, he returned to his native Ohio and won seats in the U. S. House of Representatives (1816-1819), the Ohio State Senate (1819-1821) and the U. S. Senate (1825-1828). Following his Senate term, he became America's Envoy to Columbia where he urged Simón Bolívar to consider a democratic form of government.

As the Northwest Territory's first governor and congressional delegate, Harrison was instrumental, through legislation, to have the territory divided into two parts. On part remaining the "Northwest Territory" and the other, the "Indiana Territory" named in honor of the region's original inhabitants. The portion known as the Indiana Territory was later subdivided into the states of Indiana, Illinois, Michigan, Wisconsin, and the eastern portion of Minnesota.

In 1836, sixty-three years old and feeling his age, the grand old man known as "Old Tippecanoe" received the Whig Party nomination to run against Martin Van Buren for the presidency. He did, and although he lost the election, he retained his stature as a military hero.

Four years later, he was once again the choice of the Whigs. This time with running mate John Tyler of Virginia, and the election was a contentious one. Nevertheless, with the slogan "Tippecanoe and Tyler too," Harrison and Tyler eked out a popular vote majority of less than 150,000 votes. However, a solid Electoral College win of 234-60, made Harrison at sixty-eight the oldest person up to that time elected to the presidency of the United States.

The date set for Harrison to take the oath of office was March 4, 1841. The event would be held outdoors to accommodate an unusually large crowd. Harrison was a man who wanted others to see in him, the man he believed he still was. He saw himself as a tough battle-tested military man, a man with the strength and courage to make America's most difficult decisions.

The day of the inauguration was a bitter cold day with a drizzling rain. Nevertheless, despite the inhospitable weather, or perhaps because of it, the tough ol' bird Harrison decided to forego hat and overcoat, and he refused the use of an enclosed carriage in favor of an open one.

They weren't good decisions for a man who wanted others to view him as a good decision maker.

Once at the podium and inadequately dressed for the weather, he delivered what remains to this day, the longest inaugural address in American history, 8,445 words that took nearly two hours to deliver.

After taking the oath of office, he rode through the streets of Washington in his open carriage, almost up to the time of the three inaugural balls in his honor.

Three weeks after moving into the White House, he was in a fight worse than he'd seen on any battlefield, a cold so severe that it quickly developed into pneumonia and pleurisy. The doctors tried everything they knew, including opium, leeches, and snakeweed, but nothing could stem the inevitable.

On April 4, 1841, William Henry Harrison died, entering the history books as America's shortest-term president and the first to die in office, serving a total of exactly thirty days.

On **April 4, 1968**, civil rights advocate
Martin Luther King, Jr.,
was shot to death by James Earl Ray in Memphis, Tennessee.

WAYNE WINTERTON, PH.D.

Howard Hughes
(Howard Robard Hughes, Jr.)
Dec 24, 1905 (Humble, TX) – **Apr 5, 1976** (Houston, TX)

T HERE IS NO shortage of stories, some true, some fanciful, all intriguing about the legend that is Howard Hughes. Hughes wasn't past his teen years when he inherited the bulk of his family's multimillion-dollar business. He would go on to become a billionaire when most Americans had no idea of what being a millionaire would be like.

Howard's father, Howard R. Hughes, Sr., was a highly intelligent businessman who invented, and then patented in 1909, an oil drilling bit consisting of interlocking cones. The unusual-looking rotary-bit revolutionized the drilling of oil by providing a drill head that could drill in places where traditional bits couldn't go. However, the innovative drilling bit didn't make the Hughes family wealthy, it was a shrewdly innovative decision made by its inventor. Instead of selling the bit to companies in the oil drilling industry, the bit was available only as a leased item from a single source, the Hughes Tool Company. Hughes' ownership and total control of the drilling bit turned the family into one of America's wealthiest.

In 1923 and only eighteen years old, Howard inherited the Hughes Tool Company, and unlike most who inherit millions while still in their teen years, he didn't make the mistake of frittering away the family fortune on wine and song. That's not to say he didn't engage in some frittering, but he had the good sense to set limits. Like his father, Howard Jr. had a brilliant mind and he accomplished more than a few things that left the rest of the world scratching its head.

Like others not known for their educational excellence in formal settings, such as Thomas Edison, of whom a teacher once said was "too stupid to learn anything," or Winston Churchill whose poor academic record brought regular punishments and the need to repeat the sixth grade, Howard's formal education wasn't bragging material.

However, at the age of eleven (1916), Howard built what is today considered as Houston, Texas' first radio transmitter. A year later, a newspaper wrote him up as the first boy in Houston to have a motorized bicycle. Not because his rich father went out and bought him one, but because he built one from parts borrowed from a steam engine.

Of course, neither the radio transmitter nor the powered bicycle bought much in the way of respect from his teachers. After all, a real education includes learning that a gerund is a verb that functions as a noun and ends in "ing." The word "flying," functions as a gerund in the sentence, "When Howard turned fourteen, he took his first flying lesson." Now, there's a piece of useful information! Knowing what a gerund is.

A year later and too young to enroll at Caltech, he slipped into the back of Caltech's classrooms and secretly sat in on the school's aeronautical engineering classes. He finished the year strong with two more gerunds under his belt, "chasing" and "catching," as in, "Howard quickly discovered the joy of not only "chasing" college girls, but in "catching" them. Yes, Howard loved his gerunds.

In 1926, three years after inheriting the family fortune, he began financing, and afterward producing his own motion pictures, including the now-classic *Hell's Angels* (1930). The movie, a World War I epic, featured expensive and highly choreographed aerial sequences and introduced an unknown starlet, Jean Harlow, to the American public. However, producing films was not enough for Hughes. He eventually bought RKO Pictures, but never once took the time to visit the studio.

His love of flight coupled with incredible confidence in his own abilities and an imagination without limits, made him one of the world's best-known aviators, and one of the world's most respected aeronautical engineers. To do what he wanted to do, he founded Hughes Aircraft in the mid-1930s including a flight test facility near Santa Ana, California.

In 1935, he set an airspeed record of 352 mph flying the Hughes H-1 Racer.

In 1937, in the same aircraft but with longer wings, he set a transcontinental airspeed record (Los Angeles to Newark) of 7-hours, 28-minutes, 25-seconds, for an average ground speed of 322 mph.

WAYNE WINTERTON, PH.D.

In 1938, he set a new record by flying around the world in 3 days and 19 hours. Some say his H-1 Racer influenced the design of numerous World War II fighter aircraft.

During the height of the aviation portion of his life, he set many records and received numerous awards, some he never bothered to acknowledge, such as a "Congressional Gold Medal" that was eventually mailed to him, personally, by President Harry S. Truman.

Hughes most famous aircraft was the "Spruce Goose," the largest aircraft ever built. It was called the Spruce Goose because Spruce rhymes better with Goose than does Birch, the type of wood actually used in its construction. Its intended use was as a cargo plane to transport military equipment and men across the Atlantic but World War II ended before the Goose was completed.

The gigantic plane with its 320-foot wingspan (twenty-feet longer than a football field), was flown once, by Hughes on November 2, 1947, for one mile. It now resides in McMinnville, Oregon, as a part of the Evergreen Aviation Museum.

Before ending this little story, let's play "what if."

For instance, what if you were nearing the end of your life and you had more money than some countries have. What would you do?

In 1966, ten years before his death, Howard Hughes went on a shopping spree. The first thing he bought was a place to live. It was the Desert Inn and Casino in Las Vegas. He redesigned the entire top floor and rarely, if ever, left its confines. He conducted all of his business by telephone. Then he bought the Sands, then the Stardust, the Castaways, the Silver Slipper, the Frontier, and finally, the Landmark, all hotels and casinos, none of which he ever stepped foot inside.

Howard Hughes died of malnutrition and kidney failure on April 5, 1976.

In 1983, his $2.5 billion dollar estate belonged to twenty-two cousins and a few others.

In 1985, General Motors purchased Hughes Aircraft, owned by the Howard Hughes Medical Institute, for $5.2-billion.

Howard Hughes was buried in a silver casket at an undisclosed location.

"I've found a sure way to lose happiness
is to want it at the expense of everything else."
Bette Davis (**Apr 5, 1908** – Oct 6, 1989) Actress

WAYNE WINTERTON, PH.D.

APRIL 6
A real 'hands-on' sort of guy

Evan O'Neill Kane
Apr 6, 1861 (Darby, PA) – Apr 1, 1932 (Kane, PA)

E VAN O. KANE was the son of a notable Pennsylvania family. His mother, Elizabeth, his brother, Thomas L. Kane, Jr., and his sister, Harriet Amelia, were all physicians. His father, Major General Thomas L. Kane, was the one who mediated a solution between the federal government and the Mormons to end the Utah War (1857-1858). Kane, Pennsylvania, and Kane County, Utah, as well as Utah's Kane Springs and Kane Canyon all derive their names from General Thomas Kane.

Dr. Evan O. Kane was an innovator who combined a mix of pragmatism, medical common sense, and unorthodoxy into his practice of medicine. After you've finished this story, you'll not only find Evan Kane interesting, but that he was a real "hands-on" sort of guy.

In 1887, the Kane family, led by matriarch Elizabeth, founded Woodside Cottage Hospital in the town named after the family, Kane, Pennsylvania. Within five years, the needs of the community had outgrown the small hospital, so Elizabeth moved the facility to a larger site, added square footage, and renamed it Kane Summit Hospital, with her physician son, Dr. Evan Kane serving as the hospital's chief of surgery.

The change from a "cottage" to a "regional" hospital brought changes. At the cottage facility, Dr. Kane controlled everything from admissions to final treatment. When he tried to impose his rules on the other physicians at the regional hospital, he experienced opposition, although he remained an influential voice at the facility.

As mentioned, Kane was an innovator and sometimes applied rather unorthodox solutions to problems. For instance, there was his practice of tattooing. Kane was aware that although baby mix-ups were rarely a problem in a cottage hospital, they could be a problem in a regional hospital. To remedy the possibility of a mix-up, Kane practiced the inconspicuous tattooing of newborn infants, likely on the bottom of a foot, with a matching tattoo on the mother.

Kane's solution in 1900 to the collapse of veins in patients who had experienced severe hemorrhaging, was a transfusion device he invented that could handle up to ten connected needles, thus replacing lost blood in a patient at a rate ten times faster than with a single needle.

He served as a railway surgeon for several railroads, and the emergency conditions he found in treating railway victims led to his creation of bandages made not of cotton gauze, but of asbestos fabric. Bandage sterilization, always a problem in treating railway accident victims, was done by passing the asbestos bandage through an open flame. The bandage might not have been pretty, but it greatly reduced infections.

Kane also proposed the use of mica, a marginally transparent mineral, as a protective covering for head wounds, its use providing a "window" for the physician to observe problems in the healing process.

On February 15, 1921, Dr. Evan O. Kane did something that really set him apart from his colleagues as a truly unique physician. As he lay on an operating table in the hospital awaiting the removal of his appendix by another physician, he sat up and made an unusual announcement.

He decided to conduct an experiment to determine if a man such as himself could remove his own appendix, using local anesthesia only. As the hospital's chief surgeon, and a man that others had learned was nearly impossible to argue with, those in the operating room reluctantly nodded agreement.

Having performed the operation about 4,000 times, Kane was fully confident in his ability to do it once more. He propped his back with pillows to allow himself a good view of his abdomen, and with the aid of a mirror and a relatively new anesthesia called Novocain, he injected the fluid into his abdominal wall. He quickly cut through his own skin and underlying tissue, located the diseased appendix, and expertly excised it from his body. There was an anxious moment when he leaned too far forward and his intestines popped out of his stomach. Waving everyone off, he replaced his intestines and began the work of suturing the incision. The entire operation took thirty minutes.

The self-surgery created a news sensation in 1921 with numerous newspaper and magazine articles.

Dr. Kane was not through making headlines.

In 1932, eleven years after the self-removal of his appendix, he was once again his own patient. This time it was the repair of an "inguinal hernia," a protrusion of abdominal cavity contents through the inguinal canal. He invited the press, including a photographer to record the self-surgery. At least one photograph of Dr. Kane intently performing this self-surgery is available on the internet.

By this time in his career, the seventy-one year old Dr. Kane was signing his surgeries by tattooing the letter "K" in Morse code (dash-dot-dash) near the surgery. The operation, which took just under two hours to perform, left Dr. Kane too drowsy to suture the incision, so a colleague, Dr. Howard Cleveland closed the incision and tattooed, in India ink, the letter "K" as Dr. Kane would have done.

Unfortunately, following his second self-surgery, Dr. Kane never regained his strength, came down with pneumonia, and died a few months after the operation.

On **April 6, 1830**, Joseph Smith and five others founded the Church of Jesus Christ of Latter-day Saints (the Mormons) in Fayette, New York.

APRIL 7

He supported his government

Haym Salomon

Apr 7, 1740 (Leszno, Poland) – Jan 6, 1785 (Philadelphia, PA)

HAYM SALOMON OF Poland was a multi-lingual Jewish financier who immigrated to New York in 1772 and quickly established himself as a successful merchant.

Shortly after his arrival, he met Alexander MacDougall, the leader of the New York Branch of the *Sons of Liberty*, an organization of patriots that, within the year, would take part in a Tea Party they would help to organize in Boston Harbor.

Between 1773 and the beginning of the Revolutionary War in 1776, two things had already happened and a third was about to happen.

First, Salomon met and married Rachel Franks, whose brother Isaac was a colonel on General Washington's military staff. Second, he received a profitable military contract to provide supplies to American troops in New York.

Then the thing that was about to happen, happened. The British arrested Salomon as a spy.

Salomon, however, was neither a spy, nor a typical prisoner, but he was clever and although detained by the British for eighteen long months, he won a pardon by agreeing to serve as the interpreter for a group of British-sponsored German mercenaries.

When the mercenaries stood before him for instructions on what to do next, Salomon, instead of translating into German what a British officer was telling him to say, spent his time convincing the Germans in their native language that involvement with the British wasn't a good idea. After the lengthy "translating" session, Salomon told the British he had done the best he could do, and he walked out the door with his pardon in hand.

When the British realized Salomon had made fools of them, they were furious. They recaptured Salomon, held a sham court, sentenced him to hang, and locked him up.

When it came time to carry out the execution, they discovered he had escaped, this time with help from his friend, Alexander MacDougall and the *Sons of Liberty*.

By 1781, Washington was closing in on Cornwallis near Yorktown, but the federal coffers were empty and the government was out of money. Washington asked his head of finance, Robert Morris, to find Haym Salomon, and fast!

The short of what happened next was that Salomon raised $20,000, enough for Washington to defeat Cornwallis at Yorktown, the final battle of the Revolution. However, Salomon didn't stop raising money, raising a total of $3.5 million from France and the Dutch Republic. Then, using his own money to purchase medical supplies, he established a hospital at Valley Forge.

There's a myth, or perhaps a true story, connected to Salomon's efforts on behalf of America. Before you determine the veracity of the story for yourself, take out a dollar bill.

Look at the back of the bill. There are two circles, one containing a pyramid topped with the symbol of the all-seeing eye, the other containing an eagle holding an olive branch and some arrows. Immediately above the eagle's head is a circle, and within the circle is a grouping of stars.

There's a story that when the dust from the Revolutionary War settled, Washington asked Salomon what kind of return compensation would be fair for the personal wealth and other sacrifices he made on behalf of the fledgling nation.

Salomon reportedly replied, "I wish nothing for myself, but I would like to have something for my [Jewish] people," and he explained his wish to General Washington.

Washington approached the engravers whose task it was to design the Great Seal of the United States, the eagle with the outstretched wings. He then personally directed that the thirteen stars, representing the original thirteen states, be arranged in the shape of a Star of David. Thus, from that time until the present, Americans have been honoring the man who raised money when the country needed it most, and who gave freely of his personal wealth to help win the Revolutionary War.

It's your call as to whether the story is myth or fact, but regardless, Salomon stands out as one of America's true patriots.

In 1976, the two hundredth year of the founding of the nation, Haym Salomon was honored on a commemorative postage stamp as one of the *Contributors to the Cause,* and indeed, he was most definitely one of the "contributors" to the cause.

"The best part of a good man's life is his little, nameless,
unremembered acts of kindness and love."
William Wordsworth (**Apr 7, 1770** – Apr 23, 1850) Poet

WAYNE WINTERTON, PH.D.

APRIL 8

Pintsize pioneering parachutist

Georgia 'Tiny' Broadwick

(Georgia Ann Thompson Broadwick)

Apr 8, 1893 (Oxford, NC) – Aug 25, 1978 (CA)

O N DECEMBER 17, 1903, Orville Wright became the first person to make a sustained flight in a heavier-than-air aircraft. Ten years later, June 21, 1913, an eighty-five pound, five-foot tall, wisp of a lady nicknamed Georgia 'Tiny' Broadwick jumped into the record books as the first female to exit an airplane in flight and parachute back to earth. She was twenty years old.

That jump on June 21 wasn't Tiny's first jump from an aircraft, which includes hot air balloons, but it was the world's first jump from a powered aircraft by a woman.

Although the elfin-sized daredevil claimed to have made her first jump in 1908 at the age of fifteen, and billed as "The Doll Girl," her first documented jump may be the one reported by the Knoxville Daily Journal and Tribune on May 19, 1910 when she was seventeen.

High Diver's Close Call

"Knoxville, Tenn., May 19. Wednesday was a banner day for the Knoxville Police Relief Association carnival. The feature was the balloon ascension by Miss Tiny Broadwick. Miss Broadwick is probably the youngest aeronaut in the world, said to be but seventeen years of age. She made her ascension about five o'clock and there were thousands of people to witness it.

"She left earth with, 'Oh, you comet,' and was soon a mere speck against the sky. When those watching her could see nothing but the large balloon and a dot trailing far below, she leaped and descended in a parachute. She alighted in the top of a tree on Fouche Street and the balloon fell on East Jackson Avenue.

"Miss Tiny made her way back to the show grounds and will make another ascension this afternoon about two o'clock. In falling through the limbs of the tree, she sustained several scratches."

Nine days later, and this time reporting her age as fourteen (three years younger than she was nine days earlier), the same newspaper reported an ill-fated jump in the town of Bristol, Tennessee in which she was fortunate to survive:

Girl Aeronaut Badly Hurt in Making Parachute Leap at Bristol, Friday. Landed on a Building; Then Fell to the Ground. Her Left Arm Broken and She Sustained Other Painful Injuries.

"Bristol, Tenn., May 27. 'Tiny' Broadwick, the fourteen-year-old girl aeronaut, who was making daily ascensions during the carnival week here, dropping from three parachutes, descended upon the roof of a grist mill this afternoon and being unable to get a hold on the roof, fell two stories, breaking her left arm near the elbow and sustaining other injuries. She was hurried to the hospital.

"This little aerial artist made several ascensions in Knoxville during the week of May 16-21 when she appeared with the Johnny Jones Carnival Company under the auspices of the Police Relief Association. Her act was a very daring one and she had at least one narrow escape from serious injury during her engagement there."

Tiny Broadwick would go on to achieve a number of spectacular parachuting firsts, including becoming the first woman to jump from a hydro aeroplane and the first woman to parachute over a body of water. She also entered the record books as the first person, male or female, to freefall from an aircraft before engaging the parachute. It

WAYNE WINTERTON, PH.D.

wasn't something she had planned to do. It was a spur of the moment decision for her own safety.

In 1914, while demonstrating the usefulness of parachutes to the U.S. Army by jumping out of an airplane with a "chute" attached to her back, the static line (a line attached to the aircraft to open the parachute pack once the jumper is free of the aircraft) became entangled in the tail assembly of the aircraft.

Although her parachute safely deployed, the problem could have led to her death. On her next demonstrated jump, she cut the static line free of the aircraft, making it just long enough for her to pull the parachute pack open after she was clear of the aircraft. The jump made her the first person in the world to make a premeditated freefall jump from an aircraft. Following her demonstration, the U.S. Army Signal Corps ordered "Broadwick Coatpack" parachutes, initiating a new era of aviation safety.

When Tiny Broadwick retired from jumping at the age of twenty-nine (1922), she had made over 1,100 jumps and was the first female to be inducted into the *Early Birds of Aviation,* an organization dedicated to early pioneers of aviation.

On November 16, 1972, the Adventurers Club of Los Angeles celebrated *Tiny Broadwick Night,* in honor of her contributions to aviation, and during which the seventy-nine year old aviation trendsetter charmed the audience with stories of those early days of flight.

Prior to Tiny's death on August 25, 1978 at the age of eighty-five, she presented one of her parachutes and packs to the Smithsonian Institution.

"Winning isn't everything. Wanting to win is."
Jim 'Catfish' Hunter (**Apr 8, 1946** – Sept 9, 1999)
Baseball player

APRIL 9

The man behind the Blue Suede Shoes

Carl Perkins

Apr 9, 1932 (Tiptonville, TN) – Jan 19, 1998 (Jackson, TN)

T HOSE WHO LOVE country music revere Carl Perkins. There are those who consider his contributions to the early days of rockabilly no less significant than the early contributions of Elvis Presley.

To say that Carl Perkins grew up dirt poor would be an understatement. Fonie 'Buck' and Louise Perkins didn't own the dirt they walked on. They were sharecroppers. Buck, Louise, and their sons lived in a drafty, three-room shack. When that became more than they could afford, they moved into a single room above a dilapidated storehouse.

At the age of six, Carl was working the cotton fields alongside his brother Jay, together earning fifty-cents a day, a seemingly small sum these days but money desperately needed by the family to help make ends meet.

On Saturday night, Carl and his father would listen to the *Grand Ole Opry* and when Carl told his father he wanted a guitar, his father fashioned one from a cigar box and a broomstick. Later, when an equally destitute neighbor needed to sell his scuffed and dented Gene Autry model with worn-out strings, Buck bought it for two dollars. It was with that guitar that Carl learned to play.

Another sharecropper, 'Uncle John' Westbrook, a black man in his sixties and an accomplished musician befriended young Carl and taught the boy the secret to playing the guitar by telling him to "get down close to it." He told Carl, "You can feel it [the music] travel down the strangs, come through your head, and down to your soul where you live. You can feel it. Let it vib-a-rate!"

As it turned out, Carl was a quick learner, musically speaking, and it wasn't long before Uncle John had Carl well beyond the basics, and the instruction continued.

Things wear out and when the "strangs" of his guitar broke, he tied and re-tied them. When the knots on the strings started cutting into his fingers, making it impossible to play a given note, Carl learned to "bend the notes," creating what musicians call "blue notes," notes played slightly below the intended frequency for creative expression. Carl knew nothing about intended frequency or creative expression, but he knew that what he was doing was keeping the bandages off his fingers. Without realizing it, Carl was quietly developing a sound that would be uniquely his own.

In 1947, the family moved near Memphis, and Carl took advantage of the city's musical opportunities. In 1955, he signed a recording contract with Flip Records (a subsidiary of Sun Records) and he became a regular performer as an opening act for a friend of his named Elvis.

Once, in Parkin, Arkansas, he saw an angry dancer warning his very pretty, but very careless girlfriend that she could do whatever she wanted to do on the dance floor, but that she'd doggone better stay off his blue suede shoes. Carl jotted the words down on a napkin and in December 1955, he wrote and recorded *Blue Suede Shoes.*

The song quickly climbed the charts and put twenty-three year old Carl Perkins in the national limelight. Arrangements for him to appear on the Ed Sullivan and Perry Como shows meant that he was making an impact on the music scene and he could almost taste the big time. When his recording of *Blue Suede Shoes* reached Gold Record status, plans were to present Carl with his Gold Record award on the Perry Como show.

While traveling to New York to make the appearance, Carl was in a horrible automobile accident. His vehicle struck the back of a pickup truck and veered into a ditch of water. Carl, thrown face down in the water, was saved when his drummer, "Fluke" Holland turned him over to see if he was okay. Carl's brother, Jay, suffered a broken neck and other injuries, and died shortly after the accident.

While recuperating, Carl's recording of *Blue Suede Shoes* hit No. 1 on the Pop, Rhythm & Blues, and country charts, and made it to No. 2 on the Billboard Hot 100 chart. From a hospital bed, he watched Elvis Presley perform the song on his first appearance on *The Milton Berle Show,* a song that turned out to be an even bigger hit for the future *King of Rock and Roll,* than it had been for Carl Perkins.

Carl continued to perform, but he never recovered the momentum lost from the accident, but his place in musical history lives.

On **April 9, 1959**, NASA introduced America
to its first astronauts:
Scott M. Carpenter, Gordon L. Cooper,
John H. Glenn, Virgil I Grissom,
Walter M Schirra, Jr., Alan B. Shepard, and
Donald K. Slayton.

WAYNE WINTERTON, PH.D.

Joseph Pulitzer
Apr 10, 1847 (Makó, Austria) – Oct 29, 1911 (Charleston, SC)

ON LIBERTY ISLAND, alongside the Statue of Liberty, is a second, much, much smaller statue. It's the statue of a gaunt, bearded, studious-looking fellow busy reading a newspaper. A closer look reveals he's wearing a pair of old-fashioned glasses, the kind that sit precariously on the bridge of the nose. The statue is that of Joseph Pulitzer, the publisher of the *New York World,* the *St. Louis Post Dispatch,* and others.

Why a statue of Joseph Pulitzer on Liberty Island, and why does it occupy a place where it is hardly noticed, dwarfed by the nation's largest and most commanding statue, Lady Liberty?

Besides being the publisher of newspapers, Joseph Pulitzer is the person behind the Pulitzer Prize, America's most prestigious award for excellence in the fields of journalism, literature, and music. Every year the world has twenty-one new "Pulitzer" winners. There is one for each of 21 award categories, as judged by 102 judges selected for their expertise by the Pulitzer Prize Board, and each year $200,000 from the Pulitzer Endowment Fund is divided among the winners.

Besides his newspapers and the Pulitzer Prize, Joseph Pulitzer also played a part in the Statue of Liberty story. It wasn't a small part, and yet it's likely something of which most people are unaware and it's the reason why his statue stands next to Lady Liberty.

In school, we learned that the statue came to America as a gift from the people of France in recognition of the friendship established between the two nations at the time of the American Revolution.

We might also have learned that an artist-sculptor named Frédéric Auguste Bartholdi designed the statue and gave it the name, *Liberty Enlightening the World*. We might have also learned that the statue's torch and fire are symbolic of the enlightening power of knowledge.

There are other items of symbolism as well. The statue, symbolically based on the Roman goddess *Libertas*, represents freedom from tyranny. Lady Liberty's slightly raised right foot represents forward movement, bringing freedom ever closer to others and at the base of her feet lay the broken chains of oppression. The crown represents the halo of divine inspiration and the seven rays that radiate outward represent the seven continents.

Many believe that Bartholdi modeled the face of *Lady Liberty* after the face of his mother, although there is no official proof of this.

However, *Liberty Enlightening the World*, or whatever your preferred name is for the lady on Liberty Island, it almost didn't happen.

The statue wasn't the cut-and-dried gift that we assumed in fifth grade.

It was actually a joint project between France and the United States. The "gift" being Bartoldi's artistic and creative genius, but to carry out such an international undertaking, an organization, the French-American Union, planned and coordinated the project. It called for the people of France to pay for the statue, and for the people of America to build the pedestal upon which the statue would stand.

Fund raising would take place on both sides of the Atlantic.

Donations toward the project began in France in 1875 with money coming in from towns, villages, and from children who chipped in their allowances. When the hand and torch of the massive statue arrived in Philadelphia in 1876, Americans caught the spirit and donations from cities, towns, and from American schoolchildren started to trickle in. The costs for the statue and pedestal were, in 1880s dollars, $400,000 for the statue and $300,000 for the pedestal, very large sums at the time. However, money in France, as in America, was tight and there were many stops and starts to the project.

In America, when it didn't appear that New York would get the statue, Boston, Philadelphia, Cleveland, Baltimore, San Francisco, and Minneapolis all got in the act, each offering to pay the tab, but only if the statue would be erected in their cities.

That's when New Yorker Joseph Pulitzer and his newspapers became involved.

Pulitzer didn't believe the statue belonged anywhere but in New York harbor and on March 16, 1885, he wrote an editorial that said as much. Under his guidance, his newspapers started an all-out attack on wealthy New Yorkers for their cavalier attitude toward the project.

He was also merciless in attacking the lackadaisical public for its willingness to stand by, expecting the rich to pay the bill.

Pulitzer's campaign wasn't limited to New York alone, but he and his news organization hit up every corner of the country, asking everyone to "assist in averting the shame of rejecting," what he considered, "the most generous gesture one nation had ever offered to another."

Suddenly America came to life. Hometown fund-raisers raised money, fancy balls generated revenue, and corporate America chipped in big time.

Pulitzer even mounted an energetic drive of his own, promising to print the name of every donor, no matter the size of the donation. Millions contributed and Pulitzer kept his word, even publishing the $1.35 donation from a class of Iowa kindergarteners.

In August of 1885, five months after his March 16 editorial, the final $100,000 for the statue's pedestal was in the bank.

Now, you know why a statue of Joseph Pulitzer stands right alongside Lady Liberty.

As an aside to the above story, and a fitting way to close out a story of true national friendship, know this. In France, within sight of the Eiffel Tower, there is another Statue of Liberty, a small version of her big sister in New York Harbor. However, unlike America's eastern facing Lady Liberty, aligned to face incoming immigrants, the statue in Paris faces west, toward America a half a world away.

The positioning of the two statues, gazing at each other from across the Atlantic didn't happen by accident, it was the result of intentional and purposeful design.

The two Ladies are in perfect geographical alignment with one another, a quiet everlasting reminder of the close relationship between the two countries.

"Being a woman has only bothered me in climbing trees."
Frances Perkins (**Apr 10, 1880** – May 14, 1965)
1st female Cabinet member

APRIL 11
First Lady of the Navajo Nation

Annie Dodge Wauneka
Apr 11, 1910 (Sawmill, AZ) – Nov 10, 1997 (Toyei, AZ)

O N DECEMBER 6, 1963, Annie Wauneka, a woman of the Navajo Nation became the first Native American to receive the Presidential Medal of Freedom.

Established by President John F. Kennedy a half-year earlier, on July 4, 1963, President Lyndon B. Johnson made the presentation due to Kennedy's assassination just two weeks prior to the scheduled ceremony.

Annie Wauneka, the Navajo Nation's most recognizable female in the 1960s, was a fine choice as one of the award's first recipients. It acknowledged Annie as the "first woman elected to the Navajo Tribal Council," and it noted her "long crusade for improved health programs [that] helped dramatically to lessen the menace of disease among her people and to improve their way of life."

Annie Wauneka, in any culture would have been an outstanding proponent of good, and within her own culture, that of the Navajo, her contributions are legendary.

Annie was born Annie Dodge, the daughter of Henry Chee Dodge who helped to create the Navajo Tribal Council in 1922, afterward becoming its first chairman and serving in office from 1922 to 1928. Now, lest you think that chairing the concerns of the Navajo people is small potatoes, consider the following. The Navajo Reservation is roughly the size of West Virginia, even more rural, with far more than its share of social and economic problems.

In the 1920s, nearly all of the roads on the reservation were dirt and transportation was largely horse and wagon. Shopping for most families meant going to the local trading post for clothing, canned goods, and other household items, paying for the items on a barter-credit type arrangement using wool, rugs, and turquoise jewelry as a means of exchange.

Although Annie was born in a hogan, the Navajo traditional one-room dwelling, her early life was atypical of Navajo children. Henry Chee Dodge was wealthy by Navajo standards, owning a large ranch and a residence with modern conveniences, but he was adamant that his children learn and understand responsibility.

Each child did chores, including herding sheep, and each was educated in government boarding schools. Formal education for Annie began at the Fort Defiance Boarding School, then the Albuquerque Indian High School, and later, the University of Arizona in Tucson where she earned a degree in Public Health Administration.

In 1929, Annie married George Wauneka, a man she met while both were in boarding school. Twenty-two years into their marriage (1951), through an unusual set of circumstances, Annie and George ended up as rival candidates for a single vacancy on the Navajo Tribal Council. Annie, by then well known for her work on behalf of reservation health, defeated her husband and a third-party candidate, thus becoming the first woman to sit on the Tribal Council.

She held the office for three four-year terms, leading the effort to rid the reservation of tuberculosis, helping to demystify non-traditional medical practices and bringing traditional medicine men and the physicians of the Public Health Service together to achieve a spiritual-medical balance. She worked to improve the sanitation of family food preparation, and she oversaw to completion, the development of a Navajo-English dictionary of medical terms.

In 1959, she received the Arizona State Public Health Association's "Outstanding Worker in Public Health" award. And then in 1963, the Crown Jewel when she and a small group of others, including former Supreme Court justice Felix Frankfurter, artist Andrew Wyeth, novelist Thornton Wilder, and Polaroid camera inventor Edwin H. Land all stood before the nation to receive its highest civilian honor, the Presidential Medal of Freedom.

Well done Annie Dodge Wauneka, the very highly respected *First Lady of the Navajo Nation.*

"A woman who laughs is a woman conquered."
Oleg Cassini (**Apr 11, 1938** – Mar 17, 2006)
Fashion designer

APRIL 12
Recluse, custodian, artist

Henry Darger
Apr 12, 1892 (Chicago, IL) - Apr 13, 1973 (Chicago, IL)

D URING HIS LIFETIME, no one knew what Henry Darger was doing inside his creepy second-floor flat at 851 W. Webster Avenue in the Lincoln Park section of Chicago. Actually, no one cared what the unkempt man was doing, and as long as he paid his rent on time, which he did, no one, not even his landlord would look inside.

As far as is known, Darger had only one friend in the world, a man named William Schloeder, but it's not known if Schloeder was ever inside Darger's apartment. He may have been, but it wouldn't have mattered. Schloeder was as down and out as was Darger, and whatever might have been inside wouldn't have been anything that Schloeder would have made a fuss over, certainly not to someone else.

Henry faithfully worked as a hospital janitor for forty-one years, doing the same thing day after day from the time he was thirty in 1922, until his retirement at the age of seventy-one in 1963. After his retirement, Darger lived another ten years in the same dilapidated second-floor apartment until his death in 1973.

He is currently at rest in the *All Saints Catholic Cemetery* in Des Plaines, Illinois, in a plot known as "The Old People of the Little Sisters of the Poor Plot." His marker reads, line by line, *Henry Darger – 1892-1973 – ARTIST – Protector of Children.*

Illinois records show that Henry was born at home to Henry and Rosa Darger, the third of four children. Rosa died giving birth to the fourth child, a girl, whom someone adopted. Henry lived at home with his older siblings and a badly crippled father in a state of dire impoverishment until placed in a Catholic boy's home at the age of eight.

When his father died in 1905, Henry ended up at the Illinois Asylum for Feeble-Minded Children in a rural part of the state. His placement, at least in part, was the result of a doctor's highly unscientific diagnosis that "Little Henry's heart is not in the right place."

At the asylum, Henry didn't get along well with the staff or his asylum-mates. Discipline was harsh, although in accordance with the asylum's accepted practices, including threats or the use of severe punishment. Henry tried to escape from his uncomfortable environment a number of times, and in 1908 and sixteen years old, he was finally successful.

Free of the Asylum, he found his way back to Chicago where he took a job in the maintenance and custodial department of a Catholic hospital. Except for a brief stint in the army during World War I, his life was one of virtually no variance. A devout Catholic, he attended Mass without fail every day, sometimes multiple times a day, collecting street garbage as he walked. Although his appearance was rumpled and shabby, he kept himself and his patched clothing quite clean.

Darger was a loner with the exception of his one friend, William Schloeder, the two often talking at length about the care of helpless children as if they were wealthy men. Much of their talk centered on a desire to found a "Children's Protective Society," where needy children could be adopted by good families, but it was all just talk. In about 1935, Schloeder moved away from Chicago, but their friendship continued with correspondence until Schloeder's death in 1959.

Darger continued to work at the hospital, picking up whatever people dropped on the sidewalk as he walked to and from work. After his retirement in 1963, his daily walks were limited to attending Mass.

In 1973, no longer able to make it to Mass, he walked into St. Augustine's Catholic Mission, the same place where his father had died, and awaited death himself. The final entry in his diary reads, "I had a very poor nothing like Christmas. Never had a good Christmas all my life, nor a good New Year, and now I am very bitter but fortunately not revengeful, though I feel should be how I am ...."

Henry Darger died on April 13, 1973, one day after his eighty-first birthday, and the world was about to discover the artistic genius of a man that almost no one knew existed.

A day or two after Darger's death, his former landlord, a photographer named Nathan Lerner entered the one-room apartment to clean and prepare it for a new tenant. His would be the first eyes to look upon Darger's art. Not a few, but hundreds of pieces, varied in taste from beautiful sweeping landscape panoramas to erotic fantasies. There was also a huge, 15,145 page, single-spaced manuscript titled, *The Story of the Vivian Girls, in What is Known as the Realms of the Unreal, of the Glandeco-Angelinian War Storm, Caused by the Child Slave Rebellion.* The manuscript contains hundreds of line and watercolor illustrations.

Darger's art, for which he never shared nor received any praise during his lifetime, is today included in the permanent collections of numerous art museums, including: The *American Folk Art Museum* in New York, *The Center of Intuitive and Outsider Art,* the *Chicago Museum of Contemporary Art,* the *New Orleans Museum of Art,* the *Milwaukee Art Museum,* the *Collection de l'art brut,* the *Walker Art Center,* the *Irish Museum of Modern Art,* the *Smithsonian American Art Museum,* and dozens of other locations.

If you're interested in owning a Darger original, you need to begin saving now as an original piece commands more than many folks earn in a year.

Prints, however, are affordable from numerous internet sites.

On **April 12, 1934**, a gust of wind atop
Mount Washington, NH was recorded
at 231 mph, making it the strongest wind gust recorded in the
United States.

APRIL 13

Krum the Fearsome, Krum the Dreadful, et al.

Krum the Horrible

c. 775 (Bulgaria) – **Apr 13, 814** (Bulgaria)

THE BULGARIANS HAVE a proud history.
Their history as a country began when Kahn Asparukh established the first Bulgarian Empire in 680-681, by leading 45,000 Bulgars into the Danube Delta where they settled briefly before relocating further south in the Balkan Mountains. Asparukh ruled until about 695 AD. Today, in the city of Strelcha, a statue of Kahn Asparukh shows the leader heroically astride a spirited horse in commemoration of the founding of Bulgaria.

Two hundred years later (893-927), Tsar Simeon I led the Bulgars in a series of successful military campaigns against the Byzantines, Magyars, and Serbs, greatly expanding the land holdings of Bulgaria and establishing it as a nation of importance. His thirty-four year rule is known as the *Golden Age of Bulgarian Culture.*

Between those two periods of generally prosperous rule, comes the reign of Kahn Krum, known historically by a number of rather descriptive nicknames, including *Krum the Horrible*, *Krum the Fearsome*, *Krum the Dreadful*, and others. He ruled Bulgaria during the period from about 799 to 814 AD.

Krum the Horrible instituted a few good things during his reign, including the codification of Bulgaria's first-ever written laws, and he used those laws to unite factions of independent Bulgars into a cohesive, almost European-like country. He showed concern for the country's poor and instituted an early form of welfare assistance for beggars.

Nevertheless, Krum was also a man with limited patience and a nasty streak. For instance, get caught stealing and the punishment was having both ankles broken on the spot. Make a slanderous comment regarding his Kahnship and suffer imprisonment or death. Once, he even considered a ban on alcoholic beverages, but being the forward-thinking man he was, decided that prohibition might be more of a problem than it was worth, and besides he really liked his wine.

After crowned the leader of the Bulgars, he spent the next few hours considering the pros and Kahns of expanding Bulgaria's borders. He decided it was something that needed done and that he was just the guy to do it. He began by establishing an army of horsemen in the manner of that other notable expansionist, Attila the Hun. With his agile warriors, he crossed the Carpathian Mountains and began carving out chunks of land in places like Transylvania and Macedonia. With each victory, he collected the heads of the slain kings or tribal leaders.

To the south of Bulgaria lay the Byzantines. In 800 AD, the Byzantine Emperor, Nicephorus I, having just been deposed and exiled, made Krum's capture of Thrace, the capital city, easy pickings. Krum's army, not equipped to scale the city's walls, simply surrounded Thrace and waited until the people began to die of starvation. Then he offered them the deal of a lifetime, "Surrender your city to me," he told them, "and I'll grant you safe passage to leave."

The starving Byzantines opened their gates, stumbled, and hobbled outside. Then, as soon as they were beyond the protective walls of the city, Krum ordered his horsemen to ride into the exodus with swords flashing. The slaughter ended with approximately 6,000 Byzantines dead and the city on fire.

When Nicephorus I, the deposed ruler of the Byzantines learned of the city's destruction, he took matters into his own hands and organized a massive army of his own. The following year, during a time when Krum and his army were busy raping and pillaging elsewhere, Nicephorus made his move and marched straight into the Bulgarian capital of Pliska.

With the previous destruction of his own capital city and the massacre of its citizens still fresh in his mind, Nicephorus attempted to set a new standard for cruelty and savagery! What happened in Pliska wasn't pretty. After raiding Bulgaria's treasury, and killing all of the men, he ordered unspeakable forms of death against women, children, and the elderly. Then, just as Krum had done the previous year to his city, Nicephorus set Pliska ablaze.

WAYNE WINTERTON, PH.D.

When Krum returned to Pliska, incensed by the savagery of Nicephorus's retaliation, he decided it was time to teach the Byzantine leader a lesson he wouldn't soon forget.

Krum paused only long enough to dust off some of the nicer heads in his collection and apply a fresh coat of varnish to others, before ordering his army to intercept Nicephorus and his slow-moving Byzantine army before it could reach the safety of Constantinople.

At dawn on July 26, 811, Kahn Krum and the Bulgarian Army had Nicephoros's Army trapped at a killing-field called Vărbica Pass, and the result was ugly. Think, no, don't think, just know that not a single Byzantine soldier survived, and Nicephorus was dead as well.

Krum personally removed Nicephorus's head from its body and placed it on a pike as a trophy. Back in Bulgaria, Krum had the skull lined with gold, after which it became his personal drinking cup.

In 813, Krum the Horrible warred once again against the Byzantines, besieging the capital city and devastating the surrounding farmland. The following winter (813-814), while preparing for another siege, Krum suffered a brain hemorrhage and died.

The date was April 13, 814 AD, and thus ended the rule of Krum the Horrible.

"I learned that often the most intolerant and narrow-minded
people are the ones who congratulate themselves
on their tolerance and open-mindedness."
Christopher Hitchins (**Apr 13, 1949** – Dec 15, 2011) Author

---

APRIL 14
Blink of an eye shootout

The Four Dead in Five Seconds Gunfight
Apr 14, 1881 (El Paso, TX)

T HE *FOUR DEAD in Five Seconds* gunfight that took place in El Paso, Texas, on April 14, 1881, required about as much time to play out as it took for you to read this sentence. Yes, there were some who claim the shootout took twice as long, as many as ten seconds, and if it did, that's about as much time as it took you to read the first and second sentences of this paragraph.

As with most everything in life, the Four Dead in Five Seconds gunfight didn't grow out of thin air, so here's the dime store version of what led up to it, and remember, in the wild west not everything that happens needs a reason:

The participants and their occupations in order of appearance:

The Manning Brothers, cattle thieves
Ed Fitch, Texas Ranger
Sanchez and Juarique, Mexican farm hands
John Hale, a rancher of dubious character
An angry 75-person Mexican posse, multiple occupations
Gus Krempkau, Spanish-speaking constable
George Campbell, Former El Paso marshal
Dallas Stoudenmire, the new El Paso marshal

The events leading up to the shootout:
The three Manning Brothers, notorious for rustling cattle, had stolen thirty head of cattle from somewhere in Mexico and driven them across the border to El Paso where they intended to sell them, likely to rancher John Hale.

The rustling came to the attention of Texas Ranger Ed Fitch who, with Mexican farm hands Sanchez and Juarique, set out to investigate. The investigation led them to the ranch owned by

John Hale. The Ranger and the farmhands split up to check the brands on Hale's cattle and the farmhands, ambushed, left Ranger Fitch to return alone.

From Mexico, a posse of about seventy-five men rode across the border demanding (1) the bodies of the farmhands, (2) an investigation into their deaths, but (3) they mostly wanted their cattle back, if said cattle could be located.

The following day Gus Krempkau, a Spanish-speaking lawman led the Mexican posse to John Hale's ranch where they located the bodies of the two farmhands. Rancher Hale, as you might suppose, claimed no knowledge of the killings or of the whereabouts of any Mexican cattle.

A day or two later an inquest was held into the deaths of the two Mexican farmhands with Constable Gus Krempkau serving as the court interpreter.

Then, the inquest was either bound over to the following day, or recessed, and . . .

The shootout:

Constable Gus Krempkau left the courthouse and headed next door to Keating's Saloon where, as was his custom, he'd left his two pistols for safekeeping while he was in court.

Inside Keating's Saloon was George Campbell, a former El Paso marshal and friend of John Hale. By himself and drinking heavily was rancher John Hale. Prior to Krempkau's return to the saloon to get his two pistols, it's likely that Campbell had been given an earful from John Hale, whose name had been a hot topic at the inquest.

Former marshal Campbell, upset, confronted Krempkau, claiming he had not accurately handled the translation duties at the inquest. The Constable defended his translating and was trying to calm Campbell down when John Hale, clearly intoxicated, came up from behind Krempkau and pulled one of Krempkau's two pistols from its holster, pointed it at Krempkau and yelled, "George, I've got you covered!" and the gunfight was on.

John Hale shot Krempkau who crashed through the saloon's double doors and into the street.

Hale, suddenly sober, made a dash for a saloon support post just as Dallas Stoudenmire, El Paso's new three-days-on-the-job marshal, burst from the courthouse to see what the shooting was all about. Seeing Hale scrunched behind the support post, Stoudenmire fired off a round that missed Hale but killed an innocent bystander.

Hale peeked to see where the marshal was, Stoudenmire saw Hale's eyes, fired again, and Hale dropped like a sack of potatoes, shot cleanly through the head. Before Hale hit the ground, ex-marshal Campbell, yelled for the action to stop, but Krempkau, shot seconds ago by Hale, fired at Campbell at the exact same time that Stoudenmire fired at Campbell. Campbell died instantly with five bullet holes.

When the dust from the dust-up cleared, dead were Constable Gus Krempkau, rancher John Hale, ex-marshal George Campbell, and a Mexican peddler known in the records only as Ochoa, the victims of the Four Dead in Five Seconds gunfight.

It's not known if any of the rustled cattle were ever recovered.

On **April 14, 1913**, the worst of many black blizzards that
occurred throughout the Dust Bowl era took place
on this day, giving the date its name, *Black Sunday.*

Edward Gorey
(Edward St. John Gorey)
Feb 22, 1925 (Chicago, IL) – **April 15, 2000** (Hyannis, MA)

WHAT DO AUTHORS Edward Gorey, E. G. Deadworry, Raddory Gewe, Dogear Wryde, Mrs. Regera Dowdy, Ogdred Weary, and the *Soho Weekly* movie reviewer, Wardore Edgy have in common, besides the fact that each name consists of exactly eleven characters? We can also toss Eduard Blutig into the "what do these names have in common" mix, if we wish, but his will have to be a "sideways" entry because Eduard Blutig's name consists of twelve, not eleven characters, but that's ok. Nothing's perfect.

Edward Gorey was the son of Edward and Helen Gorey who divorced when little Eddie was eleven, giving him the opportunity to pass through several different, and indifferent, stepmothers before he was old enough to pack his bags and leave home on his own.

One of those stepmothers was Corinna Mura, the cabaret guitarist-vocalist inside *Rick's Café Américain* in the Humphrey Bogart classic, *Casablanca,* useless trivia for sure, but included here on the assumption that since you're reading this book, you're probably okay with useless trivia.

At the age of five, the precocious Gorey claims to have read Bram Stoker's *Dracula,* and if true, that might explain his fascination with the macabre and his own curiously out-of-whack mind. Take his illustrated alphabet book, the *Gashlycrumb Tinies* (1963) for instance:

A is for Amy who fell down the stairs
B is for Basil assaulted by bears
C is for Clara who wasted away
D is for Desmond thrown out of a sleigh
E is for Ernest who choked on a peach, and
F is for Fanny sucked dry by a leach.

If you're not familiar with an Edward Gorey book, think small (his books are typically mini-sized) and imagine each of the above ABC situations illustrated by a morbidly funny pen-and-ink drawing. Obviously, *Gashlycrumb* isn't for small fry trying to learn their ABCs, but for adults needing a bizarre break from the troubles of the real world.

If *Gashlycrumb* contains just the right amount of offbeat humor for your taste, you're going to love others of his more than 100 grotesquely strange books with equally strange titles. Here are a few worthwhile titles: *The Doubtful Guest* (1957); *The Beastly Baby* (1962); *The Recently Deflowered Girl* (1965); *The Loathsome Couple* (1977); *The Universal Solvent* (1989); and *The Twelve Terrors of Christmas,* the latter written by John Updike but illustrated by Gorey (1999) as only Gorey can illustrate.

The Twelve Terrors of Christmas contains enough off-kilter Yuletide mayhem to last through the holidays, and maybe even a lifetime. To wit, the book suggests for example, that Santa's high-flying reindeer are quite likely "laden with disease-bearing ticks."

Gorey worked for eight years at Doubleday, providing artistic services for other people's books, but he never lost hope of one day seeing his own disarmingly charming dark humor in print and in 1953 it all came together. The small company of Duell, Sloan and Pearce published *The Unstrung Harp* for $2.00. Today, an original copy in fine condition, that is, if you can find one, can bring upwards of, well, a lot of money.

Oh, and remember the names of all of those other authors mentioned up front?

Gorey loved word games, particularly anagrams, and many of his titles used anagrams of his name on the cover to show authorship. Thus, Raddory Gewe, E. G. Deadworry, Dogear Wryde, Regera Dowdy, and Ogdred Weary, are all anagrams of Edward Gorey, as was the name of *The Soho Weekly* movie reviewer Wardore Edgy.

Besides anagrams, Gorey used other ways to show or hide authorship. Remember the name, Eduard Blutig from the opening paragraph, where it was suggested that Blutig's name could be added to the mix, but only as a "sideways" entry? It's because the surname "Blutig" in German means "bloody," a sort of sideways synonym for "gory," which of course is pronounced exactly like "Gorey."

WAYNE WINTERTON, PH.D.

When Gorey died in 2000, he left the bulk of his estate to a charitable trust benefitting cats, dogs, bats, and insects.

He was an unusual man indeed.

"He who wishes to be rich in a day,
will be hanged in a year."
Leonardo da Vinci (**Apr 15, 1452** – May 2, 1519) Polymath

APRIL 16

The greatest jockey of all time

Isaac Burns Murphy

Apr 16, 1861 (Frankfort, KY) – Feb 12, 1896 (Lexington, KY)

IF YOU'RE A horse racing enthusiast, you may have heard of the Isaac Murphy Trophy, given every year to the jockey with the highest winning percentage by the National Turf Writers Association; or perhaps you're aware that since 1997, the former American Derby (Chicago, Illinois) has been renamed the Isaac Murphy Stakes. Even if you know one or both of those two horseracing facts, there's a good chance you still don't know much about Murphy, so you've come to the right place for a little elucidation.

To set the stage, when the *National Museum of Racing and Hall of Fame* in Saratoga Springs, New York, established its listing of Hall of Fame jockeys, the very first jockey voted into the Hall of Fame was Isaac Burns Murphy, and there's a very good reason for that.

Isaac Murphy's riding career extended over 19 years. During that time, he officially rode 1,538 horses, bringing 530 of those horses across the finish line ahead of the pack. That's a winning percentage of 34.5%, meaning he won a solid one-third of the races he competed in, and those are verifiable statistics. From Murphy's own hand-written records, in which he includes unofficial races, as well as official races run, he shows a lifetime winning percentage of 44%.

Here's the text honoring Isaac B. Murphy taken directly from the Hall of Fame award.

> "Many consider Isaac Murphy the greatest American jockey of all time. The son of a former slave, Murphy rose to prominence in a field that was dominated by African-American jockeys at the time. By his own account Murphy won 44% of his races. Only 34.5% can be verified in chart books from the era, but it's likely that some of Murphy's races were not covered in the chart books. Either way, Murphy has set a standard that no other jockey has met.

"Isaac Murphy won more than a third of his mounts year after year. He won the Kentucky Derby three times, the Latonia Derby five times, and four of the first five runnings of the American Derby, once the richest 3-year-old race in America.

"Not only was Murphy known for his skill on horseback but also for his honesty and loyalty. He once refused to let champion 'Falsetto' lose the 1879 Kenner Stakes, even though gamblers enticed him with bribes."

Here are a few more facts about this incredible man.

Isaac's father, also Isaac, was in the Union army during the Civil War. At some point, he was taken captive by the Confederates and imprisoned at Camp Nelson, Kentucky until his death. With the loss of his father, young Isaac and his mother and siblings moved to Lexington where they lived with their maternal grandfather, Green Murphy. When Isaac became a jockey at the age of fourteen, he changed his surname to Murphy in honor of his grandfather, thus becoming Isaac Burns Murphy.

To the present date (2015), there has been only one horse owned by an African American that has won the Kentucky Derby. In 1892, Isaac Murphy was the jockey on *Kingman*, winning the race for African American owner Dudley Allen.

Murphy's style was his own and stood in marked contrast to the accepted practice of using a rider's crop and/or spurs to urge the horse on. Murphy rarely used either, preferring to talk to the horse, persuading it to win for him. At least that's how his fellow jockeys tell the story, and they should know, they were closest to the action.

At the height of his career, he was well-paid for the era, earning $10,000 a year.

Eddie Arcaro, who won 19.8% of his races and Willie Shoemaker who won 21.9% of his races, may well be the first two names who come to mind as Hall of Fame jockeys; but both fall well below Isaac Murphy's numbers. When asked about Murphy, Arcaro once said, "There is no chance that his record of winning will ever be surpassed."

Murphy died of pneumonia in 1896 at the age of thirty-six and was buried in an unmarked grave in "African Cemetery No 2" in Lexington, Kentucky.

In the 1960s, Frank B. Borries, Jr., a University of Kentucky press specialist spent three years searching for Murphy's unmarked grave and found it.

Today, Murphy is at rest near the entrance to the Kentucky Horse Park in Lexington where a nearby marker describes his racing accomplishments.

"All I ask is the chance to prove that money can't make me happy."
Spike Mulligan (**Apr 16, 1918** – Feb 27, 2002) Comedian

APRIL 17
First baseballer with over 3,000 hits

Adrian "Cap" Anson
(Adrian Constantine Anson)
Apr 17, 1852 (Marshalltown, IA) – Apr 14, 1922 (Chicago, IL)

CAP ANSON, WITH his meticulously brushed handlebar mustache, was a dominating figure on and off the baseball field. Like many ball players of his era, he considered it unmanly to wear a glove and did his fielding barehanded. Unfortunately, his baseball legacy, which is substantial, is marred by his prejudice against African-American players. With his superstar stature and his bellicose voice intimidating others who may not have shared his views, it is likely he drove away from baseball, many African-Americans who might have become the Satchel Paiges, Willie Mays, and Willie Stargells, of their day.

Aside from his personal feelings, Anson was involved in two of the most ridiculous plays that ever took place inside the confines of a baseball park, and they seem even funnier today than they did a hundred plus years ago because, well because baseball back then wasn't like it is today.

The first incident took place in 1892 when Anson was playing first base for the Chicago Colts (today: the Chicago Cubs). Tom Brown of the Louisville Colonels hit the ball to the second baseman for what should have been an easy out. However, the second baseman's throw to Anson went wide.

Anson chased the ball into foul territory to near where Sam, the groundskeeper's horse was pastured when it wasn't pulling the grass-mower. Anson and the horse had already had several run-ins and the nag had never taken kindly to Anson, a situation that wasn't about to change. As soon as Anson and Sam saw each other, Anson stopped chasing the ball and Sam started chasing Anson. Meanwhile, Tom Brown circled the bases while watching Anson trying to get to the ball and stay out of Sam's way at the same time.

In just a moment, the second ridiculous play, but first a little more about Anson.

Anson was baseball's first superstar in an era before the word "superstar" was coined. He was the player that set most of the hitting records that Ty Cobb and Babe Ruth would later break. He was also the first player to hit over 3,000 lifetime hits, punching out 3,435. He agreed to his first baseball contract in 1871 and as a nineteen-year-old rookie, hit .325 that season for the Rockford Forest baseball team. At year's end, the Rockford team disbanded and Anson was picked up by the Philadelphia Athletics, a team he rewarded by hitting .415, the third best percentage in the league.

Anson alternated playing first and third base, and most of the other positions as well, and if called on, he might have pitched a couple of innings as well.

While playing for Philadelphia (1873-1876) Anson dated fourteen-year-old Virginia Fiegal, the daughter of a Philly restaurant owner, and Anson was smitten, cute little number that she was. When he signed to play for Chicago the following year, the youthful Virginia, showing wisdom beyond her years, refused to go to Chicago with Anson unless they were married. With her father's blessing, they were married on November 21, 1876, a marriage that lasted until her death thirty-nine years later in 1915.

Anson was big (6 foot 9 and 200 lbs.), powerfully built, and still considered one of baseball's strongest players. Besides being big and handsome, he had eyes that could follow with ease, the ball from the pitcher's hand to the plate. During the entire 1878 season, he only struck out once; and to prove it wasn't a fluke, he only struck out twice the following season. In 1881, he won the league batting title with a .399 percentage.

If you're interested in baseball trivia, in 1892, Anson became the last barehanded first baseman in the major leagues.

Now, as promised, here's that second ridiculous play.

In 1892, in the top of the eighth inning in a game against Philadelphia, Anson hit a soaring fly ball to center field. The ball struck a pole and plopped right inside a small storage shed where the scorekeepers kept the over-sized numbers they manually posted to the center field scoreboard. The shed was nicknamed the doghouse.

Outfielder "Big Ed" Delahanty, nicknamed for his oversized body, tried to retrieve the ball which was still in play by reaching into the doghouse. When his reach wasn't long enough, he tried to get his upper body into the small shed and he became hopelessly stuck. By the time teammate Sam Thompson freed Big Ed and retrieved the ball, Anson had crossed the plate on what Bruce Nash and Allan Zullo's "Baseball Hall of Shame," now refer to as baseball's only "inside-the-doghouse home run."

On **April 17, 1970,** the Apollo 13 spacecraft returned to Earth safely after an oxygen tank ruptured and exploded, and America had a new catch phrase: *Houston, we have a problem.*

Albert Einstein

Mar 14, 1879 (Ulm, Germany) – **Apr 18, 1955** (Princeton, NJ)

A LBERT WAS SEVEN or eight years old when his father let him play with a pocket compass. It didn't take long for Albert to realize that every time he locked the needle in position and turned himself a quarter or half-turn, and released the needle, something in the "empty space" caused the needle to quickly move back to its original position. When he was finished playing with the compass he returned it to his father.

In 1894, when his father's business failed, forcing the family to relocate to Italy, Albert, fifteen, remained in Munich. It was his intention to complete his studies at the Luitpold Gymnasium (secondary school), but a clash with school authorities over its method of strict memorized instruction ended his school year early and he traveled to Italy to rejoin his family.

With time on his hands, and based on his experience with the pocket compass, he wrote a scientific paper titled, *On the Investigation of the State of the Ether* [pure air] *in a Magnetic Field*." To suggest that Albert Einstein was your typical fifteen-year-old would be a stretch of enormous proportions.

In 1896 and sixteen, Albert took the entrance exam for acceptance at the Swiss National Polytechnic in Zürich, failed to pass the general education portion of the examination, but scored so high in physics and mathematics that he was admitted to the Argovian Gymnasium in Aarau, Switzerland. He would complete their program, establishing new high scores in, of course, physics and mathematics. Now, seventeen, he once again applied to the Zurich Polytechnic and this time he was welcomed into a four-year mathematics and physics "teacher preparation" program, graduating in 1901.

After graduation, Albert spent two frustrating years in search of a teaching position. When he couldn't find work as a teacher, he accepted a job as a clerk in the Swiss Patent Office. It was his role to evaluate patent applications for electromagnetic devices. In his spare time, he worked toward a PhD at the University of Zürich, graduating in 1905. His doctoral dissertation was titled, "A New Determination of Molecular Dimensions."

That same year, 1905, was known in the scientific world as Einstein's *annus mirabilis*, or his "miracle year." He would publish four groundbreaking papers in less than a year, a feat he would never duplicate, and one entirely out of the question for anyone else on the planet.

Paper #1: "The Photoelectric Effect." He applied the quantum theory developed by physicist Max Planck to light, explaining the phenomenon known as the "photoelectric effect," by which a material will emit electrically charged particles when hit by light.

Paper #2: Brownian Motion." He provided experimental proof of the existence of atoms by analyzing the phenomenon known as "Brownian Motion," in which tiny particles are suspended in water.

Paper #3: "The Electrodynamics of Moving Bodies." He resolved an apparent contradiction between Isaac Newton's concept of absolute space and time; and James Clerk Maxwell's idea that the speed of light was a constant.

Paper #4: "Special Theory of Relativity." He explained the relationship between mass and energy, concepts previously viewed as mutually exclusive with his now famous equation $E=mc2$, where "c" represents the constant speed of light.

Einstein, the man whose powers of reasoning and scientific intellect is legendary, could also be very down to earth, and he once offered the following to help a group understand the concept of relativity, "When you're courting a nice girl, an hour seems like a second. When you sit on a red-hot cinder, a second seems like an hour. The difference is relativity."

In 1952, Einstein declined an offer to become the President of Israel, stating that he was both "deeply moved" for the opportunity and "at once saddened and ashamed" that he could not accept it.

Einstein died on April 18, 1955, fifty years after his *annus mirabilis* of 1905. He was about to give a speech in commemoration of the State of Israel's Seventh Anniversary, and was working on that speech, when he died. Here is his unfinished speech, written in a hospital bed at Princeton University, ending abruptly as his own life came to an abrupt end.

> "In essence, the conflict that exists today is no more than an old-style struggle for power, once again presented to mankind in semireligious trappings. The difference is that, this time, the development of atomic power has imbued the struggle with a ghostly character; for both parties know and admit that, should the quarrel deteriorate into actual war, mankind is doomed.
>
> "Despite this knowledge, statesmen in responsible positions on both sides continue to employ the well-known technique of seeking to intimidate and demoralize the opponent by marshaling superior military strength. They do so even though such a policy entails the risk of war and doom. Not one statesman in a position of responsibility has dared to pursue the only course that holds out any promise of peace, the course of supranational security, since for a statesman to follow such a course would be tantamount to political suicide. Political passions, once they have been fanned into flame, exact their victims. . . . . ."

Albert Einstein, the modern world's greatest scientist, was dead at the age of 76.

"Whoever is careless with the truth in small matters
cannot be trusted with important matters."
Albert Einstein (Mar 14, 1879 – **Apr 18, 1955**) Physicist

Israel Bissell
(Outrode Paul Revere on **April 19, 1775**)
1752 (East Windsor, CT) – Oct 24, 1823 (Middlefield, MA)

Paul Revere owes a debt of gratitude to Henry Wadsworth Longfellow, the poet who seared Revere's name into America's collective psyche. You remember the poem that begins . . .

> *Listen, my children, and you shall hear*
> *Of the midnight ride of Paul Revere*

For if Longfellow had given poetic life to another Bostonian, one who had embarked on a ride from Boston to Philadelphia, rather than Revere's puny by comparison ride through the streets of downtown Boston, he just might have begun his epic poem along these lines:

> *Listen, my children, and I shall tell*
> *Of the five day ride of Israel Bissell*

Even though Longfellow's poetry didn't work out in Bissell's favor, Bissell didn't care because the Revolutionary War turned out in everyone's favor. Everyone, that is, except King George. What follows is a piece of American history that your civics teacher probably didn't teach you.

You learned that Paul Revere, an American patriot of importance, rode through the streets of Boston warning the residents of the arrival of British ships in Boston harbor. That's true. However, Revere wasn't the only rider responsible for alerting the folks, there were others, each with their own assignments of who to alert, and one of those was Israel Bissell.

At the same time that Revere began yelling, "The British are coming! The British are coming!" to the locals, Bissell was leaving on a 345 mile ride to yell the same warning to colonists in nearly every town from Watertown, Massachusetts to Philadelphia, Pennsylvania.

To make it to Philadelphia in five days, Bissell had to average from 70 to 82 miles per day with a fresh horse awaiting in most towns. His exhausting five-day race to alert the colonists easily surpasses, distance and saddle-sore wise, Revere's ride through Boston's curvy streets.

Like Revere, Bissell shouted, "To arms! To arms! The British are here!" every time he approached a new town. Unlike Revere, Bissell also carried a message, handwritten by General Joseph Palmer that was hand copied at each stop for reprinting in newspapers and onto posters. Here is that message:

> "Wednesday morning near 10 of the clock – Watertown.
>
> To all the friends of American liberty be it known that this morning before break of day, a brigade, consisting of about 1,000 to 1,200 men landed at Phip's Farm at Cambridge and marched to Lexington, where they found a company of our colony militia in arms, upon whom they fired without provocation and killed six men and wounded four others. By an express from Boston, we find another brigade are now upon their march from Boston supposed to be about 1,000. The Bearer, Israel Bissell, is charged to alarm the country quite to Connecticut and all persons are desired to furnish him with fresh horses as they may be needed. I have spoken with several persons who have seen the dead and wounded. Pray let the delegates from this colony to Connecticut see this.
>
> J. Palmer, one of the Committee of Safety."

Bissell, mounted and carrying the above message, departed Watertown (now a suburb of Boston) and rode to Marlboro and Worcester, arriving two hours after his start. After delivering his message, his horse died of over-exertion. He received a fresh mount and then rode south to the residence of Israel Putnam, a patriot and veteran of the French and Indian Wars.

After sharing the information with Putnam, who then carried the news elsewhere, Bissell on yet another fresh mount continued in like manner for four days. His route took him through New Haven, thence through the seaport town of Manhattan, New York, across the length of present-day New Jersey, past Princeton, sharing his message at every town. When he finally arrived in the City of Brotherly Love, he nearly collapsed from exhaustion as he delivered General Palmer's message for the last time.

Although different historians assign slightly different distances to Bissell's ride, most are around the 345-mile mark. Regardless of the actual miles, there is no doubt it was a ride for the history books.

At any rate, Israel Bissell, an unrhymed American hero was eventually honored in verse, and here are a few lines from a couple of the offerings.

Israel Bissell's Ride
By Gerard Chapman

Listen, my children, and you shall hear
Of Israel Bissell of yesteryear:
A poet-less patriot whose fame, I fear,
Was eclipsed by that of Paul Revere.
Etc. etc. etc.

And one more:

Israel Bissell's Ride
By Clay Perry

Listen, my children, to my epistle
Of the long, long ride of Israel Bissell,
Who outrode Paul by miles and time
But didn't rate a poet's rhyme.
Etc. etc. etc.

After his long ride, Israel Bissell fought in the Revolutionary War alongside his brother Justis. He died in 1832 and is at rest in the Maple Street Cemetery in Hinsdale, Massachusetts.

"It is the most wonderful feeling in the world,
knowing you are loved and wanted."
Jayne Mansfield (**Apr 19, 1933** – June 29, 1967) Actress

APRIL 20

Hank the angry drunken dwarf

Henry Joseph Nasiff

Apr 20, 1962 (Fall River, MA) – Sept 4, 2001 (Fall River, MA)

IN MAY 1998, in a promotion for an upcoming issue of *People Magazine,* the editors conducted a poll to determine the "50 Most Beautiful People" in the world. It was a foregone conclusion that heartthrob Leonardo DiCaprio, the star of the film *Titanic* would ace the field in the male category. After all, the movie was still drawing well, making him foremost on the minds of lady moviegoers.

In an effort to maximize participation in the poll, the magazine decided to allow readers to submit write-in candidates. It seemed like a good idea, but the old saw, "Be careful what you ask for because you just might get it," was about to come true.

When the results were tabulated, top box-office draw DiCaprio had garnered 14,471 votes, a reasonable response, but only enough to put him in third place behind second-place finisher, wrestler Ric Flair who had a headlock on 17,145 votes. However, what surprised everyone was the total number of votes cast for the winner, a lowly write-in candidate who had never competed in a popularity contest before, anywhere.

The voting public, at least that part of the voting public interested in playing in *People Magazine's* sandbox, had just voted Hank the Angry Drunken Dwarf to the top of the list with an astounding first-place finish of 230,169 votes. That's right, over a quarter of a million votes, and exactly 215,698 more votes than received by DiCaprio.

The executive editor at *People Magazine* wasn't amused.

So, how did it happen and who was Hank the Angry Drunken Dwarf?

Let's take the second question first. Hank was, as he referred to himself, a dwarf, a person defined as someone less than 4-feet 10-inches tall, and he did have a drinking problem, but he wasn't angry with anybody. His anger was only a part of a theatrical persona that served him well.

Hank, born Henry Joseph Nasiff, Jr., was diagnosed with *achondroplasia dwarfism* a week after his birth. His parents, both of normal height, encouraged him from the start to get involved in the typical things that youngsters do. He learned to ride a bicycle. He played Little League baseball. Best of all, he really enjoyed acting in local theatrical productions.

As he grew into adulthood he acquired a taste for alcohol and at four-foot-ten inches tall and ninety-five pounds soaking wet, it never took much alcohol to affect him negatively.

In 1996, after an evening at a Boston dinner theater, he and a friend decided to drive to New York to see if they could get on the *Howard Stern Radio Show.* They arrived in New York in the middle of the night and spent several hours binge drinking until the studio employees showed up for work.

Stern's producer, Gary Dell'Abate recalled his first encounter with the obviously intoxicated Hank Nasiff, Jr.

> "There was a dwarf standing there, and I remember he was wearing a Hawaiian shirt and one of those Hawaiian leis. And he had a vodka bottle in his hand . . . and he was drunk beyond belief."

You, the reader, as a sober intelligent person, might think that arriving intoxicated would be counterproductive to the objective of wangling oneself a seat in Howard Stern's audience, but you would be mistaken. When Hank, bolstered by several too many drinks, realized that the man standing in front of him was the show's producer, he demanded a meeting with the show's star, Howard Stern. "A good way to get tossed out on your ear," you're probably saying to yourself. Not so! "Follow me," Dell'Abate told the intoxicated little person, and as they say, the rest is history.

As Stern was preparing to open his show that day, he told his co-hosts, "I've always wanted an angry, drunken dwarf on my show, and now I've got one." Hank didn't disappoint, not then nor on any of the shows that he appeared on over the course of the next five years. He was articulate, funny, and although he came across as, well, as an angry, drunken dwarf, he found an endearing audience who sensed more sensitivity than toughness and they loved him.

WAYNE WINTERTON, PH.D.

Hank, who dropped his real name in favor of Stern's initial assessment of his guest, became *Hank the Angry Drunken Dwarf.* The relatively polite, soft-spoken guy, who most often wore a big smile on his face, knew exactly how to play his audience, and he was a darn good actor.

Then, in 1998, the topic of *People Magazine's,* "50 Most Beautiful People" showed up on a Howard Stern fan website. Next, someone suggested casting votes for Hank, and even Stern helped to propel it along by mentioning the promotion several times on the air.

The idea didn't just catch fire; it became a conflagration, a four-alarm light-up-the-sky idea.

Nevertheless, even Hank's landslide win wasn't enough to sway the single-minded powers at *People* to put Hank on the cover, and as predicted, *Titanic* star Leonardo DiCaprio won out over the rest of the guys. The magazine did photograph Hank and gave him a few inches of space on the website along with other participants.

To the credit of Stern and others on his staff, there were a number of genuine attempts made over the years to help Hank with his alcoholism problem, but it was never going to happen. Hank was too far inside the bottle. He died at home, not awakening from his sleep, the cause of death a seizure disorder and ethanol abuse.

The day after his death, Stern dedicated the show to tributes and remembrances of the life of Hank, the Angry Drunken Dwarf, who was a mostly happy-go-lucky likable little guy with a big problem.

"Gratitude is when memory is stored in the heart and not in the mind."
Lionel Hampton (**Apr 20, 1908** – Aug 31, 2002)
Jazz musician

APRIL 21
From Romulus to Pope Gregory XIII

The Evolution of the Calendar
The founding of Rome: **Apr 21, 753 BC**

A B URBE CONDITA is a Latin phrase meaning, "From the founding of the city." The city is Rome and the traditional date of its founding is April 21, 753 BC.

From the founding of Rome in 753 BC to today, the calendar has gone through not one, but four evolutions. They are in order, (1) Romulus's original calendar in 753 BC; which was (2) revised by Numa Pompilius in 713 BC; which was (3) revised by Julius Caesar in 46 BC; and which was (4) revised by Pope Gregory XIII in 1582 AD. The latter, known as the "Gregorian Calendar," is the calendar we use today.

In telling the story of the calendar's evolution, we begin with Rhea Silva, the lovely daughter of King Numitor. Rhea was a free-spirited tart who spent more time than good sense in the arms of the Roman god Mars. As happens during unchaperoned dalliances, the comely Rhea became pregnant and gave birth to twins Romulus and Remus.

Rhea's uncle, Amulius, who had recently wrested the throne away from Rhea's father, knew right away that it wasn't in his best interest to keep the twins around. To solve the problem, he had the infants tossed into the Tiber River. Fortunately, the little tykes simply floated downstream until a fig tree snagged them by their diapers. It was at that moment that a kindly she-wolf wandered by and nursed the twins to health, assisted by a woodpecker that Roman storytellers somehow felt lent credence to the legend.

The bottom line is that the she-wolf and woodpecker kept the little guys alive long enough to hand them over to Faustulus, a local shepherd who, with his wife, raised the boys.

The short of the story is that the twins, a couple of hellions, grew up, killed Uncle Amulius, and returned the throne to their Grandpa, Numitor.

In 753 BC, anxious to establish a new city, Romulus and Remus returned to the place by the Tiber where Faustulus had found them, but each preferred a different piece of real estate. To establish some property lines, Romulus set about building a wall around his chosen piece of land. When Remus dropped by to see how his brother was doing, he mocked his brother's wall by jumping over it and saying something like, "That piddlin' little wall ain't big enough to protect your city," and that's when Romulus whopped Remus up the side of the head with a shovel, killing him.

Romulus continued to build the city that became *Rome*. In his spare time, he tinkered with a lunar calendar, and since he liked things in orders of ten, the original Roman calendar had ten months, each corresponding to a lunar cycle of 29.5 days, for a total of 295 days.

In 713 BC, Numa Pompilius, one of the seven kings of Rome, added two months (Ianuarius and Februarius) to the front end of Romulus's calendar, and then believing odd numbers lucky, adjusted the number of days per month to give each month either 29 or 31 days. Pompilius also preferred a year of 355 days, so to accommodate the situation he sliced a day from Februarius, giving that month an even number of days (28). To account for differences between Numa's man-made calendar of 355 days, and the earth's non-adjustable cycle of 365.24219 days, the month of Februarius received a few extra "leap" days whenever the astronomers so dictated.

In 46 BC, Julius Caesar introduced the Julian calendar. It consisted of twelve months totaling 365 days, with a "leap" day added to Februarius every four years. This meant that each year averaged 365.25 days long. Although the Julian calendar was more accurate than Pompilius's calendar, it still gained eleven minutes a year, and if you don't consider that a big deal, Pope Gregory XIII did.

When Pope Gregory XIII looked into the calendar situation over a century later, he found the Roman calendar off by a whopping ten days. The Pope, however, being a stickler for accuracy, applied a couple of fixes to the problem.

He figured out (or had his mathematicians and astronomers figure it out) that by adjusting the rules governing leap years, he could narrow the margin of error to a very small factor. Thus, he dictated the following rule change: Century years (e.g. 1700, 1800,

1900, 2000, etc.) would only be a leap year if cleanly divisible by 400, as was the year 2000 (making it a leap year); but 1700, 1900, and 2100 would not be leap years because they are not divisible by 400.

That tiny adjustment means that the Gregorian calendar we use today is so accurate that it needs adjustment (the addition of one day) only once every 3,323 years, something that shouldn't be a problem to any of us.

However, there was still the matter of the shortage of the ten days, and Pope Gregory, being a master problem solver took care of the problem in a swift and painless manner.

Had you been alive in 1582, you would have gone to bed on the evening of October 4 and awakened on the morning of October 15. Thus for the year 1582, October 5 through 14 never happened. It wasn't a problem for most folks, although a handful of Germans in Frankfurt took issue with the Pope and accused him of stealing ten days from their lives.

However, once the rest of the calendar-keeping world followed the Pope's example, everything settled down and chances are good that you've heard very little grumbling about those ten lost days during your lifetime.

That folks is how the calendar got its start, and we have Pope Gregory to thank for a very accurate calendar.

"A ruffled mind makes a restless pillow."
Charlotte Brontë (**Apr 21, 1816** – Mar 31, 1855) Novelist

Margaret J. Winkler
Apr 22, 1895 (Hungary) – June 21, 1990 (Mamaroneck, NY)

AROUND 1915, MARGARET Winkler became Harry's executive secretary, and she was good and she was organized. If you've worked around secretaries, you'll know the type, super-efficient, fearless, and never sick. Harry was Harry Warner, one of the Warner Brothers of motion picture fame. However, back in the earliest days of silent pictures, the brothers owned a company that distributed movies to the theaters, Warner's Film Exchange.

In 1917, Harry cut a deal for the rights to the *Mutt and Jeff* animated cartoons, and then he turned the deal over to Margaret to manage. Later, when Harry brought cartoonist Max Fleischer and his "Out of the Inkwell" cartoon characters, *Betty Boop* and *Popeye* to Warner's, he did the same thing, turned them over to Margaret to manage. Again, when cartoonist Pat Sullivan needed a distributor for *Felix the Cat,* Harry made the deal and told Margaret to take care of Pat and the cat.

Around 1922, Harry Warner and his brothers grew tired of distributing films and decided to start making them. By now, Margaret had so endeared herself to the Warner organization that Harry made a gift of Fleischer and Sullivan's contracts to her. This generous act made it possible for Margaret to open her own distribution company with two of the silent era's hottest cartoons.

In a male dominated industry, Margaret gave her company the gender-free name of the M. J. Winkler Company. Within a year her company had become a dependable distributor of cartoons, travelogues, and short subjects, all anchored with her big name attraction, *Felix the Cat.* However, when the business relationship with Felix's creator, Pat Sullivan, started to show signs of wearing thin, she suspected the artist might be exploring a new place to put Felix's sandbox.

Although the prospect of losing *Felix* might not rate high enough to be considered a tragedy, it was enough to motivate Margaret to begin looking for a replacement for the anthropomorphic cat with the giant grin. That's when someone in the office stuck a copy of a submitted cartoon titled *Alice's Wonderland* in her hand.

She liked what she saw, and with time of the essence, she hired the unknown cartoonist sight unseen, which was a good thing.

Had she visited the cartoonist, she would have been surprised and likely disappointed to find, not an artist's studio, but the smelly corner of a dilapidated one-car garage owned by a man named Robert S. Disney.

Bob Disney had been kind enough to allow his skinny nephew, twenty-year-old Walt to use a corner of his garage as a workshop. There, young Walt had an easel, paints, and whatever else aspiring artists use in hopes of one day impressing someone with their talent.

Walt went to work for Winkler using *Alice's Wonderland* as a springboard, eventually producing thirty-one Alice cartoons and making a name for himself as a credible illustrator and a doggone-good cartoonist in the process.

If it hadn't been for Margaret Winkler, a go-getter of a gal who offered an unknown talent named Walt a job, we might all have grown up in a Disney-less world.

Walt may never have had the opportunity to "draw close" to his future alter ego, a mouse named Mickey, and that folks, would have been a tragedy.

"The optimist thinks this is the best of all possible worlds.
The pessimist fears it is true."
J. Robert Oppenheimer (**Apr 22, 1904** – Feb 18, 1967)
Physicist

WAYNE WINTERTON, PH.D.

APRIL 23
It's not easy being 3-foot-11

Hervé Villechaize
(Hervé Jean-Pierre Villechaize)
Apr 23, 1943 (Paris, France) – Sept 4, 1993 (Los Feliz, CA)

A S A SMALL man in a big world, Hervé Villechaize found an endocrine disorder called "proportionate dwarfism," to be even more difficult to live with than the green colored skin with which Sesame Street's Kermit the Frog complained.

After all, people expect frogs to be green; but people don't expect people to be less than four feet tall. As a fully-grown adult, Hervé stood three foot eleven, and as a child of mixed heritage (English and Filipino) and in a world in which children are often unwittingly cruel, he experienced years of relentless playground taunting and bullying.

Hervé's father, André Villechaize, a successful surgeon, tried desperately to find help for his son, including specialized surgery at America's Mayo Clinic. However, the surgeries, numerous and painful, were unsuccessful in correcting his problem.

Villechaize, teased into a quiet life, discovered a talent for painting and photography. He studied at the famed Beaux-Arts Museum in Paris, and there gained the confidence he didn't have during his formative years. At eighteen, he became the youngest artist to have his work displayed at the prestigious Museum of Paris.

There was another side to Hervé, and on one occasion after too much alcohol, he viciously attacked one of his paintings with a knife. It was, perhaps, a harbinger of things to come. The painting, you see, was a self-portrait.

He later moved to America where he found his unique size not so much a disadvantage. His size and his confidence helped him land some parts in a number of Broadway productions. Next, came a few movies and a major break in the role of Nick-Nack in the 1974 James Bond thriller, *The Man with the Golden Gun*. Life for Villechaize only got better and wealthier with stardom as Tattoo on television's *Fantasy Island*.

Unfortunately, Villechaize was a difficult actor to direct. He was unbridled around women and quarrelsome with management. When he demanded a salary equal to that Ricardo Montalbán, the star of *Fantasy Island*, the producers dropped him from the show.

He went through the $3.5 million he earned on *Fantasy Island* as though money would never be a problem and then his health took a turn for the worst. His oversized internal organs inside an undersized body began to hurt, requiring too many painkillers to go to sleep. His alcohol consumption increased and he became hopelessly depressed.

On the final day of his life, he wrote a note to his longtime companion, Kathy Self, stating, "I can't live like this anymore. I've always been a proud man and always wanted to make you proud of me. … I'm doing what I have to do."

In the early morning hours of September 4, 1993, he leaned backward against a sliding glass patio door, placed a pillow against his chest and fired a pistol into the pillow.

Hervé Villechaize was a free man. The health and addiction problems that had plagued him were over.

"For all your days, be prepared,
and meet them ever alike.
When you are the anvil, bear –
when you are the hammer, strike."
Edwin Markham (**Apr 23, 1852** – Mar 7, 1940)
Poet

WAYNE WINTERTON, PH.D.

APRIL 24
Captain of the Mary Celeste

Benjamin Briggs
Apr 24, 1835 (Unknown, MA) – November 1872 (Atlantic Ocean)

C APTAIN BRIGGS WAS an experienced mariner, as respected as any captain of his day and known for his seafaring ability and fairness. He was also devoutly religious and a firm believer in abstinence from strong drink.

When he married in 1862, he took his bride to Europe aboard his schooner, the *Forest King*, and six years later, he took his wife and his five-year-old son, Arthur, to Marseilles, France, returning in time for their daughter to be born on October 31, 1870. Thus, one can see that the Briggs family was quite accustomed to making ocean voyages.

In 1871, Briggs was considering hanging up his captain's cap for a clerk's apron, going into the hardware business with his brother, another seasoned seaman, but one who had already retired. Just before closing the deal on the hardware store, along came another opportunity.

It was a chance to buy into a brigantine with a friend, James Winchester, who had already procured the ship and changed its name from the *Amazon* to the name of his daughter, *Mary Celeste*.

Then, 1872, and another opportunity, this time to transport 1,701 barrels of alcohol to the wine growers of Genoa, Italy, intended for use in fortifying Italian wines.

On November 5, the *Mary Celeste* with Briggs, his wife Sarah and two-year-old daughter Sophia aboard (his son Arthur remaining behind to attend school), and a crew of seven sailed out of New York harbor and into the place where legends are made, as one of the strangest sea-faring stories on record.

Somehow, the ship made it across the ocean to Portugal, arriving with the greater portion of a six-month supply of food and water, but without its crew or passengers.

An examination of the ship showed the crew's personal possessions intact, and all 1,701 barrels were present, although nine of them, the only barrels made of red oak, were empty, and a single lifeboat was missing. The ship, with unwashed dishes in the galley and still under sail as if its crew was still aboard, suggested an unexplained abandonment with no hint of violence. Why?

There has never been a shortage of theories as to what might have happened to the *Mary Celeste* and its crew and passengers, including piracy, a perfect storm, a mutinous crew, an under-the-sea earthquake, and an elaborate insurance scam, none of which seem consistent with the nature of the captain and crew.

One of the most interesting and perhaps more plausible of the theories is the one that was offered by James Winchester, Captain Briggs partner in the ownership of the *Mary Celeste.*

Winchester suggested that the key to the mystery may well rest with the answer as to why there were nine empty red oak barrels.

According to Winchester, red oak is more porous than white oak and perhaps the alcohol in the red oak barrels had been evaporating with the vapor gradually building up in the ceiling of the hold. Then, what if someone opened the hold at the instant that the metal band of one barrel struck the metal band of another, and the friction caused a spark to ignite the ceiling-bound vapors. The resulting and highly unexpected explosion may well have convinced Briggs and company to lower a lifeboat and to board it, at least for as long as it would take to determine if the *Mary Celeste* was going to sink.

Then, in the confusion of the moment, no one attached a towline from the ship to the raft, a towline that would have kept the raft at a reasonable distance until the seaworthiness of the *Mary Celeste* was determined. With no towline, it's plausible that a wind could have blown the lifeboat and its passengers further and further away from the ship with its supply of food and water. The theory would certainly explain the fact that nothing seemed out of place when the *Mary Celeste* reached its destination.

Yet, when the *Mary Celeste* arrived in Portugal, there was no record of anyone observing the smell of alcohol fumes, nor of any explosive damage reported to the hold or to the nine red oak barrels. In fact, the empty red oak barrels might simply have been going to Genoa for another purpose and had never been filled with anything.

Thus, the mystery of what happened to Captain Benjamin Briggs and the *Mary Celeste* is still just that, a mystery.

"The greatest rogues are those who talk
most about their honesty."
Anthony Trollope (**Apr 24, 1815** – Dec 6, 1882) Novelist

Nicolas Jacques Pelletier
Unknown (France) – **Apr 25, 1792** (Paris, France)

O N OCTOBER 14, 1791, Nicolas Pelletier and his gang of toughs mugged a man on Bourbon-Villeneuve Street in Paris. They took the man's money and most of what happened next is lost to history, although we know the victim put up enough of a struggle to alert a nearby gendarme who arrived in time to detain Pelletier, but not in time to save the life of the victim.

Whether it was Pelletier or one of the other hoodlums who actually killed the victim, there was no way to know, but Pelletier found himself arrested, charged with murder, and locked up.

When his case came before the court, he went before Judge Jacob Augustin Moreau who, after considering all of the evidence banged his gavel and found the defendant, Nicolas Pelletier guilty. In cases like Pelletier's, a common street thief, Parisian justice was always swift. An execution date of December 31, 1791, less than 3 months after the crime, was set. Pelletier would die on the gallows.

On December 24, 1791, in accordance with French law in capital cases, a Second Criminal Court with a different judge heard the case. The new judge listened to a public defender argue on behalf of Pelletier, and Pelletier himself might have made a plea for his life, but a judge's gavel struck wood for a second time, and the execution date was confirmed.

Then, just a day or two before December 31, there came a stay of execution. It was most unusual for a street thief like Pelletier, a down-and-outer who didn't have the money to buy a new pair of underwear for the execution, let alone retain a fancy attorney, to receive a stay.

What happened, was that just prior to Pelletier's scheduled execution, the French National Assembly had voted to make decapitation by guillotine the state's only approved method of execution, and construction had just begun on the first of the new-fangled contraptions.

Then there would be the required testing of the equipment by public executioner Charles Henri Sanson using unidentified corpses from the Paris morgue, and finally, installation of the guillotine in the *Place de Grève*, a large outdoor area under preparation to handle the thousands of visitors who were expected to attend the guillotine's debut, and Pelletier's exit.

As might be expected, everyone was anxious to get started, everyone of course, except Pelletier.

To speed up the process, Judge Moreau sent a plea to the French Minister of Justice. The plea stated (edited), "In the name of humanity and . . . for the sake of the unfortunate man condemned to death, who realizes his fate and for each moment that prolongs his life must be death to him," closed by asking the Minister to put the guillotine project on a fast track.

Assuredly, this was not a letter approved by Pelletier, not that he had any voice in the matter, but the Minister did speed up the construction, testing, and the installation of the new-fangled killing machine.

Just when everything was running smoothly, there were among the local populace, some who were concerned about the execution. Not as to whether the execution should take place, but whether all of the paperwork approving the use of guillotine had been legally approved.

On January 24, 1792, a Third Criminal Court heard arguments, with everyone assured that execution by guillotine was not only legal, but also humane. Another date, March 23, 1792, was set for Pelletier's execution.

On March 23, a special unit of soldiers under the command of American Revolutionary War hero General Marie-Joseph Lafayette stood guard as thousands of onlookers milled about the *Place de Grève*, awaiting the execution.

On schedule, Nicolas Jacques Pelletier, the man whose blood was about to christen the guillotine, climbed the steps and stood on the platform. Executioner Charles Henri Sanson wasted no time in adjusting Nicolas Pelletier's neck on the block before releasing the weighted blade.

For the crowd, some of whom had traveled long distances, the execution was anticlimactic. It had been too clinically clean, too quick, and the crowd remembering the good old days of death by hanging, began to chant, "Bring back our wooden gallows! Bring back our wooden gallows!"

Street tough Nicolas Jacques Pelletier earned a place in history the hard way. He was literally on the cutting edge of the newest in human execution technology, and the first of many to die by the swift, anticlimactic blade of the guillotine.

"When two people love each other,
they don't look at each other; they look
in the same direction."
Ginger Rogers (July 16, 1911 – **Apr 25, 1995**)
Actress, dancer

Gypsy Rose Lee

(Rose Louise Hovick)

Jan 9, 1911 (Seattle, WA) - **Apr 26, 1970** (Los Angeles, CA)

TEENAGER ROSE ELIZABETH Thompson and Jack Hovick, a reporter for *The Seattle Times,* married, and before long Rose gave birth to a little girl they named Rose Louise. Ten months later, a second girl came along that they named Ellen Evangeline, although she would grow up as June.

Rose and Jack's marriage was stormy. Rose wanted show business careers for her daughters, a goal not shared by Jack who preferred a white picket fence, hot apple pie, and a tidy house.

When the marriage failed, Rose quickly had two-year-old June ready and appearing on stage with ballerina Anna Pavlova and playing uncredited bit parts opposite silent film star Harold Lloyd. Rose even produced a short Vaudeville act for June, *Baby June and Her Farmboys.*

A decade later, as was bound to happen, baby June blossomed into adolescent June. The act became *Dainty June and her Newsboys*, and older sister Rose, thought by mom to be the less talented of her daughters, performed as one of the chorus girls.

By the 1920s, Vaudeville was struggling but mother Rose remained her confident, domineering self. When June turned fourteen, she had become so resentful of her mother's unyielding control that she and *Newsboy* Bobby Reed eloped.

The Vaudeville act was over, or was it?

It was over for only as long as it would take mother Rose to move daughter Rose from the role of a plain-vanilla chorus girl into the star of the act. She knew Rose had neither a strong singing voice nor the natural dancing ability that June had, but what Rose did have, she had in spades. She had natural beauty, lots of it, stunning head-turning beauty. The act, *Rose Louise and her Hollywood Blondes* featured a barely-covered fifteen-year-old Rose and a bevy of busty chorus girls dancing to mildly risqué musical numbers.

However, as late-stage Vaudeville acts went, the show was ho-hum at best.

By the 1930s, Vaudeville was on life-support except for the one form of entertainment that always drew an audience, and the ever-pushy stage-door mother fast-talked a seedy nightclub manager into giving the *Hollywood Blondes* a second chance.

Then, it happened.

The club's star was so intoxicated she could neither stand up nor talk coherently. Enter mother Rose, stage left, who quickly volunteered daughter Rose to take the place of the stewed stripper. The club manager, without a replacement and hearing the ominous threats of an audience demanding its money back, weighed his options, and ….

. . . fifteen-year-old Rose Louise, her heart beating wildly, stepped onto the stage wearing a grass skirt and a skimpy top. She was now face-to-face with an older, mostly male audience who had paid to see a woman remove her clothing. Rose slowly, tantalizingly, created an onstage persona that was all tease and no strip. By the close of her act, with her grass skirt and top still in place, the young and beautiful Rose had so fired the imagination of the audience that when she exited the stage, she did so to wildly approving applause.

She had accomplished the impossible.

Rose Louise would continue to refine her act. Graceful and appealing with a hypnotic smile and the uncanny ability to make every man in the audience feel as though she were dancing just for him. Imagining what they couldn't see, her all-tease presence became the magic that became Gypsy Rose Lee, the eventual top drawing entertainer at *Minsky's of New York*.

Once, when a shoulder strap accidentally broke and caused her costume to begin to fall away, she looked at the audience, gasped in feigned horror, caught the strap at the last possible moment, retied it, and went on with the show. The audience went wild.

She afterwards devised a trick strap to simulate the effect, and when it broke, she still looked at the audience in feigned horror as if she didn't know what to do next, caught the strap at the last possible moment, and you get the picture.

Gypsy was married three times; her final marriage was to noted Spanish-born artist Julio de Diego. She was also the author of *Gypsy,* a best-selling autobiography that inspired the 1959 hit musical of the same name. She also wrote two whodunits; *The G-String Murders* (1941) and *Mother finds a Body* (1943), and she hosted *Gypsy,* a San Francisco talk show on KGO-TV until she was diagnosed with lung cancer in 1969.

Gypsy and her younger sister, June, who became famous as Hollywood actress June Havoc, reunited after Gypsy's cancer diagnosis. After no contact for nearly their entire adult lives, they reconciled their differences, and June took care of Gypsy until her death in 1970.

On **April 26, 1803,** thousands of meteor fragments fell from
the sky over L'Aigle, France, convincing
European scientists that meteors actually exist.

Ulysses S. Grant
(Hyram Ulysses Grant)
Apr 27, 1822 (Point Pleasant, OH) - July 23, 1885 (Wilton, NY)

W HEN HIRAM ULYSSES Grant wanted to go to West Point, family friend and Congressman Thomas L. Hammer erroneously wrote the young man's name in his letter of nomination as "Ulysses S. Grant." Seventeen year old Hiram Ulysses Grant, all 5-foot-1 and 117 pounds dripping wet, merely shrugged his shoulders, discarded his given name, Hiram, and adopted the middle initial 'S.'

There was no need to make a federal case out of the error, he decided. After all, he would simply return to Hiram Ulysses once his military obligation was out of the way. West Point only represented a means for an education, repayable by a few years military service, about which he once wrote, "A military life had no charms for me."

At West Point, Ulysses was an average cadet who afterward paid his dues by serving in the Mexican War and a few comfortable posts in New York, Detroit, and California. When his time was up he resigned his commission and with his wife and kids, began farming near St. Louis, Missouri.

After four years of hard work (1854-1858), the farm failed, so he tried selling real estate. He quickly realized he wasn't a businessman. With prospects dim, he accepted a clerking position in his father's leather business in Galena, Illinois, earning $800 a year and living in a modest home next to the town cemetery, a neighborhood with no noisy neighbors, but few other amenities.

When the Civil War broke out in 1861, Grant, as a West Point graduate, received a colonel's commission in the 21st Illinois Infantry. Two months later, he was a Brigadier General, and a year after that, a Major General. In 1864 Lincoln appointed him General in Chief of all U. S. Armies, and on April 9, 1865, he accepted Robert E. Lee's surrender at the Appomattox, Virginia, courthouse.

In 1866, Congress created the rank of four-star General (*General of the Army of the United States*) and Grant was the first to be so commissioned.

In 1868, Grant was nominated by the Republican Party to run for the office of President, resigned his general's commission so he could run, and eventually won two consecutive terms (1869-1877).

In 1883, he fell at his residence and was bedridden for weeks.

In 1884, a firm he helped establish, the "Grant and Ward Brokerage" failed and he lost virtually all of his wealth. A few months after that, diagnosed with untreatable throat cancer, he began to suffer from bouts of deep depression.

By 1885 Grant was penniless (presidential pensions didn't begin until Congress enacted the "Former Presidents Act" in 1958), and since he had resigned his four-star general's commission instead of retiring, he wasn't eligible for military retirement. As his health continued to decline, he found the strength, somewhere, to write his memoirs.

General William Tecumseh Sherman lobbied hard for Congress to reinstate the former general on the army rolls, an action that would have made Grant eligible for a federal pension. The action, blocked by unsympathetic southern Democrats who felt no love for the former Union general, failed.

As if things needed to be more difficult for Sherman in his attempt to help Grant, in the 1884 election just decided, Grover Cleveland, Democrat, had just defeated the incumbent, Chester A. Arthur, and what little interest there may have been among the Democrats to help Grant, there was even less interest now.

As Grant lay near death, Sherman made one last ditch effort to secure a pension for Grant. Minutes before noon on the morning of March 4, 1885, Sherman got the bill through the House of Representatives. However, as noon marked the closing hour of the Senate so inauguration festivities could begin, it appeared there would be no way to get the bill through the Senate.

That's when Sherman convinced a lowly Senate clerk to turn the hands of the clock back just long enough, with no one noticing, to allow the Senate to take up the matter one final time while Chester A. Arthur was still president.

When the vote was counted, the bill had squeaked past the Senate.

President Arthur signed the bill into law, his final official act before exiting the Senate chamber to pass the baton of national leadership to the incoming Grover Cleveland.

With the doors to the Senate chambers closed, the clerk reset the Senate clock to the correct time and went outside to join the festivities.

Four months later, July 23, 1885, Ulysses S. Grant was dead. But former first lady Julia Grant received a widow's pension, all because for one hour on March 4, 1885, time stood still just long enough for America's law makers to do the right thing.

On **April 27, 1981,** the computer mouse, developed by the
Palo Alto Research Center (PARC), was
introduced as an integral part of the Xeros Alto
computer.

APRIL 28
The Amazing Dunninger

Joseph Dunninger
Apr 28, 1892 (New York, NY) – Mar 9, 1975 (Cliffside Park, NJ)

THE NAME HARRY Houdini (1874-1926) conjures up mental images of the most famous magician in history, in part, because of the attention that Houdini received over the years from movies made about his life.

Another magician of the same era is hardly remembered at all. His name was Joseph Dunninger, a mentalist and a man that Houdini had once tried to prove a fraud, and when he couldn't, the two became friends.

When radio became a commercial reality in the late 1920s, with sponsors willing to pay to have their products advertised over the airwaves, Joseph Dunninger became radio's first paid entertainer.

Although the radio audience could only hear what he was doing, he still commanded a sizeable audience. So, you might ask, how did he convince his listening audience that what they were hearing wasn't simply broadcast-sleight-of-hand? He had a standing offer of $10,000 for anyone who could prove that he used paid assistants or stooges of any kind. Although there were those who tried to expose his mentalist claims, no one ever successfully did.

Dunninger became interested in magic as a child and by the age of seven was performing at a Masonic Lodge in New York as *Master Joseph Dunninger, Child Magician.* At a youthful sixteen he signed a one-year contract at New York's famed *Eden Musee,* an entertainment mecca that hosted living notables such as Sitting Bull, an automaton (robot) that played chess against the likes of O. Henry and Sara Bernhardt, and vaudeville acts such as the two-person mind-reading act of Mr. & Mrs. John Fay.

Dunninger, impressed by the Fays' two-person mentalist act, did them one better by creating a one-person mind-reading act that was truly astounding.

When his one-year contract at the *Eden Musee* ran out, he found himself invited into the homes of Theodore Roosevelt and Thomas A. Edison, both admirers of his incredible mentalist skills.

With his seemingly impossible mind-reading successes, he soon caught the attention of Harry Houdini and another well-known magician, Howard Thurston (1869-1936). Houdini and Thurston spent a great deal of time and effort, independent of each other, in attempting to uncover Dunninger's mind-reading secret, but neither were successful and afterward Dunninger joined Houdini's crusade against fraudulent mediums and mentalists.

Dunninger never claimed any psychic or supernatural powers, and often said, "Any three-year-old could do what I do – with thirty years practice."

Television sets were becoming affordable in the 1940s, and as the three existing networks (ABC, CBS, and NBC) were expanding, Dunninger prepared for prime time. On September 12, 1943, his first television broadcast, *Dunninger, The Master Mind*, became an overnight success. In fact, his series was so popular that he appeared on all three networks at different times.

At the height of his television success, he proved to be a marketing genius, writing a vast array of articles for popular magazines and authoring a number of best-selling books, including, *What is Telepathy? Dunninger's Secrets: Inside the Medium's Cabinet, The Complete Encyclopedia of Magic* and others, all of which kept his name in the public eye.

The format for his *Master Mind* television broadcast was deceptively simple. There was no grand entrance, no elaborate stage sets, he just walked on stage and sat on a stool, his only prop, a pad of paper and a pencil. As he doodled and talked to the audience, he would call out a name or a set of initials or even a random thought.

When someone from the audience with the name, or the initials, or the thought identified themselves, he might ask them to "think of" their social security number, or he might ask them to take a dollar bill from their wallet and look at the serial number. Then he would tell them their social security number or the serial number from the dollar bill. He might ask someone to write down a random phrase; and when the person was through writing, he would recite the phrase.

Sometimes he missed the mark, but more often or not, he was spot-on correct.

He claimed 90% accuracy in his ability to know what someone was thinking, and assessed his work as 60% mind reading, 10% psychology, 10% hypnosis, 15% self-hypnosis, and 5% magic, all of which, he would say, "adds up to 100% entertainment."

His television sign-off was, "For those who believe, no explanation is necessary; for those who do not believe, no explanation will suffice."

Joseph Dunninger took his remarkable talent to the grave when he died in 1975 of Parkinson's disease.

How did he do what he did?

Not even Harry Houdini, the most famous magician in history was able to figure out how Joseph Dunninger did what he did. He was that good.

"Half the people in Hollywood are dying
to be discovered
and the other half are afraid they will be."
Lionel Barrymore (**Apr 28, 1878** – Nov 15, 1954) Actor

APRIL 29
The Father of American Slang

Tad Dorgan
(Thomas Aloysius Dorgan)
Apr 29, 1877 (San Francisco, CA) – May 2, 1929 (Great Neck, NY)

SHORTLY AFTER THOMAS Aloysius Dorgan passed away, a sketch appeared in Bill Shannon's Biographical Dictionary of New York Sports. In it, Dorgan, who signed his cartoons "TAD" was recognized as "more than a cartoonist [but also] a sportswriter of some note and a phrasemaker who contributed much to the language and slang of the nation for three decades of this century."

The biography concluded with a few of the slang expressions attributed to Dorgan that endeared him to the hearts of the American public, along with the story of how the hot dog came to be called the "hot dog." Keep in mind that Dorgan passed away in 1929. The biography also credits Dorgan as the person who created such slang expressions as "'23-skidoo" and "Yes, we have no bananas," neither of which have any meaning today, but were extremely popular during the Roaring Twenties.

Dorgan's "Yes, we have no bananas" catchphrase became so popular that a novelty song of the same name was written by songsters Frank Silver and Irving Cohn for the 1922 Broadway show, *Make it Snappy.* In 1923, the song held the Number 1 slot for vocals for a full five weeks. Billy Jones, known as one of the "Happiness Boys," and vaudevillian Irving Kaufman, both sang the song. Later, Benny Goodman and his Orchestra recorded it. Spike Jones and His City Slickers parodied the song as only Spike and company could do. In 1924, Billy Jones returned with a follow-up, titled, *I've Got the Yes! We Have No Bananas Blues,* a song that also became the finale for the 2014 Broadway musical, *Bullets over Broadway.* Now, that's a lot of mileage for a song originating as a single Tad Dorgan catchphrase!

Let's return to the biography and Dorgan's role in naming one of America's favorite snacks, the "hot dog." The biography mentions Polo Grounds concessionaire Harry M. Stevens as the person who introduced "a hot sausage on a roll" for Giants' fans. Nothing is said about what Stevens might have called his culinary delight, perhaps just *Hot Sausage on a Roll*, but it was a great idea, selling a sausage inside a bun, perfect for keeping the fingers free of grease in the event a foul ball should come the fan's way.

Because a cooked sausage looked like the body of a dachshund, the so-called wiener dog, the biography went on to state that "Dorgan drew a dachshund wrapped in a frankfurter roll in one of his cartoons, titled it a 'hot dog,' and the name stuck!"

Let's look at some of the words or expressions attributed to or popularized by Dorgan,

The "cat's meow" didn't refer to the sound made by a cat, but to something outstanding, as in, "Hey good-looking, that dress is the *cat's meow!"*

The "cat's pajamas" referred to something of value or something strikingly fancy, usually an inanimate object, such as, "Isn't that snazzy bicycle just *the cat's pajamas!"*

The term "fab" was short for something considered as, what else, but *fabulous.*

The "bee's knees" was something along the line of the *cat's pajamas,* referring to almost anything in a positive way, such as, "That new sweater is just the *bee's knees* and it looks simply *fab* on you."

A "dumbbell" wasn't a bodybuilding tool, but someone with the IQ of a dumbbell.

"Applesauce" meant something absurd as in, "It's just *applesauce,* the idea that man will ever set foot on the moon."

"Cheaters" were eyeglasses, as in, "I wish the girl wearing the *cheaters* would go out with me."

"Threads" were clothes, as in, "Wow! Those new *threads* look great on you."

A "skimmer" was a straw hat with a stiff brim and a flat crown, as in, "Nothing sounds better than a barbershop quartet wearing matching *threads* and *skimmers."*

A "Hard-boiled egg" was someone with a tough outlook on life and little flexibility, as in, "Stay clear of Officer O'Reilly, he's one *hard-boiled egg.*"

"Solid ivory" referred to a thickheaded stupid person, as in, "Can you believe what Mike told Marge? He's *solid ivory* I tell you, *solid ivory*."

The above slang, credited to the fertile mind of Tad Dorgan, and largely through his fab cartoons and sports articles, he added something special to the Roaring Twenties. There is no other way to say it, his way with words was the *cat's pajamas*, and its pure *applesauce* to think there will ever be another Tad Dorgan.

His imaginative mind and colorful pen were both quieted on May 2, 1929, the result of years of battling heart disease followed by a life-sapping bout with pneumonia.

"Make no mistake about why these babies are here –
they are here to replace us."
Jerry Seinfeld (**Apr 29, 1954** –) Comedian, producer

APRIL 30

She won der Führer's favor, but lost her life

Eva Braun
Feb 6, 1912 (Munich, Germany) - **Apr 30, 1945** (Berlin, Germany)

I N 1929, THE year Eva Braun met Adolph Hitler, she was a naïve seventeen-year-old beauty from a respectable Bavarian family. She knew her face and athletic figure had been useful in attracting the attention of the young men in her hometown, and typical of other young ladies her age, she was flirty and fun.

Eva went to work for photographer Heinrich Hoffman, a loyal member of the Nazi party, a respected photographer, and a close friend of the politically up-and-coming Adolph Hitler. Eva's duties in the shop included waiting on customers, managing the office, helping in the shop's darkroom, and whenever Herr Hoffman needed a pretty face and figure, she was available as a photographic model. It was an enviable job for the vivacious Eva and she enjoyed it.

She was in the shop on a ladder putting away some seldom-used files, when her boss, Herr Hoffman and a mustached man, walked in and sat on the opposite side of the room. From the corner of her eye she could see the mustached man watching as she leaned to place the files into their proper storage slots.

Once finished, she descended the ladder and her boss, Herr Hoffman, introduced her to his longtime friend, Herr Wolff. When forty-year-old Wolff had seen the winsome seventeen year old in the store a few days earlier, she had not paid attention to him. However, today and formally introduced by her boss as a "longtime friend," she agreed to go out with the man. It wasn't long before the two were often in each other's company and something else, his name wasn't Herr Wolff at all, it was Adolph Hitler.

Miss Braun would not be Hitler's first mistress, nor his second or third.

His first mistress was a sixteen-year-old shop clerk from Obersalzberg named Mimi Reiter. Hitler came on strong, told her he wanted to marry her, and then ignored her for months. She attempted suicide by hanging herself, but before the deed was done, her brother-in-law cut her down and saved her life. Mimi and Adolph saw each other on and off for years, including during the time that Eva Braun believed herself to be Adolph's lone lover.

After Mimi came English socialite Unity V. Mitford, an ardent supporter of Nazism and a devotee of Hitler. Unity's sister, Diana, was the wife of Oswald Mosley, leader of the British Union of Fascists, so fascism was in the family, so to speak.

During a trip to Germany in 1934 with Diana, Unity met Hitler, later commenting, "The first time I saw him (Hitler) I knew there was no one I would rather meet." Then, after following his movements (stalking might be a better word) for ten months, the two "accidentally" met in a restaurant where Adolph picked up more than the tab for dinner. Hitler loved her Germanic middle name, Valkyrie, and he invited her to attend Nazi party rallies where he would introduce her as "a perfect specimen of Aryan womanhood."

In mythology, "the Valkyrie" were maidens who carried the souls of slain warriors to Valhalla where they would join the god Odin for eternity, the Valkyrie caring for their needs.

While Hitler was out romancing Unity, Braun seethed, writing in her diary, "Unity is known as the Valkyrie and looks the part, including her legs. I, the mistress of the greatest man in Germany and the whole world, sit here waiting while the sun mocks me through the window panes."

Desperate times called for desperate measures so Braun decided to show Adolph how much she loved him. She would attempt suicide, the operative word being "attempt." The bullet barely grazed her shoulder, and although Adolph professed affection for Eva, her weak attempt at suicide had no effect on his wandering eye.

As his interest in Unity Mitford waned, his lust took center stage with a popular German actress named Renate Müller. The romance was short-lived however, when Renate jumped from a Berlin hospital window after refusing to appear in Nazi propaganda films.

Does her "jump" sound fishy? Whom are you going to believe, your personal intellect or the collective intellect of the Gestapo?

In 1936, Braun still desperate for Hitler's undivided attention, decided to take another crack at suicide, this time with an overdose of sleeping pills. She was halfway successful. She didn't die, but she did succeed in getting a marriage commitment from der Führer, along with a chauffeured Mercedes and a three-bedroom villa with a maid, in a posh suburb of Munich.

In spite of the commitment, Hitler still had Unity to deal with. He decided the best way to break off his relationship with Unity was to warn her that war between Germany and England was inevitable. He was right. Britain declared war on Germany on September 5, 1939.

Unity was beside herself. She walked into the English Gardens in Munich, took a pearl-handled pistol given to her as a gift by Hitler, placed the pistol to her head and pulled the trigger. To her astonishment, she survived and ended up in a Munich hospital where Hitler visited her, took care of her hospital bills, and arranged for her speedy return to England.

Throughout most of the war years, life was good for Eva in her cozy villa. Her bills were paid and she saw Adolph whenever he felt like it. Then, in 1944, Germany's war machine broke down and the Third Reich came apart at the seams.

On April 29, 1944, Hitler and Eva were together in the Führerbunker when Adolph, good to his word, took Eva for better or for worse in what was one of history's briefest marriages.

After speaking their vows, they walked the bunker, bidding farewell to everyone before retiring to their private quarters. Then, a single gunshot! When the door was opened, the Führerbunker reeked of gunpowder and almonds.

Blood seeped from a hole in Hitler's forehead.

Eva, seated upright, still had the broken cyanide capsule lodged between her teeth, her third attempted suicide a definite success.

On **April 30, 1789**, on the balcony of Federal Hall in New York, George Washington took the oath of office and officially became the first president of the United States.

COMPREHENSIVE ALPHABETICAL INDEX
FOR VOLUMES 1-3

Berners' Street Hoax	3: Nov 27
Beswick, Hannah	2: Jul 22
Bierce, Ambrose	2: Jun 24
Bigg, John	1: Jan 30
Biggs, Ronald A.	2: Aug 8
Bissell, Israel	1: Apr 19
Blay, Ruth	2: Jun 10
Blazek, Rosa & Josefa	1: Mar 30
Bombard, Alain	3: Oct 27
Bong, Richard Ira	3: Sep 24
Bonney, William	3: Nov 7
Boop, Betty	2: Aug 9
Booth, Edwin Thomas	2: Jun 7
Boston Tea Party	3: Dec 16
Bowdler, Thomas	2: July 11
Boycott, Charles C.	2: Jun 19
Boyd, Belle	2: May 9
Braille, Louis	1: Jan 4
Braun, Eva	1: Apr 30
Briggs, Benjamin	1: Apr 24
Broadwick, Georgia Ann	1: Apr 8
Brennan, Walter	3: Sep 21
Browne, Samuel J.	3: Oct 3
Browning, John	3: Nov 26
Brunel, Isambard K.	3: Sep 15
Buckles, Frank	1: Feb 1
Burns, George	1: Jan 20
Burton, Richard Francis	1: Mar 19
Butchell, Mary Ann	1: Jan 14
Butterick, Ebenezer	2: May 29
Canova, Antonio	3: Nov 1
Chadwick, Cassie	3: Oct 10
Chapman, John	3: Sep 26
Chapman, Ray	2: Aug 17

WAYNE WINTERTON, PH.D.

Charles, Jacques	3: Nov 12
Cherry Sisters, The	2: May 28
Cheval, Ferdinand	2: Aug 19
Christmas Day Truce	3: Dec 25
Church, Ellen	3: Sep 22
Cincinnati, Society of the	2: May 13
Clayton, William H.	3: Dec 4
Cline, Patsy	3: Sep 8
Cochran, Jacqueline	2: May 11
Cochrane, Josephine G.	2: Aug 3
Colette	1: Jan 28
Collyer Brothers, The	1: Mar 21
Cooke, Sam	3: Dec 11
Coolidge, Calvin	2: Jul 4
Corbin and Wakeman	1: Jan 16
Corey, Giles	3: Sep 19
Corby, William	3: Dec 28
Corey, Irwin	2: Jul 29
Cotton, Becky	2: May 5
Cox, Wally	3: Dec 6
Crippen, Hawley	3: Sep 11
Cunningham, Glenn	2: Aug 4
Curtis, Charles	1: Jan 25
Custer, George A.	2: Jun 25
Dare, Virginia	2: Aug 18
Darger, Henry	1: Apr 12
de Laroche, Raymonde	2: Aug 22
Dean, Dizzy	2: Jul 17
Demara, Ferdinand Waldo	3: Dec 21
Dexter, Timothy	1: Jan 22
Dickson, Margaret	3: Sep 2
Diesel, Rudolf	1: Mar 18
Dixon, George E.	1: Feb 17
Dorgan, Tad	1: Apr 29

Doss, Desmond	1: Mar 23
Doss, Nannie	2: Jun 2
Doubleday, Abner	2: Jun 26
Doyle, Arthur Conan	2: May 22
Drake, Edwin L.	1: Mar 29
Dunninger, Joseph	1: Apr 28
Duryea, Charles	3: Dec 15
Eaton, Peggy	3: Nov 8
Ebson, Buddy	1: Apr 2
Edmonds, Sarah Emma	3: Sep 5
Einstein, Albert	1: Apr 18
Erdos, Paul	3: Sep 20
Erskine, Albert	1: Jan 24
Escalante, Jaime	3: Dec 31
Evolution of the Calendar	1: Apr 21
Fairbanks, Jason	3: Sep 25
Falk, Peter	3: Sep 16
Farnsworth, Philo T.	1: Mar 11
Farragut, David	2: Aug 14
Fawcett, Farrah	1: Feb 2
Fields, Mary	3: Dec 5
Fillmore, Millard	1: Mar 8
Fisher, Lavinia	1: Feb 18
Flake, William Jordan	2: Aug 10
Fleming, Ian	2: Aug 12
Fleming, Sandford	1: Jan 7
Fleming, Williamina	2: May 15
Fluckey, Eugene Bennett	2: Jun 28
Follis, Charles	1: Feb 3
Ford, Harrison	3: Dec 2
Forestiere, Baldassare	3: Nov 10
Forrest, Nathan B.	2: Jul 13
Four Dead in Five Seconds	1: Apr 14
Foy, Eddie Sr.	1: Mar 9

Freeman, Edward	3: Nov 20
Funicello, Annette	3: Oct 22
Gagarin, Yuri	1: Mar 27
Gage, Phineas P.	2: May 21
Galton, Sir Francis	1: Jan 17
Garber, Paul E	2: Aug 31
Garfield, James A.	3: Nov 19
Garn, Jake	3: Oct 12
Garnerin, Andre-Jacques	1: Jan 31
Gass, Patrick	2: Jun 12
Gatling, Richard Jordan	3: Sep 12
Gerry, Elbridge	3: Nov 23
Gillette, King C.	1: Jan 5
Girard, Stephen	2: May 20
Gish, Lillian	3: Oct 14
Glidden, Joseph	3: Oct 9
Goodyear, Charles	3: Dec 29
Gorey, Edward	1: Apr 15
Grant, Ulysses S.	1: Apr 27
Gray, Pete	1: Mar 6
Great Moon Hoax	2: Aug 25
Greenhow, Rose O'Neal	3: Oct 1
Greenough, Horatio	3: Sep 6
Guest, Edgar A.	2: Aug 20
Gunby, John	1: Mar 10
Hale, Girard Van Barkaloo	3: Oct 29
Hall, H. Tracy	3: Oct 20
Halliburton, Richard	1: Jan 9
Hamilton, Margaret	3: Dec 9
Harrison, William Henry	1: Apr 4
Hart, Pearl Taylor	3: Dec30
Harvey, Paul	3: Sep 4
Haydn, Franz Joseph	2: May 31
Hayes, Frank	2: Jun 4

Hayes, Ira	1: Jan 12
Hayes, Rutherford B.	3: Oct 4
Heisman, John	3: Oct 23
Henry, Joseph	3: Dec 17
Henry, O	2: Jun 5
Hickam, Homer	1: Feb 19
Hilton, Daisy & Violet	1: Feb 5
Holmes, H. H.	2: May 16
Hooker, Joseph	3: Oct 31
Hopkinson, Francis	3: Oct 2
Hughes, Howard	1: Apr 5
Hyman, Flo	2: Jul 31
Ignatow, Mel	3: Sep 1
Inouye, Daniel	3: Sep 7
Irving, Washington	3: Nov 28
Jarvis, Ann Marie Reeves	3: Sep 30
Jenkins' Ear, War of	3: Oct 19
Jenkins, Micah	3: Dec 1
Jobs, Steve	3: Oct 5
Johnson, Charles K.	2: Jul 24
Johnson, Howard	2: Jun 20
Johnson, Jack	1: Mar 31
Johnson, Samuel	3: Sep 18
Kaiser, Henry J.	2: Aug 24
Kane, Evan O'Neill	1: Apr 6
Keene, Laura	2: Jul 20
Kehoe, Andrew	2: May 18
Kellerman, Annette	3: Nov 6
Kemmler, William	2: Aug 6
Kennedy, Robert Cobb	1: Mar 25
Kilroy, James J.	3: Nov 24
Knotts, Don	2: Jul 21
Kovacs, Ernie	1: Jan 13
Krum the Horrible	1: Apr 13

Kyselak, Joseph	3: Sep 17
LaLaurie, Delphine	3: Dec 7
Lamarr, Hedy	3: Nov 9
Land, Edwin H.	1: Mar 1
Lane, Joseph	3: Dec 14
Last Great Race on Earth	1: Jan 27
Laurel, Stan	2: Jun 16
Leatherman, The	1: Mar 24
Lee, Gypsy Rose	1: Apr 26
Levant, Oscar	3: Dec 27
Lewis, Ida	1: Feb 25
Liddell, Alice P.	2: May 4
Lincoln, Abraham	1: Feb 12
Louis, Antoine	1: Feb 13
Lovelace, Ada	3: Dec 10
Lunt, David	1: Mar 22
Lyon, Matthew	2: Jul 14
MacDougall, Duncan	3: Oct 15
Mantz, Paul	2: Aug 2
Marble, Alice	3: Dec13
Marovich, Pete	2: Jun 22
Mature, Victor	1: Jan 29
McCurdy, Elmer	3: Oct 7
McGuffey, William H.	3: Sep 23
Meeks, Wilbur "Bub"	3: Nov 22
Merrick, Joseph	2: Aug 5
Mesmer, Franz Anton	2: May 23
Mikan, George	2: Jun 18
Miller, Roger	3: Oct 25
Missile Mail	2: Jun 8
Mitchell, Margaret	2: Aug 16
Moniz, Antonio Egas	3: Nov 29
Moondog	2: May 26
Moore, Clayton	3: Sep 14

Morrison, Walter	1: Jan 23
Mostel, Zero	1: Feb 28
Mott, Ralph L.	3: Nov 14
Mudd, Samuel A.	3: Dec 20
Muggs, J. Fred	1: Mar 14
Murphy, Isaac Burns	1: Apr 16
Nash, Ogden	2: May 19
Nasiff, Henry Jr.	1: Apr 20
Newby, Dangerfield	3: Oct 17
Niepce, Joseph N	1: Mar 7
Nobel, Alfred	3: Oct 21
Norton, Joshua A.	1: Jan 8
Oakley, Annie	3: Nov 3
O'Hair, Madalyn Murray	3: Sep 29
Old Abe	1: Mar 26
Olsen, Ken	1: Feb 20
Orton, William	2: Jun 14
Paul, Alice	1: Jan 11
Paulsen, Pat	2: Jul 6
Peace, Charles	2: May 14
Pearse, Richard	3: Dec 3
Peek, Kim	3: Nov 11
Peel, Sir Robert	2: Jul 2
Peeping Tom	2: Jun 11
Pelletier, Nicholas Jacques	1: Apr 25
Pemberton, John	2: Jul 8
Perdicaris, Ion	1: Mar 12
Perkins, Carl	1: Apr 9
Pig War, The	2: Jun 15
Plunkett, Roy J.	2: May 12
Poe, Edgar Allan	1: Jan 19
Ponzi, Charles	1: Mar 3
Powell, Dick	1: Jan 2
Powers, Francis Gary	2: Aug 1

WAYNE WINTERTON, PH.D.

Prefontaine, Steve	2: May 30
Pulitzer, Joseph	1: Apr 10
Puller, Lewis "Chesty"	3: Oct 11
Quantrill, William	2: Jun 6
Randles, Slim	2: Jul 27
Raskova, Marina M	1: Mar 28
Rathbone, Henry	2: Jul 1
Ray, Johnnie	1: Jan 10
Reese, Pee Wee	2: Jul 23
Reichelt, Franz	1: Feb 4
Reilly, Sidney	3: Nov 5
Rey, H. A.	2: Aug 26
Rickenbacker, Eddie	3: Oct 8
Ringenberg, Margaret	2: Jul 28
Ripley, Robert LeRoy	2: May 27
Robert-Houdin, Jean	2: Jun 13
Roberts, Bartholomew	2: May 17
Roberts, Timp	2: Jul 9
Robinson, Bojangles	2: May 25
Robinson, Eddie	1: Apr 3
Rockefeller, Michael	3: Nov 17
Rohwedder, Otto F.	2: Jul 7
Rolls, Charles Stewart	2: Jul 12
Rooney, Andy	3: Nov 4
Ross, Betsy	1: Jan 1
Saint Patrick	1: Mar 17
Saint Scholastica Day Riot	1: Feb 10
Saint Urho	1: Mar 16
Saint Valentine	1: Feb 14
Salomon, Haym	1: Apr 7
Sandburg, Carl	1: Jan 6
Sarnoff, David	3: Dec 12
Schieffeling, Eugene	2: Aug 15
Schmeling, Max	3: Sep 28

Segar, E. C.	3: Oct 13
Selfridge, Thomas E.	1: Feb 8
Sheppard, Jack	1: Mar 4
Shore, Dinah	1: Feb 29
Shuster, Joe	2: Jul 30
Sickles, Daniel Edgar	2: May 3
Sikorsky, Igor	3: Oct 26
Sinclair, Upton	3: Nov 25
Skelton, Red	2: Jul 18
Skinner, B. F.	1: Mar 20
Smith, Soapy	3: Nov 2
Smithson, James	2: Jun 27
Snow, John	1: Mar 15
Soo, Jack	3: Oct 28
Spencer, Percy LeBaron	2: Jul 19
Spooner, William A.	2: Aug 29
Stanford, Leland	2: Jun 21
Stapp, John Paul	3: Nov 13
Stauffenberg, Claus von	3: Nov 15
Stead, William Thomas	2: Jul 5
Steele, Alison	3: Sep 27
Stempel, Herb	3: Dec 19
Stewart, Elinore Pruitt	2: Jun 3
Stone, Lucy	2: Aug 13
Straus, Isador and Ida	1: Feb 6
Strauss, Levi	1: Feb 26
Sutton, Willie	2: Jun 30
Swan, Walter J.	3: Sep 10
Sylbaris, Ludger	2: May 8
Taylor, Annie Edson	3: Oct 24
Taylor, Elizabeth	1: Feb 27
Teed, Cyrus Reed	3: Dec 22
Tell, William	3: Nov 18
Tesla, Nikola	2: Jul 10

WAYNE WINTERTON, PH.D.

Thayer, Ernest	2: Aug 21
Thumb, Tom	2: Jul 15
Tibbets, Paul W	1: Feb 23
Till, Emmett	2: Jul 25
Toft, Mary	1: Feb 21
Turing, Alan Mathison	2: Jun 23
Turner, Lana	2: Jun 29
Twain, Mark	3: Nov 30
Valentino, Rudolph	2: Aug 23
Vallandigham, Clement	2: Jun 17
Veeck, Bill, Jr.	1: Feb 9
Verdon, Gwen	3: Oct 18
Vernon, Edward	3: Oct 30
Villechaize, Herve	1: Apr 23
Waddell, James Iredell	2: Jul 3
Wake, Nancy	2: Aug 30
Walters, Larry	3: Oct 6
Waring, Fred	2: Jun 9
Washington, George	1: Feb 22
Wauneka, Annie Dodge	1: Apr 11
Webster, Noah	3: Oct 16
Welch, George	2: May 10
Wells, Horace	1: Jan 21
Wells, Kitty	2: Jul 16
West Point Eggnog Riot	3: Dec 24
Wharton, Edith	2: Aug 11
Wild, Jonathan	2: May 24
Williams, Daniel Hale	1: Jan 18
Wilson, Charlie	2: Jun 1
Wilson, Flip	3: Dec 8
Wilson, Sam	3: Sep 13
Winkler, Margaret J.	1: Apr 22